THE ZOM-B CHRONICLES

ZOM·B

ZOM·B UNDERGROUND

ZOM·B CITY

DARREN SHAN

Ⓛ Ⓑ LITTLE, BROWN AND COMPANY   NEW YORK   BOSTON

Collected edition copyright © 2014 by HOME OF THE DAMNED LIMITED
Zom-B text copyright © 2012 by HOME OF THE DAMNED LIMITED
Zom-B Underground and *Zom-B City* text copyright © 2013 by HOME OF THE DAMNED LIMITED
Zom-B illustrations copyright © 2012 by Warren Pleece
Zom-B Underground and *Zom-B City* illustrations copyright © 2013 by Warren Pleece
Excerpt text from *Zom-B Angels* copyright © 2013 by HOME OF THE DAMNED LIMITED
Zom-B Angels illustration copyright © 2013 by Warren Pleece

Little, Brown and Company

Hachette Book Group
237 Park Avenue, New York, NY 10017
Visit our website at lb-teens.com

Little, Brown and Company is a division of Hachette Book Group, Inc.
The Little, Brown name and logo are trademarks of Hachette Book Group, Inc.

The publisher is not responsible for websites (or their content) that are not owned by the publisher.

First Collected Edition Printing: September 2014
Zom-B first published in the U.S. in October 2012 by Little, Brown and Company
Zom-B first printed in Great Britain by Simon & Schuster in 2012
Zom-B Underground first published in the U.S. in January 2013 by Little, Brown and Company
Zom-B Underground first printed in Great Britain by Simon & Schuster in 2013
Zom-B City first published in the U.S. in April 2013 by Little, Brown and Company
Zom-B City first printed in Great Britain by Simon & Schuster in 2013

ISBN 978-0-316-28489-9

Library of Congress Control Number: 2014939690

10 9 8 7 6 5 4 3

RRD-C

Printed in the United States of America

For:

Zom-Bas, my undead lass!
Mrs. Shan!!!

OBE (Order of the Bloody Entrails) to:
Laura Zi Giuseppe, for a brace of
carefully coordinated Irish jobs!
Kathryn "Spielberg" McKenna
Elisa Offord—queen of the mutant babies

dead good editors — Venetia GoZling
and Kate Zullivan

my heart goes out, as always, to the
ChriZtopher Little brainiacs

BY DARREN SHAN

THE THIN EXECUTIONER

ZOM-B SERIES

ZOM-B

ZOM-B UNDERGROUND

ZOM-B CITY

ZOM-B ANGELS

ZOM-B BABY

ZOM-B GLADIATOR

ZOM-B MISSION

ZOM-B CLANS

THE SAGA OF LARTEN CREPSLEY

BIRTH OF A KILLER

OCEAN OF BLOOD

PALACE OF THE DAMNED

BROTHERS TO THE DEATH

THE DEMONATA SERIES

LORD LOSS

DEMON THIEF

SLAWTER

BEC

BLOOD BEAST

DEMON APOCALYPSE

DEATH'S SHADOW

WOLF ISLAND

DARK CALLING

HELL'S HEROES

THE CIRQUE DU FREAK SERIES

A LIVING NIGHTMARE

THE VAMPIRE'S ASSISTANT

TUNNELS OF BLOOD

VAMPIRE MOUNTAIN

TRIALS OF DEATH

THE VAMPIRE PRINCE

HUNTERS OF THE DUSK

ALLIES OF THE NIGHT

KILLERS OF THE DAWN

THE LAKE OF SOULS

LORD OF THE SHADOWS

SONS OF DESTINY

CONTENTS

Zom-B
1

Zom-B Underground
185

Zom-B City
369

BOOK 1:

ZOM-B

THEN...

It was the darkest, most wretched hour of the night when the dead came back to life and spread like a plague of monstrous locusts through the village of Pallaskenry. The luckier victims were slaughtered in their sleep, their skulls ripped open, their brains devoured. The others suffered a far more terrible fate.

The living and the undead shared the village for a short, frantic time, but it was a balance made in hell and it could not last. One side would surely wipe out the other. As the demented, demonic beasts tore into their unsuspecting prey, killing or infecting, it soon became apparent that this was a war the living had never been destined to win.

Brian Barry watched sickly as his mother dug through the shredded remains of her husband's face to scoop out his brains. Mum had often joked about killing Brian's dad, on nights when he had stumbled home from the local pub, or when he wouldn't shut up about soccer. Brian and his dad had always laughed when she made her outlandish threats. But neither was laughing now.

Brian couldn't understand how the world had changed so abruptly. It had been an ordinary Sunday night. He'd watched some TV, finished his homework just before going to bed, and settled down for a night of sweet dreams before another school week kicked off.

Screams had disturbed his slumber. Brian wasn't a light sleeper, but even the dead were unable to sleep through the uproar in Pallaskenry that night.

Brian had thought at first that somebody was throwing a party. But he lived on a quiet stretch of road. His neighbors weren't party animals. Had teenagers driven out from Limerick city to bring noise and chaos to the countryside?

As his head cleared and he turned on the light in his bedroom, he quickly realized that this was no party. The screams were genuine roars of terror. Looking out of his window, he spotted some of his neighbors running, shrieking, fighting. He watched, awestruck, as Mrs. Shanahan stabbed one of her sons in the chest with a long knife, then staggered away, keening sharply.

The stabbed son should have died instantly, as the knife had pierced his heart. But to Brian's astonishment he yanked out the knife, tossed it aside, then fell upon his mother with a bloodthirsty howl. Mrs. Shanahan had time to scream once more. Then her son somehow cracked her head open with his fingers and began pulling out lumps of her brain.

Brian turned away and vomited as Mrs. Shanahan's son stuffed bits of his dead mother's brain into his mouth and swallowed gleefully. Then Brian rushed to his mum and dad's room to seek protection.

They weren't there.

As if in a nightmare, Brian shuffled towards the kitchen, where he could see a light. Pushing open the door, he spotted his parents, but he didn't call out to them. There was no point, he saw that immediately. His father would never hear anything again. His face had been ripped apart and his body was deathly still.

As for Brian's mother, she was too busy eating her dead husband's brain to care about anything her son might have to say. There was a nasty cut on her left arm and a green fungus was creeping across the wound. There was something strange about her teeth and fingers too, but Brian didn't focus on those details. He could stomach no more. Weeping softly, he backed away from the kitchen of death and fled into the night of blood and screams.

Brian headed for the main street of Pallaskenry, crying, moaning, shivering. He could see atrocities unraveling wherever he looked, corpses littering the road, people – neighbors, family members, friends – feasting on the dead, tucking into their brains.

Fighting was rife, brother struggling with sister, wife with husband, child with parent. It made no sense. It was as if a great madness had swept through the village and struck at random. Anyone who tried to reason with the cannibalistic crazies was knocked down and ripped apart. The only ones who stood any chance of survival were those who didn't stop to ask questions, who didn't try to help, who simply turned tail and ran.

But Brian was a child and he believed that adults had all the answers, that you should always seek assistance if you found yourself in trouble. So he pushed on, searching for a police officer, a teacher, a priest... *anyone.*

All he found was more horror, blood everywhere, corpses everywhere, undead monsters everywhere. Nobody could help Brian Barry. It was every man, woman and child for themselves.

Brian somehow made it to the top of the main street, ducking challenges, skipping past the lunges of bloodthirsty abominations. In the middle of the killing frenzy, there was no shortage of targets, so the undead creatures didn't take much notice of an eleven-year-old boy.

At the top of the street, where the road branched, a man was standing, feet spread wide apart, hands on hips, studying the violence. Lots of undead creatures were gathered at this point, scrapping with the living or feeding on the brains of the freshly killed. None attacked the man in the middle of the road. Some growled suspiciously at him, but all of the monsters let him be.

Brian was young but he was no fool. He saw his best chance of survival and launched himself at it, desperation lending him one last blast of speed when he'd been sure that his lungs were about to burst.

Slipping past the frenzied, sharklike killers, Brian threw himself at the feet of the man who was immune to the attacks. He looked up and got ready to beg for his life. But when he saw the man's face, he paused. The tall man was very thin, with a large potbelly and extraordinarily unsettling eyes. They were double the size of Brian's, the largest eyes the boy had ever seen, unnaturally white, with a tiny dark pupil set in the center of each. Brian was immediately reminded of an owl.

"Yes, little boy?" the man murmured. He had a soft, pleasant voice, like one of the announcers on the TV shows that Brian had been watching earlier that night. It didn't really suit those eerie eyes.

"Please," Brian gasped, grabbing hold of the man's legs. "Help me. Please. My dad's dead. My mum..."

"She killed him?" the man asked, then tutted when Brian nodded. "How sad that you had to bear witness to such a shocking scene. No child should ever be put in so unfortunate a situation. You have my condolences."

7

One of the undead creatures darted at them, reaching for Brian, drooling as it moved in for the kill.

"Back!" the man with the large eyes barked. The monster snarled at him but retreated as ordered.

"You . . . you can . . . help me?" Brian wheezed.

The man frowned. "I could, but with so many in your perilous position, it hardly seems fair that I should single you out for special treatment."

"Please!" Brian wailed, clutching the tall man's legs even tighter. "I didn't do anything wrong. I don't want to die. *Please!*"

The man sighed and looked around at the dead, the dying and the undead. He hesitated, then decided to be merciful. "Very well," he muttered. "But I'll only do it for you. The others will have to fend for themselves. What is your name?"

"Brian Barry."

"You need to let go of my legs, Brian, move back and kneel in front of me."

"Kneel?" Brian echoed uncertainly.

"Yes," the man said. "Then close your eyes and say a silent prayer, any prayer will do, or none at all if you're not religious, although I find that even the most agnostic individual gains a measure of comfort from prayer at a time like this."

"You'll help me if I kneel and pray?" Brian asked.

"Yes," the man smiled, and although it was a cold smile, it filled the boy with hope.

"Okay," Brian said, releasing the man's legs. The undead noticed this and started to move in for the kill. Brian gulped, then closed his eyes and prayed manically. He couldn't remember the words very well but he did the best he could, trying not to think about his mum and dad and how he used to complain when they took him to church.

The tall man looked down tenderly at the boy. Then he spotted the monsters closing in and wiped the smile away. He would have to act swiftly if he was to honor his promise and spare the boy the agony of death at the hands of these foul beasts.

"You have been a brave boy, Brian," the man whispered. "I am sure you will be reunited with your parents in the next world."

Then his hands snaked out. Brian didn't see the long, bony fingers, and only barely felt them as they gripped his head and twisted left then right. He heard a sharp cracking noise but felt no pain and was dead before he knew it.

The man let the corpse drop and bade Brian a silent farewell as the living dead moved in and tore into the boy's skull. He watched for a while, then checked his watch and grunted. There was still a long way to go until morning.

With a small cough he adjusted the ends of his sleeves, then started down the road into the village, leaving the undead leeches to carve up Brian Barry's skull and feast upon the hot, sweet brain within.

ONE

NOW...

Zombies, my arse! I've got a *real* problem on my hands. Dad's been drinking and I can tell by his beady eyes that he's close to tipping over the edge.

We've been watching the news, a report about the alleged zombie attack in Ireland. Dad takes a swig of beer, then snorts and switches channels.

"I was watching that," Mum complains.

"You're not anymore," Dad grunts.

"But it's important," Mum presses. "They might attack here. We need to know what to do, Todd."

"B knows what to do, don't you?" Dad says, winking at me, and it's a relief to see he's still at the stage where he can crack a joke.

"Of course," I grin. "Put my head between my legs and kiss my arse good-bye!"

We crack up laughing. Mum tuts and makes a face. She doesn't like it when we swear. She thinks foul language is a sign of ill breeding. I don't know how she ended up with Dad—he could swear for a living.

"Don't be silly, Daisy," Dad says. "It's all a con. Zombies? The dead returning to life to feast on the living? Give me a break."

"But it's on the *news*," Mum says. "They showed pictures."

"They can do anything with computers these days," Dad says. "I bet B could knock up something just as realistic on our laptop. Am I right, B?"

"Dead on," I nod. "With a few apps, I could out-zombie George Romero."

"Who's that?" Mum frowns.

"The president of South Africa," Dad says seriously and we both howl at her bewildered expression.

"It's all very well for the pair of you to laugh like hyenas," Mum snaps, face reddening. "But what happens if zombies attack us here? You won't be laughing if they kill me and B."

"I'll happily chuck *you* to them if you keep on moaning," Dad says, and there's an edge to his voice now, one I'm all too familiar with.

Dad stares at Mum, his eyes hard. I tense, waiting for him to roar, or maybe just throw a punch at her without warning. If he does, I'll hurl myself at him, the way I have countless times in the past. I love him, but I love Mum too, and I can never stand by and let him lay into her. The trouble is, there's not much I can do to stop him. We could both be in for some serious battering tonight.

But instead, after a dangerous pause, Dad smirks and switches back to the news. That's Dad all over — unpredictable as the weather.

I scratch the back of my head – I had it shaved tight over the weekend and it's always itchy for a few days when I do that – and watch the footage from Ireland. It's a helicopter shot. They're flying over Pallaskenry, the small village where zombies apparently ran wild on Sunday.

The village is in ruins. Buildings are being burned to the ground by soldiers with cool-looking flamethrowers. Corpses all over the place. At least they *look* like corpses. Dad reckons they're dummies. "That's a waste of good ketchup," he said when Mum challenged him about the blood.

"I mean," Dad says as we watch, "if it had happened in London, fair enough, I might believe it. But bloody Ireland? It's one of their Paddy jokes. *There was an Englishman, an Irishman and a zombie…*"

"But they've shown dead people," Mum persists. "They've interviewed some of the survivors who got out."

"Never heard of actors?" Dad says witheringly, then turns to me. "You don't buy any of this, do you?"

"Not a word." I point at the TV. They're showing a clip that's already passed into legend on YouTube. One of the zombies is biting into a woman's head. He's a guy in pajamas. His eyes are crazy and

14

he's covered in blood, but apart from that you wouldn't look at him twice in a crowd. The woman screams as he chews off a chunk of her skull and digs his fingers into her brain. As he pulls out a handful and stuffs it into his mouth, the camera pans away and, if you listen closely, you can hear the cameraman vomiting.

The clip had gone viral on the Web by Monday morning, but they first showed it on TV that evening. There was an uproar the next day, papers saying it shouldn't have been aired, people getting their knickers in a right old twist. It gave me a fright when I first saw it. Dad too, even if he won't admit it. Now it's just a bit of fun. Like when you see a horror film more than once—scary the first time, but the more you watch it, the lamer it gets.

"He should have dipped that bit of brain in curry sauce," I joke.

"B!" Mum gasps. "Don't joke about it!"

"Why not?" I retort. "None of it's real. I reckon it's a trailer for a new movie. You wait, another few days and they'll admit it was a publicity stunt. Anyone who fell for it will look a right idiot, won't they?"

"But the police and soldiers…" On the TV, a tank fires at a church, blasting holes out of the walls, exposing zombies who were sheltering inside—these guys are like vampires, they don't come out much in the day.

"They're part of the campaign," I insist. "They've been paid to go along with the act."

Mum frowns. "Surely they'd get in trouble if they lied to the public like that."

15

"Trouble's like a bad stink," Dad says. "Throw enough money at it and nobody cares. Any lawyers who go after these guys will be given a big fat check and that'll be the end of that."

"I dunno," Mum says, shaking her head. "They're talking about a curfew here."

"Course they are," Dad sneers, knocking back another slug of beer. "The government would love that. Get everyone off the streets, terrify us into holing up like rats. It'd leave them free to do whatever they wanted at night. They'd ship in more immigrants while we weren't watching. That might be what the whole thing's about, a plot to make us look away while they sneak in a load of scabs who'll work for peanuts and steal our jobs."

Mum looks dubious. "You can't be serious, Todd."

"I'd bet my crown jewels on it," he says firmly.

She stares at him, maybe wondering how she ended up marrying such a paranoid nutter. Or maybe she's trying to convince herself that he's right, to avoid any arguments and associated beatings.

The worst thing about this zombie scare is talk of a curfew. I'd go mad if I had to stay home every night, locked in with Mum and Dad. I mean, most nights I stay in anyway, watching TV, surfing the Web, playing computer games, listening to music. But I know that I *can* go out, any time I please. Take that choice away and I'd be no better off than a prisoner.

I shiver at the thought of being caged up and get to my feet. "I've had enough of zombies. They're boring me. I'm heading out."

"I'm not sure that's a good idea," Mum says. "What if there's an attack?"

"Don't be daft," I laugh.

"But if they struck there, they could strike here. We're not that far from Ireland." She looks like she's about to cry. "They come out at night, the reporters all say so. If they attack London and catch you on the street..."

"Dad?" I look to him for support.

"I dunno..." he mutters, and for the first time I see that he's not so sure that this is the work of sneaky liberals.

"Don't tell me you're gonna start too," I groan.

Dad chews the inside of his cheek, the way he does when he's thinking hard.

"Put your foot down, Todd," Mum says. "It's dangerous out there. You can't –"

"I can do whatever the bloody hell I want!" Dad shouts. "Don't tell me what I can and can't do."

"I'm not," Mum squeaks. "I was only –"

"Shut it," Dad says quietly and Mum zips up immediately. She knows that tone. We both do. I gulp as Dad sits forward, putting down the can of beer. He cracks his fingers, eyeballing Mum. She's trembling. She's not the sharpest tool in the box. She missed the earlier warning signs, his expression, the clip to his words. But now she's up to speed. Dad's in a foul mood. There could be some thuggery in the cards tonight.

I start to edge towards Mum, to do my best to protect her. I hate it when Dad hits me. But I hate it even more when he hits her. Mum's soft. I'm more like Dad, a tough little nut. I'll distract him if I can, draw his attention away from Mum. If I'm lucky he'll only slap me. If not, and he starts punching and kicking, I'll curl up into a ball and take it. Won't be the first time. Won't be the last. Better he does it to me than Mum.

"B!" Dad barks, making me jump.

"Yeah?" I croak, trying not to shake.

He glares at me — then snorts, picks up the can of beer and settles back again. "Go do whatever the hell you feel like."

"Sure thing, boss," I smile and tip him a stupid salute.

Dad smirks. "You're an idiot," he says.

"I know where I get it from," I chuck back at him, feeling safe enough to wind him up a bit. I can do that to Dad when he's in the right mood. He's a great laugh when he wants to be.

"Oi!" he roars and throws a cushion at me.

I laugh and duck out, knowing Mum will be fine now, delighted at this unexpected swing, feeling on top of the world. There's nothing sweeter than a narrow escape. I don't know why Dad laid off at the last moment, and I don't try to figure it out. I gave up trying to read his mind years ago.

The last thing I see is Mum getting up to retrieve the cushion. Dad doesn't like it if she leaves stuff lying around. Doesn't matter if he left it there. Cleaning up is *her* job.

TWO

Out of the flat, down three flights of stairs, taking the steps two at a time, four on the last set. I slap the wall on my right as I fly past. Someone spray painted a giant arse on it months ago and I always slap it for good luck when I pass. Some of the neighbors have tried scrubbing it off but it's hanging in there, faded but defiant. I love graffiti. If I could paint, I'd be out covering the walls of London every night.

I land like a cat, cool in my new, totally black sneakers. There was a bit of red running through them when they first came out of their box, and the brand name shone brightly, but I carefully went over everything with a heavy-duty Sharpie. B Smith is nobody's advertising pawn!

It's not yet six, plenty of daylight left. I

don't know what Mum was panicking about. Even if zombies were real, and even if they did attack here, they wouldn't show their faces for another hour, not if the news teams have got it right.

I check myself out in shop windows. Plain black T-shirt and jeans, no tags to show what make they are, threadbare in places, but worn in naturally by me, none of your bloody designer wear and tear.

I'm almost past Black Spot when I stop and backtrack. Vinyl's in there with his old man. Black Spot is a retro freak's paradise. They only stock vinyl records, along with clothes, toys, hats, and other bits and pieces from the dark ages. I even saw a video recorder in the window once.

Vinyl's dad loves all that twentieth-century crap. He won't let CDs or DVDs in his house, and as for downloads, forget it! They have a computer but all the music sites on it are blocked. He says the crackle of old records is what real music is all about, that digital tracks don't make the air throb.

I lean close to the window and tap on it softly. Vinyl looks up and scowls. He hates it when we spot him with his dad. Vinyl's old man is all right – he does his own thing and doesn't make a song and dance about it – but he's a weirdo. I think Vinyl secretly likes the records that his dad makes him listen to but he never admits that to us or defends his dad when we slag him off. As long as we don't take it too far. I started to make a joke once about his dad liking the small holes that you find in the middle of records. Vinyl very quietly told me to shut up. He didn't have to say any more. I'm not afraid of Vinyl but I know he'd wipe the floor with me if we fought. Why sign up for a beating if you don't have to?

I make a face and stick out my tongue. Vinyl gives me the finger, then says something to his dad. Old man Vinyl looks up, nods at me and smiles. I salute him, the same way I saluted Dad a while ago. Vinyl comes out, nudging the door open with his head.

"You're so cool," I gush, squeezing my hands together and making doe eyes at him.

"Get stuffed," Vinyl sneers.

We grin and knock knuckles.

"I like the hair," Vinyl says. "Number 3?"

"Sod that. Number 2."

"Hard-core."

Vinyl's got long, curly hair. He'd love to shave it but his mum would cry and he doesn't want to upset her. He's a soft git, Vinyl. But hard when he needs to be. There aren't many who get the better of him in a punch-up.

"How's the new school?" I ask.

Vinyl rolls his eyes. "I should have failed that bloody test."

"Bad?" I laugh.

"You wouldn't believe it."

Vinyl took a Mensa test in the summer. Turns out he's smarter than the rest of us put together. His mum went gaga – she thinks he's the new Einstein – and begged him to switch to a posh school. He hated bailing on us but she turned on the tears and he caved.

"What's it really like?" I ask as we stroll, punching each other's arm every now and then.

"All right," he shrugs. "I thought they'd be full of themselves but most aren't much different from us. I'm doing okay, not the best, not the worst."

"What about the teachers?"

He shrugs again. "They wouldn't last long in our place. I'd give them a week—they'd be head cases after that."

Vinyl still thinks he's one of us. And at the moment he is. But that will change. You can't switch schools and carry on as if nothing's happened. He'll make new friends soon and start hanging out with them. Another few weeks and we won't see a lick of him. Way of the world.

"You must be crapping yourself," I tell him.

"What are you talking about?" he frowns.

"The zombies."

"What about them?"

"They go for freaks with big brains."

He laughs sarcastically. "Know what I like about you, B?"

"What?"

"You'll be dead one day."

We snicker, knock knuckles and head for the park.

THREE

Some of the gang are already in the park, as I guessed they would be. We're too young to get into pubs and there's not much else to do around here. They're hanging out by the swings, trying to look cool. Dipsticks! I mean, how the hell are you supposed to look cool in a *park*?

"Strewth, it's the B-ster," Trev hoots. "And who's that with our cheery old chum? Strike me pink if it ain't our old mate Vinyl! Evening, guv'nor."

Trev loves a bit of old-time cockney slang. Sometimes it's funny but it gets stale quick. "Anything happening?" I ask, taking one of the swings and lifting my feet up so that everyone can admire my sneakers.

"Sod all," Copper says.

"Looking for zombies," Kray yawns.

"We thought Vinyl was one of them," Ballydefeck says.

"Eat me," Vinyl retorts.

"I wouldn't even if I was a zombie," Ballydefeck sniffs.

"Anyone else coming?" I ask.

Trev shrugs. "Talk of a curfew has scared a lot of people. I'm not expecting many more. Surprised to see you, B. I thought you'd have been kept in."

"It'd take more than the threat of a few zombies to keep *me* in," I sneer.

"Aren't you afraid of the living dead?" Kray asks.

"I'm more afraid of your killer breath."

Laughter all round. I grin. It's great to have friends to slag off.

Copper produces a packet of cigs and passes them around. He's good that way. He'd share his last butt with you. He used to take a lot of flack for being a ginger before he butched up, but I always liked him. I slagged him off, sure – and I gave him his nickname – but in a nice way.

I've given a few of my friends nicknames over the years. I'm good at it. You'd be amazed how some people struggle. It doesn't take a stroke of genius to look at a redhead and call him Copper, but even that simple task is beyond a lot of the kids I know.

I'm prouder of Ballydefeck. His family's Irish. Most of us have a bit of Paddy in our blood, but his lot act like they still live in the bog, spuds for dinner every night of the week, Irish dancing competitions on the weekend, Daniel O'Donnell blasting out loud in every

24

room of their house if you pop round. He was known as Paddy or Mick for years. Then one night I was watching a rerun of *Father Ted*. An old priest in it kept cursing, saying, "Feck!" I put that together with the name of an Irish village and came up with Ballydefeck. He's answered to that ever since.

Kray digs out an iPod with a plug-in speaker. It's brand-new, the latest model. I whistle appreciatively. "Fall off the back of a truck?" I ask.

"I don't know what you mean," Kray says indignantly, but his smirk ruins his show of innocence. We've all nicked a bit in our time but Kray would have been Fagin's star student.

We listen to some good tunes – Kray has great taste – and talk about TV, zombies, music, sex. Vinyl tells us about the girls in his new school. He says they're hot and easy. Trev, Copper and Ballydefeck listen with their mouths open as he describes what he's been getting up to with them. Me and Kray look at each other and roll our eyes — we know bullshit when we smell it. But we don't tell Vinyl to shut up. It's fun listening to him stringing the fools along.

After a while I spot a skinny black teenager entering the park. It's Tyler, a kid from our year. He stops when he sees us, hesitates, then backs up.

"Tyler!" I shout. "Get your arse over here!"

He grins nervously and taps his watch. Vanishes before I can call to him again.

"A pity," I sneer. "I fancied a lynching."

"That's a bit harsh, isn't it?" Vinyl says.

"Only joking," I reply.

"Tyler's all right," Vinyl mutters.

"No, he's not," I growl.

"What's wrong with him?" Vinyl challenges me, then smiles with icy sweetness before I can answer. "It's not the color of his skin, is it?"

I scowl at Vinyl but don't say anything. Because to an extent he's right. Dad's a racist and proud of it. He hates anyone who isn't from England, especially if they're dark-skinned. In his ideal world the ruling party would be the Ku Klux Klan and he'd go riding through the streets of London on a horse every day with a load of hood-wearing buddies, keeping law and order with a thick length of rope.

Dad's always warning me of the dangers of racial tolerance. He pushes Aryan books and pamphlets my way. The first picture book I remember reading by myself was *Little Black Sambo*.

I don't believe the same things that Dad does. I don't want to be like him, not that way. But at the same time I've got to live with him. I learned early on not to challenge his word. So I put up with the ranting and raving. I read the hate lit. I laugh at his crude jokes. I've even gone to a few meetings with him, rooms full of angry white men muttering bloody murder.

The trouble with putting on an act is that sometimes it's hard to tell where the actor stops and the real you begins. It's rubbed off on me to an extent, the years of pretending to hate. Vinyl's black as the ace of spades, but he's my only friend who is. And it's not just because I know Dad would hit the roof if he saw me hanging out with black kids or Muslims. Part of me genuinely fears the menace of those who are different. I've read so much and heard so much and been forced to say so much that sometimes I forget that I don't believe it.

To be honest, I'm amazed I'm still friends with Vinyl. We hung out together when we were tiny, before I started selecting my associates more cautiously. When Dad beat me a few times and told me to stop having anything to do with *that horrible little black kid*, that should have been the end of it. I tried to avoid Vinyl after that but I couldn't. We got on too well. He made me laugh, he never teased me, I could talk to him about anything.

I learned to sneak behind Dad's back, never mention Vinyl at home, not be seen with him close to where we live. He's my secret friend. If Dad knew, he'd knock the stuffing out of me. Even one black friend is one too many as far as he's concerned.

"Come on," Vinyl says again, bristling now. "What's wrong with Tyler?"

"I don't like his face," I snap. "What difference does it make?"

"I ran into your dad a few days ago," Vinyl says. "He recognized me, which was a surprise. I thought we all looked the same to him."

"Hey," Trev says uneasily. "Let's drop it."

"He told me he'd heard about my new school," Vinyl goes on, ignoring Trev and staring hard at me. "Said it was amazing what they could teach chimps these days. Asked me if I could peel my own bananas now."

I feel my face flush. I'm ashamed of my mean-spirited, foul-mouthed father. But I'm even more ashamed of myself, because I instinctively want to defend him. I know it's wrong. He shouldn't have said that to Vinyl – to anyone – but part of me wants to take his side, because no matter what, he's my dad and I love him.

"I can't control what he says," I mutter, dropping my gaze.

"But do you agree with it?" Vinyl growls.

"Of course not!" I spit. "Tyler's a whiny brat. He gets up my nose. It's got nothing to do with him being black."

Vinyl eyes me coldly for a long, probing moment. Then he relaxes. "That's all right then." He winks. "You should tell your dad that you want to move in with me."

"Wishful thinking!" I snort.

We laugh, bump fists and everything's okay again. In a weird, messed-up, uncomfortable kind of way. It's not easy sometimes, having a racist for a dad.

FOUR

We meet Suze and La Lips outside a kebab shop. They're sharing a bag of fries and Suze has a kebab that she's saving for later.

"Lovely ladies!" Trev croons. "What does a guy have to do to get a fry and a kiss around here?"

"Sod off," Suze growls as he drapes an arm round each of them. La Lips smiles and cuddles into him.

"What's up?" I ask, eyeing the fries hungrily. I had dinner before I came out but I always get the munchies when I spy a bag of steaming-hot fries.

"We were supposed to be meeting Elephant and Stagger Lee, but they never turned up," La Lips pouts.

"What are you doing with them?" Copper asks suspiciously. La Lips has kissed just about every boy she's ever come into contact with – I snogged her too, a while back, to see what it was like, though she tells me to shut my trap whenever I bring that up – but Copper has been sort of going steady with her for the last few weeks.

"Stagger Lee was going to give us new ringtones for our phones," Suze says.

"More Nick Cave, I bet," Copper scowls (Stagger Lee's a Nick Cave freak—he was nicknamed after one of the singer's most famous songs) and drags La Lips away from Trev.

"Careful!" she shouts, spilling a couple of fries. She rubs her arm where he pinched her and glares.

"You won't be copping a feel tonight," Kray laughs.

"He doesn't cop a feel *any* night," La Lips says, tossing her hair indignantly, but nobody buys that for even a second.

"Here," Suze says, handing me the bag of fries. "I can't bear to look at you drooling any longer."

"Cheers, ears." I tuck in and the others crowd around me. Thirty seconds later the fries are gone and we're licking our lips.

Suze shakes her head. "Like a pack of dogs," she sighs. Then she smiles at Vinyl, the only one who didn't grab any fries. "How's the new school?"

Vinyl shrugs. "You know. All right."

"Is it very different from ours?" La Lips asks.

"Yeah. They have gold-rimmed toilet seats."

"No way!" she gasps.

Everyone laughs.

"You're an idiot," I tell her.

"Less of that," Copper says, draping a protective arm around her.

"My hero," La Lips simpers and stands on her toes to stick her tongue down his throat.

"Not in public!" I roar and we keep on going down the street, jostling and laughing.

The girls don't have much news. They're as bored as we are. Suze and I walk a little ahead of the others, chatting about our mums—they used to be best friends when they were our age. But then Ballydefeck starts telling us to kiss each other, so I round on him and give him a slap to shut him up. He covers his head with both hands. "Not the face, B! Not the face!" In the end I kick him playfully and leave it at that.

We come to a liquor store and pause by the window, enviously studying the bottles. Most of us have had a drink or two in our time – Dad let me sip beer when I was a baby, for laughs – but it's hard to get hold of. Another few years and we'll be able to pass for eighteen and go to parties and drink ourselves stupid. But for now we can't do much apart from ogle and dream.

"Wait here," I tell the others, deciding to stir things up a bit. I push into the shop and walk straight to the beer fridge. I pick up a six-pack of the cheapest brand I can find – in case I get lucky – then lug it to the counter. The Pakistani guy behind the till stares at me, unimpressed. "Ring it up, boss," I tell him.

"You are underage." He doesn't even ask to see my ID.

"No I'm not. Go on, ring it up, I'm good for it." I dig out a tattered wallet that once belonged to my dad and slide out a tenner that I've been holding on to since Friday.

"You are underage," he says again. "It is illegal to sell alcohol to anyone under the age of eighteen. Please leave my shop immediately."

"*Please leave my shop immediately*," I echo, mimicking his accent. I know it's petty but I can't stop myself.

"If you do not leave, I will call the police," he says.

"Call them what?" I smirk.

He points to a security camera. "This is all being recorded. I would advise you to return the alcohol to its shelf and –"

I let the six-pack drop. The cans fizz but don't explode. "Stick them back on the shelf yourself, numbnuts."

His face darkens and he leans forward to strike me. Then he stops and points at the door. "Out!" he screams.

I laugh and shoot him the finger. I give the finger to the camera too, then take my time heading for the door. I plan to tell Dad about this later, knowing he'll laugh, lovingly run his hand over my head and tell me I did good.

"You're crazy," Kray yells when I get outside, then he bumps my fist hard. They're all laughing and Trev gives me knuckles too.

"Same old B," Vinyl smiles tightly. For a moment I think he's going to have a go at me again, but he says nothing more.

"You didn't really expect him to sell you any beer, did you?" Suze asks.

"No." I whip out a bar of chocolate from beneath my T-shirt. "But he was so wound up about the beer, he never saw me palming this."

Lots of cheers. They all lean in for a square. I push them away, then dole it out, a piece for everyone, a quick prayer of thanks to Mr. Cadbury, then on we go, the others still cooing over what I did.

Later I head home alone through the dark. And do I worry about zombies? Do I bugger. I'm B Smith. This is my turf. Any zombies on the loose should be worried about *me*!

FIVE

That night I have the nightmare again. I've been tormented by it for as long as I can remember. Always the same, and always as terrifying.

I'm on a plane. We haven't taken off yet. I'm by the window but I don't look out. In the dream I never look out.

There's a woman next to me and a baby in the aisle seat. The baby's sitting alone, strapped in by a normal belt. I know that's not right — they have special straps for babies on planes – but in the dream it doesn't seem strange.

The woman's chatting to her child, cooing, making nonsense noises. The baby ignores her. It's staring straight ahead. I don't know if it's a boy or a girl—it's dressed in white clothes.

We taxi down the runway. The engine roars. The plane tears free of the ground and whines like a dying dog. I shake in my seat. My stomach clenches. I don't mind flying but I hate takeoff. We go abroad most years, Costa del Sol, Cyprus, Ibiza. Each time we rise, I'm sure that the engine will stall, that the plane will drop sickeningly, that I'll die from an explosion or burn to death slowly. The fear passes when we level out, but for that first minute or two... absolute terror.

It's no different in the dream. Except in a way it is. Because I know something worse than a crash is coming. I sense it in the air. The roar of a plane engine is always menacing, but this sounds worse. It sounds *hungry*.

The woman starts to cry. She doesn't raise her hands, just sits upright, sobbing, tears streaming down her cheeks. I stare at her, wanting to say something but struck dumb by fear of what's to come.

Then the baby speaks.

"don't cry mummy."

Its voice is tinny, barely a whisper, but it carries above the roar of the engine. The woman doesn't look at the baby or stop crying.

"don't be frightened mummy," the baby says. *"we're with you. we'll always be with you."*

The baby's head turns. But it's not looking at its mother. It's looking at me. It has no pupils, just balls of white for eyes.

"you're yummy mummy," the baby whispers. It should be funny but it isn't. The unnatural infant has a full set of teeth, all sharpened

into fangs. Drops of blood drip from the sides of its mouth as it speaks.

The baby stands. (I don't know what happened to the belt.) I stare at it and it stares at me. The woman between us has vanished. The baby looks like a doll, not moving, not breathing, white eyes, sharp teeth, blood.

"*don't be frightened mummy*," the baby says. Except its lips don't move. After a confused moment I realize the voice came from the seat in front. I tear my gaze away from the baby and look ahead.

Another baby is clinging to the top of the seat. I can see its face and shoulders, its perfect, tiny hands. It has the same type of clothes as the baby next to me. Same white eyes and sharp teeth. But no blood on this one's lips. Not yet.

"*we'll save you mummy*," the baby in front whispers.

"*we'll always be with you mummy.*" Another voice, from behind.

The baby in my row is in the seat next to me now. The top of its head doesn't quite reach my chin. It's leaning forward. I should be able to knock it away with a single swipe. But I don't move. I can't.

"*you have to die now mummy*," the baby says, and *die* is echoed in whispers around the cabin.

I half rise and look over the top of the seats ahead of me. Babies everywhere, all standing, climbing the seats, looking at me, whispering *die*.

I glance back—more of the same. Scores of babies clambering

over the seats, but calmly, smoothly, faces blank, eyes white, mouths open, teeth flashing.

I cringe away from the monstrous babies and press hard against the window. I think I'm crying but I can't be sure. The babies crawl over the seats, closer and closer, a tide of them, all looking the same. Only their fingers move, little flickers of flesh and bone. Otherwise they could be gliding.

The baby next to me climbs into my lap and stands, feet planted on my thighs, face right in front of mine now. Others crowd around it. Unnaturally slender fingers fasten on my legs, my ankles, my wrists, my arms. A baby grabs my ears and pulls back my head, exposing my throat. There are more babies on the ceiling, hanging from it like angels or vampires.

"*join us mummy*," the baby directly in front of me says. The blood on its chin has dried. It falls off in flaky scabs.

"*die mummy*," the others croon.

"*you're one of us*," the baby in my lap snarls, and suddenly its face changes. Its eyes glare red. Its lips contort into a sneer. Lines of hatred warp its clammy flesh. "*you're one of us mummy*," it shrieks.

The baby thrusts forward and latches on to my throat. Those clinging to the ceiling drop. The rest press in around me. All of their mouths are open, rows of tiny, shiny teeth. All make a sickening moaning sound.

Then they bite...

SIX

…and I wake up.

I'm shaking and sweating. I always am after the nightmare. I feel like I've been screaming, but in all these years I've never made a sound. Mum and Dad would have told me if I had.

I only wear underpants and a T-shirt to bed. I used to wear pajamas, but I'd always sweat through them when I had the dream and have to dump them the next day.

I get up and stagger to the bathroom. I take off the T-shirt on the way and drop it by the foot of my bed, knowing Mum will stick it in the laundry basket in the morning.

I sit on the toilet, shivering. I don't need to pee. I just have to wait somewhere outside my bedroom for a bit, until the shakes pass.

I hate that bloody dream. Apart from when Dad is on the rampage, it's the only time I ever feel truly scared, lost, out of my depth, helpless. What's worse, I can't tell anyone about it. What would it look like, someone my age admitting they're scared by a dream about babies? I mean, if it was cannibals or monsters or something, fair enough. But bloody *babies*!

Dad would skin me if he heard I still have the nightmare. When I'd go crying to him as a kid, he'd tell me not to be stupid, there was nothing scary about babies. When I kept bothering him, he whipped me with his belt. He asked a few weeks later if I was still having the dream, I forced a grin and said I wasn't.

When the shakes stop, I get up and wash my face and hands. I wipe sweat from my back with a towel, then pause and study myself in the mirror. My eyes are bloodshot and blurry with traces of fear – I think I sometimes cry quietly in my sleep – so I splash water over them and rub them with my knuckles until it hurts. Next time I check, I just look angry. That's better.

I study my light blue eyes and admire my stubbled head. Flex my biceps. Rub a faded yellow bruise on my left arm where Dad thumped me a week ago when I didn't hand him the remote quick enough. I wink at myself and mutter, "Looking good, B."

I massage my stomach, to loosen the tightened muscles, then pick at the faded white scar near the top of my right thigh. It's a small *c* shape, from an injection I had when I was two or three years old. It was a new type of flu vaccine. Dad volunteered me for it—

they were paying good money for guinea pigs. Mum was worried but Dad said there was no way they'd test it on babies if there was any chance it would cause harm.

He was right and it worked a treat. I've never even had a cold. I don't know why it didn't make it to the shops. Maybe there were side effects and I'm one of the lucky ones who didn't suffer any. Or maybe they have to wait a certain amount of time before they can put it on the market.

I scowl and stop picking the *c* scar. The things that go through your mind at – I check my watch – 3:27 in the morning. I should be sleeping, not analyzing a dumb bloody scar. I grin at myself "You're a stupid…"

I stop. In the mirror I spot a baby standing on the laundry basket, hands red with blood, eyes white, teeth glinting. It breathes out and a small cloud of red mist rises from its mouth.

I shut my eyes and count to five, taking quick breaths, cursing myself for my weakness. When I look again, there's nobody behind me.

I stomp from the bathroom and back to bed. I grab a fresh T-shirt from my wardrobe and glare as I pull it on, mad at myself for letting the nightmare freak me out so much.

"It was only a dream, B," I whisper as I lie beneath the covers, eyes wide, knowing I won't get a wink of sleep again tonight. "Only a dream. Only a dream. Only a…"

SEVEN

School. Tired and grumpy. I hate the nightmare more than ever. I'm a teenager. I should be dreaming about getting hot and steamy with movie stars, not about killer babies. I was sure I'd leave the dream behind as I got older, but no such luck. I still have it two or three nights a week.

I barely listen in class at the best of times. Today I tune out completely and scribble crude drawings over my books. I suck at art but I like to doodle when I'm bored.

Most of my teachers ignore me. They know I'm a lost cause and they don't try to reach out to me. They also know I'm not someone you mess with. One of them crossed me a couple of years ago. I'd been in a fight and had been sent to the principal's office. The teacher saw me waiting outside and whispered something to one of his colleagues. Both men sniggered. Then he said out loud, "But what can you expect from someone with a father like *that*?"

Someone punctured the tires on that teacher's car. Someone found out where he lived and threw a brick through his window. Someone stuck up pictures of him around the local area with his phone number and the message, *Ring for a good time!*

I'm not saying who that *someone* was, but after he came creeping up to B Smith in school one day and meekly said, "Sorry for what I said about your dad," he was left in peace.

I fall asleep in history. Jonesenzio is duller than most of our teachers. I'm not the only one to snooze in his class.

"Fire!" someone hisses in my ear and I jolt awake, almost falling off my chair.

Meths and Kray laugh their faces off as Jonesenzio scowls at me.

"Sods," I spit at them, rubbing my elbow where I hit it on the desk.

"If you're *quite* finished..." Jonesenzio murmurs.

"Sorry, Mr. Jones," I simper. "I thought I saw a mouse."

He drones on. I don't mind Jonesenzio. He's given me a C on every essay we've been assigned for the last three years, even though I've never handed one in.

Mum sometimes grouches about my lousy grades. "How come you don't do as well in the other subjects as you do in history?" Dad tosses me a wink when she goes on like that. He had Jonesenzio when he was younger. He knows the score.

"I bet you were dreaming about me," Meths chuckles, keeping his voice low so as not to disturb the teacher. Jonesenzio doesn't complain if you talk loudly in his class, but he stops talking and stands there silently, looking at you politely, which is even worse. A couple of us tested him once and found that he's happy to do that for an entire class. You'll never out-patient the Jones.

"Yeah," I tell Meths. "It was a real nightmare."

Meths is the biggest guy in our year, and the oldest. He started school a year later than most of us and has been held back twice. That's where he got his nickname, short for Methuselah. I wish I could lay claim to that but it wasn't one of mine. I'd no idea who Methuselah was until someone explained it to me.

"You can copy my notes later," Kray says seriously.

"Notes?" I take the bait.

He holds up a drawing. Kray's a much better artist than me. The picture is of La Lips, naked, being given some after-school tuition by a very animated Jonesenzio.

I smother a laugh and raise my knuckles for him to knock. "Don't let Copper see it," I gasp.

"I was hoping he could correct any anatomical inaccuracies," Kray says.

"Like you haven't seen La Lips in the swimming pool," Meths snorts, and this time we all have to smother laughs. It's an old story that

La Lips shows everything in the public pool if you give her a quid. No truth in it as far as I know, but when did that ever stop a good story?

History ends (if only!) and we roll out into the yard for lunch. I swipe a bag of chips and nick a bar of chocolate from a girl in a lower year. She tries to fight me for it but her friends pull her off. I sneer as they haul her away. She had a narrow escape. In my current mood I'd have happily taken her into the toilet and half drowned her. If her friends hadn't pulled her clear when they did...

I spend most of the break with Meths, Kray, Trev, Ballydefeck, Suze, La Lips, Copper, Dunglop and Elephant. The usual gang, except for Linzer and Pox, who are off somewhere else.

There's a new zombie clip circulating on the Internet. Copper shows it to us on his phone. It's footage of an undead soldier. If the clip is genuine, it looks like he was one of the team sent in to eliminate the Pallaskenry mob. He must have been infected, got away, tangled with some humans later.

In the clip, several men are pounding the zombie with shovels and axes. One of them strikes his left arm a few times and it tears loose. Another of the men picks it up and starts whacking the zombie over the head with it, cheered on by his team.

I laugh the first time I watch the clip. Most of the others do too. It's comical, a guy being slapped around with his own severed arm.

Then, as Copper replays it a couple of times, I start focusing on the finer details. The terror in the men's eyes. The rage and hunger in the soldier's. The flecks of dried blood around his mouth, a sign that he must have fed prior to his run-in with the vigilantes. The long bits of bone sticking out of his fingers. His fangs.

The clip stops with the guys hitting the zombie, leaving us to guess how it ends. I imagine one of the group chopping off the soldier's head with an ax, the men pulping it beneath their feet, not stopping until every last scrap of brain has been mulched. That's how they kill zombies in films, by destroying their brains. Does that work in real life too? I assume so but I'm not sure.

There's silence when Copper turns off his phone. We're all troubled by what we've seen. We can't even make a joke about it. Not yet. It feels too real at the moment. We need time to absorb and then dismiss it.

Elephant starts rabbiting on about soccer in order to break the solemn spell. He's a real fanatic, goes to matches all the time. I watch the highlights on TV most weeks, so that I can discuss the goals with the others, but soccer bores me.

Elephant finishes moaning about the weekend's match and pauses for breath.

"Enough already," I snap. "You're driving me crazy."

"Who rattled your cage?" Elephant scowls.

"You did," I tell him. "And if you don't shut it, I'll cut you down to size."

Lots of catcalls, everyone relieved to have something else to think about, welcoming the distraction. Elephant didn't get his nickname because he's tall or fat, but because of what his mates saw the first time he undressed for a shower after gym.

"Leave my trunk alone," Elephant smirks, crossing his hands protectively in front of himself.

"Are you all right?" Trev asks me. "You're like a tiger today."

"Knackered," I growl. "Didn't get much sleep."

"Worried about zombies?" Suze asks sympathetically.

"Don't be daft," I tell her. "I'm dreading the exams."

Everyone laughs, forgetting about the clip, putting it behind us, slipping back into our normal routines as if we'd never been disturbed.

"You won't get into Oxford if you don't get straight A's," Dunglop says.

"I prefer Cambridge anyway," I sniff.

"God, imagine if you *did* get in," Meths says, and we stare at him. "I mean on a sports scholarship or something."

"You ever see me playing any sports?" I jeer.

"No, but maybe there's some other…" Meths pulls a face and tries to remember what he wanted to say. I fail classes because I don't give a damn. Meths, bless him, really *is* thick.

The bell rings and I slap Meths's back. "Come on. I don't think either of us has to worry about Cambridge or Oxford. I'll be amazed if we make it out of this place."

"Yeah, but…" Meths shrugs and smiles, letting go of whatever crazy thought it was that he had. Thoughts never stick long with Meths. If zombies ever do attack, he has nothing to worry about. With that tiny brain, he's the last one they'll target!

EIGHT

Biology. One of the few classes where I pay attention. Not because I'm fascinated by the digestive system of the worm (give me strength!) but because I like the teacher, Mr. Burke.

Burke impressed me the first day he walked into class and said, "I know most of you couldn't give a toss about biology, but if you don't give me any grief, I'll do my best to make it interesting for you."

Burke's the best of our teachers, maybe the only really good one that we have. I don't know what he's doing in this dump. He should be at a good school like the one Vinyl moved to. He's wasted here, stuck with mugs like Meths and Kray and... yeah, I can admit it... me.

Dad doesn't share my high opinion of

Mr. Burke and has tried a few times to have him drummed out, or at least confined to teaching kids of his own race. Which is odd, because the lightly colored Burke is of a mixed background. I would have thought that meant he could claim membership to either side, but Dad doesn't see it that way. He moans about Burke all the time and I nod like the obedient little puppy that I am and simper, "Yes, Dad. No, Dad. Three bags full, Dad." It sickens me but what can I do? If I told him Burke's a cool teacher, he'd hammer me. Easier to say nothing and keep my head down.

Burke is trying hard to make the dissection of a worm seem like an earth-shattering event but it's hard to keep us interested in crap like this. After a while Trev puts up a hand. "Sir?"

"Go on," Burke sighs, looking up from the worm with an expression that seems to suggest he finds this particular lesson as boring as the rest of us.

"Can we dissect a zombie next, sir?"

Laughter.

"If you bring me one, I'll certainly help you cut it up," Burke says drily, then pushes the worm aside. I grin at Trev and give him a cheesy thumbs-up. It's great when we sidetrack Burke. He doesn't let it happen often – he insists on covering the course inside out – but every now and then he'll relent.

"Who believes that zombies are real?" Burke asks.

A few hands go up, but not many. It's not that we don't believe, just that we don't want to be seen to be enthusiastic in class.

"Come on," Burke snaps. "A real show of hands or it's back to the worm."

We groan, then hands start creeping up. Soon most of them are in the air.

Burke does a slow count, then says softly, "Why?"

We gape at him.

"Why?" he says again. "Because they're on TV? Because you've seen photos and video clips?"

"Yeah," someone says.

"But they can do anything with digital equipment these days, can't they?" he smirks.

"Don't you believe, sir?" I ask. I was one of the few to keep their hand down.

"Actually, I do," he says. "But let's explore alternatives." He turns to the whiteboard, grabs a pen and writes *Media hoax? Publicity for a film or TV show?* then looks over his shoulder at us. "Any other ideas?"

"It's a conspiracy," Stagger Lee snorts.

"The government?" Burke asks.

"Yeah."

"The Irish? Ours? America's?"

Stagger Lee shrugs. "The whole bloody lot."

"What for?" Burke asks. "Why go to all that trouble?"

Silence for a moment, then Linzer – one of the smartest in our year – puts up her hand and says, "Experiment gone wrong."

"Good," Burke beams and adds it to the whiteboard. "What sort of experiment?"

"Chemical weapons," Linzer says. "Maybe they were testing something and it accidentally got into the water or air. Or they released it on purpose."

"Which is more likely?" Burke asks, nodding at Elephant.

"Dunno," Elephant says.

"B?"

"A test," I say confidently.

"Why?" he presses.

"Pallaskenry's in the middle of nowhere. They wouldn't have any labs around there. It's all bog land."

"Excellent, B."

I find myself grinning goofily. Nobody has a dig at me to bring me down to size either, like they would if this was any other class.

"More ideas," Burke says, pointing to Suze.

"God, I don't know." She blushes, then coughs. "My dad thinks it's terrorists."

Burke blinks. "Come again?"

"He thinks the army went in looking for terrorists. Got carried away and killed civilians by mistake. Then cooked up this zombie story to give them an excuse to kill the witnesses."

"Far-fetched," Burke hums, "but let's run with it." He adds the theory to the board and asks for more suggestions.

Someone thinks the zombies are robots gone wild. Another says

54

maybe it's aliens, that the rabid crazies were taken over by bodiless beings from another planet. Kray comes up with a twist on the experiment angle, only he figures people are being controlled by satellite signals.

"They're gonna use it on the Arabs," he says. "No more sending our troops in to sort out their messes. Drive the buggers mad and leave them to it. They'll wipe themselves out, and good riddance to them."

The Muslim kids don't like that. Angry mutterings. Burke shushes them.

"That's not one of the more far-fetched ideas," he says. "Certain politicians would do just about anything to cling to power and disable our enemies. Kray was insulting – grow up and stop acting like a thug – but he might have a point."

"I don't think it's terrifying," I snort, evil-eyeing the Muslims. "In fact I hope Kray's right, that we *are* going after them. They'd do it to us if they could."

"We'll have that argument another day," Burke barks, stopping a war before it can erupt. "Let's stick to zombies. Any other proposals?"

There are a few more, then Burke stands back to study what he's written. "It's a horrible world, isn't it?" he mutters and I'm not sure he knows that he's spoken out loud.

He turns to us. "I'm not saying I believe any of these exotic, unfounded theories. But these are questions we should be asking.

55

Life's complicated. Answers rarely come wrapped up nice and simple. There are plenty of people out there ready to tell us what we should and shouldn't believe. We always need to be skeptical, to look for the sting in the tale."

Burke looks around slowly and it seems like he's staring at each and every one of us in turn. "Trust no one. Always question what you're told. Don't believe the lies that people feed you, even if they're your teachers or parents. At the end of the day you have to work out for yourself what's right or wrong."

He glances back at the board and sighs. "But bear in mind. There are lots of black-hearted, mean-spirited bastards in the world." There are some gasps when he swears but most of us take no notice. "It's important that we hold them to account. But always remember that *you* might be the most black-hearted and mean-spirited of the lot, so hold yourself the most accountable of all."

As we try to make sense of that, Burke chuckles, shakes his head and wipes the board clean. "Enough preaching," he says brightly, then adds, to a chorus of groans, "Back to the worm..."

NINE

The last class ends and we churn out, shouting, laughing, cursing. Normally I can't escape the building quick enough, but today I head deeper into it. There's a five-a-side soccer tournament in the gym. I'm not playing, and I'm not really bothered about watching, but it'll be more fun than hanging out on the streets.

Kray, Elephant, Trev, Linzer and I wind our way through the labyrinth of corridors. Our school's massive. It holds over a thousand students, and it used to be even bigger. It wasn't always the cesspit it is now. Once upon a time they sank money into this place, kept adding on new rooms. It's not very wide but it's deep. Takes several minutes, with all the twists and turns, to get from one end to the other.

No outdoor spaces apart from a few small courtyards. The gym's a huge room at the rear of the building, solid walls all around, a few narrow skylight windows high overhead, lots of artificial light. The phys-ed staff keep it in good shape. You can play soccer, basketball, hockey, badminton. They have foosball and pool tables stacked at the sides— they bring them out at lunch for those who are so easily amused.

We hit the gym and spread out. There's already a crowd and the first game has kicked off. The teams are from the year above ours, so we give them loads of abuse, trying to distract them. One player shoots us the finger and we cheer.

"Bloody idiots," I laugh. "Running round like maniacs."

"It's the beautiful game," Elephant argues. He loves soccer but hasn't played in ages, still recovering from breaking his foot a few months back.

"Beautiful waste of time," I tease him, but he's too engrossed in the game to pay me much attention.

I get bored quickly and look around for something else to do. There's a small group to our left, cheering on the players, a mix of kids from different years. I don't know most of them, but one catches my eye—Tyler Bayor.

My dad had a bust-up with Tyler's old man a while back. Tyler's dad had accused me of stealing from his son. It was true – I took money from him a few times, like I took the bar of chocolate from the girl today, because Tyler's soft and the cash was there for the taking – but I denied it until I was blue in the face.

My dad was furious that a black guy had dared point the finger at me. Marched round to their home, dragged Tyler's dad outside, fought with him in the street. Others separated them before it got nasty. We retreated with our heads held high, and Tyler's dad didn't push the charges any further.

I stopped stealing from Tyler, even though my dad told me he didn't care what I did to *that walking fart of a kid*. I didn't stop because I'd been challenged. I stopped because I knew my dad thought that I was targeting Tyler because of his race. I wasn't. I picked on Tyler because he was weak and I could get away with it. But I felt uneasy, seeing myself through my dad's eyes, like I was the same as him.

I never told any of the others about what happened, which is why Vinyl didn't realize it was personal when I was having a go at Tyler in the park. I'm not sure why I kept it secret. I guess I was ashamed, not of stealing, but of my dad turning it into a racial thing.

Even though I don't steal from Tyler anymore, I don't like him. The sight of him reminds me of that night, my dad squaring up to Tyler's old man, me feeling proud and mortified at the same time, all of it brought on by Tyler not keeping his mouth shut and putting up with the theft as any good victim should.

"Hey, Tyler," I shout. "Why didn't you come play with us the other night?"

Tyler looks at me and forces a laugh. Turns back to the game, hoping I'll let it drop. But I'm not in the dropping mood.

"Oi! Don't ignore me."

"I'm not ignoring you, B," he sighs.

"You bloody are."

The kids around him back away and focus on the game. None of them wants to get sucked into this.

Tyler gulps and faces me. "I was looking for a mate. He wasn't there. So I left."

"But you didn't even stop to say hello," I remind him.

"That was rude," Kray chuckles, giving me a dig in the ribs, egging me on.

"I know your kind aren't the most civilized in the world," I continue, taking a few steps towards the small, nervous kid, "but I thought you'd have the good manners to –"

"What do you mean, *your kind*?" someone snaps.

I halt and blink. A tall black girl has stepped forward. She's glaring at me. She's from the year above mine, Nancy something-or-other.

"You got a problem?" I snarl.

"Yeah," she says, stepping in front of Tyler, who can't believe his luck. "You just said that blacks are uncivilized."

"Not me," I grin.

"Yes you did," she huffs. "I heard what you said. *Your kind.*"

"Maybe I was talking about his family," I chuckle. "Or the fans of the team he supports."

"No," Nancy says. "I know exactly what you meant."

I shrug and fake a yawn. Nancy's got me dead to rights, but I can't admit that in front of the others. It's not in my nature to back

60

down. You can never show weakness. You have to fight every fight that comes your way. Otherwise you end up being picked on, like Tyler.

"Let's say you're right," I drawl. "So what?"

"I won't stand for racism," Nancy says. "Apologize or I'll report you."

"Me?" I gasp. "Racist? You're nuts. Isn't she, Kray?"

Kray chuckles weakly but says nothing. He doesn't want the hassle.

"Tell her I'm not a racist, Tyler. Tell her you and me are good friends and were just having a laugh."

"Leave him alone," Nancy says. "Pick on me if you want to pick on someone."

I grin tightly. "All right." I move closer and get in her face, even though I have to go right up on my toes. "I *was* talking about blacks," I murmur. I know it's madness, that I won't be able to justify this if she grasses me up. But I've only two choices here — apologize or push through with the hard-nosed, racist routine. And I wasn't brought up to apologize. Certainly not to the likes of her.

Nancy pushes me away. "You're scum," she sneers.

"At least I'm white scum," I toss back at her, slipping into hateful character with alarming ease.

"You'll be suspended scum once I tell a teacher what you said."

"Is that how you deal with people who wind you up?" I jeer. "You run to the teachers?"

61

"Yeah."

I shrug. "Go on then. It's my word against yours. But while you're complaining about me, I'll complain too. You pushed me. That's physical assault and everyone saw it."

"Rubbish," she snorts.

"You raised your hands and pushed me. That's a direct attack." I step up close to Nancy and smile. "If you're gonna get done just for pushing me, you might as well go the whole hog. Go on, knock my block off, you know you want to. You lot love to fight, don't you? It's what you were born for. Well, that and basketball."

Nancy's fingers bunch into fists. She's trembling. She wants to hit me but she'll lose the moral high ground if she does. If she strikes the first blow, she won't be able to turn me in. It doesn't matter if you're provoked — school policy is that you should never react.

"Go on," I whisper, then sink lower than I ever thought I would, and make a few soft, gorilla-like grunting noises.

Nancy shrieks and slaps me. I laugh.

"Is that the hardest you can hit?" I mock her.

She slaps me again, a flurry of feeble blows. I don't even bother to raise my hands to protect myself. "Help me!" I yell theatrically. "She's gone mad. I think she has rabies. Don't let her bite. I'm afraid she'll —"

One of Nancy's rings catches my cheek and tears into it. I hiss and slap her away. A thin trickle of blood flows from the cut. The sight of it goads Nancy on. She throws herself at me and grapples

for my eyes with her nails, kicking my shins, screaming shrilly. I put a hand on her face to push her away. She bites my fingers.

I grit my teeth and tear my hand free. Nancy goes for my eyes again. Losing my temper, I step back and let fly, a real punch. My fist hits the side of her face and she goes down. She lands hard and cries out. I start after her to finish her off, but Elephant and Kray get in my way.

"Easy, B," Kray says. "She's not as tough as you."

"I don't care," I shout. "She bit me. I'm gonna –"

"B Smith!" someone roars.

I look up and groan. It's Stuttering Stan, one of the PE teachers. He doesn't really stutter but he trips over his tongue sometimes.

"You're in for it now," Nancy cackles, smiling through her tears of pain and anger.

"You hit me first," I snarl.

"Tell it to Stuttering Stan," she crows.

I spit at her as if I were a child, then turn and stand to attention, staring directly at Stuttering Stan as he strides towards me, acting as if I've done nothing wrong. I know I should feel ashamed of myself, and to a degree I do. But to my surprise and dismay, I also feel smug, because I know Dad would be proud if he could see me now, bringing an interfering black girl down a peg or two.

TEN

Stuttering Stan takes me to the principal's office. Very neat, everything in its place. A shining computer in one corner. Diplomas on the walls. A small plaque on her desk, MRS. LYNNE REED, PRINCIPAL, just in case anyone is in any doubt.

Nancy's already outside, waiting her turn. I'm sitting across from Mrs. Reed, gaze glued to the floor, waiting for her to start in on me. She transferred here the year that I started, and I was one of the first students she had to discipline, just a couple of days into her new job. I've had to explain myself to her a lot of times since then, though in my defense it's been a while since I was last hauled before her.

Mrs. Reed flicks through a file, slowly. I'm guessing it's about me. I try not to fidget. My face is red and I keep my hands tucked under my legs, in case she spots them trembling. I shouldn't be worried. I'm in trouble, sure, but Dad won't give me any grief, not when he hears what it was about. Still, I'm in the wrong and Mrs. Reed isn't the sort of person who makes you feel at ease in a situation like this. She looks like something from an ancient movie, black cape, silver hair, thin-rimmed glasses.

"I don't like it when my students fight," she finally says, putting the file aside.

"Nancy started it," I say evenly, careful not to sound like I'm whining.

"I'll let Miss Price state her case once I'm through with you," Mrs. Reed says. "I suspect her story will differ significantly from yours. Please tell me what happened, and try to be honest if you can."

I was going to spin it, but that last line stings me. It's like she's challenging me. So I decide to hit her with the facts. If I'm going down, I might as well go down with my dignity intact, not whimpering and making up stories.

"I was having a dig at Tyler."

"Tyler Bayor?" she asks.

"Yeah. Nancy stuck her nose in and told me I was being racist."

"Were you?"

"No." I scowl. "I mean, yeah, in a way I was, but nothing bad. I said something about his kind not being civilized."

"That was stupid," Mrs. Reed murmurs.

66

I bristle but don't retort. Because she's right—it *was* stupid.

"Anyway," I mutter, "Nancy squared up to me. I told her to butt out. She didn't. Then she slapped me."

"She struck first?" Mrs. Reed asks.

"Yeah. Everyone saw her."

"And you hit back?"

"No. I let her slap me a few times. I tried to make a joke out of it. But then she cut me and I lost it."

"I see. Is there anything else you wish to add?"

I think about stopping there, but Mrs. Reed is looking at me archly, like she still doesn't think I'm capable of telling the truth. "I made some gorilla noises," I sigh, my blush deepening.

Mrs. Reed hums, picks up my file again and glances through it.

"I know your father," she says out of the blue.

"My dad?" I frown.

"Yes," she says. "We share concerns about our nation's disintegrating morals and have attended many of the same meetings over the years."

I blink, confusion turning into outright bewilderment. Dad has never talked about Mrs. Reed. I can't imagine where they could have run into each other, except at parent-teacher evenings.

"Your father is an upstanding member of the community," Mrs. Reed continues, and I have to choke back a scornful laugh. "He works tirelessly for the things he believes in. Always there to lend his support when it is needed, giving selflessly of his time and energy.

We need people like him. People like *you*. People who want to make Britain great again, who are prepared to fly in the face of public apathy and political correctness."

She pauses to make sure I'm on her wavelength. And I am. Mrs. Reed must share Dad's low opinion of foreigners. I wouldn't have thought someone in her position could be as small-minded and bigoted as my old man, but thinking back to the meetings he's made me attend, there were all sorts present. I guess racists come from every walk of life.

"This is not where we fight our battles," Mrs. Reed says as I gape at her. "You achieve nothing by stirring up trouble like this. You merely hand ammunition to those who wish to undermine our cause. When you get into difficulties of this nature, it reflects poorly on your father, and by extension on the rest of us."

"I wasn't fighting any battles," I wheeze. "I was just having a go at Tyler and then Nancy got in my way and…"

Mrs. Reed smiles gently. "I know it can be frustrating when people like Nancy interfere. Like your father, I am critical of this government's immigration policies. They have let in too many people of Nancy's caliber, and afforded them far too prominent a voice. But we must fight sensibly for a sensible Britain. When you are older, you can vote and campaign and express your concerns politically. The tide is turning. Public opinion is swinging our way, and will continue to do so, but only if people can trust us, if we behave calmly and responsibly. We must rise above insults and petty fights. We're better than that.

"You can return to class now," Mrs. Reed says. "I'll have a talk with Miss Price. Since she slapped you first, I'm sure I'll be able to convince her to let the matter drop. But, to be safe, tomorrow I want you to take her to one side and apologize."

"But –" I start to object.

"It's that or a suspension," Mrs. Reed snaps.

I fall silent. I wasn't going to argue about the apology. I was going to say that this isn't fair. I thought she was going to chew me a new arsehole. I didn't expect her to sympathize with me. I wasn't fighting for a cause. I'm not like my dad. I don't give a stuff about any of that crap. I expected her to bawl me out, suspend me, maybe expel me. Instead she's commending me. For making gorilla noises to a black girl.

It's wrong. I lost my head and did something I shouldn't have. That was bad, but this is worse. It's disturbing to think that a woman in Mrs. Reed's position would praise me for losing my temper and saying such a thing.

But how dumb would I need to be to criticize my principal for being a racist? She's giving me a get-out-of-jail-free card. I'd have to be a moron or a martyr to turn that down. And I'm neither.

"All right," I mutter and get up and go.

I don't look at Nancy as I pass. I can't meet her eyes. She probably thinks it's because I'm upset at having been punished. But it's not. It's because I'm ashamed that Mrs. Reed thinks I'm a racist. And because I'm worried that she might be right.

ELEVEN

On my way home, I choose to tell Dad about what happened with Tyler, Nancy and Mrs. Reed, figuring it's better that he hear about it from me rather than someone else.

To my surprise, Dad is already there when I arrive. He must have clocked off early. He's in the kitchen, talking with someone. No sign of Mum.

Dad often has people over to the flat. As Mrs. Reed noted, he's heavily involved with local movements to stem the tide of immigration and keep Britain white. He does a lot of canvassing for politicians, works hard behind the scenes, helps stir things up.

I've always tried to stay out of that area of his life, but it's getting harder. Now that

I'm older, he's started taking me to meetings. I've been to a few rallies with him too, and once he took me to a house packed with Muslims. I stood outside while he went in and had a long conversation with them. Well, it was more of a screaming match. I could hear them from outside, the Muslims shrieking, Dad shouting even louder. I felt small and afraid, no idea what was going on or what would happen next, standing in the middle of the street like a lemon, wondering what I should do if Dad never reappeared.

But he did emerge in the end, and I saw a Muslim guy glowering behind him. Dad pointed to me and said, "That's who I fight for—my kid, my wife, my friends. Anything ever happens to any of them, I'll come back here and burn the lot of you down to the ground."

Then Dad hugged me hard. I glared at the Muslim and shot him the finger. Dad laughed, clapped my back, took me for dinner and bought me the biggest hamburger I'd ever seen. I felt bad about it afterwards but at the time I was on cloud nine.

Part of me knows I should stop acting, that I'm on thin ice, growing less sure of where the actor ends and the real me begins. When I grunted at Nancy, that wasn't part of an act. That came from the soul.

I should tell Dad I don't share his views, that I'm not warped inside like he is, start standing up to him. But how can you say such a thing to your father? He loves me, I know he does, despite the beatings when he's angry. It would break his heart if I told him what I really thought of him.

Dad doesn't like to be disturbed when he's discussing the state of affairs with his friends and associates, so even though I'm hungry, I slide on by the kitchen, planning to head straight to my room. But Dad must hear me because he calls out, "B? Is that you?"

"Yeah."

"Come here a minute."

He sounds more subdued than usual. That tips me off to the fact that there might be somebody important with him. Dad's loud and bullish most of the time, but quiet and submissive around people he respects.

I head into the kitchen, expecting someone in a suit with a politically perfect smile. But I stagger to a halt halfway through the door and stare uncertainly. The guy with Dad is like nobody I've ever seen before.

The man is standing by the table, sipping from a cup of coffee. He sets it down when he spots me and arches an eyebrow, amused by my reaction.

He's very tall, maybe six foot six, and thin, except for a large potbelly. It looks weird on such a slender frame, and the buttons on the pink shirt he's wearing beneath his striped jacket strain to hold it in. He has a mop of white hair and pale skin. Not albino pale, but damn close. Long, creepy-looking fingers.

But it's his eyes that prove so startling. They're by far the biggest I've ever seen, at least twice the size of mine. Almost totally white, except for a dark, tiny pupil at the center of each. As soon as I see him, I immediately think, *Owl Man*. I almost say it out loud, but catch myself in time. Dad would hit the roof if I insulted one of his guests.

"So this is the infamous B Smith," the man chuckles. He has a smooth, cultured voice. He sounds like a radio presenter, but one of the old guys you hear on a Sunday afternoon on the station your gran listens to.

"Yeah," Dad says. He runs a hand over my head and smiles as if he's in pain and trying to hide it. "How was school?"

"Fine," I mutter, unable to tear my gaze away from Owl Man's enormous, cartoonish eyes.

"Some people think it's rude to stare," Owl Man says merrily, "but I've always considered it a sign of honest curiosity."

"Sorry," I say, blushing at the polite rebuke.

"No need to be," Owl Man laughs. "The young *should* be curious, and open too. You should have nothing to hide or apologize for at your tender age. Leave that to decrepit old warhorses like your father and me."

Dad clears his throat and looks questioningly at Owl Man. "Anything you'd like to ask?" he says meekly.

"Not just now," Owl Man purrs and waves a long, bony hand at me. "You may proceed. It has been nice seeing you again."

"Again?" I frown, certain I've never met this guy before. There's no way I could have forgotten eyes like that.

"I saw you when you were a child. You were a cute little thing. Sweet enough to eat."

Owl Man gnashes his teeth playfully, but there's nothing funny about the way he does it and I get goose bumps up my arms and the back of my neck.

"I'm going to my room," I tell Dad and hurry out without saying anything else. I half expect Dad to call me back and bark at me for not saying a proper good-bye, but he lets me go without a word.

I find it hard to settle. I keep thinking about the guy in the kitchen, those unnaturally large eyes. Who the hell is he? He doesn't look like anyone else my dad has ever invited round.

I surf the Web for a while, then stick on my headphones and listen to my iPod. I shut my eyes and bop my head to the music, trying to lose myself in the tunes. Sometime later, opening my eyes to stare at the ceiling, I spot Owl Man standing just inside the door to my room.

"Bloody hell!" I shout, ripping off the headphones and sitting up quickly.

"I did knock," Owl Man says, "but there was no answer."

"How long have you been standing there?" I yell, trying to remember if I'd been scratching myself inappropriately over the last five or ten minutes.

"Mere moments," he says, his smile never slipping.

"Where's my dad?" I ask, heart beating hard. For a crazy second I think that the stranger has killed Dad, maybe pecked him to death, and is now gearing up for an attack on me.

"In the kitchen," Owl Man says. "I had to come up to use the facilities."

He falls silent and stares at me with his big, round eyes. At the back of my mind I hear Mum reading that old fairy tale to me when I was younger. *All the better to see you with, my dear.*

"What do you want?" I snap, not caring about insulting him now, angry at him for invading my privacy.

"I wanted to ask you a question."

"Oh yeah?" I squint, wondering if he's going to make a pass at me, ready to scream for Dad if he does.

"Do you still have the dream?" he asks, and the scream dies silently on my lips.

"What dream?" I croak, but I know the one he means, and he knows that I know. I can see it in his freakish, unsettling eyes.

"The dream about the babies," Owl Man says softly. "Your father told me that you had it all the time when you were younger."

"Why the hell would he tell you something like that?" I try to snap, but it comes out more as a sob.

"I'm interested in dreams," Owl Man beams. "Especially dreams of monstrous babies. *mummy*," he adds in a high-pitched voice, and it sounds just the way the babies in my nightmare say it.

"Get out of my room," I moan. "Get out before I call my dad and tell him you tried to molest me."

"Your father knows I would never do anything like that," Owl Man sniffs and takes a step closer. "I'm not leaving until you tell me."

"No," I spit. "I don't have it anymore, okay?"

Owl Man studies me silently. Then his lips lift into an even wider, sickening smile. "You're lying. You *do* still have the dream. How interesting."

The tall, thin man pats his potbelly, then presses his fingers to his lips and blows me a kiss. "Good evening, B. It has been a pleasure meeting you again after all these years. Take care of yourself. There are dark times ahead of us. But I think you will fare well."

With that he turns and slips out of my room, carefully closing the door behind him. I don't put my headphones back on. I can't move. I just lie on my bed, think about his enormous eyes, wonder at the nature of his questions and shiver.

TWELVE

I don't see much of Dad over the next few days. It's like he's avoiding me. I want to ask him about the strange visitor, find out his real name, where he's from, why he was here, why Dad told him about my dreams. But Dad clearly doesn't want to discuss it, and what Dad wants, Dad gets.

So I say nothing. I keep my questions to myself. And I try to pretend that my surreal conversation with Owl Man never happened.

On Friday we visit the Imperial War Museum. I've been looking forward to this for weeks and my spirits lift for the first time since my run-in with Nancy and the rest of that bizarre afternoon. We don't go on many school trips — the money isn't there, plus we're buggers to control when we're let loose. Twenty of our lot were taken to the Tate Modern last year and they ran wild. The teachers swore never again, but they seem to have had a change of heart.

"I don't expect you to behave like good little boys and girls," Burke says on the Tube, to a chorus of jeers and whistles. "But don't piss me off. I'm in charge of you and I'll be held accountable if you get out of hand. Don't steal, don't beat up the staff, and be back at the meeting point at the arranged time."

"Do we get a prize if we do all that, sir?" Trev asks.

"No," Burke says. "You get my respect."

I love the War Museum. I was here before, when I was in primary school. We were meant to be looking at the World War I stuff, but the tanks and planes in the main hall are what I most remember.

"Look at the bloody cannons!" Elephant gasps as we enter the gardens outside the museum. "They're massive!"

"You can have a proper look at them later," Burke says.

"Aw, sir, just a quick look now," Elephant pleads.

Burke says nothing, just pushes on, and we follow.

80

The main hall still impresses. I thought it might be disappointing this time, but the tanks and planes are as cool as ever. The planes hang from the ceiling, loads of them, and the ceiling's three or four floors high. Everyone coos, necks craned, then we hurry to the tanks. They're amazing, and you can even crawl into some and pretend that you're driving them. We should be too old for that sort of stuff, but it's like we slip back to when we were ten years old — the lure of the tanks is impossible to resist.

Burke gives us a few minutes to mess around. We're the second group from the school to arrive. As the third lot trickle in, we form a group and head upstairs to where the Holocaust exhibition starts.

This is the reason we're here. We haven't focused much on the Holocaust in class – at least not that I remember, though I guess I could have slept through it – but our teachers reckon this is important, so they've brought us anyway, regardless of the very real risk that we might start a riot and wreck the place.

Burke stops us just before we go in and makes sure we're all together.

Kray sniffs the air and makes a face. "Something's burning."

I expect Burke to have a go at him, but to my shock it's Jonesenzio – I didn't even know he was here – who speaks up.

"One of my uncles was Polish. He was sent to Auschwitz in the thirties. Not the death camp, where they gassed people, but the concentration camp. He was worked like a slave until he was a skeleton. Starved. Tortured. The bones in one of his feet were smashed with a hammer. He survived for a long time, longer than most. But in the end he was hung for allegedly stealing food from a guard. They let him hang for nearly ten minutes, without killing him. Then they took him down, let him recover, and hung him again until he was dead."

Jonesenzio steps up to Kray, stares at him until he looks away, then says softly but loud enough for everyone to hear, "If there are any more jokes, or if you take one step out of line from this point on, you'll have to answer to *me*."

It should be funny – pitiful even – but it isn't. Everyone shuts up, and for the first time that I can ever remember, we stay shut up.

The exhibition is horrible. It's not so bad at the start, a bit boring even, where we learn about the buildup to war, how the Nazis came to power, why nobody liked the Jews. But it soon becomes a nightmare as we dip further into the world of ghettos, death camps and gas chambers.

Old film footage of Jews being rounded up and chased by Nazis hits hard. So does the funeral cart on which piles of corpses were wheeled to mass graves. And the rows of shoes and glasses, taken from people before they were gassed and cremated.

But what unsettles me most is a small book. It belonged to a girl, my sort of age. She wrote stories in it and drew sweet, colorful pictures. As I stare at it I think, *That could have been me.* Sitting in my room, writing and drawing. Then dragged out, shipped off to a death camp in a train, shaved bare, stripped naked, gassed, cremated or buried in an unmarked grave with a load of strangers. And all that's left of me is a stupid book I used to scribble in, in a cold, empty room where no one lives anymore.

Some of the others cry as we walk through the chambers of atrocity. I don't. But I feel my throat tighten and I have to look away more than once and blink until I'm sure my eyes are going to stay dry.

Coming out of the exhibition is like emerging into sunlight after being in a dark tunnel. The museum doesn't look so much like an adventure park now. The planes and tanks, the cannons, guns and swords that lie scattered around the place... They were used to kill people. Not actors, like in the movies. But real people like me and my mum. Like that little girl.

"Sobering stuff, isn't it?" Burke says to a few of us standing silently nearby.

"They were monsters," I growl.

Burke raises an eyebrow. "You think so?"

"Nobody human could have done that."

Burke shrugs, then leans in and whispers so that only I can hear, "Maybe that's what we should do with the immigrants."

I gasp and draw back from him, shocked.

Burke raises an eyebrow. "You look surprised."

"You can't say things like that!" I protest.

"Why not?" As I stare at him, he says, "I heard about your fight with Nancy and how Mrs. Reed *white*washed it because of her friendship with your father."

"How do you know about that?" I growl.

"It's no big secret," he says. "Aren't the gas chambers where it will all end if the likes of Mrs. Reed and your father get their way?"

"No!" I shout, then lower my voice when the others look at me strangely. "How can you even suggest that?"

"Because it's true," he snaps. "This is where hatred and intolerance lead. Don't be a child, B, and don't act like you're naive."

"You're wrong, they just want a society where –"

"Don't," Burke stops me. "I've heard all the arguments before. I'm not going to tell you which side you should be on. You're old enough to choose. All I'm saying is be aware. Know what you're signing up for and accept the consequences. Mrs. Reed and your dad are modern-day fascists. Only a fool would think otherwise."

Then he walks off and leaves me trembling.

I think about the Nazis. I think about my dad.

"It's not true," I whisper. "They're not the same."

But a voice inside my head snickers slyly and asks the question that I don't dare form out loud. *Aren't they?*

THIRTEEN

I wander off by myself, thinking about the Holocaust and what Burke said. I want to come back at him with a watertight argument, show him he was wrong to make such accusations about my dad. But I can't think of anything.

I don't pay much attention to the exhibits. Some of my mates rumble by, calling for me to join them, but I shake my head and stick to myself. I can't get that girl's book out of my mind. I keep imagining myself in her place, head bent over the pages, concentrating hard, unaware of the army of hateful Nazis bearing down upon me, surrounding the house, crashing in, taking me.

I push lower into the building, down the stairs to the World War I section, familiar from my previous visit. I wish I'd paid more attention before. If I had, maybe I'd understand about the two wars, how one led to the next, how other nations let the Nazis build and spread and do whatever they liked.

There's a trench re-creation that I vaguely recall, a life-size model of what part of a real trench was like, to give an idea of the hellish conditions soldiers lived in before they went over the top to be ripped apart by machine guns. I stroll through the narrow, nightmarish maze, pausing to study the details, holes where soldiers slept, things they ate, fake rats.

In a strange way I feel better here. It helps distract me from the horrors upstairs. This war was brutal but human. Soldiers fought other soldiers. Millions died, but there were no death camps, no gas chambers. No little Jewish girls were rounded up, humiliated, tormented, and executed.

If I could go back in time, I wouldn't mind stopping here, in the years before the truly horrific war began, before people found out just how demonically vile they could be. I could live with a war like this. But not the one that followed. And for Burke to say that my dad was no better than a Nazi...

My blood boils and rushes to my cheeks. I won't let that insult drop. I'll tell Mrs. Reed. Burke can't say things like that. If I rat on him, he'll be out of a job, and good riddance to the bugger.

But as much as I'd like to hurt Burke, I don't want to do that. Partly because nobody likes a grass. But mostly because the stuff that he said got under my skin. I've always liked to think that I see things as they are. I know Dad's no saint but I've never thought of him as a monster. But if Burke's right, and I take Dad's side, the way I've gone along with him for all these years, won't that make me a monster too?

I've told myself it doesn't matter that I never stood up to Dad. For the sake of a quiet life I've pretended to be on the same racist page as him. I didn't think it made a difference, letting a minor bigot spout off without challenging him. But I've been questioning that recently, even before what happened with Nancy.

Did people like me go along with the Nazis that way in the early days? Did other children put on an act for their fathers, figuring nothing bad could come of it? Can the terrors of that war in some way be traced back to the kids who didn't put their parents on the spot?

As I'm pondering my twisted relationship with Dad, I turn a corner and spot a struggle ahead. Two men are fighting with an Indian woman. She has a head scarf, a painted dot in the middle of her forehead, long flowing dress, the works. One of the men has a hand over her mouth. As I gape at them, the other man hits her hard in the stomach, and she goes down like a doll that's been dropped.

There's a baby in a stroller, maybe a year old, a boy. He's crying. One of the men picks him up.

"Hey!" I shout. They glance around. It's dark in here and they're not that close to me. They're both wearing hoodies. I can't see their faces. "What the hell are you doing?"

The men dart away from me, taking the baby. The woman moans and reaches out desperately, fingers opening and closing, clutching for the stolen boy.

I race after the men, not stopping to see if the woman's all right. There's no time to help her. If I lose sight of them, they'll disappear into the warren of the museum and that'll be the last I see of the child.

I hit the ground floor and hurry after the kidnappers. They've slowed slightly, so as not to draw attention to themselves. I want to roar but I'm out of breath from fear and the race up the stairs.

I've almost caught up with them when one of the men stops and turns before the museum shop. He tackles me and tries to wrestle me to the floor. No time to fight fair. I scratch at his eyes. He hisses and his grip loosens. I make a bit of space for myself and knee him in the groin. He groans and collapses. I jump over him and push on, ignoring the astonished crowd around us, people staring, slack-jawed, a few of my friends among them.

Out front. No sign of the man with the baby. I look right, then left, and spot him streaking towards the giant cannons and the road beyond. I shout, "Stop!" Then I run after him again.

The man halts before he gets to the cannons. Turns and waits. He's holding the baby close to his chest.

I come to a wary halt a few yards from him. He's not much

bigger than me but I don't want to take any chances. He might have a knife or a gun.

"Put down the baby," I snarl.

In response the man pushes back his hoodie with his free hand. I feel my face go pale. He looks like a mutant out of a horror film. His skin is disfigured, purplish in patches, pustulant, some strips of flesh peeling from his cheeks. Straggly gray hair. Pale yellow eyes. He's missing some teeth, and those still intact are black and cracked.

He points at me and I note absentmindedly that he doesn't have any fingernails, just filthy, bloodstained flaps of skin. He stares, eyes widening, and crooks one of his fingers, like he's trying to hypnotize me.

I think about tackling the mutant but I'm not gonna make the sort of dumb mistakes that people do in horror flicks. Taking a step back, I scream as loudly as I can, hoping that guards will come running.

Footsteps behind me. The man I knocked down outside the shop rushes past. He half twirls and spits at me. He looks like a mutant too, like he's survived a nuclear war and is suffering from radiation poisoning. I think for a moment that the pair of freaks is going to attack me. But then I hear lots of people coming, muttering and shouting. A woman shrieks, "My son! Don't hurt my son!"

The mutant holding the baby looks past me and his face twists with fury. He sets his sights on me again and leers. He licks his lips lewdly — his tongue is shriveled and scabby.

As the footsteps draw closer, the man raises the baby high, then throws him at me. I grab the boy like a ball, cushioning him as best I can. I fall backwards and land on my bum. The baby sits in my lap and laughs, poking at my nose with his chubby little fingers.

I look up. The mutants have fled. They're moving fast now that they don't have the baby. They reach the gate and seconds later they're gone, out of sight.

Just before the crowd catches up with me, I stare into the baby's face. I half expect him to smile sinisterly and say, "*don't be afraid mummy,*" like the babies in my dreams. But of course he doesn't. This is the real world, not a nightmare.

Then I think of the two men, their unnatural skin and yellow eyes. And I wonder.

FOURTEEN

I'm hailed as a hero by the baby's mother. She hugs me and thanks me through her sobs, saying I'm wonderful, I saved her child, I should get a reward. Strangers look on and beam. Guards and staff from the museum congratulate me. My mates from school watch, astonished. Burke is smiling. He winks when I catch his eye.

The guards try to get descriptions of the men from me. I tell them I didn't see much, that they didn't let their hoods drop. I don't tell them about the odd skin, the yellow eyes, that they looked like mutants. I'd sound like a lunatic if I did.

I shrug off the compliments on the Tube back to school, scowling and saying nothing. Burke tells the others to leave me alone and I sit in silence, listening to the rumblings of the train, staring out of the window at the darkness of the tunnels, unable to forget the men's lips, their skin, those eyes. If I *did* imagine all that, I have a more vivid imagination than I ever gave myself credit for.

Back at school, Burke asks if I'm all right. When he sees that I'm not, he offers to take me home early. I don't want any special treatment, so I tell him I'd rather stay and I sit in an empty classroom for the rest of the afternoon. Burke and Mrs. Reed pop in to see me a few times – Mrs. Reed says I've done the school proud – but otherwise I'm alone with my thoughts. And if I could get away from them, I would.

The minutes drag but eventually pass and I slip out of school ahead of the bell, so as not to have to face my friends. I feel strange, like I've been violently sick. I just want to go home, rest up, stay in for the weekend, and hopefully return in better form on Monday.

Mum has already heard about the incident at the museum when I get back. She squeals when I walk in and calls me her little hero. Hugs and coos over me, asks if I want anything special for dinner. I grin weakly and tell her I don't have much of an appetite, I'll just have whatever she's having.

She wants me to tell her all about it, the kidnapping, the rescue, how I stood up to two grown men. I try to shrug it off but she keeps on and on about it. Eventually I give in and start talking. I hold back the bit about how the men looked. I don't plan on telling anyone about that.

Dad gets home before I'm finished. He's grinning when he

comes in and sees us chatting—he thinks we're gossiping. When Mum starts to tell him what happened, he frowns, tells her to shut up and makes me go through it again from the start.

Mum serves up dinner—fish and chips, usually my favorite, but they taste like cardboard in my current state. She keeps saying how brave I was, how she's proud of me, how the staff at the museum shouldn't have let me face a pair of dangerous criminals by myself.

Dad doesn't say much. He's got a face on him, the sort of scowl I know all too well. He's brooding about something. Mum's so excited, she doesn't notice it, but I do and I keep my trap shut, not wanting to wind him up any further. It's best to say as little as possible when he's in a mood like this.

It finally comes out when we're watching TV after dinner. Mum's still babbling about the baby and how I should get a medal. Dad sighs irritably and says, "I wish you'd drop it, Daisy."

"But aren't you proud, Todd?" Mum replies, surprised.

Dad grunts and shoots me a dirty look. I act as if I'm fascinated by the chef who's showing us how to cook a meal for six people in less than thirty minutes.

"Of course I'm pleased that you stood up for yourself," he says to me. "But..."

"What?" Mum huffs when he doesn't go on. I groan. Why doesn't she know when to keep quiet?

"They were Indian," Dad says softly, and I look around. I didn't know what was gnawing at him before. Now it becomes clear.

"What's that got to do with anything?" Mum asks, bewildered.

"We'd be better off if they took a dozen little Indians and dumped them in the Thames." Dad laughs, like he's only joking, but I know he's genuinely angry.

Mum frowns. "Don't say things like that, Todd. It's not funny. It's not the poor baby's fault it's Indian."

"It's not mine either, is it?" Dad snaps. He glares at Mum, then looks at me and grimaces. "I like that you tried to help, but if it had been an English kid..."

"That's outrageous," Mum says frostily. "Babies are innocent. Would you have left the child to those two beasts?"

"Nobody's innocent," Dad says. "It's us against them. Always has been, always will be. If we start fighting their battles for them, where will it stop? Do we let them stay because they have cute babies? Keep on giving them benefits, so they can spit out more of the buggers, until they have enough to out-vote us? Babies grow up. They infest good schools and ruin them. They buy houses and destroy neighborhoods. They import drugs and sell them to our kids. They blow things up.

"They were all babies once," Dad says. "Every last terrorist and job-stealing scab was like that boy in the museum. We can't be soft. We can't give ground. *Ever.*"

"You're wrong," Mum says, and I think Dad's even more amazed than I am. She's never spoken to him like this before. I wouldn't have thought that she could. "There are bad people in the world,

Todd, white as well as colored. We can't let people steal babies. We'd be cruel if we –"

Dad's hand shoots up and he slaps her, hard. Her head cracks back and she cries out. He grabs her throat and squeezes. His eyes are wild. I throw myself at him, roaring at him to stop. He hits me with his free hand, slaps me even harder than he slapped Mum. I'm knocked to the floor by the force of the blow, but Dad barely notices. He's fully fixed on Mum.

"Don't ever talk to me that way," Dad snarls. "I won't have you turn on me. If you ever stick up for those bastards again, I'll kill you. You hear me, woman? Do. You. Bloody. Well. *Hear.* Me?"

He shakes her with every word. Mum makes a choking noise and tries to nod. Her fingers scratch at his arms. For a moment I think he's gonna finish her off, that this is how it will end. All these years, all the beatings, all leading to this. I push myself to my feet, ready to lunge at him again, desperate to stop him, to save Mum, to escape with her before he can make good on his threat.

But then Dad's fingers relax and withdraw. He clutches Mum's chin and gives her the evil eyeball. She's weeping. Her nose is bleeding. The flesh under her left eye is already starting to puff up. Dad wipes blood from her lip and smiles tightly.

"You'll be all right," he says as if she'd just tripped and hurt herself. "Go make us all a cuppa. Have a cig out back. You'll be fine when you come in. Won't you?"

Mum gasps repeatedly like a dying fish. Dad's fingers clench.

"*Won't you?*" he barks, sharper this time, wanting to hear an answer.

"Yes...Todd," Mum wheezes.

Dad releases her. She gets up and stumbles to the kitchen, trying not to sob, knowing that if she makes too much noise it will infuriate him and maybe set him off again.

Dad looks at me and I wait for him to follow up his first blow. If he lays into me, I'll just stand here and let him beat me. It's the best thing to do. He loses his head completely if I fight back. I don't mind the beatings, the pain. As long as Mum's out of the way and safe, he can hit me as hard as he likes.

"I'll say this, though," Dad says slowly, then pauses, letting me know that he could swing either way right now, that he can laugh this off or come down hard on me, that he has the power, that me and Mum are his to control. "I wish I'd been there to see you knee that sod."

We both laugh, Dad loudly, me weakly. He switches channels to a quiz show, gets a few answers right and chuckles proudly, delighted with himself. Mum brings the tea and he pats her bum as she places it before him. She smiles crookedly, sits by his side and kisses the hand he struck her with.

Later, in my room, sitting up in bed, listening to tunes on my iPod. Crying. I hate tears but tonight I can't hold them back. I'm not in much pain – the slap didn't even leave a mark – but inside I feel wretched.

I don't want to blame Dad for what he did. I make excuses for him, the way I always do. Mum shouldn't have challenged him. She knows what he's like. She should have read his mood and...

No. I can't put the blame on her. I was wrong too. I shouldn't have risked my neck for an Indian kid. I should have left the baby to the mutants. One less for us to kick out of the country. Dad was right. He was trying to help us see the world the way it really is. We should have listened. It wasn't his fault. I shouldn't have saved the baby. Mum should have kept her mouth shut.

I tell myself that over and over. I make every excuse for him that I can. And I try to believe. I try so bloody hard to justify his actions, because he's my dad and I love him. But deep down I know it's a load of bull.

When I'm crying so hard that I'm making moaning sounds, I channel the music through my speakers so that Dad won't hear. Then I weep harder, fingers balled into fists, face scrunched up with hate and confusion.

He's a bully. A wife beater. A racist. A hateful, nasty sod. I want to hang him up by his thumbs. Sneer at him as he writhes in agony. Ask him if he's proud of himself now, if he still thinks it's all right to beat up a woman and child.

Then I despise myself for thinking such a terrible thing. He wants what's best for us. He's trying to help, doing all that he can to steer us the right way. He only hits us when we let him down. We have to try harder. We...

"I hate him," I moan, burying my face in my hands.

But he's my dad.

"I hate him."

But he's my dad.

"I hate him."

But...

FIFTEEN

Saturday drags. I stay in all day. A few of my mates call and ask me to come meet up, but I tell them I don't feel well. They say everyone's talking about me and how I rescued the baby. I laugh it off like it's no big deal.

Dad takes us out to a Chinese restaurant for dinner. Mum dresses up and slaps makeup over her bruise. She and Dad share a couple of bottles of wine. He lets me have a sip when nobody's watching. Laughs when I grimace.

"Don't worry," he says. "You'll get used to it."

Dad's polite as he can be to the staff. Funny how he doesn't have a problem with foreigners when they're serving him food. Most of his favorite grub comes from overseas, Chinese, Italian, Indian. I consider pointing that out to him, but I don't want to set him off again.

Mum and Dad head to the pub after the meal, leaving me to guard the fort at home. Dad gives me a fiver and tells me to treat myself to some chips and sweets. He scratches my head and grins. I grin back. The aggro of yesterday isn't forgotten by any of us, but we move on, the way we always do. No point living in the past. We'd have burned out long ago if we held grudges.

I watch a film, surf the Web, download some new tracks, play a few games, go to bed late. I don't hear the old pair come home.

I get up about midday. Dad's still asleep. Mum's working on a Sunday roast. We're a bit stiff with each other. It always takes us a while to return to normal after Dad loses his temper. We're both embarrassed.

We eat at two. Dad's hungover but he still manages to polish off his plate. He loves roasts, never leaves more than scraps. He drinks beer with the meal, saying that's the only way to combat a hangover. Normally he praises Mum's cooking but he doesn't say much today, nursing a headache.

"That was nice," I mutter as Mum clears up.

"I've got dessert for later," Mum smiles. "Pavlova. Your favorite."

It's actually Dad's favorite, but I don't mind. We share a smile. Things are getting better. The air doesn't feel so tight around me now.

Dad watches soccer in the afternoon. I watch some of the match with him. I make a few scathing comments about Premiership players and how they're overpaid prima donnas. That's usually guaranteed to set him off on an enthusiastic rant, but today he just grunts, wincing every now and then, rubbing his head as if that will make the pain go away.

Some of Mum's friends come to visit. They don't say anything about her face, don't even ask if she had an accident. They start chirping about what happened at the War Museum but Mum shushes them before Dad kicks off again. They retreat to the kitchen and carry on in whispers.

I go to my room when the soccer's over and phone Vinyl, hoping he won't have heard about the museum. No such luck.

"I hear you're London's newest superhero," he chuckles.

"Get stuffed."

"They should send you over to Ireland to stamp out the zombies."

"Don't make me come and give you a kicking," I warn him.

He asks if I've heard the latest rumors. Apparently Pallaskenry wasn't the first place the zombies struck. According to supposedly classified documents that have somehow surfaced on the Internet, there were at least three other attacks in small, out-of-the-way villages, one in Africa, two in South America.

"If that's true," Vinyl says, "you can bet there's been even more of them in places we haven't heard of yet."

"It's all crap," I tell him. "They're trying to scare us."

"Maybe," he hums. "But it looks like the curfew's going ahead. They've already introduced it in a lot of towns in Wales, since that's so close to Ireland. London nightlife's gonna be a thing of the past soon."

"That won't last," I snort. "You think people here will stand for a lockdown? I give it a week or less. The rumors will die away, the curfew will be lifted, everything will go back to normal."

"I hope so," he sighs.

We chat about TV and music. I tell Vinyl how Nancy confronted me at school, treating me like a racist. I get huffy about it, conveniently not mentioning the fact that I made gorilla noises. Vinyl isn't in the least sympathetic.

"Well, you *are* a racist," he notes.

"No I'm not," I snap. "I'm talking to you, and you're hardly Snow White."

"I'm your token black friend," he chuckles.

"No," I sniff. "You're my token retarded friend."

I hang up before he can yell at me. Giggling wickedly, delighted to have trumped him, I punch the air, then go take a long, hot bath. There's nothing like a good soak when it comes to relaxing. I lie in the tub for an hour, staring at the drops of condensation on the ceiling and window, feeling peaceful. The old scar on my thigh is itchy, so I scratch it, then turn on my side and let the air at it. When it stops annoying me, I lie flat again.

Mum and I watch TV together later. Dad's gone out to the pub. Mum opens a box of chocolates and we share them. Belgian chocs. They're nice, but I prefer Roses or Quality Street. You can't beat a good Strawberry Cream.

Dad gets back with a few of his mates not long after ten. My stomach tenses when they enter – I think Owl Man is going to be with them – but these are just some of his campaign buddies. They have posters and leaflets. Local elections aren't for another three or four months, but they've been asked to start canvassing early. One of the posters has a picture of a zombie, set next to a photo of a Muslim bomber. WHICH DO YOU FEAR MOST? it asks.

Dad and his mates love the poster. Mum and I pretend to admire it too. Then we go to bed early. Dad doesn't like us hanging around when he's talking shop. I'm sure that I'll struggle to drop off, or have the nightmare again, but I don't. I'm out in a minute and sleep the sleep of the dead after that.

SIXTEEN

I could do without school on Monday. I think about giving it a miss – wouldn't be the first time – but I don't fancy the idea of trudging around the streets by myself. If I'd met up with my mates over the weekend, I could have arranged for a few of them to skip school with me. But it's too late to organize that now, so I decide to struggle through and maybe take tomorrow off instead.

Everyone's still talking about the museum, the way I rescued the baby. Suze and La Lips shiver when they ask me to re-create it for them, eyes wide, wanting a tale of blood, treachery and heroism.

"It wasn't much," I mutter. "The guys weren't that big."

"Rubbish," Kray says. "I saw the one

you tackled outside the shop. He was well over six foot. That knee put him down sweet though."

Kray's not the only one living in awe of my trusty right knee. I reckon some of the fools would kneel down and kiss it if I gave them the chance.

The praise goes to my head a bit but my mood doesn't lift. No matter how many times I'm told that I'm a hero, I can't forget about Dad, the contempt in his expression, the way he hit Mum and me. If ever there was a time to stand up to him and tell him I'm not a racist, it was then. I could have said that I thought all babies were equal. Attacked him for being so heartless, so inhuman.

Instead I just stood there, head low, saying nothing. As always.

It's almost a relief to get to class. I can escape from the adulation there. We have biology first. I'm worried that Mr. Burke might make a song and dance about what I did at the museum, but he's not in today, must be sick. Mrs. Reed takes our class instead.

The morning rolls along drearily. I trudge from one class to the next, ignoring anyone who tries to talk with me about Friday, scribbling during lessons, paying little or no attention to the teachers.

I meet up with some of the gang during the break and I'm delighted when Elephant draws their attention away from me.

"I'm playing soccer at lunch," he beams. "Saw the doctor on Friday and she gave me the all-clear. Said it'll probably hurt for a few days, and not to tackle too hard, but I've got the green light."

Elephant's so excited, you'd swear he was about to play in a cup final, not in a poxy five-a-side tournament. We slag him a bit but he laughs off our jeers, vowing to score a hat trick and come back bigger and better than ever.

"*Bigger?*" La Lips says, batting her eyelids innocently.

We all laugh, even the normally jealous Copper.

Elephant makes us promise to come and cheer him on. I normally wouldn't bother with footie at lunch, but to keep Elephant happy, I agree to watch him make a fool of himself.

"Just don't elbow anybody," Suze warns him, "or B will go for you."

Elephant looks blank. He must be the only person not to have heard about the incident on Friday. Luckily, before I'm forced to go through it again for his benefit, the bell rings and it's back to class.

More pointless lessons, teachers droning on, trying to amuse myself by drawing crude cartoons and coming up with nicknames for the few of my friends who don't have any. Then lunch.

I head to the gym with Copper, Kray, Suze, La Lips, Ballydefeck and Stagger Lee. We meet Pox, Trev and Linzer there. Elephant's warming up. Meths is on his team and the two of them hold a hushed conversation, discussing tactics. What a pair of clowns!

Stuttering Stan is the ref. He blows his whistle and the teams take to the pitch. Other kids move out of their way and either line up along the sides to watch or go find somewhere else to hang out.

The game kicks off and Elephant gets stuck straight in. If anyone expected him to take things easy in his first game back, they're instantly corrected as he goes into a tackle feetfirst and barges one of the other players over.

Stuttering Stan blows for a free kick and gives Elephant a warning. Elephant rubs his leg and looks worried. As soon as Stuttering Stan's back is turned, he winks at Meths. I see now what they were cooking up — play the wounded soldier angle, use Stuttering Stan's sympathy to get away with as many dirty tackles as they can.

"Go on, Elephant!" I roar as he chases the action. "Do him!"

The others cheer along with me. The goalie pulls off a save and launches the ball up the field to Elephant. He turns, shoots and almost scores the goal of his life, but it flies just a few inches over.

We're having a great time. For once I'm immersed, keen to see who Elephant targets next, if he can cap his comeback with a goal, how much grimacing and sighing Stuttering Stan will stand for before he brandishes a yellow card.

Then Tyler Bayor spoils it all. He comes up to me and gives my sleeve a tug. I glance at him suspiciously. He's never approached me like this before. I figure I must be in trouble, that he's delivering a message for someone.

"What do you want?" I snap.

Tyler grins shakily. "I just wanted to say well done for the other day."

I stare at him incredulously. The others are amazed too. He must have fallen out of bed and hit his head this morning. It's madness, tagging me like this, acting like we can be friends, like a compliment from him can make everything right between us. Who the hell does he reckon he is, Nelson bloody Mandela?

"Do you think I give a damn what you think of me?" I snarl.

Tyler's face creases and he gulps. "No, B, of course not. I just wanted to –"

I poke him in the chest and he takes a quick step back. I follow and the gang closes around me, their focus switching from the game to the new, more highly charged action.

"Who gave you permission to breathe the same air as me?" I sneer, poking Tyler again.

"Why are you doing this?" he whines. "I only wanted to tell you that I thought it was great, the way you saved that kid."

"I didn't do it to please the likes of you," I tell him. "In fact, if I'd known the baby was Indian, I'd have let them take him."

Snickers and theatrical gasps from the gang. They think I'm joking, saying it to wind Tyler up. They don't know about what happened at home, how serious this is. If I let Tyler praise me, it'll be like I'm taking his side against Dad.

"All right," Tyler sighs. "I'm sorry. I won't congratulate you again."

He turns to leave. I grab his arm and swing him back to face me.

"You're not going anywhere." I poke his chest a third time. "You started this. Let's take it all the way."

Tyler's eyes fill with panic. I've given him a rough ride over the years, but I've never gone all out for him. He's small. I don't usually pick fights with no-hopers. I go for opponents who stand a chance,

who are worth beating. Tyler isn't a fighter. He probably thought he'd never get called out by me.

But he rubbed me the wrong way at the wrong time. I know it's unfair. It's my dad I should be squaring up to, not a wimp like Tyler. Or, if not Dad, then one of Tyler's bigger buddies, someone who could give as good as he gets. But I can't help myself. I've been bottling up my anger all weekend. I have to lash out at someone, and Tyler's placed himself in my line of fire.

"Easy, B," Trev mutters, seeing something dark flash across my face.

"You want some of this too?" I bark.

He shakes his head and goes quiet.

I focus on Tyler again. I'm snarling like a dog. Tyler looks like he's about to faint. Before he passes out, I slap him, the way his mate Nancy slapped me when I made the gorilla noises.

"Come on," I hiss. "Show me what you've got."

"I don't want to fight," Tyler says, backing up.

"Too bad." I slap him again. "Give me your best shot."

"No," he squeals. "I don't want to."

I make a fist and jab him in the stomach. It's not a hard punch, just a taste of things to come. But he doubles over, then drops to his knees and starts crying, hugging himself as if I'd swung a cricket bat into his ribs.

I stare at Tyler uncertainly. I'm not used to this sort of a reaction. It throws me. The others are looking away, clearing their throats, disgusted and embarrassed at the same time. This is doing more harm to my image than to Tyler's. Everyone knows he's soft. But for me to pick a fight with a harmless crybaby...

"Forget about him," I snap, turning my back on Tyler and looking for another target. I spot a group of Muslim kids standing in a huddle, unaware of any of this, sharing a joke. They're from the year above ours, big buggers, well able to fight their own corner.

"Let's do those bastards," I snarl, looking to my gang for support.

Nobody responds. They're startled by my sudden mood swing, my thirst for a fight. They've seen me fired up before, but not like this.

"What's wrong?" I sneer. "Frightened?"

"Of course not," Kray says. "But why don't we leave it and have a go at them after school instead? We'll get in trouble if we attack them here."

He's right but I can't pull back now. "Okay, cowards," I spit. "I'll do the sods myself."

I start towards the group. I don't know if the others will follow once they see that I'm serious. I'll get hammered to a pulp if they don't — without backup I won't stand a chance. But I don't care. Let them kick the crap out of me. At least I'll be able to go home to Dad and be sure of a warm welcome. He'll make me a cup of tea, rub my head, tell me I'm one of his own. He might criticize me for picking a fight I couldn't win, and tell me I have to be savvier. But he'll be proud of me. He'll love my fighting spirit. He'll love *me*. And right now that's all in the world that matters.

But I haven't taken more than three steps when everything goes to hell and all natural fights are forgotten.

Screams ring out loud over the other noises. Everyone stops and stares at the main doors into the gym. They're hanging open and we can see the corridor beyond. The screams get louder. My eyes widen and my heart beats fast. I instinctively know what this means but I can't admit it. Nobody can. That's why we stand like a bunch of dummies, doing nothing.

A boy staggers into the gym. He's bleeding. Terrified. Moaning. He falls and I see that a chunk has been cut – *bitten* – out of the back of his neck. Blood spurts from the wound. As we gape, more kids spill into the gym. All screaming. Some bleeding. Everyone in shock.

One of the girls looks wild-eyed at the rest of us, as if just noticing we're there. Gazes at us in horrified silence. Then shrieks hysterically—"*Zombies!*"

SEVENTEEN

I want it to be a joke, some smartarses screwing with the rest of us. I'd be so happy if they were winding us up, I wouldn't care that I'd been made a fool of. I'd laugh, admit I fell for it, hail them as champion pranksters.

But the blood's real. The terror. The screams.

And the zombies.

I spot the first of them coming. A boy I don't recognize. His sweater and shirt are ripped. His stomach has been carved open. Guts ooze from holes as he lurches forward. His eyes are unfocused, his lips caked with blood. He moves stiffly but purposefully.

The undead boy grabs the girl who screamed. Pulls her hair back. Sinks his

teeth into her throat. Rips out a strip of flesh and gurgles happily as blood sprays his face.

I've seen blood fly in fights, movies and computer games. But never like this. Nothing I've ever seen before has prepared me for *this*.

The spell breaks and pandemonium erupts. Everyone's screaming at once. People run in circles, crash into one another, fall, thrash around on the ground, lash out with their feet and fists.

More zombies stream into the gym, boys, girls, a couple of teachers. They zone in on the living, hunting like wolves. They have a sweet time of it. In all the mayhem, lots of kids try to rush by them. Easy prey. The zombies just reach out and snatch.

I haven't moved. I'm watching sickly, numbly studying the undead as they feast on their victims. Some of the kids writhe and curse as they're bitten, moan and weep and beg for mercy. The zombies don't care. They tear with their fingers and teeth, bite, claw, rip, chew.

"Stop that!" Stuttering Stan roars. He strides forward, blowing his whistle, trying to wave back the zombies. The fool thinks that he can control this, the same way he can control violence on the pitch.

A zombie boy my age butts Stuttering Stan in the chest. As the teacher falls back, winded, the boy sticks his fingers into the adult's left eye and pokes it out. As Stuttering Stan screams, the boy gobbles the eye. Then he falls on his victim and digs through the hole where the eye should be, burrowing through to Stuttering Stan's brain.

"Come on!" Trev shouts, grabbing my arm. "We have to get out of here!"

"What?" I blink.

"They're gonna kill us, B!"

I look at the zombies and shake my head. "Not all of us. There's a pattern."

"What the hell are you talking about?" he barks.

I point. The zombies aren't killing everyone. As each one enters the gym, he or she cuts or bites a few people, leaving them to yell and flee. Only then does the zombie settle on a target, break their skull and dig into their brain. Once they start to feast, they sit there, gorging, ignorant of everything going on around them.

"There's a pattern," I mutter again.

Before I can make sense of it, Trev shouts, "We're going. You can stay and let them eat you if you want."

I glance at him and the others in our gang. They're racing towards the rear left corner of the gym. My senses click—there's an emergency exit there.

I stare at the carnage, the kids going wild, the zombies tucking in. I was in a daze before this, detached and calm. But now that I focus, I realize I'm dead if I don't move quickly.

"Sod this!" I moan, then tear after the others as fast as I can.

EIGHTEEN

The gym is situated at the back of the school. There are several buildings behind it, shops and a factory. No direct way through, except for a narrow alley included at the insistence of the local authorities.

Trev's ducking through a small door when I catch up. The others have gone ahead. He looks back as I rush after him, afraid I'm a zombie. He smiles fleetingly when he recognizes me, then stands aside and lets me pass.

"This way!" he yells, waving his arms over his head.

"What are you doing?" I snap.

"We've got to help the rest of them," he pants.

I study the scores of students fighting

with those who've been turned into zombies. Lots are trying to escape through the main doors. Some are trying to climb the walls, to get to the skylight windows that lead to the roof, but they've no hope—too smooth, too high, no ladders or ropes. Others have collapsed mentally and huddle on the floor, weeping, praying, shaking their heads, hoping the zombies will leave them alone or that they'll wake up and find out this was just a dream.

"Forget about them," I tell Trev.

"But we can't just —"

"If you keep on shouting, you'll alert the zombies. You want them coming after us?" He stares at me, tears in his eyes. "Best thing we can do is get out and call for help, Trev. It's their only hope."

Trev looks around the gym, then curses and shoves through after me.

We're in a small corridor, me, Trev, Ballydefeck, Suze, La Lips, Elephant, Meths, Linzer, Copper, Stagger Lee, Pox, Dunglop. Tyler's with us too, and a few others, two black guys, an Indian, three Muslims, a white kid called Rick.

"Where's Kray?" Trev asks.

"One of them got him," Suze sobs. "It cracked his head open. I saw it... his brains... it..."

"What the hell's going on?" the tallest of the black kids roars. "How'd they get in? Where'd they come from? I thought they only came out at night."

We stare at him in silence. Then I shrug. "We'll ask questions later. Let's get out of here before the brain-munching bastards find us."

We hurry down the corridor. The emergency exit's at the end. It opens out into the alley that runs between the two buildings behind the school. I've been through it a few times during fire drills. Never thought I'd have to do this for real, or that I'd be running from zombies, not a fire.

Ballydefeck gets to the door first. He slams down on the access bar and pushes.

Nothing happens.

"Out of the way," the tall black guy snaps. He bangs the bar down and shoves hard.

Nothing happens.

"Everyone," I shout. "Push together."

We crowd around the door. I get some fingers on the bar. It slides down smoothly when we push but the door doesn't give, not even a crack.

"Forget the bar," Trev says. "Focus on the door."

We strain, silent, red-faced, sweating, shoving with everything we have.

The door doesn't move.

"It's jammed shut," Ballydefeck says.

"Can we cut through?" Tyler asks.

"With what?" Pox yells. He got his nickname because of the spattering of facial scars left behind when he had the chicken pox.

The scars aren't normally very prominent, but now that his face is scrunched up with terror, he looks like a rabid monkey. I almost make a joke out of it, but this isn't the time to be a wiseass.

"We're all gonna die," La Lips wails.

"Shut up," I tell her. "Trev?" I look to him, hoping he'll have an answer.

"There's another exit to the alley on this side of the building, on the floor above," he says. "Or there's the front door."

"Which do you think we should —"

A scream stops me. My head whips around. A small girl is dangling from Pox's right arm, teeth locked on his flesh, chewing her way down to the bone.

Pox screams again and slams the girl into the wall. She doesn't let go. He jabs at her face with the fingers of his free hand. In a swift movement she releases him and snaps at his fingers. Catches them and grinds down. Pox screams louder and falls to his knees.

I start towards them but the black kid who beat me to the bar beats me to the girl too. There's a flick knife in his right hand. He slashes the blade across the girl's chest. She loses interest in Pox and pushes her attacker away. Looks at the gash in her chest. Gurgles, then throws herself at the teenager with the knife.

He keeps his cool. Ducks the girl's attack, then jabs the knife at her face. She winces when it strikes. He winces too. I can see horror in his eyes. He's never done anything like this before. But when the zombie snaps at his fingers, he thrusts the horror away, grits his teeth and digs the knife deeper into her head. She swipes at him, squealing and snapping at his fingers.

"Hold her down!" he roars.

Trev and I react quickest and wrestle her to the floor. She snaps at the black kid again but he keeps his fingers clear of her mouth. Drives the knife deep into her head, panting like a dog. Again. Blood flows. Bone splinters. He doesn't stop. Moments later he's gouging out chunks of brain, making sobbing noises. The girl shudders, moans, spasms. He keeps it up, face grim, silent now, teeth bared. Finally she stops moving and her eyes go steady in their sockets.

"Is she dead?" Trev asks.

"Yeah," he croaks, getting up, wiping tears from his cheeks. He's trembling wildly, his left hand shaking like mad. But his right hand – his knife hand – is steady as the blade itself.

"How can we be sure?" Stagger Lee asks.

"I destroyed her brain," the black kid grunts.

"That works in movies, but we don't know for sure that it happens that way in real life," I note, eyeing the dead girl nervously. "What if she comes back to life and attacks again?"

He laughs edgily. "Then we're screwed."

I look up, shocked, then laugh with him. It's that or go mad.

"How'd you sneak in the knife?" I ask.

"I never leave home without it. Been mugged too many times."

"If the teachers found it..."

"That lot don't know how to find their own arseholes."

My smile spreads. "I'm B," I tell him.

"Cass."

"Isn't that a girl's name?"

"Short for Cassius. After Muhammad Ali's real name."

"Sweet." I show my knuckles and let him knock them.

"We killed her," Suze cries.

"We had to," Cass says, then takes a deep, steadying breath. "We've gotta get out of here."

"But —" Suze says.

"Shut it," Meths snarls. He's still holding the ball, which he must have picked up when the game stopped.

"Are you all right?" I ask Pox.

He's bleeding, shaking like an old geezer with Parkinson's, even worse than Cass was, but he nods. "I'll live," he moans, taking off his sweatshirt and using it to wipe blood from his arm and fingers.

"But as what?" Cass says, blade still extended, pointing now at Pox.

"What do you mean?" Pox frowns.

"We've all seen zombie films. You've been bitten. If you turn into one of them…"

"I won't!" Pox squeaks. As Cass glares at him, Pox looks for support. "B? You're not gonna let him do me, are you?"

I glance at the others but nobody meets my eye, happy to leave the decision to me now that it's been placed in my hands. Bloody cowards.

127

"B?" Pox wheezes, real terror in his eyes, fresh tears trickling down his cheeks and gathering in the pockmarks in his flesh. "Are you gonna…?"

"No," I mutter. "But keep behind the rest of us, all right? And if we think you're starting to change, we'll have to cut you loose."

"But —"

"No time to argue, Pox. Accept the rules or it's the knife." I turn to Cass. "What do you reckon—make a break for one of the exits, or find a place to hole up and wait for help to arrive?"

"Nobody helped those buggers in Pallaskenry," Copper says. "The only ones who made it out alive were those who got out early. The soldiers surrounded the place once they hit the scene and shot anyone who moved, normal people along with the zombies."

"Run?" Cass asks.

"Run," I agree.

And we're off.

NINETEEN

We don't get very far. This corridor stretches along the side of the gym. We hurry to the end of it and start down the next passageway, off of which lie a series of classrooms. But we're less than a quarter of the way along when we hear a mob racing towards us, screaming and wailing.

"They must be heading for the exit or the gym," Stagger Lee says.

"They'll be on us in a sec," Copper mutters.

"We have to tell them to go back," Suze pants.

"Don't be stupid," I snarl. "They're being chased. They won't stop and listen calmly."

"We won't get through them," Cass says.

"Even if we do, zombies must be right behind," Copper says.

There's a door to my left. I open it and glance into a small classroom for younger kids. It's empty.

"In here," I decide. "We'll hide, wait for them to pass, then sneak out."

"What if the zombies smell us?" Cass asks.

I shrug. "It's a gamble one way or the other."

The first few kids of the mob surge into the hallway. Zombies are among them, snapping, tearing, maiming, killing. "In!" I bark and everyone pushes into the room after me, no complaints.

When we're all inside, I slam the door shut. There's no key, of course. "We need to barricade it," I shout, but some of the others are ahead of me. Copper and Ballydefeck arrive seconds later with a desk each, which they prop against the door. More furniture is added to the pile and moments later there's a mountain of desks and chairs between us and the door.

"Won't do much good if they come through the windows," Trev says, nodding at the frosted glass on either side of the door.

"They can't see us through the glass," I mutter, stepping back. "And if we keep quiet, they can't hear us either."

"What about smell?" Cass asks.

I frown. "What is it with you and zombies smelling us?"

"I've seen movies where they can sniff out the living," he says.

"Well, let's hope they all had really bad colds when they were turned," I growl and we all squat quietly.

Screams in the corridor. Sounds of fighting. Someone slams into the glass and it rattles. At first I think it's a zombie trying to break through, but it must have just been someone crashing into it, because there aren't any more assaults on the window.

"Please don't eat me!" I hear a kid beg. "Please don't eat me! Please don't –"

A high-pitched shriek. I shut my eyes and feel tears build behind my eyelids. This can't be happening. Zombies aren't real. Pallaskenry was a joke. We were so sneery, laughing about it in class, coming up with alternative theories. I must be dreaming. Babies will come crawling over the desks any minute now, calling me their mummy, and I'll know it's a nightmare.

But that's wishful thinking. This is reality. I always know when I'm having a dream. No matter how real it seems at the time, it never *feels* completely real. This does.

I open my eyes and look around. Everyone's shaking and either crying or close to it. La Lips is clinging to Copper, weeping as he whispers soothing words in her ear. Linzer's praying. She's not the only one — Dunglop, Tyler, Ballydefeck and two of the Muslims are also openly praying. I figure some of the others are too, but privately.

Pox is squatting a couple of feet away from the rest of us, weeping over his wounds, shaking his head, muttering something under his breath. Cass is keeping an eye on him, flick knife open and glinting, ready to leap on Pox at the first sign that he's turning into a zombie.

131

"You know the worst thing about this?" Elephant whispers. When a few of us stare at him, he says glumly, "It ruined my comeback."

I stifle a giggle. "Idiot!" I snort.

"You were crap anyway," Meths says.

"Was not," Elephant growls.

"We need a plan," Trev says, and we look at him expectantly. "We can't just go charging about the place."

"So what should we do?" Cass asks.

"Stay here," Trev says. "Keep our heads down. Wait for the police to find us."

"But in Pallaskenry –" Copper starts to object.

"This isn't Pallaskenry," Trev snaps. "It's a school. They're not going to stand by and let soldiers kill a load of kids. There'd be riots if they did. They'll come as soon as they can, flush out the place, protect the survivors. If we can stay hidden for an hour or two, that's all we'll need. Maybe less."

We consider Trev's plan.

"If police and soldiers raid the school," Linzer says, "we'd be safer here than out there. They shot anyone who moved in Ireland. They won't know who's a zombie and who isn't, and they won't want to take chances."

"It'll be a free-for-all," Copper agrees.

"But if the zombies find us first…" Stagger Lee mutters. "I say we make a break for it. Head for the stairs, get to the floor above, find the exit, let ourselves out, don't look back."

"What if that door's shut too?" one of the Muslim boys asks.

"It won't be," Stagger Lee says.

"The one by the gym was," the Muslim reminds him.

"That was bad luck," Stagger Lee says. "There's no chance that two of the exits will be jammed at the same time."

"Who says it was luck?" the Muslim asks. "Am I the only one who thinks this is too much of a coincidence? The janitors check those doors regularly — they have to be sure they're working, in case of a fire. And on the very day we need them, one just happens to be stuck? I don't buy it."

"What are you talking about?" Trev snaps.

"Someone sealed it shut," the Muslim says. "We've been locked in."

A scary silence settles over us. I find myself looking at Cass, and he looks back at me. His eyes are wider with fear than they were a minute ago.

"What's your name?" I ask the Muslim.

"Seez," he says.

"Seez, do us all a favor and shut up," I tell him.

"Why?" he scowls.

"If you're right, we're screwed," I say evenly. "So let's not think about it, and keep our fingers crossed that you're wrong."

"But —"

"If we're locked in here with a pack of rotten zombies, what good will worrying about it do us?" I challenge him.

"We can come up with a plan," he says.

I laugh bitterly. "If someone's blocked all the exits, there's no plan, we're done for. We have to believe that the door back there was a one-off. If it wasn't, we'll find out soon enough, and we won't have to worry about it for long."

Seez stares at me, then nods reluctantly.

"So what do we do?" I ask. "Hole up or try for the exits? Let's vote. Who wants to stay?"

Everyone looks around, hesitant to be the first to vote. Then Linzer sticks up her hand. A few more start to rise. But before a decision can be made, Pox groans, turns aside and vomits.

"Gross," Dunglop chuckles — he's closest to Pox.

There's a strange creaking sound, like a plank being bent to snapping point. As I'm trying to place it, Pox shudders, then falls still. The noise comes again. Cass takes a cautious step towards the motionless Pox, rolling his knife lightly between his fingers.

"Everyone stay back," Cass says. "I'm gonna make sure –"

Pox lurches to his feet, leaps at Dunglop and bites a chunk of flesh out of his cheek.

Dunglop screams and staggers into Cass, knocking him aside. Pox is already moving. He scrabbles after Rick, the kid from a lower year, and grabs his foot. Rick kicks out but Pox bites into his ankle. As Rick screams, Pox turns on Suze and goes for her throat.

Cass gets in the way and jabs at Pox with his knife. Pox lowers his head and charges. I tackle him before he connects with Cass. Drive him sideways. He crashes into a desk and goes sprawling.

"Clear the bloody door!" I roar. As the others hurry to the piled-up desks and chairs, I face Pox, who's back on his feet, snarling. There's a strange green fungus growing over the places where he was bitten by the zombie. Only thin wisps, but I note their presence like some supersleuth with a keen eye for detail. And his fingernails are longer than they were.

No... hold on... those aren't nails. Bits of bone are sticking out of each finger, scraps of flesh and nails shedding from them. I recall the creaking noise and put two and two together. The bones must have lengthened and snapped through his flesh as he was changing. I glance down and spot bones sticking through the tips of his shoes too.

Pox closes in on me but is distracted when Cass whistles.

"Here, boy," Cass growls, beckoning Pox on. "Come and get it."

Pox scowls and goes after Cass, moving speedily. Cass stabs at him. The blade sinks deep into Pox's chest. It pierces his heart, but that doesn't matter to Pox. He pushes on and Cass goes down. Pox opens his jaws and snaps at Cass's face. His teeth are longer and thicker than I remember.

One of the Muslims grabs Pox before he can bite. Pulls him off of Cass and pushes him away. Pox falls, but one of his bony nails scratches the Muslim's chin and draws blood.

"We're out of here!" Trev shouts, and I see that the door is open. Everyone's spilling into the corridor. Meths is dragging Rick, and Dunglop is stumbling after the others.

135

"Let me help you," I pant, taking Dunglop's arm.

"Thanks," he moans, holding a hand to his bitten cheek.

"I'm so sorry," I whisper, then whirl swiftly and send Dunglop flying across the room. He smashes into Pox, who goes down again and starts biting instinctively.

"What the hell!" Trev shouts.

"Meths!" I bark. "Leave him."

Meths looks at me uncertainly.

"They were bitten," I growl. "The same thing that happened to Pox will happen to them."

"No!" Rick screams. "Don't leave me! I won't change! You can't just —"

"B's right," Copper says.

"Look," La Lips groans, pointing.

Pox is tucking into Dunglop's brain. He's broken through the skull with the bones sticking out of his fingers and is gorging himself on the juicy stuff inside, like a pig chowing down. Dunglop's still alive, shivering, eyelids flickering with terror and shock. But he doesn't scream. Just spasms.

Meths drops Rick and backs away from him. When Rick tries to crawl after him, Meths kicks him in the head and the boy collapses with a whine.

Seez is staring at the scratched Muslim, who wipes drops of blood from his chin, studies them and sighs. "A scratch might not be the same as a bite," he says.

"But we can't take that chance," Seez says quietly.

The Muslim sighs again. "I'll head for the front door. If I make it, and if I don't turn, I'll try to get help for the rest of you."

He darts through the doorway and is gone before Seez can say anything.

I glance at Pox and Dunglop one last time, my stomach turning, tears dripping down my cheeks. Then I curse hatefully and rush out after the others, leaving my dead and undead friends behind.

TWENTY

We pad along the corridor. Screams behind us, echoing, bouncing off the walls like they're never going to die away. I'm so glad I'm not in the gym. It sounds insane, way worse than when we snuck out.

At the end of the corridor we turn right. There are bodies sprawled across the floor. Students like us, scratched, torn, bitten, bloody. Dead. As we edge past, eyeing them nervously in case they spring to life, I note that their heads have been cracked open, their brains scooped out. Except one, a small girl whose skull is intact. The same can't be said for her guts — they're all over the place.

"Wait," I whisper, stopping by the girl. I look for Cass. "Give me your knife."

"No one touches the knife but me," he says coldly.

"Fine," I snap. "Then get over here and be ready to stab her in the head if she stirs."

"What the hell are we waiting for?" Linzer snarls.

"I need to find out something."

"Who do you think you are?" she screeches. "Some sort of bloody –"

There's a creaking sound. Bones thrust through the tips of the dead girl's fingers, each at least half an inch long. Her lips shake and pull back over her teeth, which are growing and getting thicker. Her arms writhe, then she sits up and hisses at us, hunger in her eyes. I shriek and fall back. She dives after me. Hooks my shirt with her fingers. Tries to dig in.

As I scream again, Cass appears by my side and drives his knife into the side of the girl's head, all the way to the hilt. She shivers, eyes rolling. He works the blade around, digs it in and out several times. The girl falls away from me and goes still.

I force myself to my feet and tug up my shirt, wildly examining my flesh for scratches, heart beating hard. The others are staring at me suspiciously. Cass's eyes are narrow, his fingers tight on the handle of the knife.

"Nothing," I moan happily, exposing my stomach to them. "She didn't cut me. See?"

"You're lucky," Cass snorts.

"Now let's get the hell out of here, or do you want to study them some more?" Linzer sneers.

"I've confirmed what I wanted to." I point at the other corpses. "*Brains.* Like in the movies. If they eat your brain, or if it's destroyed, you're properly dead and there's no coming back. That's how we kill them."

"No shit, Sherlock," Cass says. "Now let's –"

La Lips screeches. A couple of bloodstained kids have stumbled into the corridor. Their eyes light up when they spot us and they stagger forward.

"Run!" I bark, and in a second we're racing past classrooms and corpses.

The zombies follow silently. I shouldn't look back but I can't help myself. I glance over my shoulder and spot them closing in. They're not smiling or leering. They don't pant either. They run expressionlessly, like robots. Only their eyes are alive.

One of the zombies grabs La Lips, who was struggling to keep up with the rest of us. She goes down with a yelp and it tears into her.

"Don't!" I shout at Copper as he stops to try to rescue her.

"I have to!" he yells and kicks at the zombie's head. The other one leaps on him. He bellows and lets fly with a flurry of punches. But the zombie pulls up Copper's shirt and bites into the soft flesh of his stomach. As Copper screams with pain and terror, the zombie

141

rises, lips and teeth red, and comes after the rest of us again, leaving Copper to suffer, die and turn into one of the walking dead.

I want to help Copper and La Lips but I can't. They're finished. No time to feel sorry for them. If the zombie grabs hold, I'm done for too. So I leg it, trying not to think about the friends I'm leaving behind. The poor, doomed friends that I've lost.

As we come to where the corridor branches, we turn left, but I steal a glance right and then wish that I hadn't. There's another group of kids. Maybe they had the same idea as us and were making for the exit. But they've been set upon by a pack of zombies. They're trapped against a wall, dozens of transformed students holding them there, chewing through their skulls. The captured kids are screaming, sobbing, throwing up. All helpless. All damned.

A couple of zombies at the rear of the pack spot us and break away, joining the one who was already hot on our tail. They chase us down another corridor. The black kid whose name I don't know slips on a sliver of intestines. One of them is on him a moment later. He fights back manfully but the zombie bites, scratches and pushes him down. We press on and leave him.

More corpses. The floor is sticky with blood. We dash past a room. The door's open. I spot a teacher inside, pinned to the whiteboard by four zombies. They're eating her, two on her arms, two on her legs, working their way up to her torso. She's alive and sobbing softly, her fingers, lips and eyelids spasming.

We come to a set of stairs. A few bodies lie spread-eagle across the steps. We clamber over them and up. But we can't all fit at once. It's a tight squeeze. Elbows and curses fly as each of us struggles to be first to the top.

I'm next to Cass, the pair of us pushing forward, when he gives a cry of shock. I turn. The zombies have him. One's got his right leg, one the left. Both have bitten into his calves.

Cass screams and kicks at the zombies, but they hold firm. His eyes meet mine. He silently pleads with me to help him, do something, stop this. I shake my head numbly, then reach for his knife. He jerks it away from me.

"Please," I whisper. "It's no good to you now."

Cass snarls at me and starts stabbing at the zombies. I watch him for a couple of seconds, then back away slowly. Neither Cass nor the zombies pay any attention to me. They're locked in battle, but it's a fight that has only one of two possible outcomes. They tuck into his brain and he dies. Or they leave his skull alone and he becomes one of them. Either way, Cass is lost to us, so I wipe him from my thoughts as best I can and hobble up the stairs after the others.

TWENTY-ONE

We pause at the top of the stairs to get our bearings. The two zombies below are still tucking into the screaming Cass, and there are no others in sight.

"The exit's back that way," Stagger Lee pants.

I'm familiar with it. I used it once in a fire drill. If we can get through the door, it leads, via a set of steps, to the same alley as the other emergency exit.

"Maybe we should make for the front of the building," Trev says. "We could jump from the windows."

"This exit's closer," Stagger Lee says.

"But if it's blocked..." Seez mutters.

"We've got to try," Stagger Lee insists. "It's our best hope."

"Wait," Tyler says. It's the first time

he's spoken since we broke out of the gym. "The cafeteria's over there."

"You can't be hungry!" I gasp.

He shoots me a dirty look. "They've got knives in the kitchen. We can tool up."

I frown. That's not a bad idea. "What about it?" I ask the group.

"Won't the cafeteria be full?" Suze asks. "It's lunch, so it will be like the gym. If the zombies have struck there, it'll be bedlam."

"But we'll have a much better chance if we have weapons," Ballydefeck says.

"It's worth a look," Elephant agrees.

"All right." I nod at Tyler. "Lead the way."

"Me?" he squeaks.

I grin sharkishly. "It was your idea. Only fair that if we get attacked, you should be first on their menu."

It's hard to believe that I can make a joke at a time like this. But as awful as this is, as shocking as it's been, I can't shut down. At the moment I'm alive. Those of us in this group have a chance to get out and fight another day. We have to cling to life as tightly as we can, put the atrocities from our thoughts, deal with this as if it were a surprise exam. What I've learned today is that when the shit hits the fan, you can sit around and get splattered, or you can take it in your stride and do what you must to get away clean. I'll have nightmares about this later, maybe a full-on nervous breakdown, but only if I keep my cool and escape alive.

We follow Tyler along the corridors. We're the only ones on the move up here, none of the chaos of downstairs. I have visions of walking into the cafeteria, everyone eating, unaware of what's happening below. Maybe they'll think we're winding them up. They might ignore our warnings and carry on with their lunch, oblivious until the zombies come crashing in on them.

But when we get there, I immediately see that reality has struck just as hard in the cafeteria as it has downstairs. In fact, it's struck even harder.

Students, along with some teachers and kitchen staff, are backed up against one of the walls. They're moaning and sobbing, but hardly any of them are fighting or trying to break free. They seem to have abandoned hope completely.

They're surrounded by scores of zombies, maybe a hundred or more. They're picking off the living one by one, biting some to convert them, tearing into the brains of others. It's a carefully organized operation. And pulling the strings, directing the movements of the undead, is a small group of men and women in hoodies.

My breath catches in my throat. We're watching from outside the cafeteria, through two round windows in the doors, taking turns to observe the horror show. But when my turn comes and I spot the people in the hoodies, I freeze and can't be torn away.

There are several of them. Each has a whistle, which they blow every now and then to command attention. They have rotten skin, pockmarked with pustulant sores, purple in places, patches of flesh

peeling away. All have gray, lifeless hair and pale yellow eyes. I can't see inside their mouths, but I'm pretty sure that if I examined them close up, I'd find shriveled, scabby tongues.

They're the same type of creeps as the two guys at the Imperial War Museum, the mutants who tried to kidnap the baby. And they're clearly in control, dominating the zombies, using them to process the survivors neatly and efficiently.

Seez was right. This isn't bad luck or a freak attack. We've been set up. And even though I wouldn't have believed it was possible a minute ago, I feel even more fear now than I did when the zombies first burst into the gym.

TWENTY-TWO

We head for the exit, numb, and dumb
with shock. I don't think anyone now
expects it to be open. But we act as if we
hadn't seen the slaughter in the cafeteria, as
if we don't know what it means.

We're at the door a minute later. We
stare at the bar. If it works, and the door
opens, we're just seconds away from
freedom.

Nobody reaches for the bar. Everyone's afraid of being the one to fail, to
dash the hope that we all long for but
don't dare believe in. Finally I sigh and
step up to the challenge. I push the bar
down. It clicks. I pause a second, then
push.

Nothing happens.

I close my eyes and lean my head

against the door. Then I curse and push again, straining, putting everything into it. But I'm wasting my time. It doesn't budge.

"B," Trev says.

I fire one of my vilest curses his way.

"B," he says calmly. "Look."

I turn and spot something on the floor to our left. I saw it before but thought it was just a corpse. Now I see that there are actually two bodies. And one of them's moving, chewing on the head of the other, slurping down brains.

As we stare with disgust, the zombie pushes its victim away and stands. We all gasp at the same time.

"Mrs. Reed!" I shout.

The zombie that was once our principal sways from side to side, staring at us blankly, chin drenched with blood and flecked with bits of brain. I get a fix on the body beneath her and cringe. It's Jonesenzio. He won't be boring anyone with dry history lectures again. Poor old sod.

Mrs. Reed shuffles towards us. Nobody moves. She doesn't seem to pose an immediate threat. She's smiling stupidly, eyes unfocused, rubbing her stomach. She burps and giggles softly.

"This is unreal," the Indian kid sighs.

Mrs. Reed's eyes settle on him and she frowns. She raises a finger and shakes it slowly. Then she spots me. Her smile spreads again.

"*Beeeeeeee*," she wheezes.

"Bloody hell!" Elephant yelps. "How's she talking? Zombies can't talk! Can they?"

Mrs. Reed comes closer. She's within touching distance of me now but I can't move. I'm rooted. The others back up but nobody runs or screams or tries to pull me away from her. They're mesmerized, held captive by the spectacle like I am.

Mrs. Reed strokes my cheek with a finger – there's no bone sticking out of it – and leaves a trail of blood across my flesh. But she doesn't scratch me and claim me for one of her own. Her eyes are locked on mine. She looks demented but strangely peaceful at the same time.

"*Fullll*," she whispers, still rubbing her stomach with her other hand.

"What's happening?" Seez asks, distracting her. "Where did the zombies come from? Who are the freaks in the hoodies? Who locked the doors?"

Mrs. Reed snarls at him. Then she smiles at me again and taps the side of my head. "*Stayyy. Hungry again . . . sooooon.*"

"Sorry," I croak, stepping away from her. "I don't fancy being eaten."

Mrs. Reed looks disappointed, but she shrugs and sits down. Dabs at the bits of brain stuck to her chin and sucks them from her finger.

I'm backing away from the zombie principal when I stop. This isn't right. She's not like any of the others we've encountered. And it's not just the fact that she can talk and doesn't have bones sticking out of her fingers. There are no bite marks or scratches. I can't see where she was wounded.

I want to study her properly – this seems important – but Trev interrupts.

"We have to get out of here."

"But this is weird," I argue. "She's different. I want to know why."

Trev shrugs. "Then stay and have a chat with her. Me, I'm heading for the front of the building, to get the hell out. They might have barred the doors but they can't have blocked all the windows. There wasn't enough time."

"He's right," Seez says. "The windows are our best hope."

"You don't have any hope," someone snickers behind us.

I whirl and spot three people in hoodies. They're spread across the corridor, grinning viciously. I'm almost certain that the one in the middle is the louse who tried to steal the baby in the museum. Then he points at me and says, "You should have let me take the boy," and my suspicions are confirmed.

"Who are you?" I yell. "Why are you doing this?"

"Don't worry," the mutant chuckles, his voice gravelly and gurgly, nothing like a normal person's. "You're in good company. This is happening all over London. This will be a city of zombies by the time the sun sets. And it won't be the only one. From tomorrow, this world is ours."

As we stare at the mutant with the crazy skin and yellow eyes, horrified by his prediction, he puts his whistle to his lips and blows. The others blow their whistles too. Three long, sharp toots. They're so piercing, I have to cover my ears with my hands. Then the mutants drop the whistles and smirk. Lowering my hands, I fix on the sound of a flurry of feet stomping down the corridor, dozens of zombies responding to the call of the mutants, closing in on *us*.

TWENTY-THREE

No time to think. We run from the mob of zombies, tear along the corridor, knowing we don't have much time.

As we pass an open door to a classroom, Linzer ducks inside. "I'm hiding!" she screams, slamming the door shut on the rest of us.

Meths starts to slow but Stagger Lee bellows at him, "Leave her!"

We press on. My heart's hammering. I'm finding it hard to breathe. I was never the fittest—too many helpings of fries and not enough exercise. I start to drift towards the rear of the group. We turn a corner, then another. I've lost track of where we are. The zombies are drawing closer. The mutants in hoodies must be with them because I hear an occasional whistle.

I'm rushing past a window when I catch a glimpse of open space. I stop and yell to the others, "We're next to a courtyard. I'm jumping."

"We don't know what's down there," Trev roars. "It could be full of zombies."

I grin ghoulishly. "Only one way to find out." I back up from the window, then hurl myself at the glass, covering my face with my arms. There's a good chance I'll slice open a vein or artery, but I'd rather bleed to death than be devoured by the living dead.

I smash through the window and whoop insanely, half-terrified, half-buzzing. My arms snap open and flap wildly. A brief glimpse of the ground coming fast towards me. Then I land in an untidy heap and roll awkwardly. The air's knocked out of me. Shards of glass nick my hands and knees. But I'm alive. I'm not badly injured. And the courtyard's empty.

"Come on!" I shout at the others.

Seez follows first, bursting through another pane of glass. There's a wide hole now and the rest can jump cleanly. They pile after us, landing hard, picking themselves up, a few cuts and bruises but no broken ankles or severed arteries.

Suze and Ballydefeck are last. Suze stares at the drop with terror. She's crying.

"Hurry up," Ballydefeck says, grabbing her.

She shakes him off. "I can't. I'm afraid of heights."

"It's not that bloody high!"

"I –"

A scream from a window on the other side of the courtyard stops her. We all look. Linzer is pressed against the glass, her face contorted. Zombies are bunched around her. They yank her out of sight. Looks like Cass might have been right about them having a keen nose for the living.

"Get down and drop, then," Ballydefeck barks, getting to his knees and backing out, holding on to the sill.

"All right," Suze moans, shutting her eyes. "But I can't look. You tell me where I have to –"

There's a blur of motion. A zombie tackles Suze and she's gone before she can scream. Ballydefeck yelps and lets go. But hands snake out and grab his arms. He's hauled back into the room, roaring and cursing.

Several zombies lean out through the shattered windows, and I'm sure they're going to jump in and finish us off. But the sunlight unnerves them. They wince, cover their eyes and back away into the gloom. Before hungrier or braver zombies can take their place, we find the nearest door and race back inside, stumbling slightly, feet stinging from the jump, but delighted to be alive, all too aware that we could have very easily gone the same way as Linzer, Suze and Ballydefeck.

TWENTY-FOUR

Nine of us left. Me, Trev, Meths, Elephant, Stagger Lee, Tyler, Seez, the other Muslim boy and the Indian. As we run, twisting through corridors, I try to remember how many of us there were to begin with, but I can't. I've already forgotten the names and faces of the dead. I'm sure, if I sat down for five minutes, I'd be able to recall them. But right now they're vaguely remembered ghosts.

Sounds behind us again. The zombies must have overcome their fear of the light. The chase has resumed.

"Hold on," Trev pants, coming to a stop. "Where are we? I don't know if we're heading back towards the gym or close to the front."

We gaze around. There are classrooms

on both sides but I don't recognize them. All of the corridors have started to look the same. I'm as lost as Trev. By the blank stares of the others, I know that they are too.

Tyler coughs shyly and points. "The front's that way."

"You're sure?" Trev asks.

"Yeah," he says with a small smile. "I'm good at directions, me."

"Then let's go."

We head the way Tyler pointed. He'd better be right. If he's not, I'll kill him before the zombies can.

We turn a corner and I run into a boy my own size. We collide, bounce off each other and fall. Sitting up and rubbing my head, I realize it's Pox and I burst into a smile.

"Pox! I thought you were..."

I stop. Pox is staring at me with a hungry look. I remember that the last time I saw him, he was dining on Dunglop's brain. My eyes flash to the fingers of his left hand and I see a light green moss running along the bite marks. Bones jut nastily from the ruined tips of his fingers.

Rick's just behind Pox. He's limping, dragging one leg. His foot's missing. Pox or another zombie must have chewed it off before he turned. But there's not much blood.

Pox scuttles after me. Dunglop's brain obviously wasn't enough to satisfy his appetite. Like Meths, poor old Dunglop never was the brightest of sparks, so he must have made for no more than a snack.

I kick at Pox's face, driving him back. As I try to scramble to my feet, Meths wades in and kicks Pox harder. Rick hops towards Meths, arms wide, fingers flexed like a cat's claws. Meths slips. Rick ducks in for the kill –

– then there's an unnatural roar and the zombie flies backwards, stomach ripped to shreds, blood spattering the wall and floor behind him.

Pox gets up and snarls. Goes for me again. There's another roar and his head explodes. Somebody's firing bullets. Someone has a gun.

Bloody *yes*, mate!

"His head!" I roar as Rick hobbles forward, guts spilling down his legs. "Shoot him in the head! That's the only way to stop them!"

The gun fires again and Rick's temple cracks open. He drops in a lifeless heap.

I turn to face the gunman. The others have all turned too, jaws slack, hardly able to believe that this is real. I'm hoping for a squadron of soldiers but it's just a normal-looking guy with a rifle. He hasn't lowered it and is staring grimly down the barrel at *me*.

"Were you bitten?" he growls.

"No!" I scream.

"Don't lie. I saw it attack you. Stand back!" he barks at the others.

I gape at the man with the gun. This is so unfair. To survive the zombies, only to be finished off by an idiot who won't listen. I'd love to knock some sense into his thick head. But it doesn't look like I'll have a chance, because he's aiming at the middle of my face. Any second now he's gonna –

"Stop!" another man roars. "Don't shoot! That's my daughter!"

"But I saw –" the man with the rifle begins.

The rest of what he says is lost to me. Because suddenly Dad is there, pushing past the idiot with the gun, spreading his arms wide, stooping to hug me.

"Dad!" I cry with a rush of relief.

"*Becky!*" he moans, wrapping his arms around me and hugging me tight. "My girl! My girl!"

Then he's kissing me and hugging me, and I don't care how many zombies or idiots with trigger-happy fingers there are. They can't hurt me. They don't matter anymore. Dad loves me. He risked his life to find me. Everything will be all right now. Dad will save me. He'll save us all. He's a bloody hero!

TWENTY-FIVE

"Todd," the man with the gun says, interrupting our hug fest. Dad looks up, happy tears sparkling in his eyes, grinning like a loon. "Our kids aren't here. We have to push on."

Dad's grin fades. He pats my head, then stands. The two men shake hands. There are a couple of women behind the guy with the gun, one white, one Chinese. Dad smiles sadly at the white woman but only scowls at the other one.

"You're sure you want to continue?" Dad asks Gun Guy.

"I have to." He turns to the rest of us. "Any of you know Jimmy Wilkins?" Most of us nod. "Have you seen him?" We shake our heads.

"What about Lindsay Hogan?" the white woman asks.

Linzer.

"The zombies got her," I mutter.

The woman's face hardens. "No!" she snaps. "You're wrong."

"We saw them grab her."

"Where?" she screams.

I turn and point. The woman starts running. "It was on the top floor," I shout. "You're too late. She's dead."

But the woman isn't listening. She's gone.

The Chinese woman asks us if we've seen her son and daughter, but we don't know either of them. She heads off with Gun Guy, the pair advancing swiftly, checking each room as they pass.

"It's madness," I whisper to Dad. "They're gonna get killed."

"I know, love," he says. "But that's what parents do for their kids. I knew I'd probably get eaten when I came looking for you, but did that stop me? Hell no."

I beam at him, so proud. He looks around, smiles at my friends, sniffs at the Muslims, the Indian and Tyler. "Come on," he says. "I'm getting you out of here."

We follow Dad back the way he came. He's moving quickly but he isn't racing. "Slow down," he says as Trev tries to force the pace.

"But the zombies…" Trev gasps.

"You think I don't know about them?" Dad snorts.

"We have to get out," Trev insists.

"That's what we're doing," Dad says calmly. "But if we go

flapping around like headless chickens, we'll run into trouble, the way you lot did before I found you. These zombies aren't so tough if you're prepared for them. I've finished off a few of them already." He shakes a metal bar at us—it's red with blood. "But you have to go about it the right way, keep your head, make sure you have the time and space to spot them coming."

He takes a left turn and we pass the staff room. The door's open. I spot a couple of teachers inside, chewing on the remains of some of their colleagues.

"They won't be failing you again," Dad says and we both laugh.

"Straight F's in most courses," I chuckle. "But A-plus in zombie survival!"

"Been a long time since I was a student here," Dad mutters nostalgically. "But I remember the place like it was yesterday. Didn't have any trouble finding my way around."

"How'd you get over here so quickly?" I ask. It feels like we've been running for hours since the gym, but it can't have been more than fifteen or twenty minutes.

"I was working nearby," Dad says. "When I heard about the attacks on the radio, I ran like the wind. I tried calling ahead to check if things were all right but the phones aren't working."

"Then it's true?" Elephant asks. "This is happening in other places too?"

"Yeah," Dad says. "Schools, hospitals, shops, factories, all sorts and all over the place. Getting out of here won't be the end of it.

London's in an uproar. But the zombies tend to keep to the shadows. If we stick to the main streets and roads, we should be all right. At least until night."

"What about Mum?" I ask, able to think about her now that I have someone else to watch out for me.

"We'll swing by home, see if she's there," Dad says.

"Can't we call and get her to —"

"Weren't you listening?" he snaps. "The phones are dead. Cells, landlines, the lot. TV stations are down too. A lot of radio stations as well, but a guy I work with has a top-of-the-range radio that picks up all sorts of frequencies. That's how I know it's widespread. It started about..." He checks his watch. "Not quite an hour ago. But I didn't hear about it immediately. As soon as I did, I came." He flashes me a shaky smile. "You didn't think I'd leave you to be gobbled by zombies, did you?"

I want to burst into tears and hug him again, but there's no time. We have to keep moving. We'll be relatively safe in the sunlight once we get out of here. We can hug all we want then.

We move steadily through the school, drawing closer to the front of the building. For the first time since the gym I really allow myself to hope. I don't want to tempt fate but I think we've made it.

We come to a corridor that's only a few turns from the main exit. Everyone's excited. We can virtually smell freedom. There's a fire door ahead of us. Once we push through that, the corridor branches. The right turn leads back into the school. The left will lead us all the way home.

Dad shoves the door. It rattles but doesn't open. He frowns and pushes it again. No joy. "That's not right," he says. "I came through here on my way in."

The Indian kid slides up to the crack in the door and peers through. "It's been locked," he moans. "There's a chain."

"What?" Dad shouts, shoving him aside and squinting through the crack. "Who the hell did that?"

"The mutants," I sigh. As if in answer, I hear a whistle blow somewhere close behind us. "Dad! They're coming!"

Dad stares at me. He starts to ask how I know we're in trouble, then shakes his head and slams the door with his shoulder. "Keep back," he grunts at those around him. "It'll take more than a chain to hold *me* here."

We stare at Dad as he rams the door again and again. It's a thick, heavy door, designed to slow the spread of flames in case of a fire. The chain is sturdy too. Dad doesn't look to be achieving much but he keeps going, sweating like a marathon runner, totally focused.

I glance back down the corridor and spot four zombies slipping into it. They lock sights on us and slither forward.

"Dad!" I wail.

"I nearly have it," he pants.

Trev throws himself at the door, trying to help. Meths and Seez take turns too. Dad glares at them, but then there's a snapping sound and the door starts to give. "That's the way, boys!" Dad whoops. "Give it everything you have."

They hurl themselves at the door, one after the other. Their arms and shoulders will be black and blue later but they don't care. No matter how much of a battering they take, they don't back down.

Elephant, Stagger Lee, the Indian and the other Muslim kid watch helplessly as Dad and the three boys fly at the door like rabid dogs. I'm a bit farther back, Tyler by my side. I'm looking for anything I can use to fend off the zombies but I'm not having much luck. They're closing in. They could have rushed us by now, but they see that we're trapped, so they're taking their time.

"Dad!" I yell.

"Just another few blows," he wheezes, launching himself at the door again.

More zombies appear at the far end of the corridor, loads of them, a couple of whistle-blowing mutants in the middle, guiding them towards us.

"Dad!"

Dad looks back and whitens. "Holy hell," he croaks.

Meths bangs into the door and it cracks. The hinges give. Meths cheers and starts shaking the door. Dad and Seez join him. There isn't room for Trev—he's been pushed out of the way.

"They're almost on us," I shout.

Dad looks at me, then at the zombies, and curses. "You've got to stall them. We only need a few more seconds."

"How?" I scream. "There's nothing I can do to –"

"Throw them the black kid!" Dad roars.

I stare at him. Tyler stares too, both of us stunned, momentarily forgetting about the zombies.

"Do it!" Dad shouts.

"But he's Tyler," I whisper. "He's one of us. He helped us get –"

"Throw them the bloody chimney sweep or I'll whip you raw!" Dad screams.

And suddenly I'm reacting, doing what he tells me, the way I always do when he loses his temper, because it's easier to obey him than stand up to him. Years of conditioning kick in. Fear takes over. I go into my dutiful-daughter act. The racist in me swims to the fore and rejoices at being set free.

On autopilot, I grab Tyler's arm and hurl him at the zombies.

"*No!*" he shrieks as he stumbles towards them. "B! No! Help me!"

Tyler crashes into the zombies. All five go down, and the zombies sprawl like bowling pins. Tyler starts to get up. Immediately guilt-stricken and appalled, I reach out to him, desperately wanting to put right what I've done. But before I can drag him to safety, a zombie catches hold and bites Tyler's neck. Tyler chokes and stiffens, blood spurting, and I watch with horror as the other three zombies crowd around and tuck into the tasty human morsel that I've thrown them.

TWENTY-SIX

I've seen a lot of terrible things today, but nothing compares with this. It's not that Tyler dies more horribly than any of the others who've been torn to pieces. But *I* sacrificed him. I let Dad bully me, the way I've always done, and now a boy is dead because of it. Because of *me*.

As the other zombies draw closer, the scent of Tyler's blood luring them on, Dad jerks the door open and bellows triumphantly. Trev and the others squeeze through. Dad dashes back and pulls me away from the awful spectacle of Tyler Bayor being finished off by the undead.

"Come on," Dad pants. "We've got to get out of here."

Dad shoves the Indian kid away from

the door and growls at him, "Get out of it, Gandhi. My daughter goes first."

He shoves me through, then follows. The Indian boy's squealing. He tries to wriggle after us but a zombie grabs him. He screeches and reaches out to us, pleading to be saved. Dad sneers, then pushes him back and slams the door shut.

"Help me hold this," he snaps at Trev and Meths. They obey without question, shocked into submission by his viciousness, dominated by the cruelty in his voice, the same way I've been dominated by it all my life.

Dad looks around for something to jam the door with, but there's nothing. "All right," he pants, straining with Trev and Meths to hold back the zombies. "I'm guessing they'll pile up and get stuck. It'll take them a while to sort themselves out. You lot run ahead. We'll hold this a bit longer, then dash after you and hope we get enough of a start on them."

Elephant, Stagger Lee, Seez and the other Muslim boy peel away to the left. They're crying and shaking but they push on, freedom all but guaranteed now.

"Go on, B," Dad says.

I shake my head.

"Stupid girl," he mutters, then winces as the door buckles. "All right, stick with me then. Are you two ready? We'll let go on the count of three."

Trev and Meths nod nervously. Then Dad shouts swiftly, "One two three!"

The trio release the door and make a break for it. The zombies push hard on the door and it tears free. But like Dad guessed, too many try to squeeze through at the same time and they get jammed. It'll be a few seconds before they make any headway.

Dad realizes I'm not with him. He pauses and turns. Sees me backing away. "B!" he shouts. "What the hell are you doing?"

"I can't," I moan.

He starts towards me. Stops when he spots the zombies untangling themselves. "Come on!" he screams, extending a hand. "I didn't go through all this to lose you now. Get your arse over here before —"

"You know the problem with you, Dad?" I stop him, calmer than I've any right to be, wiping angry, bitter tears from my cheeks. "You're a bigger monster than any bloody zombie."

As Dad gapes at me, bewildered, I turn my back on the man I love more than any in the world, the man I hate more than any in the world, and stumble away from him, from the exit, from safety. As he roars my name, I follow the branch of the corridor that leads back into the building, preferring to take my chances among the zombies than go along with the racist beast who made me kill Tyler Bayor.

TWENTY-SEVEN

Twisting and turning, racing along corridors, tears streaming down my face, I pant and stumble, but never fall or falter. Never look back either, afraid of what I might see, zombies or Dad, one as bad as the other.

I can't believe I'm doing this. I was so close to freedom. I should have escaped with the others, dealt with Dad outside, fought my fight when my life wasn't on the line.

But I couldn't. For all these years I've said nothing when he hit Mum, when he hit me, when he demonized anyone who wasn't white. I never stood up to him. I put on an act, tried to pretend it didn't matter. And not just because I was afraid of him. Because I loved him too. He was my dad. I didn't want to admit that he was truly evil, irredeemably warped.

But he turned me into a killer. He made me throw Tyler to the zombies. I can't forgive that. I can't lie to myself, dismiss it as an isolated incident, tell myself that he'll change. Tyler and I weren't close, he wasn't a friend, but he helped us get as far as we did. We might not have found our way out without him. He didn't deserve to be killed because of the color of his skin. Nor the Indian boy, sacrificed by a man who cares for nobody except his own.

I remember something that Mr. Burke said a while back. *There are lots of black-hearted, mean-spirited bastards in the world. It's important that we hold them to account. But always remember that you might be the most black-hearted and mean-spirited of the lot, so hold yourself the most accountable of all.*

I've played a cringing neutral all my life, and it turned me into something far worse than I ever feared I'd become. But that changes here, today, now. If I get out of this alive, I'll never make a mistake like that again. I can't bring Tyler back – that will haunt me forever, and nothing can ever make up for it – but from this point on I'll do whatever I can to stand up to Dad and anyone like him. I swear on the blood I've shed, on the life I've destroyed.

I come to an intersection and turn right, but there are zombies shambling up the corridor towards me. I backpedal and push on straight. The zombies give chase.

I'm passing a room when a girl staggers out ahead of me. She's bleeding, one arm bitten off at the elbow. A zombie follows, a boy my size, his clothes almost torn to shreds. He decides I'm richer pickings and makes a grab for me.

I duck, but not quickly enough. Finger bones rake my arm and catch on the exposed flesh of my wrist. I yelp and kick at him. He snaps for my leg with his teeth but I pull it back in time. Kick him hard in the head. Race on.

I stare at the scratch as I run, terror mounting. We never found out whether a scratch was enough to turn a human into a zombie. Maybe it's harmless and they can only convert by biting, a transfer of saliva or blood. But I wouldn't bet on it. I think it's all over for me. In another minute or two I'll probably throw up like Pox did, give a shiver and a grunt, and never think clearly again.

I come to a set of stairs and start up the steps, figuring I can get to the windows at the front and jump to safety. I have to believe it's not too late. If I can get out of the school, maybe I can be helped, even if the scratch *is* infectious. I'm hoping it isn't, but if it is, maybe someone can chop off my arm or inject me with a cure or...or...*something*. It doesn't matter that I'm clutching at straws. Better I cling to some kind of hope than abandon it entirely.

But I'm not halfway up the steps when even the thinnest sliver of hope is ripped away from me forever.

"Run, run as fast as you can," someone gurgles ahead of me.

I look up and spot the mutant from the museum, the one I ran into earlier. There are dozens of zombies behind him, staring at me, drooling, fingers twitching, awaiting the order to attack.

I come to a halt and stare at the man with the yellow eyes and purplish skin. He's giggling sickly. "Where are you going, Becky?" he crows.

I take a step back, whimpering softly, looking for angles, seeing nothing but zombies. I feel dizzy and nauseous. Am I turning, or is it just fear?

"I was scratched," I moan, holding out my hand, eyesight blurring, senses going into a tailspin. "Does that mean...?"

The mutant cackles. "Yes. But you've more than a scratch to worry about. It looks to me like one of your friends wants a word."

He nods at the stairs behind me. I turn and find Tyler standing on the step just below mine. His chin is lowered. Blood and a light green layer of moss cake his shoulder and neck, and all the other places where he was bitten. I can't see his eyes.

Before I can say anything, Tyler's right hand shoots forward. His fingers are stiff, hooked slightly, the bones at the tips sticking out like small daggers. They hammer into my chest, shatter my breastbone, clasp around my heart. As I scream with shock and agony, Tyler rips my heart free of my body. I see it pulse in his palm a few times. Then he rams it into his mouth, tears off a chunk and swallows.

That's the last thing I see in this life, Tyler chewing on my heart, grinning viciously — revenge is obviously as sweet as people always said it was.

Then I'm falling, fading away. The world goes black around the edges, throbs, and all is consumed by a wave of dark nothingness.

I die.

To be continued…

BOOK 2:

ZOM-B
UNDERGROUND

was playing with a lighter and I've never forgotten that foul aroma. As my face wrinkles with distaste, an even nastier stench kicks in and I almost gag. What the hell *is* that?

As I'm trying to place the sickening scent, a tall man staggers past, face and skull ablaze, trying to slap out the flames but failing. He falls to his knees and shakes his head wildly from side to side, the flames growing thicker, glowing more brightly. And I peg the source of the smell.

It's burning flesh.

With a startled cry, I flail away from the man on fire and glance around desperately for something to quench the flames with, or someone to call for help. It takes all of two seconds to realize I'm in just as much trouble as the guy with the burning pumpkin for a head.

I'm in a large room. Not one I recognize. I should be in my school, but this is a place I've never seen before. Pure white walls, except where they've been scorched. Several oversized windows, lots of people on the other side of the glass, peering in, studying the chaos.

There's a small team at the center of the room, six people in black leather pants and jackets, faces hidden behind the visors of motorcycle-type helmets. Each is armed, a couple with flame-throwers, another pair with stun guns, two with spears.

Lots of figures surround the six in leathers. Fifteen or so men, a handful of women, a couple of teenagers, a girl no more than eight or nine years old. Except they're not normal people. They're zombies.

I categorize them even before the memories of what happened at my school click into place. I've seen enough horror films to know a fully paid-up member of the living dead when I see one. They don't move as stiffly as most movie zombies, but they have the vacant expression, they're missing body parts, some are caked in blood, their teeth are gnashing together hungrily, they're covered in scars and cuts, and wisps of green moss grow over their wounds.

Wait...I never saw moss in any of the movies. I only saw that on the zombies in the Internet clips of the attack in Pallaskenry.

188

And on those who struck when my school was attacked. When *I* was killed.

I flash on a memory of Tyler Bayor jamming his hand into my chest and ripping out my heart. I moan pitifully and my hands snake to my breast to find out if that really happened or if it was just a dream. But I'm distracted before I can check.

One of the leather-clad tormentors at the center of the room is bigger than the others, tall and burly. He breaks away from the group and sprays flames in a wide semicircle, scorching the zombies closest to him. They squeal and peel away. It seems like the dead can feel pain too.

"Rage!" one of the others barks. "Get your arse back here. We've got to stick together."

"Sod that," the tall one retorts, and pushes forward, coming towards me, letting fly with more flames.

I forget about everything else and flee from the fire, survival instincts kicking in, following a man and woman who were singed from the last burst. I try to call to the guy in the leathers, to plead with him to stop, but there's something wrong with my mouth. It feels like it's full of pebbles. All that emerges is a strangled "*Urrggghh! Ugga gurhk!*" sound.

One of the zombies—a woman—leaps onto the tall guy's back and gnaws at his shoulder. He lowers his flamethrower, grabs her hair and tugs. She claws at his helmet. He bends over to shake her off.

While I'm not naturally inclined to side with a zombie, it's clear

that we're in the same boat. An enemy of theirs is also an enemy of mine. So I dart forward to help the undead woman tackle our foe with the flamethrower.

One of the others in the center yells a warning to the suitably named Rage, but it's too late. I rush him from his blind side and throw myself at him. I probably wouldn't be able to knock him over by myself, but the weight of the woman helps drag him down.

As the guy in the helmet yelps, I grab the hose of his flame-thrower and wrestle it from him. He hangs on tightly, roaring for help, but then the woman bites his arm and digs through the leather of his jacket. With a curse, his grip loosens. A second later I've ripped the hose from the tanks strapped to his back and the device is rendered useless.

The person with the other flamethrower peels away from the group and starts towards me.

"Cathy!" someone shouts. "Don't break rank!"

"But Rage needs—"

"Forget about him. We need you to cover the rest of us."

As the woman hesitates, I heft the hose—it feels quite solid—and move in on the guy on the ground. He's pushing the female zombie away, trying to make room to kick at her. I take a couple of practice swings, then let him have it, bringing it down as hard as I can over the top of his helmet.

The guy bellows with pain and backs away from me as I swing at him again. The zombie gurgles and shoves me aside, hurrying after him, clawing at his legs like a cat as she tries to grab hold. My gaze fixes on the small bits of bone sticking out of the ends of her fingers and I'm stopped in my tracks by another flashback.

I glance down at my own hand and see bones jutting out of my fingers too. I drop the hose and clutch the hand to my chest, moaning softly. I check the other fingers and find more extended bones. I raise my head and shriek at the ceiling, a wordless cry of frustration and terror.

The guy on the floor lashes out with a foot and connects with the zombie's head. She's driven back. He forces himself to his feet and staggers towards the safety of his pack. Other zombies throw themselves in his path, clutch at him, gnash at his gloved fingers. But he's strong and moving fast. He brushes them aside as if they were mannequins, then slips behind the woman with the flame-thrower and picks at the material around the place where the zombie bit him, examining his wound.

I chuckle sickly at the sight of the guy studying his arm. The bite of a zombie is contagious. He's finished. Any minute now he'll turn into one of them, and good riddance to the bugger. I've no sympathy for anyone who tries to burn me alive.

I look at my fingers again and the chuckle dies away at the back of my throat as I'm forced to correct myself. He'll turn into one of *us*.

A siren blares and panels slide open in the ceiling. As I stare, bewildered, nets drop through the gaps and fall on several of the zombies. There must be weights attached to the nets, because the zombies stagger, then fall. They become entangled as they writhe on the floor and are quickly trapped.

More nets drop and the rest of the zombies are swiftly subdued. They hiss and roar defiantly, and some try to flee, but the nets find them all, even the little girl. Soon I'm the only one left standing. For some reason they haven't targeted me. I squint at the ceiling as the panels are replaced, waiting for the area above me to open, but I'm either standing in a spot where they can't get at me or for some reason they don't want to ensnare me.

"Do you think I should toast this one?" the woman with the flamethrower asks, advancing past the struggling zombies.

I snarl at her and try to shout a curse, but again all that comes out is a gargled noise, something along the lines of "*Fwah ooo!*"

"Hold on," somebody says, and a guy with a spear puts it down, then removes his helmet. I stare uncertainly. It's a boy, my sort of age, maybe a bit younger. The rest start to take off their helmets and I'm astonished to find that all of them are teenagers. I look for a familiar face, but they're all strangers to me.

As four of the boys drop their helmets and study me with dark, suspicious expressions, the girl called Cathy takes off hers. She's scowling. She points the nozzle of her flamethrower at me again.

"She attacked Rage," Cathy growls. "I say we finish her off."

"They don't want us to," one of the boys mutters, nodding at the ceiling, then pointing at a window, where the people on the other side of the glass are watching calmly.

193

"All the more reason to burn her," Cathy sneers.

"Hold it!" the tall one – Rage – barks. He's still wearing his helmet. He strides over to the girl with the flamethrower and stares at her through the dark lens of his visor. "Nobody breaks the rules around here."

"But she attacked you," Cathy pouts. "She tried to kill you."

"Yeah," Rage says. "You would have too in her position. She's a zom head. We have to hand her over."

"She might not be," Cathy says. She still hasn't lowered the flamethrower.

Rage tilts his head, then looks back at me. "Got anything to say for yourself?"

Unable to express myself with words, I give him the finger.

Rage chuckles drily, then takes off his helmet. He's got a big head, hair cut even shorter than mine, chubby cheeks – a chunk of flesh has been bitten out of the left cheek and a layer of green moss grows lightly around it – small ears, beady eyes. He's grinning wickedly.

"Whaddaya know," he jeers, reaching out and bending my finger down. *"It's aliiiiive!"*

As I stare at him, more confused than I've ever been, a door swishes open. Soldiers and medics spill into the room and fan out around us.

The madness begins.

TWO

I'm B Smith and I'm a zombie.

I study my face in the small mirror in my cell, looking for a monster but only finding myself. I look much the same as I did before I was killed, hair shaved tight, pale skin, a few freckles, a mole on the far right of my jaw, light blue eyes, a nose that's a bit too wide for my face. But if I stare long enough I start to notice subtle differences.

Like those blue eyes I was always so pleased about. (I was never a girlie girl, but they were my best feature and, yeah, I used to admire them every so often if I was feeling gooey.) They're not as shiny as they were. They look like they've dried out. That's because they have.

I tilt my head back and pour several

drops from a bottle into each eye, then shake my head gently from side to side to work the liquid about. Reilly gave me the bottle. He also taught me how to shake my head the right way.

"You can't blink anymore."

That was several days ago, not long after I was brought to my cell from the room of fire. I was bundled in here without anyone saying anything, no explanations, no sympathy, no warnings. After the horror show with the zombies and the gang in leather, a group of soldiers simply shuffled me along a series of corridors, stuck me here and left me alone.

For a few hours I paced around the small cell. There was nothing in it then, no mirror, no bed, no bucket. Just a sink that didn't have running water. I was wild with questions, theories, nightmarish speculations. I knew that I'd been killed and come back to life as a zombie. But why had my thoughts returned? Why could I remember my past? Why was I able to reason?

The zombies in Pallaskenry and my school were mindless, murdering wrecks. They killed because they couldn't control their unnatural hunger for brains. The zombies in the room were the same, single-minded killing machines on legs.

Except I thought that those teenagers with the weapons were zombies too. Rage had definitely been bitten by one of the undead — the moss growing around his cheek was proof of that. But they could talk and think and act the same way they could when they were alive.

What the hell was going on?

Reilly was the first person to enter my cell that day. A thickset soldier with brown hair and permanent stubble, he brought in a chair, closed the door behind him, put the chair in front of me and sat.

"You can't blink anymore," he said.

"*Uh urh ooh?*" I grunted, forgetting that I couldn't speak.

"You can't talk either," he noted drily. "We'll sort out your mouth soon but you should tend to your eyes first. Your vision will have suffered already, but the more they dry out, the worse it'll get."

He produced a plastic bottle of eye drops and passed it to me. As I stared at it suspiciously, he chuckled. "It's not a trick. If we wanted to harm you, we'd have fried you in the lab. Your eyelids don't work. Go on, try them, see for yourself."

I tried to close my eyes but nothing happened. If I furrowed my brow it forced them partly closed into a squint, but they wouldn't move by themselves. I reached for them to pull the lids down. Then I saw the bones sticking out of my fingers and stopped, afraid I might scratch my eyeballs.

"Good call," Reilly said. "Revitalizeds all come close to poking out an eye—a few actually did before we could warn them. Most reviveds instinctively know to keep their hands away from their eyes, but you guys..." He snorted, then told me how to administer the drops.

I stare at myself in the mirror again and wipe streaks from the drops away as they drip down my cheeks—the closest I'm ever going to get to tears now that I'm dead. My eyes look better, but still not as moist and sharp as they once did. I can see clearly, but my field of vision is narrower and the world's a bit darker than when I was alive, as if I'm staring through a thin gray veil.

I open my mouth and examine my teeth. Run a tongue over them, but carefully. I nicked it loads of times the first few days and I still catch myself occasionally.

After Reilly had given me the drops, he told me why I couldn't talk.

"Your teeth have sprouted. When you returned from the dead, they thickened and lengthened into fangs. That's so you can bite through flesh and bone more easily." He said it casually, as if it were no big thing.

"The bones in your fingers serve the same purpose," he went on. "They let you dig through a person's skull. Better than daggers, they are. We're not sure why it happens in your toes as well. Maybe the zombie gene can't distinguish between one set of digits and the other."

I wanted to cry when he said that. I don't know why, but something about his tone tore a long, deep hole through my soul. I made a moaning noise and hung my head, but no tears came. They couldn't. My tear ducts have dried up. I can never weep again.

Reilly went on to explain how they were going to file my teeth down. They'd use an electric file to start me off, but after that I could trim them with a metal file myself every day or two.

"It'll be like brushing your teeth," he said cheerfully. "A few minutes in the morning, again at night before you go to bed, and they'll be fine." He paused. "Although you won't really need to go to bed now...."

It's been hard keeping track of the days, but by totaling up Reilly's visits I figure I've been here at least a week, maybe longer. And not a wink of sleep in all that time. They gave me a bed, and I lie down every now and then to rest, but I never come close to dropping off.

"The dead don't sleep," Reilly shrugged when I asked him why I couldn't doze. "They don't need to."

I was nervous when a medic first filed my teeth down. I always hated going to the dentist, and this was a hundred times worse. The noise was louder than any dentist's drill, and splinters from my teeth went flying back in my throat and up my nose and into my eyes. My teeth got hot from the friction and my gums felt like they were burning. I pushed the medic away several times to snarl at him and give him an evil glare.

"Just don't bite," Reilly warned me. "If you nip him and turn him into one of your lot, you'll be put down like a rabid dog, no excuses."

The medic wiped sweat from his forehead and I realized he was more nervous than I was. He was wearing thick gloves, but as I'd seen in the room when the woman bit the tall guy in leathers, clothes and gloves aren't foolproof against a zombie attack.

I tried to control myself after that, and didn't pull back as much as I had been doing, even though every part of me wanted to.

The medic left once he'd finished. I ran my tongue around my mouth and winced as one of my teeth nicked it.

"I should have warned you about that," Reilly said. "Doesn't matter how much you file them down, they'll always be sharper than they were. Best thing is to keep your tongue clear of your teeth."

"Thash eashy fuhr you tuh shay," I mumbled.

"Hey, not bad for your first attempt," Reilly said, looking impressed. "Most of the revitalizeds take a few days to get their act together. I think you're going to be a fast learner."

"Shkroo you, arsh hohl," I spat, and his expression darkened.

"Maybe you were better off mute," he growled.

It took me a while to get the hang of my new teeth. I still slur the occasional word, but a week into my new life—or unlife, or whatever the hell it's called—I can speak as clearly as I could before I was killed.

"B Smith went to mow, went to mow a meadow," I sing tune-lessly to my reflection. "But a zombie ripped her heart out, so now she's a walking dead-o."

Hey, I might be dead, but you've gotta laugh, haven't you? Especially when you're no longer able to cry your bloody eyes out.

THREE

Lying on the bed, staring at the ceiling, thinking about Mum and Dad.

Reilly hasn't told me anything about the outside world. We've spent a lot of time together. He chats with me about all sorts of things, soccer, TV shows we used to watch, our lives before the zombie uprising. But he won't discuss the attack on my school or any of the other assaults that took place that day. I've no idea if order has been restored or if the soldiers and medics here are the only people left alive in the whole wide world. I've pushed him hard for answers, but although Reilly's been good to me, he can play deaf and dumb to perfection when he wants.

I've said a few prayers for Mum and Dad, even though I'm not the praying type. For Mum especially. It's strange. I thought I loved Dad more. He was the one I respected, the one I wanted to impress. Mum was weak in my opinion, a coward and a fool for letting her husband knock her about the place. I stood up for her and always tried to help when he'd lay into her, because that's what you do for your mum, but if you'd ask me to name a favorite, I'd have chosen Dad, despite all his flaws.

But she's the one I miss most. Maybe it's because of what Dad did the day I died. He came to rescue me. Risked his own life to try to save me. But then he made me throw Tyler to the zombies, turned me into a killer, and since then…

No. That's a lie, and I don't want to lie to myself anymore. I've done too much of that in the past. Be truthful, B. Dad didn't force me. I threw Tyler to the zombies because I was scared and it was the easy thing to do.

Dad hated foreigners and people who had different beliefs. I never wanted to be like him in that respect, but to keep him quiet I acted as if I was, and in the end it rubbed off on me. I became a monster. I don't ever want to allow that to happen again, but if I'm to keep the beast inside me under control, I have to accept that the guilt was mine for doing what Dad told me to do. You can't blame other people for sins of your own making.

I sit up, swing my legs off the bed and scowl. No use worrying about Mum and Dad until I have more information. I'm sure answers will be revealed in time. They can't be keeping me alive just

204

to hold me in this cell forever. I have to be patient. Explanations will come. If I have to mourn, I'll do it once their deaths are confirmed. Until then I need to hope for the best.

To distract myself, I focus on the throbbing noise. It's constant, the rumbling of machines in the distance, AC, oxygen being pumped in for the living. It never ceases. It drove me mad for the first few days, but now I find it comforting. Without a TV, iPod, or anything else, it's the only way I have of amusing myself when Reilly's not around. I tune into the hum when I'm bored and try to put images to the noises, to imagine what's happening outside this cell, soldiers marching, medics conducting their experiments, the teenagers in leather....

Hmm. I've no idea who they were. I'm pretty sure, judging by the green moss on the tall guy's cheek, that they're like me, zombies who can think and act the way they did before they died. Reilly refers to us as *revitalizeds*. The ordinary, mindless zombies are *reviveds*. But why were the revitalizeds in that room with weapons? Are they prisoners like me, or are they cooperating with the soldiers? Where did they come from? Why are they—we—different from the others? Is there hope for us? Can we be cured?

I sneer at that last question. "Of course you can't be cured, you dumb bitch," I snort. "Not unless you can find the Wizard of Oz to give you a brand-new heart."

I get up and stand in front of the mirror. I seem to be studying myself a lot recently. It's not that I'm vain. There just isn't anything else to do. But I'm not interested in my face this time. I was wearing the shredded, filthy remains of my school uniform when I regained consciousness. That's been replaced with a pair of jeans and a plain white T-shirt.

I pull the T-shirt up to my chin and stare at my ruined chest. I never had big tits. Vinyl used to call them bee stings. I told him I'd do worse than sting him if he kept on saying that, but I liked Vinyl, so I let him get away with it.

My right boob is the same as it was before. But my left is missing, torn from my chest by Tyler Bayor. A fair bit of the flesh around it is missing too. And my heart's been ripped out, leaving an unnatural, grisly hole in its place.

Bits of bone poke through the flesh around the hole, and I can see all sorts of tubes inside, veins, arteries and what-have-you. Congealed blood meshes the mess together, along with the green moss that sprouts lightly all over the wound. Every so often a few drops of blood ooze out of one of the tubes. But it's not like it used to be. This blood is much thicker, the consistency of jelly, and the flow always stops after a second or two.

I quizzed Reilly about that. Without a heart, there shouldn't be any flow at all. The same way that, without working lungs, I shouldn't be able to speak.

"The body remembers," he said. "At least it does in revitalizeds."

"What the hell does that mean?" I frowned.

"When you recovered your wits, your brain started trying to

206

control the rest of your body, the way it did when you were alive," he explained. "You don't need to breathe anymore, but your brain thinks that you should, so it forces your lungs to expand and collapse, which is why you can talk. You can stop it when you focus – if you shut your mouth and close your nose, your lungs will shut down after a minute or two – but most of the time your lungs work away in the background, even though there's no reason why they should.

"If you had a heart, it would be the same. Your brain would tell it to pump blood around your body. It wouldn't operate as smoothly as it did before – no more than a weak pulse every few minutes – but it would keep the blood circulating, albeit sluggishly.

"Now, you don't have a heart," Reilly said unsympathetically, "but the brain's a stubborn organ and it's doing the best it can. It's roped in some of your other organs and is using them to nudge your veins and arteries, to compensate for the missing pump. Some of the scientists here are blown away by that. They've never seen a body do it before. They think you're the coolest thing since sliced bread. They'd love to take you off to their labs to study you in depth."

"Who's stopping them?" I asked, but at that the soldier clammed up again.

I've poked my finger into the cavity in my chest a few times, dipped it in the blood and smeared it across my tongue. But I can't tell if it tastes any different. My taste buds have gone to hell. My mouth is dry – my tongue feels like it's made of sandpaper – and apart from a foul staleness that is always there, I haven't been able to identify any specific tastes.

I sigh as I stare at the hole. It shocked me the first few times. I couldn't believe that was really me. I turned my back on the image and tried to cry. Shook my head and refused to accept that this was what I'd become. But now it doesn't bother me that much. I don't let it. Why should I? After all...

"Heh," I laugh humorlessly at my reflection.

...life's too short!

FOUR

Reilly comes in with a bowl. "Grub's up," he says cheerfully, kicking the door closed behind him. I'm standing in one of the corners when he enters, so I spot the armed soldiers outside the door as it slides shut. Reilly must have been coming to see me daily for at least two weeks, usually twice a day, but they never take chances. He always has backup in case I make a break for freedom. The soldiers outside couldn't save him if I decided to bite or give him a playful scratch, but they can make sure I don't get more than a couple of steps outside the cell.

"What's on the menu today?" I ask sarcastically.

"Lamb chops."

"Really?" I gasp.

"No, you idiot," he grunts, and hands the bowl to me.

I stare at lumps of cold gray meat in a jellyish substance. It's the same thing he's given me every day.

"I'm sick of this," I mutter.

"You will be in a minute," he laughs, then scratches his head. "What difference does it make? You can't taste anything anyway."

"It has no substance," I sniff. "I might not be able to taste it, but I can feel it as I grind it up, and it feels like frogspawn."

Reilly winks. "Maybe it is."

He's never told me what the meat is, just that it's laced with chemicals that will help me adjust.

"What would happen if I refused to eat it?" I ask.

Reilly shrugs. "You'd go hungry."

"So? It's not like I'm a growing girl, is it?"

"Trust me," Reilly says, "you don't want to go hungry. The dead feel hunger even worse than the living. Makes sense when you think about it. If you're alive and you starve, eventually you die and that's the end of your suffering. But if you're dead already, the pain goes on and on and on."

"Do you feed the reviveds too?" I ask.

"Just eat up, B. I don't have all day."

I know from experience that Reilly doesn't care whether I eat the gloop or not. I threw it back at him one day, to see how he'd react, if he'd try to force me to eat. He just shrugged, turned round, exited and let me go without.

I pick up the spoon at the side of the bowl and dip in. It took a while to get the hang of my new fingers. At first I tried picking up things with the bones sticking out of them. But I soon realized that I could grip like I did before, by using the remains of the flesh beneath the tips of my fingers. The bones aren't as much of an inconvenience as I thought they'd be. The only thing I can't do is close my hands into proper fists—the bones dig into my palms—but I can keep the fingers flat and bend them down until they touch my palms, and that's almost the same.

"What's happening in the world today?" I ask around spoonfuls of the cold, oily, slimy gruel. "Anything exciting?"

"Same as yesterday and the day before," Reilly answers glibly.

"What about the soccer? Do the zombies have a team in the Premier League?"

Reilly laughs. "I'd like to see that. *Undead United*!"

I grin and carry on eating. Reilly's all right as prison warders go. I don't trust him and I'm sure he'd fire a bullet through my head without a moment's hesitation if ordered. A day might come when we have to lock horns, and maybe one of us won't walk away from that clash. But he's treating me as humanely as he can—more than I probably would if our roles were reversed—and I appreciate that.

I spoon the last of the food into my mouth, chew a few times and swallow. "All done, boss."

"Like I give a damn," he says, taking the bowl from me. He crosses to the sink and picks up the bucket beneath it. Water was supplied to the taps once Reilly had warned me not to drink any of it, just use it for washing, and the bucket was put in place before he brought my first meal.

"Give me a minute," I grumble sourly. "I want to savor the moment."

I can no longer process food or drink the normal way. Reilly says it would sit in my guts, turn putrid and decay, unaided by any digestive juices. The bits that broke down into liquids would flow through me and dribble out, meaning I'd have to wear a diaper. The solids would stay inside me indefinitely. If I ate enough, they'd back up in my stomach and throat.

"Would that harm me?" I asked Reilly once.

"No," he said. "But maggots and worms would thrive on the refuse and insects would be attracted to it. You'd become a warren for creepy crawlies and they'd chew through you. They couldn't do any real damage unless they got into your brain and destroyed enough of it to kill you, but would you want to live like that?"

The image of insects burrowing through my flesh made me shiver so much that, if I hadn't been dead already, I would have sworn that somebody had walked over my grave.

I can safely eat the specially prepared food that Reilly gives me, but I can't keep the bulk of it down. According to Reilly, when the scientists first started to experiment, they used intravenous tubes to feed nutrients to the zombies. He said that's still the best way, but since most people prefer to eat, the good folk in the labs came up with a way for us to act as if we were still capable of enjoying a meal. The gray crud is designed to release nutrients into our clogged-up bloodstream almost instantly. But we have to get rid of the rest by ourselves.

"Come on," Reilly says, tapping a foot. "You're not the only one I have to deal with."

"I won't do it until you tell me how many others you look after."

"Doesn't bother me," Reilly says, turning away. "You're the one who has to live with the stink and insects."

"Wait," I stop him. Pulling a face, I lean over the bucket and stick a finger down my throat, careful not to tear the soft lining. The gray stuff comes surging back up and I vomit into the bucket, shuddering as I spit the last dregs from my lips.

"Not very ladylike, is it?" I grunt as I pass the bucket to a smiling Reilly.

"I don't think you were ever in danger of being mistaken for a lady," he says, "even when you were one of the living."

"I could sue you for saying that sort of thing to me," I huff.

"Lawyers don't represent corpses," he smirks.

I snarl at the grinning soldier and gnash my teeth warningly, but Reilly knows I'm not dumb enough to bite him. One of the first things he told me was that I can still be decommissioned, even though I'm already dead. As I already knew, zombies need their brains to function.

Even if they didn't want to kill me, they could punish me in other ways. I don't feel as much pain as I used to, but I'm not completely desensitized. I dug one of my finger bones into my flesh, to test myself, and it hurt. When I pushed even farther, it hurt like hell. The dead can be tortured too.

"By the way," Reilly says just before he exits. "You'll be entertaining a couple of visitors shortly, so be on your best behavior."

"Who's coming?" I snap, thinking for a second that it's Mum and Dad, torn between delight and terror at the thought. Part of me doesn't want them to see me like this. If they're alive, that part would rather they believed I was dead.

"You keep asking questions," Reilly says. "About the attacks, revitalizeds, why you're different to reviveds, how you wound up here. These people can give you some answers."

"Reilly!" I shout as he steps outside. "Don't leave me hanging like that. Tell me who..."

But the door has already closed. I'm locked in, alone and ignorant, as I have been for most of my incarceration.

But not for much longer if Reilly's to be believed.

FIVE

The visitors are a doctor and a soldier.

The doctor is a thin, balding man with a carefully maintained pencil mustache. He squints a lot, like someone who needs glasses but refuses to admit it. He didn't tell me his name when he entered, or even acknowledge my presence. He just stood with his hands crossed in front of him until a table and chair were put in place, then sat and said stiffly, "I am Dr. Cerveris."

The soldier is friendlier. He brought in the table, set it down, then went out to fetch the chairs. He also brought through a mobile TV and DVD player. At first I thought he was a regular soldier, but when he sat down with the doctor and nodded to let him know it was time to begin, I realized he must be someone important.

"I'm Josh Massoglia," he introduced himself, smiling widely. "But you can stick with Josh. Everybody else does. No one can pronounce my surname. I even struggle with it myself sometimes."

Josh laughed and I smiled. He's a good-looking guy, in a rugged kind of way. Hard to tell what color his hair is, since it's shaved down to the roots. He wears a plain green sweater over his shirt and acts like he's just one of the guys, but he has an air of authority. Dr. Cerveris is snooty, like someone who thinks he's a VIP. Josh is more laid-back, so comfortable with his power that he doesn't feel like he needs to prove anything.

The doctor pulls on a pair of thick plastic gloves and asks if he can examine me. I stand still while he prods and probes my fingers and face. I hesitate when he asks me to take off my T-shirt. Josh grins and turns away. I still feel awkward—I never liked undressing in front of doctors or nurses—but I disrobe as requested.

"Remarkable," Dr. Cerveris murmurs as he studies the wretched hole where my heart once beat.

"Take a photo if you like it that much," I grunt.

"I've already seen lots of snapshots of it," he says.

I frown, wondering when the photos were taken, but I don't ask.

Dr. Cerveris sits again and Josh turns his chair around.

"You've taken to this like a duck to water," Josh notes.

"You mean being dead?"

"Yeah. Most revitalizeds struggle. It takes a lot of counseling

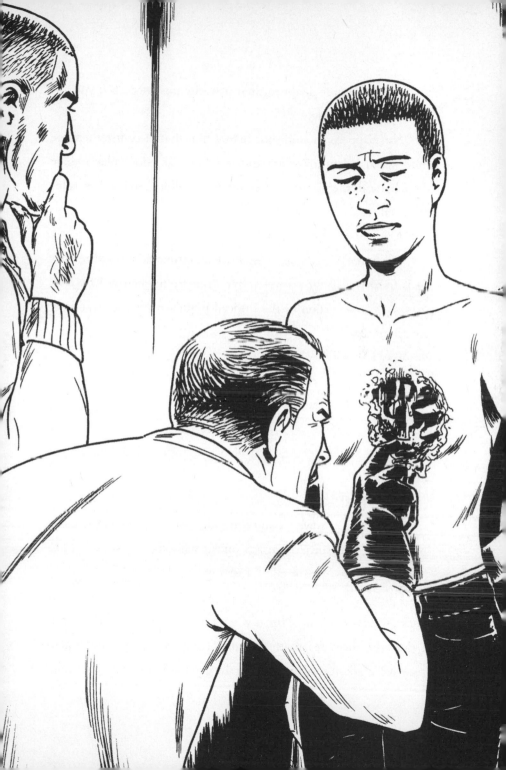

before they begin to adapt to their new circumstances. But you..."
He whistles admiringly.

"Shit happens," I sniff, not telling him that of course there are times when I want to scream and sob, but that I don't plan to give these bastards the pleasure of seeing me crumble. "So are there a lot of revitalizeds?" I ask casually.

"A few," Josh replies vaguely.

"We haven't been able to establish an estimated ratio of revitalizeds to reviveds," Dr. Cerveris says. "But from what we have witnessed, only a fraction of the undead populace appears to recover consciousness."

"Any idea why?"

"We have some theories," he says.

"Care to share them with me?"

"No."

I scowl at the doctor, then glance at Josh. "How long have I been here?"

"In this cell?"

"No. *Here.*" I wave a hand around, indicating the entire complex. "How long since the attack on the school?"

"Six months, give or take," Josh says.

I process that glumly. Half a year of my life that I can never get back. This is one of those times when I feel very small and alone, but I don't let them see that. "Do all revitalizeds take that long to recover?" I ask instead, acting like the gap in my life is no big thing.

220

"No," Dr. Cerveris says. "Most revitalize sooner."

"My teachers always used to tell me that I was slow," I grin. "Have I been here all the time since I was killed?"

Josh nods. "We brought you here directly from the school. You were in a holding cell with other reviveds before your senses kicked back in."

"There were more attacks that day. My dad told me it was happening all over London."

Josh sighs. "Yeah. It wasn't a day any of us will forget in a hurry."

"Have there been more assaults since then?" I press. "Are zombies still striking or have you put a stop to it? What's the world like out there?"

Josh shakes his head. "I can't discuss that with you. All I can say is that the situation is currently stable."

"That doesn't tell me much," I huff.

"I know, but that's the way it is. There are limits to what we can discuss. If it's any comfort, we don't tell the other revitalizeds any more than we're telling you."

"Is there a reason why you're being so secretive?" I ask.

Josh rolls his eyes. "You're a flesh-eating member of the walking dead with the ability to convert as many of the living as you can get your hands or teeth on. You scare the living hell out of us. If some of our staff had their way, we'd tell you nothing at all, only incinerate every damn one of you."

"Why don't you?" I challenge him.

Dr. Cerveris answers. "We want to learn more about you, understand what makes you tick, why your memories return, if your current state is sustainable."

I stiffen. "You mean it might not be? I could...what's the word?"

"Regress." He nods somberly. "It has happened to a couple of others."

"That's why I came packing," Josh says, tapping a gun that hangs by his side. "You'd better pay attention and stay alert. If you start to zone out, the way you might in a boring class, I'm not going to take any chances. If I think there's even a slight chance that you're turning back into a revived, I'll put a bullet through your head."

"I bet you say that to all the girls," I snarl, and Josh laughs.

Dr. Cerveris asks lots of questions, about my past, how much of the day of the attack I can recall, if I can remember anything since then. Somebody opens the door and hands him a folder—he didn't call for it, so others must be watching this on hidden cameras—and he subjects me to a Rorschach test, then word-association games and other psychological crap. I play along patiently, answering honestly, in the hope that if I help them, they can find a way to help me.

The doctor asks about my sense of taste and smell. I tell him I can smell even better than before, but I can't taste anything.

"Is that strange?" I ask.

"No," he says. "The others are the same. We're not sure why.

What about your ears? Have you noticed any difference where sounds are concerned?"

"I dunno. There hasn't been much for me to listen to."

A machine is rolled in and Dr. Cerveris tests my hearing. He puts headphones on me and I have to raise my hand when I hear a high-pitched noise in either ear.

"How'd I do?" I ask when he takes them off.

"Admirably," he says. "Every revitalized has an improved sense of hearing. The reviveds do too. Your sense of smell is probably sharper as well, as you have noted. We'll test that some other time."

I grin ghoulishly. "So I've turned into a big bad wolf. All the better to see, hear and smell you with, my dear."

"Not *see*, I think," he mutters, and lo and behold, an eye chart is duly carried in by a soldier. The test tells me what I already knew, that my eyesight has deteriorated. It's not as bad as I feared. I can still make out most of the letters, even on the lower lines, but they're more blurred than they used to be.

"Would I go blind if I didn't put the drops in every day?" I ask.

"No," Dr. Cerveris says as he jots down the results. "We haven't observed any of the reviveds losing their sight completely. But they suffer irritation and infection. It gets so annoying in some that they scratch their eyes out."

I wince and immediately try to push the image from my thoughts. I'm glad I can't sleep because I'm sure I'd have nightmares about that if I did.

"A little knowledge can be a dangerous thing," Josh chuckles. "That's another reason we prefer not to tell you too much about yourself."

"I'd rather know than live in ignorance." I lean forward. Josh pats his gun and I stop and raise my palms. "Easy, boss. I wasn't trying to freak you out."

"Like I said before, I won't take any chances." The light tone is gone from his voice. "Any move towards us will be interpreted as an aggressive gesture, so just hold on the way you were and everything will be fine."

I ease back, hands still raised. "I just wanted to ask if you knew what caused the attacks, how this is happening, why the dead came back to life."

"That's classified," Josh says shortly.

"I figured as much, but if you don't ask..."

There's silence while Dr. Cerveris writes up his findings. A couple of soldiers enter and remove everything that had been brought through, except the TV and DVD player.

"What now?" I ask, trying to sound chirpy but failing.

Josh raises an eyebrow at Dr. Cerveris. The doctor stares at his notes, hands flat on the table. Then he looks at me. "I think it will be safe to introduce you to the other revitalizeds soon."

"The kids I saw dressed in leather?"

"Yes."

"The ones who were torturing the zombies?"

Dr. Cerveris smiles icily. I thought he'd deny the charge and say that wasn't what they were doing. But all he says is, "Yes."

"But don't refer to them as revitalizeds," Josh warns me. "They prefer to call themselves *zom heads*."

"Dig that crazy new slang," I mutter witheringly. "What happens after I've joined the merry gang? Where do I go from there?"

Josh frowns. "I don't understand what you're asking."

"What's an average day like for a zom head? Do we torment zombies all the time? Go on picnics? Hang around looking cool in our leathers?" I start to lean forward, recall Josh's warning and stop myself. "What does the future hold? Do I have any chance of being set free?"

Dr. Cerveris and Josh share a smug look. It's as if they've been waiting for me to ask that question. Without a word, Dr. Cerveris turns to the TV and switches it on.

As the TV flickers to life, Josh turns on the DVD player and presses play. A grainy black-and-white image comes into focus. It's a corridor in my old school. Kids in uniform run past what must have been a security camera. Others follow, but although these look the same as the first lot, I can tell that they're zombies by the way they move. They don't shuffle along like zombies in movies, but move intently, swiftly, surely, like hunters.

Josh rewinds. He lets it play again, then pauses as the pack of zombies comes into view. "Spot anyone you know?"

"I didn't realize we were playing *Where's Waldo?*" I snap.

"Actually it's *Where's Becky Smith?*" he corrects me, and points to the lower left of the screen.

I stare hard, but with my weakened eyesight I can't be sure. It looks like me, but the picture quality isn't great and I'm not used to seeing myself in black-and-white.

"This next clip is from a helmet camera," Josh informs me. "I wasn't one of those who stormed your school, but I was part of the control team coordinating various units across London. One of my guys captured this charming footage."

He hits play again and the black-and-white clip gives way to a shaky color shot. The person with the camera is moving swiftly, jerking his head from side to side. I glimpse a rifle in his hands.

Horror images. Blood sprayed across walls. Limbs and corpses scattered across the floor. There's a blur. The rifle kicks in the soldier's hand. The camera goes out of focus for a few seconds. When it steadies again, I find myself looking at a kid whose head has been blown apart. Hard to tell if it was a boy or a girl. It's just scraps of meat now.

The soldier pushes on, then pauses. He focuses on a number of bodies to his left. I thought they were all corpses, but someone's moving in among the dead. The soldier takes a few steps forward, stops and adjusts the camera. It zooms in on the face of a zombie hunched over the remains of a dead boy.

The zombie has cut the boy's head open and is digging out bits of his brain, spooning them into its mouth with its bone-distorted

226

fingers. It looks like a drug addict on a happy high. The boy's arms are still shaking—he must be alive, at least technically. The zombie doesn't care. It goes on munching, ignorant of the trembling arms, the soldiers, everything except the slivers of brain.

The zombie is a girl.

The zombie is *me*.

"We don't know how many you killed that day," Josh says softly, "but by the variety of flesh and blood we picked out of your mouth when we were hosing you down later, we're pretty sure that boy wasn't the first."

"We can never release you, Becky," Dr. Cerveris says with just a hint of gloomy satisfaction. "You're a monster."

I don't respond. I can't. All I can do is keep my eyes pinned on the girl—the *monster*—on the screen. And stare.

227

SIX

Reilly leads me out of the cell. I've gotten so used to the cramped room over the last few weeks that I feel strange at first, almost afraid. The corridor outside isn't huge, but it feels like I'm walking down the middle of a motorway.

Four soldiers trail us, rifles at the ready. They're mean-looking sons of bitches. I think they'd love an excuse to let rip. I keep my hands tight by my sides, head down, mincing along like a lamb.

Reilly wanted to let me out several days ago, not long after my meeting with Dr. Cerveris and Josh. He was stunned when I asked if I could stay in the cell a while longer. After what I'd seen on the TV, I needed some time by myself. I felt dirty and twisted, not fit to mix with anybody else, even zombies.

I spent the last few days lying on my bed or squatting in a corner, fixating on what I'd seen, the way I'd feasted. It shouldn't have come as a shock—I know what I am and what zombies do—but it did. I'd imagined what I thought was the worst, lots of times, but nothing could have prepared me for the cold, hard reality of that film footage.

I could have tried to wipe the memory from my thoughts, turned my back on it and pretended I'd never seen the macabre film. But I remember something my teacher Mr. Burke once said. "There are lots of black-hearted, mean-spirited bastards in the world. It's important that we hold them to account. But always remember that *you* might be the most black-hearted and mean-spirited of the lot, so hold yourself the most accountable of all."

After throwing Tyler to the zombies, I vowed that I'd change, that I'd spend the rest of my life trying to make up for what I'd done. But I can't do that if I don't accept the truth about myself. I'm a vicious, cannibalistic killer. I've done plenty to be ashamed of, and I owe it to my victims to face that shame and live with it, to never forget them or what I did.

After a lot of thinking, I came to terms with my guilt and...No, that's not right. I wasn't comfortable with what I'd done, and I hope I never will be. But I found a place within myself to house the horror, somewhere close to the surface but not so close that it would get in the way of everything else. Once I'd done that, I figured I was ready to face the world again. So when Reilly offered a second time to take me to see the revitalizeds, I agreed to tag along.

We wind through a series of corridors. They all look the same, white or gray walls, fluorescent lights, lots of windows and sealed doors. I peer through some of the windows and catch glimpses of soldiers, doctors, nurses, but nothing revealing.

By the control panels set in the walls next to the doors, I can tell that they're operated by scanners, one at waist height for finger-prints, the other higher up for retinas. Some of them require a security code too.

Reilly finally stops at a door, opens it with a quick scan of his fingers and an eye, then gestures for me to enter. I step in, expecting a load of leather-clad, teenage zombies, but it's only a shower room, several vacant cubicles, towels and clothes laid on a bench across from them.

"What gives?" I ask suspiciously.

"You've been in isolation for three weeks," Reilly says. "You haven't changed your clothes. I thought you might want to freshen up before you meet the others."

"Are you saying I smell?"

"Yes."

"No peeking," I warn him.

He laughs. "Zombies don't do it for me. But others will be watching." He nods at the ceiling. "Cameras all over this place, as I'm sure you've figured out already."

"Yeah. But I thought they'd leave the bloody showers alone."

Reilly shrugs and closes the door. I gaze around, trying to spot the cameras, but they're masterfully concealed. "Sod it," I mutter and undress. If some creep gets a buzz from watching a one-boobed zombie in the buff, more power to him.

The shower's lovely, though I have to turn it up to the max to truly appreciate it. My nerve endings don't work as well as they used to. I have to crank the heat up close to boiling before I feel warm.

I scrub carefully around the hole in my chest. I pick at the green moss and try to wash it away, but it must be rooted deeply. If I pull hard, strands come out like hairs, but I'm worried I might injure myself—I don't know how deeply the moss is embedded and I'm afraid I might rip an even bigger hole in my chest if I persist—so I stop. I rinse down the rest of my body, smiling sadly as I rub the old *c* scar on my thigh. I used to hate that, since it was my only real physical blemish. Now, with a missing heart, it's the least of my worries.

I massage shampoo into my scalp and try to close my eyes, forgetting that I can't. Scowling, I tilt my head back and do my best to keep the suds away from my unprotected eyeballs.

Stepping out, I towel myself dry. The moss stays damp, except for the light layer on my right wrist where I was scratched shortly before Tyler clawed out my heart — that dries up nicely after a good bit of rubbing.

Giving up on the moss around my chest, I slip into the new clothes. Once I'm cozy, I sniff the old set and grimace. They're not as bad as I thought they'd be, but I'm surprised I didn't notice the odor before. Reilly should have told me.

I rap on the door and it opens immediately. "Any deodorant?" I ask.

Reilly cocks his head. "Are you being funny?"

"No."

"Didn't they tell you…?" He smiles. "No, I suppose it's not the sort of thing they would have thought of. Well, it's good news, B. You don't ever have to worry about your pits again. The dead don't sweat."

"Seriously?"

"Yeah."

"Cool," I chuckle. Then a thought hits me and I ask with fake innocence, "What about bad breath?"

"There's a slight smell that will always be there," Reilly says. "But it won't get any worse than that."

"And farts?" I ask.

Reilly laughs. "No. You're clear on that front too."

"A pity," I sigh. "I loved a good fart." My eyes narrow and I murmur sweetly, "What about my period?"

Reilly blushes furiously. "Without a regular flow of blood? Hardly!"

"But are you sure?" I press.

"Well, not a hundred percent," he says uneasily.

"Can you ask one of the nurses and find out for me?" I tease him.

"Ask them yourself," he huffs, ears reddening at the thought of it.

Typical bloke — so easy to embarrass!

SEVEN

A large, white room. No windows, but there's a long mirror in one of the walls. I've seen enough films and TV shows to guess that it's a two-way observation point. I bet there's a team of soldiers or scientists on the other side, watching everything.

There's a pool table and a ping-pong table down at one end of the room. A bookshelf with a scattering of books, magazines and comics. A couple of TVs, one hooked up to a DVD player, the other to a video-game console. There's a table close to that TV, loaded with games and a few iPods. A variety of couches and chairs are positioned around the place.

A couple of the zom heads are playing pool. Three are busy gaming. One – the girl called Cathy – is watching TV and

filing down her teeth. And the final zom head is slumped on a chair near the bookshelf, flicking through a car magazine.

Seven in total. One more than I saw in the room all those weeks ago.

I hover by the door—Reilly didn't say anything when he let me in—waiting for the others to notice me. Finally one of the guys playing pool looks up and shouts, "Hey! It's the girl who kicked Rage's arse!"

Everything comes to a stop and those who were sitting stand up to ogle me, all except the one in the chair with the magazine. He just glances at me, yawns, then returns to his mag.

I push forward, smiling awkwardly. "Hi. I'm Becky Smith, but everyone calls me B."

"Becky it is," one of the boys laughs, and jogs across. He sticks out a hand—it's covered by a glove and bandages. "I'm Mark," he says as we shake hands. "I wasn't there when you revitalized. They keep me out of stuff like that. Afraid I'll react badly to the flames."

"What do you mean?" I ask.

The boy gestures at himself. He's covered completely from neck to toe, heavy clothes, some sort of a padded vest, more bandages, heavy-duty boots. "I got burned to the bone while I was a revived. They don't know how. My face is okay but I'm like a skeleton under all these layers. I have to stay wrapped up. They're worried that if I lose any more internal—"

"Can it, Worm," one of the other boys says. "You'd bore her to death if she wasn't already dead." He nods at me but doesn't smile. He's dark-skinned, with short curly hair. I would have shot him the finger six months ago in response to his nod. But since I'm trying to change and accept everyone as an equal, no matter what color they are, I nod back at him instead.

"B," I tell him.

"I know," he says drily. "I'm not deaf. I'm Peder."

"Danny," the boy beside him says. Danny's tall and bony. Greasy blond hair and bad acne. He's wearing jeans and a T-shirt like mine. As I look around, I see that all of the others are similarly dressed, except for the guy in the chair. He's in the leathers he was wearing when I first saw him.

"Cathy Kelly," the girl introduces herself coldly. She sits and focuses on the video game. She has long, dark hair tied back in a ponytail. Pretty, but not in a soft way.

One of the other boys comes over and shakes my hand. "Gokhan."

"*Gherkin?*" I frown.

"Gokhan." He spells it out. "Turkish, innit?"

He's plump and relaxed-looking. Olive skin. Large, pudgy fingers. He's filed down the bones sticking out of the tips and painted them with swirling, colorful designs.

"And I'm Tiberius," the other guy who was playing pool says. He's the one who first spotted me. He's short, with ginger hair and loads of freckles.

"Tiberius?" I laugh automatically. "What sort of a dumb name is that?"

"I was named after the river Tiber in Rome," he says stiffly. Then he turns his back on me, offended, and snaps at Mark, "Are you playing or what, Worm?"

"In a minute," Mark says. "I want to show B round first. Don't you want to get to know her? She's one of us now."

"Maybe she is and maybe she isn't," the boy in the chair says. He finally stands, cracks his knuckles over his head and makes a yawning motion. I know from practicing in my cell that we can mimic the habits of the past, when we had a set of fully functioning lungs. I even find myself yawning or sneezing by accident sometimes, my body remembering happier, simpler days.

The yawning knuckle cracker is the tall guy with the big head and small ears, the chubby, rosy cheeks, a chunk bitten out of the left one. The guy I clobbered over the head when I first recovered. *Rage*.

"Of course she's one of us," Mark says. "She can talk, can't she?"

"Oh, she's a revitalized," Rage says, eyeing me beadily. "Doesn't mean she's a zom head though. You've gotta earn that right. Which *you* haven't yet, Worm, in case you'd forgotten."

Mark scowls and stares at his feet. "It's not my fault they don't let me join in with the rest of you. I would if I could. You know that."

"You say that you would," Rage sneers. "But there's saying and there's doing, and so far you've done zip. For all we know, you've

239

cried off and asked to be excused regular duties. Maybe the burns are a sham. Maybe they're just saying that because you asked them to cover up for the fact that you're a coward."

Mark stiffens, then squares himself and raises his fists. His hands are shaking, more with fear, I think, than indignation. "Say that again and I'll thump you," he squeaks. "I don't care how big you are."

Rage laughs. "Back down, Worm. I'm only messing with you."

He comes closer and circles me slowly. I say nothing while I'm being examined. When he's finished, I stare at him calmly. "Like what you see?"

"Not a lot," he sniffs. "I don't think Cathy has much to worry about."

"Why should I be worried?" the girl barks, looking up from her game.

"You've been queen bee round these parts," Rage says. "You know that all the boys fancy you, since they've no one else to lust after. Nobody would want to lose that sort of a following. And I don't think you will. No offense, *Becky*."

"Get stuffed," I snarl.

Rage cocks his head. "Are you a tough girl?" he whispers. "You are, aren't you? A fighter, yeah?"

"Wind me up and find out," I challenge him, fingers curling by my sides.

Rage glances at my fingers, then studies my eyes. "Looks like I was wrong. You *are* one of us."

"We accept you, gooble gobble," Tiberius chuckles from beside the pool table.

"What the hell does that mean?" I growl.

"Pay no attention to him," Gokhan laughs. "He's always coming out with weird crap like that."

"It's from *Freaks*," Tiberius says. "That old movie about circus freaks." He looks around for support. "Some of you must have seen it."

"Was it black-and-white?" Cathy asks.

"Yeah. It was made in the 1930s."

"Then of course we haven't seen it," she snorts. "We don't all waste our time on boring old movies."

"*Freaks*, boring?" Tiberius roars. "It's an amazing film. They used real-life freaks. It gave me nightmares the first time my dad showed it to me."

"They'd probably have found a role for *you* in it if you'd been alive back then," Cathy says frostily.

Tiberius glares at her, then turns to me. "Anyway, at one point a normal woman marries one of the freaks and they have a big party to welcome her into the family. They all start chanting, *We accept you, gooble-gobble*. They mean it nicely, but what they're really saying is that she's one of them now, a freak, an outcast, a child of the damned."

Tiberius bends over the pool table to take a shot, then says again, but glumly this time, as if he feels sorry for me, "We accept you, gooble-gobble."

241

EIGHT

I spend the rest of the day with the zom heads, getting to know them. It's awkward. None of us wants to be here. We haven't chosen each other for company. We come from different parts of London, Danny from as far out as Bromley. We don't have much in common, except for the fact that we were all killed when the zombies attacked.

"Do you remember much about that day?" I ask Mark. I'm with him, Gokhan and Tiberius on one of the couches close to the mirror.

"No," he says. "I was at school. Things went mad. I was running. I didn't even know why. I was part of a pack, doing what everybody else was. I thought someone had a gun and was shooting people, like they do in America. Then something struck the side of my head and I blacked out. Next thing I knew, I was waking up here, wrapped up tighter than a bloody Mummy."

"What about you?" I ask the others.

They shake their heads.

"We've gone over this dozens of times," Tiberius says. "It was pretty much all we talked about for the first few weeks. Everyone was at school, except Rage, who was in a shopping center with his girlfriend. Zombies attacked. We were bitten. We revitalized here."

"Were you locked into your school?"

Tiberius frowns. "What?"

"The exits were blocked in mine. We couldn't get out."

"What, someone actually stopped you from escaping?" Mark gasps.

"Yeah. We tried two different doors and they were both jammed. What about the mutants?"

"Come again?" Tiberius asks.

"There were mutants at our school, coordinating the zombies, directing them."

"Bull," he snorts.

"No, I'd seen a couple of them before. Ugly mothers with gray hair and yellow eyes. They all wear hoodies."

"You're dreaming," Tiberius insists.

"I'm dead," I snap. "We don't dream."

Tiberius clicks his tongue against his teeth. "So, what, you're saying the attacks were deliberate? That we were targeted?"

"I dunno," I shrug. "I'm just telling you what I saw."

"Hey, Rage, have you heard about this?" Tiberius yells and makes me repeat my story.

"Anybody else see hooded mutants?" Rage asks the rest of the zom heads once I'm done. Everyone's staring at me, having stopped whatever they were doing to listen.

"I didn't see any mutants," Peder says, "but one of the exit doors at my school was locked. I was furious. I'd gone through hell to make it that far. I kept kicking and punching it until the zombies swarmed me." He rubs his upper right arm, where a deep cut runs from the shoulder down to his elbow.

"It's something we wondered about before," Danny says. "How did the zombies get inside the buildings in the first place? Why were there so many of them? Where did they come from? Some of us think we might have been victims of a conspiracy."

"Terrorists," Cathy whispers.

"Get real," I laugh. "You can't think this was a terrorist attack. What, they got sick of bombs and guns, decided to use zombies instead?"

"Chemical warfare," Cathy says seriously. "It's something that terrorists have been exploring for years. Maybe they found a way to reanimate the dead. I mean, unless it's some sort of freak disease, *somebody* must have set those undead bastards loose on us."

"It could have been aliens," Mark suggests.

Tiberius nods enthusiastically. "That's my vote."

"That's why you're a pair of airheads," Rage jeers. "Aliens! Cathy's right. It was probably cooked up by mad scientists. Whether they were working for foreign powers or not, I don't know. I think it might have been our own guys, that it got leaked accidentally."

"If that was the case, they wouldn't have just struck at the schools," Cathy argues.

"They didn't," Rage responds. "I was in a shopping mall. I heard that there had been attacks at hospitals, airports, all sorts of places."

"Yeah, *attacks*," Cathy presses. "If it was an accidental breakout, it would have spread from one spot and rippled outwards. But they struck all over London at the same time. Explain that, if it wasn't planned."

There's a troubled silence. I'm disappointed that nobody seems to know any more than I do. I was hoping to find answers, but the zom heads are victims like me, ignorant of what really happened.

"Anybody know if the zombies are still running wild out there?" I ask.

"They don't tell us stuff like that," Peder says. "They don't even tell the teacher's pet what's going on outside, do they, Rage?"

"Bite me," Rage barks, and the others laugh.

"Why's he their pet?" I ask.

"He sucks up to them," Tiberius smirks.

"It's all, *Yes, Mr. Reilly, sir!* and, *No, Mr. Reilly, sir!*" Danny jeers.

"*Can I help you with anything, Dr. Cerveris?*" Gokhan adds. "*Do you want me to bend over, so you can stick your needle up my—*"

246

"One more word, eunuch boy, and it'll be your last for a while," Rage says softly, and the teasing stops instantly. He glares around and everyone drops their gaze. Except me.

"Something you want to say?" he growls.

"Yeah," I answer calmly. "Why'd you call him eunuch boy?"

Rage relaxes. "He's Turkish. Half of that lot are eunuchs."

"Hey!" Gokhan objects. "That's racist, innit?"

"Not if it's true," I smirk, and the others laugh. I grin for a moment. Then I recall Tyler and my vow to put my crude ways behind me, and my face drops. Looks like I'll have to try harder in the future. Old habits die hard.

"So nobody knows anything," I mutter. "We don't know how zombies came to be, why they attacked when they did, how they struck in so many different places at once, or what the upshot of it was. The undead might have all been killed or captured, or maybe they're still on the loose and this is the last place on earth where the living can walk around safely."

"It's not," Danny says confidently. "I overheard Reilly talking with one of the other soldiers. He was telling him to shape up or they'd ship him out to a different unit, one that wasn't as tightly secured as this place."

"Well done," Cathy says scathingly.

"What?" Danny whines.

She nods at the mirror. "You know that they're listening. You've just gone and dropped Reilly in it."

"Well, he's one of them," Danny sniffs. "I don't care what happens to him, just like he doesn't really care about any of us."

"Reilly's all right," Peder says.

"Yeah," Danny agrees, "but at the end of the day he's just doing his job. He treats us decently because he's told to. If they told him to put us down, you think he wouldn't?"

There's another long, uneasy silence.

"I thought you guys were better off than me," I say softly. "But you're not, are you? You're prisoners, just like I am."

"Yeah," Mark says when nobody else replies. "But it's not all bad. We could be reviveds. They keep them in huge holding cells, packed in tight together, none of the comforts that they treat us to. And they experiment on them. We don't have to deal with any of that."

"No?" Cathy laughs cruelly. "You're even dumber than I thought, Worm." She points at the mirror again. "What do you think all this is? We're guinea pigs, just like the reviveds. And when Dr. Cerveris and his crew have learned all that they can, we'll be discarded as casually as the others are."

We all stare at the mirror and wonder who's on the other side and what they might be thinking. Then we drift apart and everyone goes to their own part of the room to brood. Some of them shoot me dirty looks every so often, blaming me for reminding them that at the end of the day we're just fancily treated prisoners, at the mercy of those who have absolutely no human reason to show us any.

NINE

Reilly takes us back to our cells one at a time and leaves us there for what must be night. That develops into a routine. He escorts us to zom HQ (as we call it) every day, lets us mix for several hours, then returns us to our cells. We always go with him individually. Nobody ever gets to see where the other zom heads are housed. We could all be quartered in the same corridor, or in completely different parts of the complex—we've no idea.

They could leave us with each other the whole time—like me, the others don't need to sleep—but Tiberius thinks they're trying to institutionalize us, to make us easier to control.

I try to discuss the attacks and the outside situation again, but nobody wants to talk about that. They've been through it all before and are reluctant to rehash old arguments. It doesn't matter that all of the theories are fresh to me. They've been together for months now, and even though they're not tight like real friends, they share a bond that I'm not yet a true part of. They're not going to break their rules just to please the new zom head on the block.

Even Mark, the friendliest of the lot, gets prickly when I push him.

"Just leave it, B," he mutters. "What's the point? We can't do anything about it. If they want to tell us, they will. If they don't, they won't, and all the guessing in the world won't get us any closer to the truth."

Mark's the runt of the litter. The others tease him and pick on him, even Cathy. They call him Worm and mock him for not being allowed to join the zom heads when they experiment on reviveds. Mark takes it as best he can, laughs along with them, only occasionally grimaces when they go too far.

Danny tested me on my second day in zom HQ. Tossed a casual insult my way to see how I'd react.

"Say that again and you'll be picking the remains of your teeth out of your mouth," I told him, ready to back up the words with action if pushed. But Danny's no fool. He saw that I was serious and judged me a genuine threat, even though I'm a girl and he's bigger than me. Nobody's given me grief since then.

Rage is the undisputed leader of the pack. He's a big old bruiser—easy to see how he got his nickname—but clever too, reads a lot, excels at the more difficult video games, knows about all sorts of things. Reminds me a bit of my dad, a bully but sharp. It's hard to get the better of people like that. You can't beat them up and you can't outsmart them. Rage doesn't seem to be as violent as my dad, but he's not somebody you provoke lightly because there's always the chance that he'll snap and smash you up.

Having said that, he acts like a toad whenever any of the scientists or soldiers come to see us. I thought the others were exaggerating when they were winding him up that first day, but I soon see that they're not. He's like a fanboy when Josh or his team is on the scene.

Dr. Cerveris came this morning to run some routine tests on us, eyes, ears, that sort of thing. We get tested regularly, usually by nurses or low-level doctors. But today we were treated to a visit by the high and mighty one himself.

"Hey, Dr. Cerveris, how you been?" Rage beamed, running over to him like an eager puppy.

"Very well, thank you," the doctor replied, then asked Rage how things were going. Once they'd dispensed with the small talk, Rage barked at the rest of us and ordered us to line up. He walked down the line with Dr. Cerveris, glaring at us, making sure nobody said anything untoward or threatened the doctor in any way.

"Are those okay?" Rage asked when Dr. Cerveris came to the Turk and paused to study his painted finger bones.

"Yes," the doctor said. "I was just curious to see what he had drawn." He smiled at Gokhan. "You have an artistic eye."

"Art's my favorite subject, innit?" Gokhan replied.

"We'll have to give you oils and canvas, to see if your skills have been affected by your altered circumstances."

"I dunno about that," Gokhan pouted. "I'm not really into proper painting."

"You'll do whatever the hell the doctor tells you to do!" Rage roared, and shoved Gokhan in the chest.

Gokhan squared up to Rage and it looked like things were going to kick off, but Dr. Cerveris coughed politely and said, "Please, boys, no fighting."

I think Gokhan would have ignored him, but as soon as the doctor called for peace, Rage took a step back and muttered an apology.

"Why do you suck up to them so much?" I asked once Dr. Cerveris had left. I thought Rage would prickle at that but he only shrugged.

"They're the new masters now. If we're to have any hope of getting out of this place, we need to play ball. Besides, they've taken good care of us. We should be thankful. They could have left us to rot with the zombies. They're doing their best to look after us and make our lives easier. You don't bite the hand that feeds you."

I haven't seen much of the complex yet. Reilly never varies the route when he leads me to or from my cell. The others haven't seen much more of it either, though they've been to the places where the reviveds are housed.

According to Mark, there are hundreds, if not thousands, of zombies locked up in the pens. He thinks they're being held for experimental purposes. This is a giant laboratory, not a prison.

The reviveds are a mix of adults and children. But nobody's seen any grown-up zom heads. We've been segregated by age for some reason. There must be adult revitalizeds, conscious as we are, but they're either being held in a separate part of the complex or in a different building. I don't know why they'd want to divide us this way. Maybe they're worried that we'd start a big zom head family if they let us mix together freely.

There's no doubt that I'm an outsider—nothing personal, I'm sure it's purely because I'm new to the fold—but I was getting along all right with most of the zom heads until a couple of days ago. Cathy was the only one who actively disliked me. She wouldn't talk to me unless it was to say something critical. Then we had *hairgate* and I've been snubbed by the rest of them ever since.

I'd just finished filing down my teeth and was studying myself in the mirror. I ran a hand over the stubble on my head and muttered, "I hope this grows back soon. I fancy a change of style."

Cathy laughed hysterically. "Did you hear what dopey B said?" she cawed to the others.

"What's so funny about that?" I growled.

"You think your hair will grow back."

"Why the hell wouldn't…?" I stopped and groaned as I caught on.

"You're dead, dumbo," Cathy sneered. "Your hair won't ever grow again. You're stuck with that G.I. Jane look for life."

She kept on mocking me until I lost my cool. With a bellow, I rushed her, grabbed her ponytail and dragged her down onto the floor. She squealed and slapped at my hands but I was too strong for her. The others crowded round, egging us on.

"They don't let us have knives in here," I said, "but these bones sticking out of my fingers are every bit as good. If they can cut through skulls, hair shouldn't be much of a problem. I'm going to shave you even balder than I am, bitch."

"No!" Cathy screamed as I started hacking at her hair. "Don't, B, please!"

I ignored her and severed her ponytail. As it came free, I held it up in the air and whooped.

"Now for the rest of it," I jeered, waving my hand in front of her eyes, letting her see what I'd already cut away.

The fight drained from her when she saw her hair, and she started making loud moaning noises, the closest she could get to crying. I paused uneasily and watched her shaking. She reached out, took the hair from my fingers, clutched it to her chest and wailed, a dry, choking, wretched sound.

"Nice going," Tiberius snarled. "That won't grow back. She can never replace it."

"You didn't do much to stop me," I challenged him, and glared defiantly at the others, who were all looking a tad too self-righteous for my liking. "You just stood there, cheering."

"Yeah," Danny snorted. "That's right. Blame us. *You* cut off her hair, but *we're* the guilty ones."

"It's not that bad," I muttered. "I didn't scalp her."

They only stared at me with contempt until I turned my back on them and stomped away. Then they all crouched around Cathy and sympathized with her, conveniently forgetting the fact that she was the one who started the fight.

So much for my *friends*. Hypocritical jerks! I think I prefer being in my cell on my own.

TEN

In zom HQ. The others are still giving me the cold shoulder because of what I did to Cathy. I've tried apologizing but the snooty cow just ignores me. Sod her, the rest of them too. I don't care. Real loneliness is when your dad beats up your mum and you're lying in your bedroom, listening to her weep in the room next door, and it feels like the whole world's against you. A bunch of petty zombies giving me the evils? Doesn't bother me in the least.

The door opens and Reilly enters, Josh Massoglia just behind him. "You guys ready for some fun and games?" Josh roars.

"Damn right!" Rage bellows, rallying the others and shooing them towards the door. I haven't seen them this excited before.

"What about me?" Mark cries. "Can I come?"

"Sorry," Josh says. "We gave you the once-over a few days ago when we had you in for a checkup. The burns are still really bad. It's best you sit out this one."

"Don't worry, Worm," Rage chuckles. "We'll tell you all about it when we come home."

Mark looks crestfallen. If he could cry, he'd be blinking back tears.

As the others gather by the door, Josh looks over at me. "You just gonna sit there or do you want in on this too?"

"I'm invited?" I ask suspiciously, thinking it might be a trap.

"Of course," Josh says. "Why wouldn't you be?" He raises an eyebrow at Rage. "That's not a problem, is it?"

Rage smiles quickly. "Not at all. The more the merrier. Come on, B, hurry up, you don't want to make us late."

I'd like to tell the big lump to get stuffed, but I don't want to miss out on this. So I say nothing, only line up with the rest of them and follow Josh and Reilly out of zom HQ and into the heart of the complex.

Cathy cuddles up close to Josh as we're walking—well, as close as he'll let her, worried as he must be that she might accidentally scratch him and condemn him to living death. She makes cow eyes at him and actually asks if he's been working out. Give me strength! Josh laughs it off and pretends he doesn't know that she's got a crush on him.

We come to a door that requires a security code as well as the usual finger and retinal scans. Reilly opens it and we step into a room packed with weapons of all description. They're locked away in padlocked, thick steel cages, and I don't see any keys on either of the soldiers. Doesn't look like they want to take the chance of us going wild and getting our hands on a full arsenal.

Some of the weapons have been laid on a table in the middle of the room. "Take your pick," Josh says grandly. "Girls first."

I approach with Cathy and cast an eye over the loot. Flame-throwers, stun guns, spears, large knives, axes and small chainsaws. Two of each.

"Wow!" Cathy exclaims, rushing to grab a chainsaw. "These are new. They're awesome."

"Have you used a chainsaw before?" Josh asks.

"No."

"You'd better be careful. They're nasty if you swing them the wrong way. Maybe you should leave that to the boys."

"I'll be fine," Cathy smirks, pulling a cord to turn it on. She scythes through the air with the buzzing saw a couple of times, then turns it off and hangs it by her side. I hate to admit it, but she looks cool as hell.

"Becky?" Josh asks.

"I don't know." I study the weapons glumly. I've never used anything like this before. I'm worried that I'll pick something I can't use and end up looking like a mug. Maybe I should have stayed in zom HQ with Mark.

"We normally insist on pairs," Reilly explains. "Now that Cathy's chosen a chainsaw, somebody else has to choose one too. Usually, if you picked a flamethrower and Rage stepped up next and chose a knife, the final three would have to make their choice from those weapons, one each."

"But now there's seven of you," Josh says. "So there will have to be an odd one out. Tell you what, since this is your first time, you can have dibs on the exclusive weapon. So unless you fancy a chainsaw, pick from any of the others and we'll remove that choice for the rest."

I walk around the table, studying the weapons. I run a hand over a flamethrower and remember my introduction to life in this brave new world. I see Rage's eyes narrow—he wants a flame-thrower—and I nearly pick it just to spite him. But I don't like fire.

"I'll take a spear," I decide, keeping it simple. The others make their choices. When we're ready, we carry our weapons through to another room, where leather suits and helmets are hanging up for us.

The trousers feel strange as I tug them on. I was never much into leather. I owned a couple of jackets in my time but no pants or shirts. The clothes feel tight on me, uncomfortable even with my less sensitive skin.

"Are these really necessary?" I grumble.

"They'll help protect you," Josh says. "You saw the way Rage was bitten. Leather *can* be penetrated, but not as easily as regular cloth-ing. You'll be glad of it if a revived sinks their teeth into one of your legs or arms."

"But they can't infect us now, can they?" I frown. "We're zombies already."

"They can still hurt us, you idiot," Cathy snaps.

"A bite or a scratch stings like a bitch," Tiberius tells me. "And though moss will grow around it, you'll carry the wound for the rest of your life."

"Fair enough." I start to pull my T-shirt off, then pause. I don't have anything on underneath. I was never shy about my body, but I didn't go about flashing my tits to one and all. I glance around the room. The others are taking off their clothes and pulling on the leathers without any worries. The boys don't cover themselves, and Cathy doesn't either. They don't gape at one another or make suggestive comments, just get on with things, as if they're too grown-up to worry about a little nudity.

I shrug and pull off my T-shirt.

"Bloody hell!" Tiberius gasps and everybody looks up. At first I think he's staring at my boob and I prepare a hot retort. Then I realize it's the hole in my chest that caught his attention. "That's incredible."

"Not as incredible as your ginger hair," I mutter, but I feel oddly proud. The others can boast a cool variety of scars and bite marks, but nothing as outlandish as this.

Cathy comes closer and stares deep into the gaping hole. "That must have hurt like hell," she whispers.

"I can't remember," I lie, suppressing a shiver as I recall what it

261

felt like when Tyler ripped my beating heart from between the shattered bones of my chest.

Cathy reaches out to put her hand in the hole, then pauses. "Do you mind?"

"Of course I bloody mind," I snort. "That'd be like me asking if I could stick my hand up your arse."

Everyone laughs and I tug on a leather shirt.

"It's an impressive wound," Cathy says grudgingly, then winks at me. "But the breast wasn't so hot."

"Get stuffed," I grunt, but we share a grin and I think she's finally forgiven me for cutting off her hair.

"Right," Josh says when we're ready, weapons in one hand, helmets in the other. "Most of you know the drill but I'll go through it again for Becky's sake. We're going to put you in with a group of reviveds. There's a speaker system inside each helmet. We'll be issuing orders as you go."

"Let's hope nobody breaks rank this time," Reilly huffs, looking pointedly at Rage.

"I've said sorry for that already," Rage groans. "I lost my head. It won't happen again. Promise."

"To start with, stand still," Josh goes on. "Let them mill around you. If they attack, defend yourself, but don't stir them up until we tell you. And when you do, follow orders as closely as you can, as long as you can, until things get chaotic. When we think the situation's getting out of hand, we'll drop the nets and bring proceedings to a close. Any questions?"

"What's the point of it all?" I ask.

"We're testing the reviveds," Josh says. "Their reactions, what they respond to, what they ignore, how much they remember on an instinctive level from their old lives. We'll also be checking if they show signs of revitalizing, but that's not the main goal of the experiment, since it happens so rarely."

"How far can we go?" I press. "Do we draw the line at dismembering them, killing them, what?"

"You can't kill them," Josh laughs. "They're already dead."

"You know what I mean. If we destroy their brains, we'll finish them off. That's killing in my book."

"Well it shouldn't be," Josh snaps, losing his smile. "Don't think of these as people. Not even animals. They're walking corpses, monsters who would rip apart everything we know and cherish. They slaughtered friends of yours, maybe family members too, and one of them even killed *you*. There should be no room in your heart for sympathy, not where these beasts are concerned."

"Tear them to pieces," Danny snarls. "They'd do even worse to you if they had the chance."

"Well said." Josh is beaming again. "Now, if you're all ready and willing, let's do some business."

Everyone cheers and roars like gladiators. Reilly opens a

door—not the one we entered by—and we pass along a short corridor, just us seven zom heads, leaving the soldiers behind.

We enter a bare room like the one I found myself in the first time I recovered my senses. White walls, lots of windows, soldiers and scientists crowded behind them.

Rage clomps to the middle of the room and the rest of us follow. We form a tight circle. I'm nervous and I can tell that the others are too. They've been looking forward to this—it breaks the monotony—but in the quiet moments before it kicks off, they tense and wonder what will happen if it goes wrong.

Each of us tests our weapon, flexes our muscles, prepares for battle. I start to wish I'd chosen something more substantial than a spear. I don't feel as protected as the others. I wish I could swap it for a chainsaw.

Then three doors click open at the same time, in three different walls. There's a short pause, flickering shadows, the smell of blood in the air. Then about thirty zombies slip into the room, spread out, shake their heads and fix their snarling, ravenous sights on us.

ELEVEN

I instinctively raise my spear. Josh's voice comes crackling through the speaker in my helmet. "Easy, Becky. Remember what I told you. Just stand still for the time being and chill."

"*Chill* my arse," I mutter sourly, but I lower the spear and watch nervously as the zombies draw closer.

The first to come within striking distance is a woman. She's dressed in a filthy, tattered green blouse and a matching skirt. There are bite marks up and down her arms, as if her boyfriend got out of control when they were making out. Her eyes have a gray, cloudy film over them, like a blind person's, but by the way she focuses on me, I'm sure that she can see well enough.

The woman pauses in front of me and sniffs the air. Her mouth is open and her long, sharp teeth are bared. She makes a growling sound and I think she's getting ready to attack. My fingers tighten on the spear. But then she reels away to sniff the others.

I'm not sweating inside my helmet – I can't – but I feel hotter than normal. I keep a close eye on the zombies as they shuffle around, staring, sniffing, fingers twitching. I keep expecting one to realize that we're different, attack and set off the rest of their undead pack. But they don't. Because we're not *that* different, not in the most important way — like them, we're dead. Zombies clearly only have a taste for the living.

"That's good," Josh murmurs. "Let them get used to you."

"This is freaking me out," I croak.

"No," he says. "You've adjusted faster than the others did. You're the first to hold your nerve when making primary contact with reviveds. Even Rage lashed out the first time he was exposed."

That makes me feel smug. Of course it could be a load of bull and Josh might be saying it just to settle me down, but who can resist flattery like that? I treat myself to a self-indulgent chuckle, imagining Rage in a panic. I'll tease him about that later.

We hold our ground, letting the zombies move around freely. They don't have much interest in anything, not even each other. They creep in their own directions, swiveling to avoid collisions when they catch sight of one another but not communicating or cooperating in any clear way.

I start to feel sorry for them. They were real people once, with families, jobs, friends, hopes, dreams. What if some small part of them is still alive in there, if they can sense what they've become? How awful would that be?

"Okay," Josh says. "We're going to shake things up a bit. Raise your spear."

I hold it up as Josh instructs, then wave it threateningly at a passing zombie.

The zombie doesn't react.

"Do it again," Josh says. "But yell this time."

I roar at a different zombie—a man—and poke my spear at him, but he ignores me like the first one did.

The other zom heads make threatening gestures too, reacting to instructions. We must each have a separate guide, someone to direct us individually.

"Back up closer to the others," Josh says. "Form a tighter circle, so the reviveds can't pass between you."

I ease back as ordered, until my elbows brush against Danny's and Gokhan's. Danny has a chainsaw, Gokhan an ax.

"Exciting, innit?" Gokhan shouts, raising the visor of his helmet to grin at me.

The zombies close to us pause when they hear him shout and they stare at him, eyes wide and gray. "Yeah," Gokhan jeers. "You didn't expect me to talk, did you? You don't understand anything. We're gonna stomp your ugly arses. I'll cut your heads off with this ax and scoop out your brains. What do you think of that, eh?"

The zombies carry on walking, oblivious to the threat. Gokhan laughs and lowers his visor.

"Get ready for action," Josh whispers.

Rage has scorched the ceiling a couple of times, sending flames licking over the heads of the zombies. A couple of them cringed but didn't otherwise react. Now he lowers his hose, points the nozzle at a thin young woman and lets rip. Fire consumes her and she wheels away from him, screaming hoarsely, arms flapping, head shaking wildly.

The other reviveds come to a standstill. Their heads whip round and all eyes settle on Rage.

"Come on, you bastards," Rage growls.

As if in direct response to his challenge, they attack.

Instant chaos. Rage sprays the zombies with flames, and so does Tiberius, who has the other flamethrower. But they can't cover all angles and moments later the zombies are on us, digging at our stomachs with the bones sticking out of their fingers, gnashing at our faces, hissing and screeching.

I jab at a couple of my assailants, driving them back. The other zom heads are going wild. Cathy and Danny's chainsaws are alive and buzzing. Peder and Gokhan are chopping madly at the zombies, snickering hysterically.

Cathy digs the head of her chainsaw into a man's stomach and grinds it around. Blood and guts spray everywhere. The man falls away, screaming, a massive hole through his body where his middle should be. But that's not the end of him. Even though he's shrieking with agony, he crawls towards us, innards dribbling out and smearing the floor, driven to keep coming by a force beyond his control. His eyes are wild. Blood foams from his lips. He shudders and spasms like someone being electrocuted. But still he comes on.

"My go!" Peder cheers and chops at the man's neck until he severs it. With a sick laugh, he picks up the head by its hair and waves it around. The man's mouth is still opening and closing. His eyes still work. His arms still writhe on the now headless body and his legs kick out feebly at nothing.

Peder throws the head across the room and it bounces off a wall. The man's body somehow struggles to its feet and staggers around, arms flailing, trying to find his head. I'm appalled – if I had a heart, it would go out to the distressed zombie – but the others are having a ball.

"Can I go help him?" Danny yells gleefully. He must receive a positive answer because he breaks away and dashes across the room. Rage and Tiberius cover him, training their fire on the zombies who target him.

Danny grabs the headless body and hauls it over to where the head is lying. He picks up the severed head and sticks it on the neck, but back to front. With a ghoulish giggle, he returns to the ranks and restarts his chainsaw.

I stare with horror as the man swivels several times, trying to work out what's wrong. Finally his head falls off again. His body bends and his arms search for the missing head. Finding it, he puts it back in place, but the right way round this time. He holds the head in place by crooking an arm over it. With a snarl, he hurls himself back into the action and throws himself at me.

I'm frozen with shock, hardly able to believe the joy with which the zom heads have gone about their cruel business. Reacting instinctively when I'm attacked, I jab at the man's stomach, but of course there's nothing there, so my spear passes straight through the hole. Before I can pull it back, he's on me, eyes wide with crazy rage, teeth snapping together as he tries to chew through my helmet.

"Protect yourself!" Josh shouts.

I shove the man away, but he catches on the spear and doesn't fall. He bounces back towards me and his head collides with mine. His arm slips and his head falls to the floor, but the force of the collision cracks the glass in my visor. With a shriek of alarm, I push his body away, readjust my grip on my spear, then drive it down into the man's skull, all the way through his brain.

I lift the spear and the man's head rises into sight. His lips are trembling and he's making an awful choking noise. Blood drips from his neck and spatters my gloved hands. His eyes stare at me through the cracked lens of my visor. It might be my imagination, but I think I see fear in his expression.

"Cool!" Rage exclaims, then sprays the head with flames. The stench of burning flesh and hair fills my nostrils and I gag. If I'd eaten anything recently, I'm sure I'd throw up, but my stomach is empty, so I only dry heave.

"Sod this!" I cry, and throw my spear away.

"Becky," Josh snaps. "What are you doing?"

Losing all control, I step away from the others and rip loose my helmet, freeing my face.

"Replace that!" Josh yells. "Get back in line!"

In answer I scream wordlessly, a monstrous howl. The world tilts crazily around me. I can't take this anymore. I want it to stop.

I clamp my hands over my ears and try to shut my eyes. When I remember that I can't, I scream again and grab the spear. I kick the flaming head off of it, then snap the shaft in two. I point the half with the tip at my eyes, determined to blind myself to this nightmarish spectacle, maybe even dig around, rip out my brain and finish the job that Tyler started all those months ago.

Rage knocks my arm aside. I bring it up to try again but he grabs my hand and forces it down, then wrestles the spear from my fingers and tosses it away.

I curse Rage and swing for him with my fists. Zombies crowd around and tear and snap at us. I feel bones scrape down the back of my exposed neck. I shriek madly and roar them on to success.

272

Rage swears and punches me. My nose pops and blood oozes out. I choke on it, shake my head, scream again.

Then nets start to come down on the zombies. Panels are ripped aside and soldiers fire through the gaps, shooting any revived who isn't caught. I try to pull free of Rage, to hurl myself into the hail of bullets, wanting to perish along with the zombies, feeling closer to them than to any of these warped, tormenting creeps. This is a savage, dreadful world, and I want out. I wish I'd never been brought back to life. I want to end it, stop it all, get off the moving train.

A net falls around me and I get tangled up. I lash out with both arms, trying to tear free, but the net only tightens further. With another scream, this time born of frustration at being cheated out of the death I crave, I fall to the floor and thrash around weakly, trapped in this living hell, forced to continue by the soldiers and scientists who gather round me once the zombies have all been killed or subdued. They stare at me coldly and listen to me shower them with abuse.

I'm still screaming when a man pushes through the others and crouches next to me. "Stop it, B," he says softly.

I ignore him, thinking it's Josh or Dr. Cerveris.

"Stop that," the man says again. When I don't, he grabs the netting around my head, ignoring the warning cries of the soldiers, and jerks my face towards his. "Look at me!" he barks.

I try to spit at him but my mouth is too dry.

"Look at me," the man says again, quieter this time, and

273

something in his tone makes me pause. It's not Josh or Dr. Cerveris, but his voice is familiar.

Suppressing the scream that was building at the back of my throat, I focus on the light brown face in front of me and gasp. *"Mr. Burke?"*

"Yes," he says, then grabs my gloved hand and squeezes reassuringly. "You can relax now. I'm here for you, B."

I'm so astonished, I can't say anything else, and I don't resist as two soldiers haul me to my feet, cut away the net from around my feet, and force me out of the room, Billy Burke – my favorite teacher from school – incredibly, impossibly, following close behind.

TWELVE

I'm in a small room, not much bigger than my cell. Sitting at a desk, arms cuffed behind my back, legs shackled to my chair. Still wearing the leathers. Staring at the table, jaw slack, thinking back to what happened with the zombies, the way I snapped. Wincing at the memory of the man's burning head, driving my spear through his brain, helping kill him.

Burke and Josh are sitting across from me, waiting, saying nothing. I listen to the hum and crackle of the building. I like it here, away from the zom heads, zombies, all that crap. I'd be happy if they never took me back.

The door opens and Dr. Cerveris steps in. He's seething. Glares at me as if I've insulted his mother. Sits with Burke and Josh on the other side of the table.

"Is she secure?" he snaps.

"Yes," Josh says.

"You're certain?"

"We don't take chances."

Dr. Cerveris sneers at me. "You're a very silly girl."

"Get stuffed," I snort, and he quivers indignantly. Before he can retort, I lock gazes with Burke. "What the hell are *you* doing here?"

"I'm a consultant," he says in a deadpan voice.

I laugh at the sheer absurdity of it. "What happened to being a teacher?"

He smiles thinly. "There isn't much call for teachers these days. Education has slipped down the list of priorities. That's what happens when you find yourself caught in the middle of a war with the living dead."

"Careful," Josh says warningly. "Don't forget the restrictions we discussed."

"Don't worry," Burke sighs. "I won't give away any of your precious secrets, though I don't see what you gain by withholding information from her." He runs a hand through his hair. It's grayer than it was six months ago. His eyes are bloodshot, dark bags underneath. He stinks of coffee.

"What was that about in there?" Burke asks me. "Why did you flip?"

"If you'd ever stuck a spear through someone's head, maybe you'd understand," I mutter.

"It didn't bother the others," Burke says.

"Well, it should," I snarl. "We were burning and hacking up *people*. When the hell did that become acceptable?"

"I told you before you went in," Josh growls. "They're not people. They're monsters."

"No, *we're* the monsters. They can't help themselves. We can." I face Burke again. "You remember Tyler Bayor?"

He has to think for a moment. "Tyler. Yes. He didn't make it."

"That's because I threw him to the zombies."

Burke raises an eyebrow and I quickly tell him about my dad coming to rescue me, yelling at me to throw Tyler to the undead when we needed to stall them, the way I obeyed.

"You tried to warn me," I finish sullenly. "You told me I was in danger of becoming a racist and it would end badly if I didn't change my ways. I didn't listen until it was too late. But I've thought a lot about it since I came back. I'm trying hard to be a better person in death than I was in life. I've been given a second chance, and I don't want to screw it up."

"That's admirable," Burke says without any hint of condescension. "But I don't see what it has to do with this."

"Your kind were all the same to my dad," I mumble. "Blacks, Arabs, Pakis." I catch myself and make a face. "*Pakistanis*. They were something less than us, not worthy of being treated as equals.

279

I knew he was wrong, but I never called him on it. I played along. And me throwing Tyler to the zombies was the result of that.

"The way Dad thought about different races...about *you*...the way I pretended to believe those things too..." I glance with shame at Mr. Burke, then with spite at Josh and Dr. Cerveris. "It's how you lot see zombies."

"It's hardly the same thing," Dr. Cerveris protests. "Racists hate for no valid reason, because of the color of a person's skin or their religious beliefs. Reviveds, on the other hand, are unnatural beasts, savage killers brought back to life by forces beyond our comprehension. They shouldn't exist. They've wreaked irreparable damage and will destroy the world completely if we don't dissect and study them and figure out what makes them tick."

"We experiment so that we can learn and understand," Josh says. "I know it might not seem that way. It could look like torture and execution to a neutral. But there are no neutrals here. It's us against them, with you and the other revitalizeds caught between. We use the zom heads because you can get closer to the reviveds than we can, test them in ways we can't. Your input might help restore control of this planet to the living. Zombies are dead. They can't be cured. Would you rather we let them run free and kill?"

"No," I scowl. "I understand why you have to stop them, why you lock them up, even why you execute them. But there must be other ways to experiment on them." I look pleadingly to Burke. "There *must* be."

"Of course there are," Burke says.

"Billy..." Josh growls.

Burke waves away the soldier's objection. "She's not a fool. You're right, B. It *is* cruel. It's inhuman. On a moral level it's unpardonable." He shrugs wearily. "But we're at war. That's not a great excuse, I know. I certainly wouldn't have let my students get away with it in class if they'd tried to use that argument to justify war crimes. But this is where we're at. I don't call the shots and I don't have the right to pass judgment. So I do what I can to help, even if it means going against everything I once believed in." He nods at Josh and Dr. Cerveris. "These gentlemen would appreciate it if you would too."

I shift uncomfortably. "It's wrong."

"Yes," Burke says. "But we're asking you to cooperate regardless."

"You were better than that once," I whisper.

Burke winces, looks away shamefully, doesn't respond.

"A racist zombie taking the moral high ground," Dr. Cerveris jeers.

"She's not a zombie," Burke snaps.

"Thanks to you," Josh says softly.

I frown. "What does that mean?"

Burke is looking at Josh, surprised. "I thought I wasn't supposed to mention that."

"You weren't," Josh says. "But if we tell her, maybe we can get through to her...."

Burke chuckles cynically. "When all else fails, try the truth." He winks at me. "We don't know why certain zombies revitalize. It's a mystery. Based on all the studies we've conducted, it shouldn't happen. The dead lose their senses. Their brains shut down and all traces of their old selves are lost. In damn near all of them, that loss is permanent, no way back.

"But a few of you defy the laws. You recover consciousness and carry on as you did when you were alive, for however long your bodies hold up."

"Any idea how long that might be?" I interrupt.

Burke checks with Josh, who frowns, then shrugs. "Why not?" he says with just a hint of dark relish.

"We think—" Burke begins.

"It's an imprecise science," Dr. Cerveris cuts in coolly. "We have little evidence to back up our theories. But judging by what we've seen, and forecasting as accurately as we can, we anticipate an eighteen- to twenty-four-month life cycle for revitalized specimens."

"You mean I'll shut down and die for real within a couple of years?" I gasp.

"Maybe as little as a year," Josh says. "You've been with us for more than six months already, remember."

"But the revitalization process only kicked in a matter of weeks ago," Dr. Cerveris reminds him. "We're not sure if the time before that counts or not."

"Wait a minute," I snap. "Are you saying that all of the zombies will be wiped out within the next two years?"

"Sadly, no," Dr. Cerveris replies. "Only the revitalizeds. The brains of the reviveds are stable, and from what we've seen, will remain so, at least in the near future. But when consciousness returns, the brain starts to operate differently. It conflicts with the demands of its undead body and begins to decompose. Unless we can find a way to counteract that—and so far we haven't had much opportunity to study the phenomenon—the prognosis is grim."

"So I've a couple of years max," I sigh.

"If they're right," Burke says. "They might not be."

"But we usually are," Dr. Cerveris smirks.

"That's not your main worry, though," Burke says.

I raise an eyebrow. "There's worse than being told I'll be worm fodder in a couple of years?"

Burke nods solemnly. "The first revitalizeds didn't last long. They were isolated once their guards noticed the change in them, but after a week or so, they reverted. Their brains flatlined and they went back to being mindless zombies. No one has ever recovered their mental faculties a second time."

"What changed?" I murmur.

"We found a way to prolong the revitalization," Dr. Cerveris says proudly.

"How?"

"Nutrients."

"You mean the gruel you've been feeding us keeps our brains going?"

"Yes. Without it, you would deteriorate rapidly."

I stare at the doctor, then Burke. "For a bunch of quacks who don't know why the dead reanimate or how some of us regain our senses, they seem to have figured out that part pretty quickly."

Burke smiles. "Good, B. You're thinking clearly, looking for answers behind the half-truths and lies. Go on. Take it further."

"I don't know if we need to tell her that much," Josh intercedes.

"We've guided her this far," Burke counters. "There's no harm in letting her go all the way."

I try to make sense of what I've been told, but I run into a brick wall. "It's no good," I tell Burke. "I don't know what you want me to work out."

"Think," Burke groans. "What's the one thing that zombies everywhere—from those you've seen in movies to those you saw at the school—go wild for? If you had a zombie locked up, and it was bellowing and wailing, how would you calm it down?"

"I don't…"

I stop, flashing on an image of the video footage that Josh showed me, of me bent over a boy, digging around inside his skull. In all the films I saw, all the comics I read, I never came across a zombie who didn't hunger for the juicy gray matter common to humans everywhere. The kind of gray matter, I realize with a sick jolt, that Reilly has been serving me every day.

Burke sees that I'm up to speed. He grins humorlessly, then says without emotion, "They've been feeding you human brains to keep you conscious. You need them to survive."

"So tell us again," Dr. Cerveris says smugly as I stare at them with revulsion and horror. "*Who's* the monster here?"

THIRTEEN

There's a long silence while I come to terms with what I've been told. This is certainly a meeting to remember. It's not every day that you find out you've got less than two years to live, and by the way, you've been feasting on human brains for the past month. But after my initial shock it doesn't take me long to get a handle on myself.

"Where do the brains come from?" I ask.

Burke says, "I told you — humans."

"I mean, are you killing people in order to feed us?"

"Don't be ridiculous," Dr. Cerveris snorts.

"The casualties have been horrendous," Josh explains. "We can't put an exact figure on how many people have been slaughtered, but in London alone we reckon it must run into the millions."

"That's not including the hundreds of thousands who have been turned," Dr. Cerveris points out. "Just those who were killed, whose heads were cracked open, so that they couldn't revive."

"We've mopped up a lot of the corpses," Josh continues. "Reviveds rarely clean out a skull — they almost always leave bits of brain behind. Ever since we realized what revitalizeds need, we've been collecting brain matter and storing it."

There's silence again. I stare at the wall above Burke's head. This wasn't how I saw my life going when I was at school. I didn't have any great career plans, but cannibalism was *very* far down my list of options.

I chuckle drily and lower my gaze. "You know what?" I grin crookedly. "Sod it. I always wanted to go on a TV show and eat things like bugs, snakes, roadkill. This is a dream come true. Bring it on. I'll eat whatever the hell you chuck at me." I rub my stomach slowly. *"Yum."*

Burke smirks. "I told them you were a piece of work." He glances at Josh. "I bet you're glad now that you listened to me."

"We'll see," Josh mutters. "She hasn't agreed to cooperate yet."

I frown, thinking back a few minutes, then turn to Burke. "Josh said it was thanks to you that I wasn't still a zombie. What did he mean?"

"I was coming to that before you sidetracked me." Burke crosses his hands on the table and looks at me seriously. "Revitalizeds need brains to thrive. If we don't feed them, they regress. In most cases, the staff here let that happen."

I cock my head sideways. "Come again?"

"The percentage of reviveds who revitalize is minuscule," Dr. Cerveris says defensively. "But if you take a group of hundreds of thousands, even a fraction of a percent is significant."

"I figured there must be more of us," I say slowly, "that adults and younger kids were being held elsewhere."

"Of course," Dr. Cerveris says. "We keep a sample of all age groups, races, both sexes."

"A *sample*," I repeat, knowing what that must mean but waiting for them to confirm it.

"They let most revitalizeds regress," Burke says. His gaze hasn't wavered. "They separate the conscious zombies, hold them in a cell, don't feed them, then return them to the general holding pens once they've—"

"— lost their bloody minds!" I roar. I try to jump to my feet but the chains around my ankles hold me in place.

"There are limits to the numbers we can maintain," Dr. Cerveris says calmly.

"Bullshit!" I retort. "You just don't want the hassle."

"We only need a few to study and help us with our experiments," Josh says. "What would we gain by keeping the others?"

"They can think!" I scream. "They're people. They have rights."

"*Rights?*" Josh sneers. "Only the living have rights, and they're not alive, not really. You aren't either. You're a freak revived, nothing more, a threat to any normal person, never more than a few skipped feeds away from insane savagery. We keep you because we need you, but you have no rights. You lost those when you died and became a killer."

"Is that how you think too?" I ask Burke, trembling with rage.

"No," he says. "To me it's abhorrent."

"Then how can you work with them?" I snarl. "Why do you put up with this crap? Why not walk away, like anyone halfway human would?"

Burke shakes his head and doesn't reply.

"I wouldn't be so quick to criticize your old teacher if I were you," Dr. Cerveris says smoothly. "You'd be back stewing with the reviveds if it weren't for Billy Burke."

"We run a background check on every revitalized," Josh says. "We like to know who they are, where they came from. We gather as much information as we can before deciding how to process them."

"I bet that's so you can give priority to family members or people related to politicians or powerful businessmen," I sneer.

Josh shrugs. "I'd be lying if I said that wasn't a consideration, but that's the way the world has always worked. Nepotism is rampant everywhere. But if it's any consolation, very few revitalizeds fall into that bracket, so it's rare that someone is sacrificed at the expense of a minister's son or a billionaire's daughter."

"When they ran a check on you," Burke says, "they discovered your connection to me. I'm a consultant, like I told you. I've been working with the army, helping deal with undead children who are finding it hard to cope. Most are distraught at having lost family and friends. They don't all adjust as swiftly as you have."

"More's the pity," Dr. Cerveris murmurs. "Our lives would be a lot simpler if every revitalized were as cold and uncaring as Becky Smith."

I look at the doctor with contempt. "Screw you, numbnuts. I care. You don't understand me at all, do you?"

"That's why I've been kept busy," Burke says as Dr. Cerveris scowls at me. "I *do* understand, or at least I have a good idea. I never thought of it as a gift, being able to relate to teenagers, but it seems that talent is rarer than I believed. If it weren't for me and a few others, you guys would have been branded as cattle and treated the same way."

"I don't think we'd have gone quite that far," Josh smiles frostily. "Anyway, we realized you were one of Billy's ex-students, so we asked him if he wanted us to approve you for sustained revitalization."

"And you said yes." I flash my teeth at Burke in a mock smile. "Thanks. You're my hero."

"It wasn't as simple as that," Burke says quietly. "I had to pitch for you. I told them you were tough, smart, determined, that you'd be an asset."

"In short," Josh snaps, "he told us you'd fit in perfectly with the zom heads, that if we wanted someone to carry out harsh but essential tests on reviveds, you were our girl. That's why we spared you.

Otherwise..." He puts a finger to the side of his head, twirls it round and makes loony eyes at me.

"Nice to know you think so highly of me," I snarl at Burke.

"Would you rather I'd let you revert?" he asks gently. "Should I have abandoned you and left you to rot?"

I frown uncertainly. I can see where he's coming from, but still...

"You had no right to promise on my behalf," I mutter. "You shouldn't have told them I'd be willing to torture people–"

"Zombies," Josh slips in.

"– and kill them," I finish.

"I know," Burke says. "But I figured if they kept you alive, at least you'd have the chance to make that decision yourself. You're faced with a choice, B. It's not a welcome choice, and I honestly don't know how I'd react in your place, but it must be better than having no choice at all."

"And that choice is...?" I challenge him.

"Do what they ask and stay on as a zom head," he says evenly. "Or refuse to do their bidding and become a senseless zombie again."

"Not much of a choice, is it?" I huff.

"No," he admits. "But if you choose to defy them, at least you'll give up on consciousness willingly. The other way, you'd have simply regressed without any understanding of why it was happening to you."

"So I can become a vicious mercenary or a brain-dead cannibal. That's what you're telling me?"

"Boiled down to its basics, yes," Burke says.

Josh coughs politely. "I don't see any point in taking this conversation further. You know where you stand, Becky. It's time to decide. Will you help us or do we send you back to the pens?"

I stare at the three men, thinking hard. I'd like to say it's an easy choice, but it's not. I want to do the right thing and toss their offer of cooperation back into their ugly, cynical faces. I want to stand tall and proud like a hero, face true death willingly, without any regrets.

But at the same time I don't want to fade away and become a brainless member of the walking dead. They're going to carry out their experiments with or without me. Why not play along and cling to the semblance of life that I have? It wouldn't make any difference in the grand scheme of things.

When we did history at school and studied the Nazis, I was always scornful of the collaborators, those who morally objected to the cruelties but went along with them anyway, guards at death camps, doctors who were asked to experiment on live subjects, tailors who made clothes for soldiers, factory workers who provided them with guns. I thought they were cowards. There was no doubt in my mind that I'd have refused to help the Nazis just to save my neck.

Now I realize it's not that simple. If it's put to you plainly, cooperate or die, it's impossible not to have doubts. Maybe a saint would shake her head and refuse to consider the possibility of collusion, but I'm no saint. Hell, I'm not even halfway human.

But I've experienced firsthand the dreadful consequences of

meekly obeying people who are rotten to the core. Tyler's face flashes through my thoughts, as it does a dozen times a day, and I hear his cries again as the zombies bit into his flesh, see the pleading look in his eyes as he desperately begged me to save him. When I jumped at my dad's command and threw Tyler to the zombies, didn't I become a collaborator of sorts, as guilty as anyone who served the Nazis?

The man I helped kill today meant nothing to me. I didn't know him, wasn't connected to him, probably had little in common with him. Maybe he was a brute who deserved to die. But even if that was the case, he had a place in this world, a stake to existence, and I took that away from him. I vowed, after throwing Tyler to the wolves, that I'd never do it again. If I'm to honor that vow, I've got to treat everyone the same, not pick and choose those who count and those who don't. No collaboration, not if it costs me what little might be left of my soul.

"I won't do it," I moan, staring miserably at the table. "You're a pack of jackals and I won't join your sick, screwed-up cause, even if you kill me."

"Oh, we won't kill you," Dr. Cerveris says. He leans across the table and stares at me coldly. "We have a far more fitting punishment for obstinate hypocrites like you. *Nil by mouth*. This time next week, when your brain has turned to mush, you'll eat your own mother if we set her before you."

"And who knows," Josh purrs menacingly, in what I can only pray is nothing more than a nasty little dig, "maybe we will...."

FOURTEEN

Three days pass. I'm locked inside my cell. Nobody visits, not even Reilly.

No food.

My stomach doesn't rumble. I don't feel hungry. But I'm twitchy. I find myself obsessing about the gray gunk that I used to be fed, craving more. I get shooting pains through my head and insides. Sometimes I have to double over and grit my teeth until the pain passes. My vision is getting worse, even though I keep adding the drops. Conversely, for some strange reason my sense of smell and hearing are improving. The noises of the complex often grind away at my brain until I have to clamp my hands over my ears to block them out.

Last night, when I was lying on my

bed, I blacked out for a while, the way I used to when I fell asleep. The next thing I knew I was on my feet, head butting the mirror. I'd smashed it to pieces but was still butting it, snarling softly.

I've tried to stay active since then, exercising, walking around my cell, doing push-ups and squats. I won't give in to fear. I *won't*. Let them starve me. I don't care. I'm not going to play their game. I'd rather die than become a killer.

Really? a small part of me whispers.

"Yeah," I tell it.

But my voice quivers and I'm not entirely sure that I can believe myself, that I can stay strong and true.

Working out. Keeping busy. Wanting to cling to consciousness for as long as I can, hoping that if I stay focused, it will help.

I've been thinking a lot about Mum and Dad. I'd managed to put thoughts of them on hold over the last few weeks, but Josh's threat about my mum has set me wondering again. I'm pretty sure they're not prisoners here—if Josh really had a card like that up his sleeve, he wouldn't have revealed it so casually—but are they squeezing out an existence in a similar complex? Were they killed? Turned into zombies? Or have they carried on as normal in a world not much different from the way it was on the day of the attacks?

By what I was told, millions of people were killed in London,

and hundreds of thousands were turned into zombies. But maybe Josh and the doctor were lying, feeding me misinformation to make me think the situation is worse than it really is.

As I'm driving myself mad thinking about the possibilities, the door suddenly slides open and Josh and Reilly stomp into my room. They both look impassive. I was doing squats but I stop and stand. Stare at the pair of them defiantly.

"I thought you might have had a change of heart," Josh says. The sound of his voice makes me wince, it's so loud.

"You forgot," I sneer, and pull up my T-shirt to expose the hole in my chest. "I don't have a heart."

Josh sighs. "I'm not enjoying this, Becky. I can rustle up some gruel for you in a matter of minutes if you give me the word."

"I can give you two words," I tell him. "The second is *off*. Can you guess the first?"

Josh shakes his head and laughs — to my sensitive ears, it's like a jackhammer. "I really hope you relent and come to see things our way," he says. "You and I could be great friends if you cut yourself a little slack."

"I'd cut my own throat before I'd claim you as a friend," I grunt.

Josh gasps theatrically, then nods at Reilly. "Take her through."

"Where?" I ask, tensing, thinking this is it, they're taking me back to the pens to dump me with the other zombies.

"Zom HQ," Reilly says, and holds up a pair of handcuffs. "I'm going to have to ask you to wear these on the way there and back."

"What if I don't want to?"

"I have orders to force you if necessary," he says.

"I don't mean about the cuffs," I snort. "Zom HQ—I don't want to go."

"Aren't you lonely?" Reilly asks. He's speaking more softly than usual. I think he knows that noises hurt me.

"No," I lie. "Even if I was, I'd rather suffer loneliness than sit with that shower of vipers. I've no friends there. They can all go hang."

"Even Mark? He wasn't involved with any of the experiments."

I shrug. "He wants to be."

"That's because he hasn't seen what they get up to." Reilly jangles the cuffs. "It's not an option, B. They're determined to send you there. I don't want to hurt you, but if you leave me no choice..."

I roll my eyes and glare at the smiling Josh. "All right. I'll come peacefully. Give me the bloody cuffs."

The zom heads look astonished when I walk in. They also look unhappy to see me. It's a good thing I wasn't expecting a warm welcome.

"What's she doing back here?" Tiberius shouts at Reilly as he unlocks my cuffs.

"I know you've been missing her, so I brought her along to cheer you all up," Reilly deadpans, then exits.

Rage squares up to me as I head towards my regular couch.

"What was all that crap about when we were experimenting on the zombies?" he growls.

"You might call it an experiment," I spit. "I call it torture and murder."

"You can't kill zombies," Rage says, looking genuinely surprised.

"Yeah, I know, they're already dead," I sneer. "Why don't you change the track? I've heard that one too many times. It's the regular excuse round here to do whatever the hell you want."

"But they *are* dead," Cathy protests. "It doesn't matter what happens to them."

"You're dead too," I remind her.

"That's different," she growls. "*We're* different."

"Yeah, but for how long?" I sniff.

Rage squints at me. "What's that mean?"

I consider telling them what I've learned, about how we regress if we don't feed, that we're kept conscious purely to serve the whims of Dr. Cerveris and his mob, who can take our minds away from us anytime they please. But I don't think they'd thank me for enlightening them. Treat me to a beating, more likely, for being the bearer of bad news.

"Just leave me alone," I mutter, shouldering my way past Rage.

"She thinks she's better than us," Tiberius jeers. "She probably wants to spread joy and peace among the zombies. Are we savages, *Becky*? Should we be put down like rabid dogs?"

300

I ignore him, grab a file and set to work on my teeth—I wasn't allowed a file in the cell, so they've sprouted. The others toss a few insults my way but ease up when I don't bite back. I'm glad when they stop talking. It's as noisy in here as it was in my cell, but I can deal with that. Their raised voices, on the other hand, strike me like punches.

Mark slides over after a while and grins weakly. "They told me what happened," he whispers.

"And you think I'm a fool," I snap, laying the file aside. "You think I should have gone along with the rest of them, hacked off limbs, burned people alive—or burned them *dead*, or however the hell you want to phrase it."

Mark shrugs. "I can't see what the fuss is, but I wasn't there. I've never been there. I don't know what goes on, so I can't judge." He slumps beside me. "To be honest, I think anything would be better than my checkups. They're operating on me more and more. They're worried about my organs, but I don't know why. I don't feel any different."

Mark rubs his eyes and I'm stunned to see his fingers come away wet.

"I thought all of our tear ducts had dried up," I murmur, grabbing his gloved hand and studying the moisture suspiciously.

"They've given me new drops," he explains. "A side effect is that I produce liquid that looks like tears. They say my eyes will dry up completely without the new drops, that I'll go blind." He sighs unhappily.

"Sorry," I mumble. "That must be horrible."

He nods. "But they're hopeful the drops will work. And it's nice having wet eyes again. They used to sting before."

My eyes don't really pain me, but I guess we're all different.

Mark says the zom heads have been in a foul mood since they returned from the terminated experiment.

"They snap at me all the time, but at each other too. They won't admit it, but I think they're ashamed as well as angry. When you refused to harm the zombies, it made them think about how willingly they've gone along with everything. It was just the way things were. Nobody thought they had a choice, or that there was anything wrong with what they were doing. Now they've started to question what they've done."

"And they're blaming me for that," I snicker. "Nobody likes a smartarse who shakes things up. The world's a lot simpler if you don't think too much about it. I'd be mad too in their shoes. I didn't want to rock the boat. I just couldn't take it. I can't see the reviveds as monsters. They're still people in my eyes."

Mark gives my arm a squeeze. "Don't worry," he says. "They'll forgive you. Everyone's grumpy because of the diet, but once they give us back our regular rations, I'm sure—"

"What are you talking about?" I cut in sharply.

"They stopped feeding us a couple of days ago," he says, surprised by my tone.

"You mean after the others came back from the experiment?" I press.

"Yeah. They fed us the first day, same as normal, but nothing since."

I curse loudly and everyone looks at me. I start to get to my feet, to tell them of my suspicions, then pause and sit down again.

I might be wrong. Best not to say anything until I'm certain. I don't want to stir them up if there's no real reason for it.

So I keep my own counsel and sit out the shift, the hours dragging even slower than usual. When Reilly comes and takes us away, one by one, like he always does, I wait until he's leading me back to my cell, then grunt my question at him without looking around. "Are the others being starved because of what I did?"

"Yes," he says without hesitation. "It was Dr. Cerveris's idea. I don't like it, but my vote doesn't carry much weight round here."

"My fading eyesight...my improving sense of smell and hearing...that's part of the regression?"

"Yes," he says. "Reviveds rely on their nostrils and ears more than their eyes. The others haven't been denied food quite as long as you have, so they haven't deteriorated as much as you. But they'll start to notice a significant change within the next day or two."

"How long can we go without food before we turn completely?" I ask.

"It varies from one revitalized to another," he says evenly. "But nobody's ever lasted more than a week."

"Are the doctors serious about this? It's not a bluff?"

"Dr. Cerveris doesn't bluff," Reilly says with what sounds like a genuine sigh. "He doesn't need to. There are other revitalizeds he can turn to."

"So if I refuse to cooperate..."

I falter, so Reilly finishes the sentence for me. "...then they'll let Mark and all the other zom heads starve and turn back into brain-dead zombies."

FIFTEEN

I spend my time in isolation trying to decide whether or not to tell the others about the threat we face. It should be a straightforward call — they have a right to know. But I'm worried about how they'll react. They kill reviveds because they see them as monsters. If I told them that we need to eat brains to survive, and that we're being denied the gruel because of my refusal to play ball with Dr. Cerveris and Josh, they might rip me to pieces. Literally.

I've seen them do it to others. Killing gives them a buzz, and it's bull when they say that they only do it because they have to. There's a good chance they'll slaughter me if I tell them the truth, in the hope that Dr. Cerveris will restore their rations if I'm removed from the equation. A lot of normal people would sacrifice me in a situation like this, so I can't expect too much compassion from a pack of semiliving beasts.

Then again, maybe they deserve the benefit of the doubt. It's wrong to let them perish in ignorance. And if they kill me, what of it? I'll be brain-dead in a couple of days anyway. Why drag the rest of them down with me?

"Because they're bastards," I mutter, and brood about it some more.

Everyone's sour as stale yogurt the next day. The lack of *nutrients* is kicking in big-time. The zom heads are wincing at noises, groaning as hunger pangs shoot through them. They can't understand why they're being denied the gray gloop or why they feel as rough as they do.

"We must have done something wrong," Tiberius insists as they knock the issue back and forth.

"Nah," Gokhan says. "It's a test, innit? They want to see what we do when we get hungry."

"I'll rip Reilly's head off," Peder growls. "That'll show them what *I* do."

"It isn't Reilly's fault," Danny says. "He's not enjoying this. It's bloody Josh who's behind it."

"No it's not," Cathy shouts, then makes a face and lowers her voice. "It's Dr. Cerveris. Josh doesn't have any say in how they test us. It's the scientists who decide those things. I'll ask Josh what's going on the next time I see him."

"Oh, I'm sure he'll tell *you*," Tiberius simpers. "You mean so much to him."

Cathy flips him the finger, then glares at Rage. He's the calmest of everyone, watching an old episode of some American sitcom set in a bar, chuckling softly at the punch lines.

"I don't know why you're so happy," Cathy snarls. "You're part of this too. You'll starve with the rest of us, no matter how many arses you kiss."

"Chill, baby," Rage sniffs. "The Turk's right. They're testing us. Once they've compiled enough data, they'll feed us again. They need us. We're their blue-eyed darlings."

"Maybe they're feeding you on the sly," Danny challenges him. "Maybe that's why you don't seem bothered."

"Believe what you want," Rage shrugs.

"You never say a bad word against them, do you?" Peder spits. "You're a right muppet."

"I relish the easy life," Rage counters. "If we scratch their backs they'll scratch ours. You don't win any prizes for rubbing against the grain. I do what they tell me, treat them with respect and reap the rewards."

"Do you call being starved a reward?" Mark asks.

"Shut it, Worm," Rage snaps, then carries on talking to Peder as if he were the one who had asked the question. "They've got to treat me the same as everybody else when they're running a test, stands to reason. But in the normal run of things, by keeping them sweet, I get anything I ask for, films, games, magazines, even girls if I wanted."

Danny laughs out loud, ignoring the others as they moan and slam their hands over their ears. "*Girls?*" he shrieks. "What the hell would you want with those? We're all dead down below. We can't do anything with girls except look."

"That's why I said *if* I wanted," Rage replies smoothly.

Mark is frowning and staring at his groin. This is news to me. I hadn't realized the boys were impotent, though now that I consider it, it makes sense — no blood flow to stir their sleeping soldiers. If the situation weren't so dire, I'd have a good old chuckle about it. But they've more important things to worry about than dodgy machinery in their boxer shorts. And on impulse, having listened to them waffle on about this all day without saying a word, I suddenly decide to solve the mystery for them.

"It's because of me. They're starving you because I won't torture the reviveds. And they're not gonna stop until . . ."

I draw to a halt. Everyone is staring at me, even Rage, who doesn't look so cocky anymore.

"Go on," Tiberius says stiffly.

"The gray junk they've been feeding us is human brains."

308

"We know," Tiberius says.

"You *know*?" I exclaim.

He shrugs. "It's obvious. We figured that out months ago. Zombies eat brains, everyone knows that."

"You never told me," I huff.

"We didn't know that we needed to," Tiberius sneers. "How thick are you?"

"Enough of that," Rage snaps, getting to his feet. He looks uneasy. "Finish what you were going to say."

"We need the brains to stay conscious," I mutter. "Without regular feeds we'll lose our senses and become reviveds again. And if we do, we can't recover, we'll be stuck like that forever."

Rage stares at me coldly. Everybody else is gaping too.

"They told you this?" Cathy asks.

"Yeah."

"And you said nothing?" Her voice rises. "You let them starve us, knowing what would happen, not saying a word?"

"I'm telling you now."

"You bitch!" she shrieks. "That's the first thing you should have—"

"I'm calling Reilly," Rage says heavily. "I'm gonna tell him that you've agreed to do whatever they ask. Then we're gonna go tear some zombies to shreds and you'll hack them up, burn them, slice them into little pieces, and that will be that."

"No," I whisper. "They're people. I won't do it."

"You bloody well will," Rage snarls, stomping towards me.

I stand and face his challenge, hands by my sides. I don't flinch when he makes a fist and holds it threateningly in front of my face.

"A beating won't change my mind," I tell him. "I've been in plenty of fights, taken more than my fair share of thrashings. I took them at home too — my dad was handy with his fists, knocked me and Mum around all the time. You can smash me to a pulp, break my arms, snap my fingers, rip my ears off. It won't matter. I won't give in."

"I'll kill you," Rage croaks.

"Maybe," I concede. "I'll fight back, and I think Josh will stop you before it gets that far, but if you're tough enough and fast enough, maybe you can finish me off before they intervene."

"Do it," Danny says flatly, stepping up beside Rage. "I'll help."

"Me too," Gokhan growls.

"What about the rest of you?" Rage barks.

"I dunno," Peder says, looking worried. "She's not like the other zombies that we kill. She's one of us."

"But she won't be if they don't feed her," Cathy says, then frowns. "How long before we change?" she asks me.

"No one can last more than a week without being fed, so a few days at most."

Cathy's face hardens. "Kill her. If she's going to revert anyway, we should off her while we can. Otherwise we'll all turn into reviveds."

"No," Mark moans. "We can't do this. It's not right. It's murder."

"But if it's us or her..." Rage says heavily.

Tiberius pushes past Rage and glares at me. I wait for him to condemn me too, but to my surprise he comes out with something bizarre. "I was named after Captain Kirk in *Star Trek*."

Everyone stares.

"I tell people I was named after the river in Rome, but really it was after Kirk. His full name was James Tiberius Kirk. My mum and dad loved *Star Trek*. They made me watch it all the time when I was growing up. Except they didn't have to make me—I loved it as much as they did. Kirk was my hero."

"Is this going somewhere, or have you lost your marbles?" Danny huffs.

"Kirk always stood up for the underdog," Tiberius says. "Every week, him and his crew risked their lives to save others. They killed the bad guys when they had to, but they never killed innocents, not even to save themselves."

"That was just a TV show," Cathy jeers.

Tiberius nods. "I know. But it was *right*. I watched Kirk, Bones and the rest of them, and I knew they were doing the right thing. I was sure I'd do the same thing in their position. I used to hope that one day something dangerous would happen to me, so that I could prove how brave and loyal and *human* I was.

"Reviveds are different," Tiberius says, facing Rage. "I don't

311

think Kirk would have fought for a load of mindless, walking corpses. But Peder's right—B's one of us. If we kill her, we really will be monsters. And I'm not prepared to let that happen. I'll fight with her if I have to, die with her if it comes to that."

Rage holds Tiberius's gaze, deliberating. The others await his verdict. Finally he grunts and looks aside.

"We'll think it through some more," he mutters. "I'll have a chat with Reilly, see if there's another way to sort this out. But if there isn't... well, we'll discuss that tomorrow. See how we all feel about it then."

Rage returns to his couch and the others disperse, shooting me dark looks. Mark and Tiberius remain. Mark's trembling. Tiberius is stiff as a mannequin.

"Thanks," I mutter, knowing the word isn't enough.

"Screw you," Tiberius says. "You're crazy, making a stand like this. Go away and have a rethink, then start cutting up zombies like you're told. Because if you don't, I doubt I can save you next time." He glances at me and I've never seen such an expression before, torn between pride and self-loathing. "I don't even know if I'll try."

Then he storms off and Mark slips away too, leaving me alone, hated, a pariah. But, against all the odds, they didn't kill me. I'm still alive.

But not, I suspect, for long.

SIXTEEN

In my cell, lying on the bed. The pain is worse than ever. My head throbs and my fingers tremble wildly. I had the dry heaves a while ago, my body in revolt. I tried exercising and keeping active, but now it hurts too much when I move. I think I'm close to the end. All I want is to shut my eyes and drift off. I don't care if I never regain consciousness.

"I'm sorry," I whimper, but I don't know if I'm apologizing to the ghost of Tyler Bayor for killing him, my mum for letting Dad beat her up for so many years and not reporting him, myself for giving up, or somebody else. I'm not at my sharpest at the moment.

There's a screeching sound from the corridor and I jam my hands over my ears, groaning weakly. The noises have increased over the last few minutes. I've been hearing all sorts of things, explosions, tearing metal, screams. I know they aren't real. It's just my brain cascading out of control, warping ordinary sounds out of recognition.

Is this how it is all the time for regular zombies? Is that why they moan so much? I try to imagine a lifetime of this crazy noise, shaking from the hunger, nearly blind, scouring the ruins of the world in search of brains. Some life! Maybe I should end it all before I regress.

I lower my hands and stare at the sharp bones sticking out of my fingertips. It would be difficult, but I'm sure I could crack open my skull and scoop out enough of my brain to put myself out of my misery. It would be a gruesome way to die, but wouldn't it be better than shuffling around as a lost, tormented soul for the rest of my wretched years?

As I'm staring at my fingers, trying to work up the courage to end it all, the door to my room slides open. The sounds outside amplify immediately and I wince. I glance up from my hands, expecting Reilly, or maybe Dr. Cerveris and Josh. But whoever it is, he's standing in the corridor, not showing his face. I can see his shadow, but that's all.

"Don't be shy," I growl. "Come on in and have a good look."

The man giggles. It's a strange, jangly sound. It makes me grit my teeth. I start to sit up angrily. Then the man steps inside and I sink back with confusion and disgust.

314

It's a clown, but no clown that you'd ever see in a circus, not unless it was a circus in hell.

He's dressed in a pinstripe suit, but with colorful patches stitched into it in lots of different places. There are plenty of bloodstains too.

A severed face hangs from either shoulder. The faces have been skinned from the bone. I think one came from a woman and the other from a man, but it's hard to be sure.

Lengths of gut are wound around both his arms, long strands of intestines, glistening and dripping. Along his legs several ears have been pinned to the fabric of his trousers.

He's wearing a pair of oversized red shoes, a small skull sticking out of the end of each. They could be the skulls of some breed of monkey, but I don't think they are. I think the skulls came from human babies.

The clown's hair has been sourced from a variety of heads. There are all sorts of locks, every type of color, shade and length, stuck to his skull. No...not stuck. As he comes closer and giggles again, he bends slightly and I see that the clumps of hair are stapled to his scalp. There are dried bloodstains around many of them, and fresh blood flows from a few.

The clown has a painted white face, but that's the only traditional touch. The flesh around his eyes has been carved away and filled in with what looks like soot. A pair of v-shaped channels run from beneath either eye to just above his lips, which have been painted a dark blue color. The channels have been gouged out of his cheeks and the exposed bone has been dyed bright pink. Instead of the usual red ball over his nose, he's somehow attached a human eye to it. Little red stars have been dotted over it.

I do nothing as the surreal clown advances. I'm frozen in place. I'm praying that this is an illusion, a product of my fevered brain. But he doesn't look like a dream figure. By all rights he shouldn't belong to this world, but he certainly seems at home in it.

The clown hops from foot to foot, performing a strange little shuffle, still giggling, drawing closer. Now I spot a button on his chest, round and colorful, the sort a child might paint. Daubed on the button, in very ragged handwriting, is what I assume is his name.

Mr. Dowling.

He reaches the foot of my bed and beams at me, lips closed, eyes wide, looking crazier and more menacing than anything I've ever seen. His eyes continually twitch from one side of their sockets to the other. His skin is wriggling, as if insects are burrowing beneath the flesh, close to the surface.

I want to kick out at the nightmarish clown, or slide past him and race from the cell. But I can't move. It's like I'm locked down tight. I can't even whine.

The clown reaches out and slowly strokes my right cheek. His fingers are long and thin. Much of the flesh has been sliced away from them. I glimpse bones through a mishmash of exposed veins

and arteries. He's not a zombie—he has normal-looking nails, and I can feel his pulse through the touch of his fingers—so I can't understand how he tolerates these open, seeping wounds.

Withdrawing his hand, the clown—*Mr. Dowling*—leans over until his face is in front of mine. His eyes steady for a moment and he looks straight at me. Only it's more like he's looking through me. I feel as if he's reading my thoughts, stripping my mind bare, unraveling all of my secrets.

The clown's smile spreads. His eyes start dancing again. He opens his mouth.

Spiders fall from his blue lips, a rain of arachnids, small and scuttly. Hundreds of legs scrape my face as they pour upon me, over my eyes, into my mouth, up my nose.

With a scream of shock and terror, I snap back to life, hurl myself from the bed and roll across the floor, swiping spiders from my face, mashing them to pieces with the heels of my hands, spitting them out, picking them from my eyes, screaming over and over. I never thought of myself as an arachnophobe. Then again, I've never been covered with spiders until tonight.

I shake my head and wipe my hands across my face and scalp, brushing the last of the spiders away. Some scurry across the floor, seeking the shelter of the shadows under the bed. I poke the bone of my little finger into my right ear, then my left, as carefully as I can, not wanting to rupture the drums within. Then I explore slowly with my fingers.

They're gone.

With a shudder, I stand, squash a few more of the spiders under-foot and turn to face the otherworldly clown.

He isn't there. If he was real in the first place – and I wouldn't think that he was if not for the spiders – he slipped out while I wasn't looking.

And he left the door open.

Still shaking, I glance around my cell to make sure he's not lurk-ing, waiting to pounce on me from behind when I think I'm safe. Once I'm convinced that he really has gone, I call out shakily, "Hello?"

There's no answer, but the noises outside are louder than ever, the screams especially. I no longer think that they're the product of my skewed senses.

Steeling myself against every sort of imaginable horror, I edge closer to the open doorway. I keep thinking that it will slam shut, but it doesn't, and seconds later I ease out of my cell, into the cor-ridor and the middle of a blood-red storm.

SEVENTEEN

Soldiers are battling with zombies at the end of the corridor. A small group of humans, no more than four or five, against a dozen or more of the living dead. The soldiers have guns and are firing openly on their enemies, but unless the bullets strike their heads and rip the zombies' brains apart, they don't do any real damage. And the zombies aren't giving the soldiers the time or space to squeeze in many clear headshots.

My first instinct is to try to help the soldiers. It doesn't matter that they've been keeping me captive, or that they've been deliberately starving me for the last few days. I feel compelled to help the living.

The zombies have the soldiers surrounded. I start towards them, shouting,

trying to distract the undead killers. I'm not sure how I plan to help the humans, but at least I can fight off the zombies without fear of being infected. Maybe I can buy the soldiers time to retreat to safety.

But the reviveds put an early end to my half-formed plans. They press in close, dig in teeth and fingers, and it's all over before I hit the scene. They leave the humans before they fully turn, somehow knowing they've done enough.

The soldiers writhe on the ground and scream for help or mercy, but there's nothing anyone can do for them now. One puts a gun to his head and ends the nightmare before it can claim him. The others suffer on.

The zombies bunch together in front of me and sniff the air, pressing forward dangerously. I remember what happened during the experiment. The reviveds don't react to zom heads unless we attack them. It's hard, but I force myself to stand calmly as they circle me, fingers flexing, nostrils dilated.

They decide I'm one of them, lose interest in me and press on, moving with purpose. Soon I'm left with the soldiers, who are all vomiting and transforming. I can hear bones forcing their way out through fingers and toes, teeth thickening and lengthening. Turning my back on the doomed, screaming men, I make for zom HQ, hoping to find answers or safety there.

It's the first time I've been able to patrol the corridors by myself. Under normal circumstances I wouldn't get very far, but virtually all of the doors are open. The security system has either crashed or been hacked. There's nothing to hold me back. But that means there's nothing to hold back the zombies either. Or that grisly clown. Mr. Dowling could be lurking in any of the rooms that I pass or around any of the corners that I come to.

But there's no sign of the clown. I scope lots of zombies, and a few soldiers and scientists running for their lives, but that's all.

I'm close to zom HQ when a Klaxon starts to wail. The high-pitched sound is torturous and I collapse to my knees, choking with pain. Clasping my hands over my ears doesn't help. I feel like my head is about to split. I see zombies falling like ninepins, moaning and convulsing. It looks like the revolt has been quashed. Some bright spark has come to the rescue. It's probably for the best. As much as I hate the crew here for what they've done to me, I don't want to see them all slaughtered. I'll just wait, ride out the pain as best I can, and put up no resistance when they come to take me back to my...

The Klaxon dies away as swiftly as it blared into life. The zombies rise and shake their heads. They snarl accusingly at the ceiling, then press on in search of fresh victims, back in business, as hungry as ever.

I stagger on until I find zom HQ, but the door here is closed and doesn't open when I push. I pound on it and roar out names. "Rage! Reilly! Tiberius!" But nothing happens.

I'm not sure what to do now. I back away from the door, staring at it sullenly. An undead woman with one arm staggers past. She stops and turns, eyes widening with delight, lips splitting into an eager smile. Then a bullet rips through her forehead and tears her brain to shreds. She collapses with a soft wheezing noise.

I glance over my shoulder and spot Reilly and Dr. Cerveris jogging towards me. Gokhan, Peder and Cathy are with them. Reilly looks scared but in control. Dr. Cerveris just looks furious.

"How did you get out of your cell?" the doctor snaps as they draw level.

"The clown opened my door."

Everyone gapes at me.

"What bloody clown?" Reilly grunts.

"Mr. Dowling." I look around. "Nobody else saw him?"

"She's started to hallucinate," Dr. Cerveris huffs. "That's common among revitalizeds in the final stages of consciousness. We should leave her. She could regress at any time."

"They're all in bad shape," Reilly says, pointing to the others, who are shaking and dizzy-looking. "If we're going to try to save the rest, we might as well save B too."

"Very well," Dr. Cerveris mutters. "But if I give the command, blow her brains out and don't stop to think about it."

The doctor steps forward, presses his fingers to the panel on the zom HQ door, then puts an eye up to the retinal scanner. The door slides open and he looks inside. "Nobody home," he says, closing the door again.

"Why don't we hole up in there?" Peder asks. "The zombies couldn't get in if we shut the door behind us."

325

"Of course they could," Dr. Cerveris barks. "Members of staff have been turned. We know from past tests that certain operational memories remain among reviveds. Some of the soldiers and medics might recall what they need to do to open locked doors, and if they had clearance when they were alive, they still have it now."

"So what are we going to do?" I growl. "Run around like slasher-movie fodder until the zombies get us?"

"First we fetch the others," Reilly says as we pad down the corridor, following the animated Dr. Cerveris. "Then we lock ourselves into a room that requires a digital code. The reviveds won't be able to recall a string of numbers — their memories aren't *that* strong."

"How come you're bothering with us?" Cathy asks as we run. "Did Josh tell you to help us?"

"I haven't seen him," Reilly says. "I don't know if he's still alive. But it's our job to protect you. We're under attack. An outside crew has disabled our system and freed the reviveds, and their forces are still active. I thought we were safe when the Klaxon kicked in, but obviously they got to that too. I don't think they're interested in the reviveds—they can find more of them anywhere—so they must be after you guys."

"I've put too much work into this project to see it hijacked now," Dr. Cerveris says petulantly. "Once we've run off these invaders, I'll track down whoever was responsible for the attack and flay their flesh from their hides."

"So you aren't helping us out of humanitarian concern?" I jeer.

"Of course not," Dr. Cerveris says. "You aren't human."

I shake my head admiringly. He might be a son of a bitch, but at least he stays true to himself, even during a crisis.

We pick up Tiberius from his cell—it's quiet down his corridor and he had no idea that anything was amiss—then push on. A couple of corners later, we run into a pair of reviveds. They go wild when they catch the scent of Reilly and Dr. Cerveris. They hurl themselves at the humans. Reilly fires but misses. Before the zombies can take him, we wrestle them to the ground and hold them there while Reilly takes aim and shoots.

I hate doing this, helping him kill, but we have no choice. It's Reilly and Dr. Cerveris or the reviveds. And while my sympathies should lie with the zombies who've been imprisoned and maltreated, I can't stop thinking of myself as one of the living.

Mark's cell is next on our route. The door's open but he's cowering inside, hunched over in a corner, tears streaming down his face. (Those new drops are miraculous. Even with everything else that's going on, I feel a stab of jealousy and wonder why the rest of us have been denied them.)

"Mark!" Reilly barks. "Get your arse in gear. We're moving out."

Mark looks up and shakes his head. He opens his mouth to say something, but nothing emerges.

"What's wrong?" I ask, stepping towards him.

"Leave the little worm," Cathy grunts.

"Yeah," Gokhan sneers. "He's acting like a baby, eh?"

"He's coming with us," Dr. Cerveris says with unusual warmth.

He shoves past me and crouches by Mark's side. "Come on, Mark. We have to get out of here. We're going to take you to a safe place."

Mark stares at the scientist. A shadow flickers across his eyes and for a moment it looks to me as if he blinked. But of course that's impossible. The drops are good, but nothing can be *that* good, not for a zom head with paralyzed eyelids.

"Is he out there?" Mark whimpers, his gaze shooting towards the open doorway.

"Who?" Dr. Cerveris frowns.

Mark's gloved right hand is twitching by his side, fingers drumming the floor. But when I steal a closer look, I realize he isn't drumming—he's *squashing*. There are lots of dark smudges on either side of him. They could be ink blots, but I know that they're not.

They're smeared spiders.

"You saw the clown," I say, and Mark's eyes lock on mine.

"You saw him too?" he gasps.

I nod heavily. "Mr. Dowling."

"The button," Mark croaks.

It wasn't a hallucination. I'd started to doubt myself, but now I know for sure that my giggling visitor was real. There's no time to wonder at it, though. We have to get out of here and find sanctuary.

"Come on." I take Mark's hand and haul him to his feet. "We need to get away before the clown comes back."

That puts a rocket under Mark's arse and he bounces away from me and is first out the door.

EIGHTEEN

We push on, Dr. Cerveris calling the shots, leading the way. I ask Reilly about Mr. Burke, if he's safe. Reilly says he doesn't think my ex-teacher is in the complex at the moment, though he can't be sure. I start to ask Dr. Cerveris, but then he stops at another door and tells Reilly to open it.

Rage steps out, cool as you like. He raises an eyebrow at us and grins. "Are we going on a picnic?"

"This is no time for levity," Dr. Cerveris snaps. "The complex has come under attack from an unidentified enemy."

"I heard," Rage nods. "There was all sorts of fighting going on outside my door. I was confused at first. Then I figured it out." He cracks his knuckles. "How bad are things, sir?"

"Critical," Dr. Cerveris mutters. "The complex has been overrun. Our forces will regain control eventually, even if extra troops have to be summoned, but I have no confidence that stability will be resumed anytime soon. Our lives are in very real danger."

"Do we have a plan?" Rage asks as we jog on, only Danny left to gather.

"Once we're all together, we'll lock ourselves into a secure room and wait."

"That's all you've come up with?" Rage asks Reilly, chuckling bleakly.

"Just be glad we came for you," Reilly snaps. "We could have left you to rot."

"Oh, I am glad, sir, truly," Rage says. Then, to my astonishment, he slams an elbow into Reilly's nose, dropping the soldier to the floor. As Reilly slumps with a muffled yelp, Rage grabs the soldier's gun and takes it from him.

"What the hell are you—" Dr. Cerveris starts to roar.

Rage turns and jabs a finger into the doctor's eye, popping it as easily as he would a grape. As the scientist screams, Rage sucks on his finger. "Yummy," he grins. Then his face goes hard and he drives his hand through the side of Dr. Cerveris's skull, cracks it open and scoops out a handful of brain.

My field of vision narrows when I spot the fresh chunks of brain. Pain shoots through me, but it's a pleasurable pain. My mouth falls open and I advance, the other zom heads shuffling with me, all of us focused on the juicy substance in Rage's hand.

"Nuh-uh," Rage jeers, and thrusts the fistful of brain into his mouth. He chews with relish and kicks back Peder as he darts towards the one-eyed doctor. "He's all mine," Rage barks, and swiftly shovels out more of the dead man's brain.

I feel disappointment and start to turn away, looking for a victim of my own. Then my senses click back into place and I shake my head.

"What have you done?" I roar, startling the others. They lose their vacant look.

Rage is smirking. "A growing boy needs his vittles, that's what my gran used to say."

He drops the carcass of Dr. Cerveris and smiles tightly at Reilly, who is back on his feet and staring at Rage with unconcealed terror. "No need to brick it, Reilly. I'm not going to eat you. I've had my fill for the day."

"Why did you kill him?" Cathy groans, staring, nauseated, at the motionless scientist. "He was trying to help us."

"So that he could experiment on us some more?" Rage huffs. "Screw that."

"But you were always their favorite," Tiberius notes. "You did everything they asked. Their golden boy."

"Yeah," Rage says. "And they fell for it." He savagely kicks the

corpse of Dr. Cerveris. "I've hated these bastards since day one. No one locks *me* up like a lab rat and gets away with it. But there was no point hitting out at them when they had the upper hand. So I waited. I had a feeling something like this would happen, that things would break down and an opportunity would present itself. I didn't think it'd be as spectacular as this, but I was sure there'd be a bit of give somewhere along the line."

Rage looks at Reilly and cocks his head. "You still here?"

"I didn't think I was free to go," Reilly says shakily.

"Well, you are." Rage shrugs. "You weren't the worst of them. That doesn't mean I won't kill you if I have to, but at the moment you're not a threat to me, so be a sensible boy and bugger off."

"What about my gun?" Reilly asks.

"Do I look like an idiot?" Rage snorts. "You'd put a bullet through my skull the second I gave it back to you. I'm sure you'll pick up something in one of the ammo rooms. If you make it that far."

Reilly looks at the rest of us for support, but nobody says anything. "Fine," he grunts. "Damn you all too."

He takes off at top speed, desperately searching for something to defend himself with.

I focus on Rage and the gun in his hand. Rage stares back at me, then casts his gaze over the other zom heads. For a moment I think he's going to drop us all. But then he lowers the gun and smiles. "I would say it's been fun and that I'm going to miss you, but I'd be lying through my teeth."

He turns to leave.

"Where are you going?" Cathy cries.

"This way," Rage says, then points in the opposite direction. "If you follow me, I'll kill you, so I'd suggest you go that way."

"What about Danny?" Mark asks. "We haven't rescued him yet."

"Screw him," Rage says.

"You can't go off by yourself," Gokhan protests. "It's dangerous here, innit? We should stick together."

"Stick with you bunch of losers?" Rage laughs. "No way. So long, suckers!"

Then he flips us the finger and is gone.

NINETEEN

We hang around like a bunch of muppets, jaws open, senses reeling, until Tiberius finally stirs. "We've gotta get out of here."

"What about Danny?" Mark asks.

"Do you have any idea where his cell is?" Tiberius replies.

"No."

"Then forget about him."

"Wait a moment." I can't believe what I'm thinking as I stare at the remains of Dr. Cerveris.

"You want to tuck into his brain?" Cathy sneers. "Good luck—I doubt Rage left much."

"It's not that—although now that you mention it..."

Scraps of brain dot the interior of the dead doctor's head. Ignoring my feelings of disgust, I run my fingers around it, then suck them, drawing a small burst of strength from the meager blobs. When the rest of the zom heads see that, they push in and copy me. They all come away with flecks of brain on their fingers, though I got the lion's share of what was left.

When we've scraped Dr. Cerveris's skull completely clean, I return to it, stick a hand into the hole in the doctor's head, then feel around until I find the back of the eye that Rage didn't puncture. I push softly while cutting around the flesh at the front of the socket with my other hand.

"What's she doing?" Cathy squeals. "Has she gone mad?"

"I don't think so," Tiberius mutters. "The sensors... If we want to get out of here, we'll have to get through doors that require fingerprints and a retinal scan."

Dr. Cerveris's eye oozes from its socket. I wipe the goo away, cup it gently in my palm and step back. "I did the eye. Who's gonna cut off one of his hands?"

There's a pause. Then Gokhan bends and starts slicing.

"This is *so* gross," Cathy moans, but her lips are twitching and I can tell she's trying hard not to smile. I feel like chuckling too. It shouldn't be funny, but it is. I'm sure I'll feel awful later when I look back on this, but right now I'm on an unnatural high.

"Nice of him to lend us a hand," Tiberius deadpans, and I almost explode with laughter. I'm not the only one.

"Come on," Mark snaps. He doesn't find this in any way entertaining. "If we're to escape, we'll need to be quick, before they find us."

"Who are *they*, Worm?" Peder snorts.

"The soldiers or the people who attacked." Mark shrugs. "One's as bad as the other, right?"

"What if they're here to free us?" Cathy says. "Maybe it's an army of zom heads come to break us out."

I remember Mr. Dowling and the spiders. "No," I sigh. "I don't know who or what they are, but they haven't come to help us. Mark's right. We need to split ASAP, before we end up like Dr. Cerveris."

I start off in the direction that Rage sent us, not wanting to risk a run-in with him, and after a moment of hesitation the rest of them fall in behind me.

I think about the butchered Dr. Cerveris as we progress, worrying about what happened. It wasn't the fact that Rage killed him that bugs me. It's how I reacted. I was on the verge of losing control. The sight of the brain triggered something inside me, and I almost switched off and went into full-on zombie mode.

I would have eaten anybody's brain right then. If I hadn't recovered my wits by chance, I'd have gone after Reilly. If I'd killed him and feasted, that would have been the end of me. I know that fresh brains are essential for revitalizeds, that I need to eat to hold on to my senses. But if I'd given in to my baser instincts and fed in such a grisly, inhuman fashion, I think I would have regressed anyway, and gladly, all too happy to leave my conscious self behind.

I'm clinging onto my semi-humanity, but only just. It won't be long now. Soon I'll hit a critical point and then it's bye-bye, Becky Smith, *hellooooo*, zom-B!

TWENTY

We flee without any real plan in mind. I ask the others, as we run, if they have an idea of the layout of the complex, if they've seen more of it than I have. They all reply negatively. Mark has been to a lab that the rest of us haven't visited, but it wasn't far from zom HQ.

"I've always assumed we were underground," Tiberius says, "because of the lack of daylight. But that's not necessarily the case. We might simply be in the middle of a huge building."

"No," Peder says. "I once heard a soldier grumbling about being stuck down here. Reilly told him to shut up—I don't think they were supposed to mention anything about where we are—but it was too late."

"Then I guess we need to head for the top," I grunt. "Let's look for stairs."

We push open every door that we pass and peer through every window. In the dark glass of one pane I catch sight of my reflection and pause. There's a small red *z* on my right cheek. I frown, wondering how it got there. Then I recall the clown stroking my face. Shivering, I wipe the mark from my flesh and hurry on.

"Here!" Cathy shouts. She's looking through a round panel of glass in a door. I press up beside her and spot a flight of stairs. I shake the door but it's locked. There's a control panel beside it.

"Time to test our toys," I grin tightly. "Gokhan, you first. They usually press their fingers to the sensor before scanning their eye."

Gokhan holds Dr. Cerveris's fingers up to the panel. There's a small beeping noise. I open my hand and reveal the eye. I roll it in my palm until it's pointing the right way, then rest it in front of the retinal scanner. I have no confidence that it will work now that it's been ripped from its socket, but to my delight there's a second beep and the door slides open.

"Eye, eye!" Tiberius snickers, slipping past me and jogging up the stairs.

It's only a single flight of steps. Seconds later we're on a higher floor, identical to the one below, so we go looking for an exit or the next set of stairs. There are zombies loose on this level too, but they don't interfere with us. They shoot us dark looks and sniff the air

hungrily when they catch our scent, but when they realize we're not walking snack boxes, they leave us be.

We find another set of stairs and climb, this time up three levels. Once again we search for a way out. But after a couple of minutes Mark looks through an open door and does a double take. "What the hell...?" he mutters.

"Worm!" Cathy barks. "This is no time for—"

"Shh!" he snaps, and the look on his face tells us this is serious.

Curious, we crowd around Mark and gape, slack jawed, at the hellish drama unfurling within.

It's a massive room, the largest I've seen in the complex. Judging by the TV sets hanging from the walls, I'm guessing it's a relaxation area, a much grander version of zom HQ.

Quite a lot of the staff are here, shoved up against one of the walls. They're surrounded by snapping, howling zombies. But the living dead are only occasionally attacking. They're being held in check by a team of people in hoodies. The zombie masters have wrinkled flesh, an ugly mass of purple patches and pustulant, peeling skin. They have pale yellow eyes, and if their hoodies slipped I know we'd see crops of unhealthy gray hair. I also know that they have no fingernails and their tongues are scabby and shriveled.

They're the mutants I saw in my school, and before that on a visit to the Imperial War Museum. They were controlling zombies the last time I saw them, and they're in command now too, direct-

342

ing the reviveds with blasts of the whistles that hang on strings from the neck of each mutant.

In the middle of the mutants and zombies is the clown, Mr. Dowling. He towers above the rest of them, which is strange, as I didn't think he was unusually tall when I saw him in my cell. Glancing down, I see that he's on stilts, balanced elegantly.

Mr. Dowling is waving his hands above his head, swaying gently, beaming insanely.

"Come on," one of the mutants croaks at the weeping, moaning humans huddled against the wall. "Sing or we'll set the doggies on you again. *Sing!*"

The other mutants take up the refrain and start to bellow, "Sing! Sing! Sing!"

Mr. Dowling giggles shrilly and twirls his arms like an orchestra conductor. The soldiers, scientists and nurses begin to chant together, having obviously been told what to sing before we hit the scene. They're out of tune, and not all in sync, but the song is unmistakable.

> *"Jingle bells, jingle bells,*
> *Jingle all the way,*
> *Oh what fun it is to ride*
> *In a one-horse open sleigh."*

The mutants screech with delight and clap enthusiastically. Mr. Dowling sighs happily and cups his hands to his heart, then wipes a finger

343

across his cheeks as if to remove tears of joy. A couple of zombies dart forward and drag humans from the crowd. They carve their skulls open and tuck in. The survivors sing another creepy chorus of "Jingle Bells" at the rough prompting of the mutants.

While the doomed humans are singing, Mr. Dowling points at a woman and beckons her forward. She shakes her head, terrified, tears coursing down her cheeks. The clown frowns, then draws a finger across his throat. One of the mutants blows his whistle and a zombie drags the woman out and tears into her.

Mr. Dowling smiles and points to another woman. This one hurries forward, not even waiting for him to beckon. When she's in front of him, his smile widens and he bends over and opens his lips. I expect a stream of spiders to come spilling out, but this time he reaches into his mouth and pulls out a scorpion. It's alive and twisting wildly in his grip.

The clown puts a finger to the woman's lips and taps them. With a gulp, she opens her mouth. He sticks his tongue out, then nods at her to do the same. With a delirious giggle, he lays the scorpion on her tongue, then nods for her to close her mouth. With fresh tears, she obeys his command, then falls away a moment later, coughing and choking.

The mutants cackle and kick the woman. The zombies hiss and a few more dart into the fray and emerge clutching struggling, screaming humans.

Then Mr. Dowling's head turns and he trains his gaze on us. No...not on us...on *me*.

There's no doubt in my mind that he's looking at me specifically. His eyes burn into mine and his lips twitch as if he's just spotted a dear friend. When the mutants see us, they squeal and dart towards us, dragging zombies with them.

Mr. Dowling makes a high whining noise and they stop instantly. As they retreat, he extends a hand towards me, turns it upside down, then slowly crooks his middle finger, beckoning me forward.

"Not even in your sodding dreams!" I scream, then whirl and race away, not caring if the others follow, not worrying about the direction I'm taking, knowing only that I have to get far away from the clown as quickly as possible, before he takes me into his embrace and turns me into something even worse than one of the walking, undead damned.

TWENTY-ONE

I find another set of stairs and surge to the top. The others aren't far behind. We pause and listen closely. There are no footsteps. The mutants don't seem to be chasing us.

I double over and make a sighing sound. I feel like I should be panting, but of course I can't, since my lungs don't work properly.

"Who the hell was that guy in the clown outfit?" Cathy moans.

"And those freaks in the hoodies," Peder exclaims. "Were they zombies? Humans? What?"

"I don't think they're either," I tell him. "They're mutants. They were there when my school was invaded. It looks like they work for Mr. Dowling—the clown—but I've no idea what he is, or why they're here, or why the zombies obey them, or…" I shake my head and scowl. "They don't matter. We need to get out of here. We can wonder about it later."

"But what if they come after us?" Cathy whimpers.

"All the more reason to get a move on," Tiberius grunts, and off we set again.

Time seems to slow as we search for another set of stairs. We can't find any, and the longer we go on, the more our spirits dip. We're all in rough shape. The bits of brain we sucked from Dr. Cerveris's head didn't do much for us. The shooting pains are coming regularly now and I know the others are feeling them too by the way they wince and twitch every few minutes. My thoughts are starting to swim. It's getting harder to focus.

"I think we've come the wrong way," Gokhan mutters. "Just because we're underground, it don't mean the exit has to be at the top, eh? Maybe it's at the bottom, a tunnel that leads to an elevator or something."

Peder frowns. "But if we head down and don't find it, what then?"

"We come back up," Gokhan says.

"That means slipping past the clown and his mutants a couple of times," Peder growls. "I don't fancy that."

"Maybe we don't have to," Cathy says. "There must be other flights of stairs. We've been taking the first set that we've found on every floor. Let's go down a level and—"

"Wait," Mark mutters, looking at the ceiling. "Did any of you have attic stairs at home, the sort that rest inside the attic when you're not using them?"

"What sort of a question is that?" Cathy sneers.

"My parents put in a set a few years ago," Mark says stiffly, ignoring her. "If you have steps like that, you use a thin pole to open the door, which is part of the stairs. In our home, the hole you stuck the tip of the pole into looked just like that one up there."

I squint and spot the small opening that he's talking about. "So there's an attic. So what?"

"Why would they have an attic in an underground building?" Mark asks softly.

I stare harder at the hole. "You think it's something else?"

"It has to be." He shrugs. "I mean, it might just be a machine room or housing for an air-conditioning unit. But wouldn't they have signs up if that was the case, like they have elsewhere?"

"I haven't noticed any signs," Peder grunts.

"Then you haven't been paying as much attention as me," Mark says smugly, then starts looking for a pole. We search too and a minute later we find one in a nearby room, tucked away in a corner.

I try to unlock the attic door but my hands are trembling and I can't guide in the narrow tip. Peder and Tiberius try too, but both fail, their hands shaking as badly as mine.

"Give it to me," Mark snaps, losing patience, and slots it in at the first attempt. His hands are remarkably steady. He doesn't seem to be suffering like the rest of us. Maybe the doctors slipped him some nutrients on the sly when they were operating on him.

A set of steps drops smoothly as the door opens. I feel a stab of excitement. But before I can head up, Cathy pushes me aside and I stumble and fall over. "Ladies first," she chuckles.

I scowl as she trots up, Peder, Gokhan and Tiberius just behind her. Mark helps me to my feet. "Are you okay?" he asks.

"Sure. But I'm gonna give her a thumping when this is—"

Two soldiers and a female scientist spill into the corridor. The scientist is babbling, "...right here. The pole's in a room. Once we open the door, we can..." She spots Mark and me and curses.

One of the soldiers has a gun. He aims quickly and fires. A bullet rips by my head but misses.

"Up the steps!" I roar at Mark.

The soldier fires again, three times. One of the bullets strikes Mark's left arm and blood sprays from it. He cries out and whirls away from the stairs. I duck as the soldier fires again, grab Mark and hurl him at the steps. He scrambles up them. I'm about to start after him, then pause, pick up the pole and throw it up into the space ahead of me.

A bullet hits the flesh on my back where my heart used to be. If I was whole, it would open up a nasty wound. But because I'm more hole than whole in that part of my body, it only nicks a flap of skin and shoots on through the cavity and out the other side.

I hurry after Mark and pull the steps up behind me, locking them into place. The humans scream beneath us and the soldier fires a stream of bullets into the ceiling, either trying to hit us or smash the lock. I don't hang around to find out. Pushing Mark ahead of me, I scurry after the others.

We're in a corridor, not an attic, lit dimly by soft red lights. The dimness is a relief after the brightness of the complex. I hadn't realized how much the glare of the lights hurt.

We shuffle along, nobody saying anything. The corridor angles upwards, then turns back on itself and keeps rising. The noises of the complex fade the farther on we push. I feel real hope for the first time. The nurse was leading the soldiers to this place and seemed desperate to reach it. Because it's a way out? Not the main exit, but a secret escape route for those of a certain rank?

The corridor snakes around several times before the floor levels out and we step through into a large, square room. There are doorways in the middle of all four walls. Two are open, like ours, leading to corridors like the one we've stepped out of. A metal door stands in the fourth. It's like no other door that we've seen in the complex, taller, wider, more impressive.

"That must be it!" Peder whoops, racing towards the door.

"The exit!" Cathy gasps, then spins towards me. "Do you still have the eye? You didn't drop it, did you? Tell me you didn't—"

I hold up my hand and widen my fingers, letting her see the eye.

"Yes!" she shouts.

I grin and push past, giving her a sharp dig with my elbow to pay her back for pushing me aside earlier. Cathy doesn't care. She only has eyes for the door.

Gokhan presses Dr. Cerveris's fingers to the panel and it beeps. Tiberius and Peder shut their mouths as if to hold their breath, both forgetting that they can't actually breathe.

I step forward and hold up the eye. A camera scans it. There's an agonizing pause in which I convince myself that it isn't going to work, that I've shaken the eye around too much, dislodged something vital inside. Then...

Beep.

Everyone cheers as if I'd just scored the winning goal in a cup final.

The cheers stop when the system beeps again and a touch-screen calculator flashes up on the panel where Gokhan scanned in the dead doctor's fingerprints. There's a short message just below it.

Please enter six-digit authorization code.

We stare at the message, then at each other.

I clear my throat. "This is where someone says that they're a hacker and they can crack this bastard in five minutes flat."

Nobody says a word.

"Damn," I sigh, sinking to my haunches. "In that case I guess we just rot here and turn into rabid, brain-munching reviveds."

TWENTY-TWO

Tiberius starts keying in random numbers. Every time he completes a string of six figures, the screen beeps and clears itself, prompting him to try again.

"It's pointless," Mark says glumly. "There's no way you're going to key in the exact six numbers by accident."

"Shut up," Tiberius snarls, staying focused on the screen. "Maybe it's a simple code, six zeros or nines, just to stop any zombies from getting through."

Mark makes a face but says nothing. He sits beside me and tugs at the material around the wound left by the bullet. Blood is oozing out of the hole. The smell of it tickles my nostrils, and for some reason I find myself licking my lips.

I look more closely and realize Mark's

blood is different than mine. It's not congealed. It doesn't stop flowing within a couple of seconds. It's red and pure, just like...

"What's that smell?" Gokhan asks, crinkling his nose.

"Me," I say too loudly, lurching to my feet and tugging at the flesh around the hole where my heart should be. "I was shot. I'm bleeding. It'll pass in a—"

"No," Gokhan silences me. "This is different, innit? It smells like human blood. But it can't be. We're alone. Where's it coming from, eh?"

The others are sniffing the air too, even Tiberius, who isn't looking at the screen anymore. I try to think of a way to distract them before they make the same logical leap that I have. Before I can, Peder shushes everyone.

"Quiet," he snaps. "I can hear something."

"Don't be stupid," I tell him. "You're imagining things. It's just—"

"Shut the hell up!" he roars, then squints suspiciously. "That noise...it's like a drumbeat, only softer...."

It's silent in this room. Not like anywhere else in the complex, where there was always the rumbling thunder of machinery to contend with. You wouldn't hear a pin drop, but you can hear a lot of soft sounds that were masked in zom HQ and the corridors, especially if your ears are as sharp as ours. Noises like a gentle burp, a soft sneeze, someone's stomach rumbling.

Or a heartbeat.

The zom heads start to turn, nostrils flaring, eyes glassy, ears cocked, locking in on the source of the smell and noise. I shuffle my feet to distract them and start to tell them again that they're imagining things, terrified of what will happen when they figure it out.

"There!" Cathy yells, leaping across the room. I try to stop her but she bowls me aside, the excitement of the discovery lending her an extra burst of strength. Mark gapes at her as she shoves him back against the wall.

"What the hell are you doing?" he roars as she hooks her finger bones into the bandages around his chest and stomach, the fabric of his clothes, the padded vest beneath. I scramble after her but Peder grabs the back of my neck and forces me down. His eyes are bright and he's staring fixedly at Cathy.

"Leave me alone," Mark yelps, struggling feebly. "Get off of me, you nutcase. You'll expose my burns."

Cathy ignores him and keeps on ripping. Tiberius starts to close in, eyes like a shark's, lips pulling back over his teeth, fingers opening and closing.

"Please!" Mark shrieks, starting to panic now. "The doctors said I'd fall apart if I didn't stay wrapped up. Please, Cathy, don't do this. Please!"

Cathy ignores him and slices through the last of the covering. Mark clutches for the bandages as they fall away and reveal his flesh. Then he catches sight of himself and stops, frowning, one step behind everybody else.

"I don't understand," he whispers, poking at his stomach with a gloved finger. His skin is pale from being under wraps for so long, but there are no burn marks. His flesh is pure.

"Your gloves," Peder says in a choked voice, pushing himself off me, transfixed by the sight of Mark's flesh. "Take them off."

Mark frowns, then tugs at the glove covering his left hand. It doesn't detach. As he continues pulling at it, Cathy loses patience, takes hold and rips it away. Mark shouts with pain, then stares with shock. There are bits of metal attached to the ends of his fingers.

"What's happening?" Mark croaks. "I don't understand."

But this time it's a lie. The tumblers have clicked for him at last. Even without the exposed flesh, the fake finger bones, the rise and fall of his stomach as he breathes, the soft sound of his heart as it beats, he could tell by the fixed, frenzied looks in the eyes of the zom heads around him.

"Mark's alive," Cathy whispers.

Then licks her lips.

Hungry.

TWENTY-THREE

"No," Mark wheezes. "This can't be right. I'm a zom head. I was attacked. I was killed. There's been a mistake."

The zombies—and that's what they are now, all human semblance discarded—don't reply. They're shuffling closer, eyes steady, ready to feed.

"Get back," I snarl, leaping to my feet and pushing Cathy away. I step between Mark and the others. "You're not going to do this. I'm hungry too. I can smell him just like you can, and it's driving me wild. But I won't harm him and I won't let you lot either. You have to control yourselves. This is *Mark*."

"*Worm*," Cathy gurgles, grinning crookedly. "Wriggle, little worm."

"No!" I roar, slamming my hands together, trying to startle them back to their senses. "Stop. Think. Don't give in to the hunger. Peder. Gokhan. Tiberius." I turn pleadingly to the ginger-haired teenager. "You stood by my side. You fought for my life. Do the same for Mark. You have to. He's one of us." A memory clicks in. *"We accept him! Gooble gobble!"*

Tiberius pauses and his eyes clear slightly.

"It must have been an experiment," I babble. "They wanted to see if they could hide a human among us. They told him he was a zombie. They covered him up so that we couldn't smell him, hear his heartbeat or see him breathing. They must have given him drugs to keep his eyes open, dry out his mouth, stop him from sweating, make him look like he was a revitalized."

"But he's not," Peder growls. "He's human."

"I didn't know," Mark wails. "I thought…they told me…I never even guessed! B, you've got to stop them. Don't let them eat me. Please, B, I want to live, I don't want to−"

"Shh. I'm trying." I concentrate on Tiberius, hoping that if I can reach him, he can help me get through to the rest of them. "All right, he's not a proper zom head, but he's still one of us. He's been living alongside you guys for months. You can't turn on him as if he doesn't mean anything to you."

"Worm," Cathy leers again, reaching out for the trembling boy.

I slap her hands away. "I know you don't respect him, you bully him, you treat him like a worm. But he's still part of the gang. You

360

won't attack one of your own. You're not monsters. It's the hunger. You have to fight it. You—"

Gokhan smashes a fist into my jaw and I stagger sideways. Mark shrieks and the sound excites them. They press forward. Before they can target him, I'm back between them, punching and kicking, screaming abusively. I'm not going to accept this. I let Tyler Bayor die. I won't let it happen to Mark too.

"Stop!" I yell. "You don't know what you're doing!"

Peder grabs the neck of my T-shirt and pulls me in close. His eyes flash as he grins at me. "Yes we do," he hisses.

"Tiberius!" I bellow. "Help me! We have to fight together! You have to—"

Tiberius puts a finger to my lips and says, "Hush now." Then he grabs me from Peder and throws me aside.

Mark screams. "No! God! Help!"

But not even God can help him now.

The zombies fall on the boy. They dig their fingers into his skull and tear it open. Ram claws into his brain and scoop it out. They ignore his screams, his whimpers, his pleas, the feeble thrashing of his arms and legs.

And all I can do as the beasts feast and Mark dies wretchedly before my eyes, calling my name, begging for mercy, is beat the floor uselessly with my fists and howl insanely at the cruel injustices of this monstrous, twisted world.

TWENTY-FOUR

"What have you done?"

I'm backed up against the wall close to the sealed door. My finger bones are digging into the concrete, tearing at the plaster. I stare with shock and disgust at the zom heads as they squat close to Mark's remains, licking their fingers clean, dipping them back inside his emptied skull in search of any last tidbits. They look happy, sated, *full*. They pay no attention to me. Like junkies after a fix. Spaced out. In a world of their own. A world of murder, cannibalism and sweet, sweet brains.

"Oh, God, what have you sick bastards *done?*" I moan, shaking my head, trying to close my eyes to the nightmare, praying for tears that will never come.

Tiberius glances at me and frowns. He

gazes at Mark, then at his fingers. For a moment he looks like himself and he cringes. A look of regret and terror flickers across his face. Then his jaw tightens and I see him turn away from remorse. He gives himself over to the pleasure of the feed and zones out again.

Cathy is giggling. She pokes out one of Mark's eyes, the way I poked out Dr. Cerveris's earlier, and plays with it. She puts it in her mouth, sucks on it a while, then spits it up into the air and tries to catch it with her tongue as it drops. She misses. It hits her chin and bounces away. She giggles again.

Peder and Gokhan are still fishing for scraps of brain. Gokhan is muttering, "Innit. Innit. Innit." Peder nudges him aside, crouches over Mark like a dog and sticks his face into the cavity of the dead boy's head to lick out any last morsels.

"You're monsters," I sob. But they're not really. They're just hungry creatures who fed when prey was presented to them. I identify with the zom heads too closely to condemn them completely. I had to fight hard not to turn on Mark. If it had been five minutes later, or ten or thirty or however long I have left before my senses crumble, I would have joined in.

I could be harsh and say that they haven't regressed, they're still revitalizeds, they had a choice. But who am I to judge? I was able to fight temptation because I can naturally hold out longer or because I ate slightly more of Dr. Cerveris's brain than they did. Maybe they weren't able to resist the way I was.

Either way, I'm sure they'll feel guilty later, once the feeding frenzy passes and they recover their wits. They'll probably spend the rest of their conscious days regretting the way they gave in to their base instincts. That won't do poor Mark any good, but at least they'll suffer. I think they'll probably envy me once I lose my grip and regress. The only way they're ever going to escape the awful memory of their crime is by shedding their humanity entirely and becoming dumb reviveds again.

As I pause between moans, I hear a noise in one of the corridors. Footsteps. I tear my gaze away from the vile spectacle and watch sluggishly as Josh Massoglia enters the room, a small team of soldiers spreading out to flank him.

Two of the soldiers are carrying flamethrowers.

The zom heads pay no attention to the soldiers. Mark's brain was enough for them. They don't need any more at the moment. They don't even react when the pair with flamethrowers takes aim.

"Wait," Josh says. He's staring at me. My fingers are still scratching the wall. My head is shaking softly.

Josh crosses the room and stops in front of me. He looks at my fingers, my lips, then into my eyes. His right hand comes up slowly and stretches out towards the calculator on the screen. He keys in six numbers and it makes a beeping sound.

The door slides open.

Josh steps away from me and lowers his hand. He doesn't say anything. My fingers fall still. My head turns towards the open door. Bewildered, I look to Josh for confirmation, but he doesn't give me any signs.

I peel myself away from the wall and stumble through the doorway, into a corridor that rises like the one I was in before. I feel as if I'm in a dream, but I can't be. The dead don't sleep, so the dead can't dream.

The door starts to slide shut behind me. I step to the side, looking for Josh one last time, searching for answers. But all I see is a sudden blossoming of red and yellow flames.

There are agonized screams, the voices of four teenagers blending into one as the zom heads pay the ultimate price for turning on Mark. The stench of burning flesh, flames consuming all, both the monsters and their victim.

Then the door clicks shut and there's nothing.

Only me.

My cheeks are dry but I wipe a hand across them anyway, brushing away nonexistent tears. Then I turn and stagger up the corridor. I expect it to twist back on itself like the other one did, but this just keeps rising until it levels out into a tiny room. There's a plain wooden door in one of the walls, no scanners, locks or anything. I can smell the outside world, a rich, pungent, overwhelming scent after the clinical, carefully maintained atmosphere of the complex.

With a moan born more of confused dread than delight, I shuffle forward, push open the door, leave the nightmarish gloom of the underground behind me and step out into sunlight.

To be continued...

BOOK 3:

ZOM-B

CITY

ONE

The sunlight is blinding to my undead, sensitive eyes. I try to shut my eyelids, forgetting for a moment that they stopped working when I was killed. Grimacing, I turn my head to the side and cover my eyes with an arm. I stumble away from the open door and the nightmare of the underground complex, no idea where I am or where I'm going, just wanting to escape from the madness, the killing and the flames.

After several steps, my knee strikes something hard and I fall over. Groaning, I push myself up and lower my arm slightly, forcing my eyes to focus. For a while the world is a ball of lightning-sharp whiteness. Then, as my pupils slowly adjust, objects materialize through the haze. I ignore the pain and turn slowly to assess my surroundings.

I'm in a scrapyard. Old cars are piled on top of one another, three high in some places. Ancient washing machines, fridges, TVs and microwave ovens are strewn around. Many of the appliances have been gutted for spare parts.

A few concrete buildings dot the landscape, each the size of a small shed. I came out through one of them. I guess that the others also house secret entrances to the underground complex.

I pick my way through the mess of the scrapyard, steering clear of the concrete sheds, ready to run if any soldiers appear. I still don't know why I was allowed to leave when the others were killed. Maybe Josh felt sorry for me. Or maybe this is part of a game and I'm going to be hauled back in just when I think that freedom is mine for the taking.

A stabbing pain lances my stomach. I wheeze and bend over, waiting for it to pass. The ground swims in front of my eyes. I think that I'm about to lose consciousness and become a full-on zombie, a brain-dead revived. Then my vision clears and the pain passes. But I know it's only a short respite. If I don't eat some brains soon, I'm finished.

I search for an exit but this place is a maze. I can't walk in a straight line because it's full of twisting alleys and dead ends. It feels like I'm circling aimlessly, trapped in a web of broken-down appliances.

I lose patience and climb a tower of cars. On the roof of the uppermost car I steady myself then take a look around, shielding my eyes with a hand. Exposed to the sunlight, my flesh starts itching wherever it isn't covered, my arms, my neck, my face, my scalp, my bare feet. I grit my teeth against the irritation and keep looking.

The scrapyard feels like a cemetery, as if no one has been through it in years. I came out of one of the secondary exits. The main entrance must be housed elsewhere, maybe in a completely different yard or building. I'm glad of that. I don't want to run into Mr. Dowling or any of his mutants as they're trotting back to wherever it is they came from.

The yard is ringed by a tall wire fence. I spot a gate off to my left, not too far away, maybe fifty feet as the crow flies. I start to climb down, to try to find a path, then pause. One of the concrete sheds is close by and there are a few piles of cars between that and the fence. If I leap across, I can get to the gate in less than a minute.

I gauge the distance to the shed. It's leapable, but only just. If I don't make it, the ground is littered with all sorts of sharp, jagged castoffs that could cut me up nastily, even…

I grin weakly. I was going to say, *even kill me*. But I'm dead already. It's easy to forget when I'm walking around, thinking the way I always did. But I'm a corpse. No heart—that was ripped out of my chest—and no other properly functioning organs except for my brain, which for some reason keeps ticking over. If I misjudge my jump and a pole pierces my stomach and drives through my lungs, what of it? I'll just work myself free and carry on my merry way. It will hurt, sure, but it's nothing to be scared of.

I back up, spread my arms for balance, then race forward and jump. I expect to come up short, or to just make the edge of the roof. But to my shock I overshoot it by ten or twelve feet and come crashing back to earth with a startled shriek. My fall is broken by a stack of dishwashers, which scatter and shatter beneath the weight of my body.

Cursing, I pick myself up and glare at the shed. I didn't do much leaping around when I was captive underground. It seems the muscles in my legs are stronger than they were in life. I think I might have just broken the women's long-jump record. B Smith— Olympic athlete!

I climb onto the roof of the shed and jump to the next set of cars, putting less effort into the leap this time. I still sail over my target, but only by a yard. The next time I judge it right and land on top of an old Datsun, a short hop away from the gate.

I stare around uneasily before getting down. I'm expecting soldiers to spill out of the sheds, guns blazing. But I appear to be all alone in the yard.

At the gate I pause again. It's a simple wire gate and it isn't locked. But maybe it's electrified. I stick out a wary hand and nudge the wire with one of the bones jutting out of my fingertips. The gate swings open a crack. Nothing else happens.

One last glance over my shoulder. Then I shrug.

"Sod it," I mutter, and let myself out, slipping from the scrapyard into the silent, solemn city beyond.

TWO

The area outside the scrapyard is deserted. Old boarded-up houses, derelict for years. Faded signs over stores or factories that closed for business long before I was born. The only thing that looks halfway recent is the graffiti, but there's not even much of that, despite the fact that this place boasts all the blank walls a graffiti artist could dream of. It feels like a dead zone, an area that nobody lived in or visited anytime in living memory.

I stagger along a narrow, gloomy street, seeking the shade at the side. The worst of the itching dies away once I get out of the sunlight. My eyes stop stinging too. The irritation's still there but it's bearable now.

Halfway up the street, the stabbing pain in my stomach comes again and I fall to my knees, dry heaving, whining like a dying dog. I bare my unnaturally long, sharp teeth and thump the side of my head with my hand, trying to knock my senses back into place.

The pain increases and I roll over. I bang into a wall and punch it hard, tearing the skin on my knuckles. That would have brought tears to my eyes if all my tear ducts hadn't dried up when I died.

My back arches and my mouth widens. I stare at the sky with horror, thinking I'll never look at it again this way, as a person capable of thought. In another few seconds I'll be a brainless zombie, a shadow of a girl, lost to the world forever.

But to my relief the pain passes and again I'm able to force myself to my feet, mind intact. I chuckle weakly at my lucky escape. But even as I'm chuckling, I know I must have used up all nine of my lives by this stage. I can't survive another dizzying attack like that. I'm nearing the end. Even the dead have their limits.

I stumble forward, reeling like a drunk. My legs don't want to support me and I almost go down, but I manage to keep my balance. Coming to the end of the street, I grab a lamppost and swing out into a road.

Several cars are parked along the pavement and a few have been stranded in the middle of the road. One has overturned. The windows are all smashed in and bones line the asphalt around it.

The sun is blinding again now that I've left the gloom. I hurry to the nearest car in search of shelter. When I get there, I find two people lying on the backseat. Both boast a series of bite marks and scratches, each one of which is lined with a light green moss.

The zombies raise their heads and growl warningly. This is their turf and they don't want to share it with me. Fair enough. I don't really want to bed down with them either.

I lurch to the next car but that's occupied too, this time by a fat zombie who is missing his jaw—it was either ripped off when he was killed, or torn from him later. He looks comical and creepy at the same time.

The third car is empty and I start to crawl in out of the light, to rest in the shade and wait for my senses to crumble. For all intents and purposes, this car will serve as my tomb, the place where B Smith gave up the ghost and became a true member of the walking dead.

But just as I'm bidding farewell to the world of the conscious, my nostrils twitch. Pausing, I pull back and sniff the air. My taste buds haven't been worth a damn since I returned to life, but my sense of smell is stronger than ever. I've caught a whiff of something familiar, something that I was eating for a long time underground without knowing what it was.

Three cars farther down the road is a Skoda, the source of the tantalizing scent. As weary as I am and as agonizing as it is, I force myself on, focusing on the Skoda and the sweet, sweet smell.

My legs give out before I get to the car, but I don't let that stop me. Digging my finger bones into the asphalt, I drag myself along, crawling on my belly like a worm, baking in the sun, half-blind, itching like mad, brain shutting down. Every part of me wants to give up and die, but the scent lures me on, and soon I'm hauling myself into the Skoda through the front passenger door.

The driver is still held in place by her seat belt, but is lying slumped sideways. Most of her flesh has been torn from her bones, and her head has been split open, her brains scooped out and gobbled up by the zombies who caught her as she was trying to flee. She's not entirely fresh but she's not rotting either. She must have been killed quite recently.

I should feel sympathy for the woman and curiosity about how she survived this long and where she was headed when she was attacked. But right now all I'm concerned about is that those who fed on her didn't scrape her dry. Bits of brain have been left behind. Slivers are stuck to her scalp and meatier chunks rest inside the hollow of her skull.

Like a monstrous baby taking to the teat, I latch on to the shattered bones and suck tendrils of brain from them. I run my tongue the whole way round the rim, not caring about the fact that it's disgusting, that I'm behaving like an animal. In fact I'm ecstatic, getting an unbelievable buzz from the gray scraps, feeling myself strengthen as I suck, knowing I can keep the senseless beast inside me at bay for a while longer.

When I've sucked the bones dry, I pull back a touch, wipe my lips, then steel myself for what I have to do next. "For what I am about to receive..." I mutter, trying to make a sick joke out of the even sicker deed.

Then I stick my fingers into the dead woman's head, scoop out every bit of brain that I can find, and stuff myself like a cannibal at Christmas.

THREE

Once I'm done dining, I lean out of the car and force myself to vomit. If I keep food inside my system, it will rot and attract insects. I've no wish to become a sanctuary for London's creepy crawlies.

I pull back inside and shelter from the sunlight as best I can, staring glumly at the ceiling of the car, thinking about the underground complex, Rage killing Dr. Cerveris and leaving us to our own devices, poor Mark being eaten, the zom heads being burned alive. What a horrible, pointless mess, the whole bloody lot of it.

The road outside is deserted. Nobody moves. The zombies are lying low, hiding from the sun like me.

I'm itching all over. I scratch gently, careful not to slice through my skin with the bones sticking out of my fingers. I catch sight of my injured knuckles and peel some of the ruined flesh away from them. The damage isn't bad but I'm probably stuck with the wound for life. (Or whatever passes for life these days.) The hole in my chest where my heart was ripped out hasn't healed fully, so I don't think this will either. I'm dead. Your body doesn't regenerate when you're a zombie.

Still, I won't have to bear the open scars too much longer. Normal zombies can live as long as an ordinary person. Those of us who recover our senses aren't so lucky. Dr. Cerveris told me that the brains of revitalizeds start to decompose once they fire up again. I've got a year, maybe eighteen months, then I'm toast.

The day passes slowly. I think about the past, where Mum and Dad might be now, if they're alive, dead or wandering the streets of London as zombies. I recall the attack on my school. I wonder about the freaky clown and his mutants, why they tore through the compound, slaughtering all in sight, but freeing the zombies.

I wish I could sleep and kill some time that way, but the dead can't snooze. We're denied almost all of the pleasures of the flesh. The only thing we can still enjoy is food—as long as it's brains.

"You had it easy," I tell the corpse on the front seat, moving into the back as the sun swings round. "A couple of minutes of terror and pain, then it was all over. You probably didn't think you were one of the lucky ones as your skull was being clawed open, but trust me, you were."

The woman doesn't respond, but I go on speaking to her anyway, telling her my story, my thoughts, my regrets, my fears. It's the first time I've talked about my feelings since I recovered consciousness. There was nobody in the compound I could confide in. Mark was the closest I had to a friend, but I couldn't trust him completely. For all I knew he was working for the doctors, a plant. And in fact he was, only he didn't know about it until it was too late.

The dead are the best listeners in the world. The corpse takes it all in, never interrupts, doesn't criticize me, lets me waffle on for as long as I like.

Finally the sun dips and night falls on London. I feel nervous as I slide out of the car. I've no idea what to expect. The soldiers and scientists told me nothing about the outside world. I don't know how much damage the zombies caused when they went wild, or if the living managed to suppress them. By what I've seen on this road—the lack of activity, the silence, the zombies sheltering in deserted cars—I assume the worst. But I won't know for sure until I explore some more.

The other zombies come out as I do, free to move around without irritation now that the sun has set. They don't shuffle like movie zombies—they walk almost as freely as when they were alive—but you couldn't mistake them for the living. Their eyes are glassed over, bones stick out of their fingers and toes, their teeth are too big for their mouths, they sniff the air like dogs.

The fat guy I saw earlier gets a whiff of me and moves in closer, head twitching as he sniffs and listens. I let him come as close as he likes, curious to see what he'll do, if he can tell that I'm different from him.

Something must register inside his chaotic mess of a brain, telling him I'm not entirely the same, because he circles me warily, studying me with his cold, dead eyes.

"Take it easy, boss," I grunt, pulling up my T-shirt to reveal the hole in my chest. "I'm one of you, honest I am."

The zombie growls when he hears me talking, then frowns when he spots the hole where my heart once rested. He peers into it for ages, as if he thinks it might be a trick. Then he turns away and goes looking for dinner elsewhere.

"We accept you, gooble-gobble..." I murmur, remembering something Tiberius used to say. Then I press on, leaving my temporary shelter behind, to find out if London truly has become a city of the dead.

FOUR

The streets are mostly deserted and the only people I glimpse are zombies. They seem to be drifting aimlessly, sniffing the air, looking for living humans to feed on. Many groan or whine, scratching at their stomachs or heads, suffering hunger pangs. Some have accidentally clawed through to their guts or poked an eye out. They're pitiful beasts in this sorry state. They'd be better off properly dead, no doubt about it.

Lots of zombies stop me as I draw close. They can tell I'm not exactly the same as them, maybe by my scent or the way I move. In almost every case, their face lights up with excitement, then creases with doubt, then returns to blankness once they realize I'm dead like they are.

The reviveds become a nuisance after

a while. If I try to push on without stopping to be examined, they get angry and snap at me. I'm pretty sure I could take any one of them in a fight – it shouldn't be too difficult to outwit a brain-dead zombie – but I don't want to spend the whole night wrestling with the undead. It's easier to stand still, let them give me the once-over, then move on when they lose interest.

To clarify my situation, I rip a hole in my T-shirt to expose the left half of my chest. That speeds things up a bit, but some still stop me to make absolutely sure I'm not one of the living. With all the interruptions, I make little headway. It's been about a couple of hours since I left the car, but I haven't gone far.

I spot a newsstand and let myself in. It's dusty. Shelves have been knocked down, broken bottles litter the floor, the glass of the refrigerated section has been shattered. There are a few newspapers on the counter, all dated the day of the zombie attacks, the world's last normal day. The cash register is open, notes lying undisturbed inside it. I guess money doesn't matter much anymore.

The electricity is off but I can see fairly clearly. My eyes work well in the dark, better than they do in strong light.

I find a large *A to Z* guidebook and take it outside. I look for a street sign, then do a quick check in the book. I'm in the East End. I don't know this area well, but I'm not far from more familiar territory. It's probably pointless, but with nowhere else to head for, I figure I might as well go home. I doubt I'll find anyone there, but at least I'll be in more comforting surroundings.

I replace the *A to Z* with a smaller map and stick it in the back of my jeans. Then I set off in a slight northwest direction, picking my way through the streets, stopping whenever I'm challenged by one of the roaming dead.

I endure the stop-start process for another hour before I get sick of it. It'll take forever if I keep going like this. There has to be a better way and I think I know what it is. I could try a motorbike or car, of course, but I never learned to drive, and anyway, the roads are cluttered with crashed vehicles.

I find a street packed with shops and go on a scouting mission. First I slip into a drugstore and hunt for eyedrops. My eyes don't produce tears now, so I need to keep moistening them or they'll dry out and my vision will worsen. Once I've doused them, I load a bag with several bottles and look around, wondering if I need anything else. I think about bandaging over the hole in my chest, but it's not a medical necessity—apart from the green moss, I haven't seen any signs of infection—and besides, the open hole makes it easier for the walking dead to identify me as one of their own.

I move on and spot a hardware store. I spend a bit longer in this shop, testing a variety of tools, looking for weapons in case I have to fight at any point. The zombies haven't bothered me so far, but I can't rely on them leaving me alone forever. I know from the tests underground that they'll attack revitalizeds if they feel threatened. I don't plan on antagonizing anyone, but sometimes things can get out of control. Better to be safe than sorry.

I settle on a hammer, a couple of screwdrivers and a chisel. Light, easy to carry and use, effective. I spend a long time among the drills, playing around with them, wincing at the shriek they make – my sense of hearing is much better than it was when I was alive – but loving their sheer ferocity. It would be cool to become a drill-packing zombie, but the bulky machines aren't practical, so in the end, reluctantly, I leave them behind.

A file, on the other hand, is vital, and I spend even longer testing out the goods in that section. My teeth are constantly growing and need to be filed back every day or two. Otherwise they'll fill my mouth and I won't be able to speak. When I find a file that does the job, I give all of my teeth a thorough going-over, then stick it in my bag, along with replacements, and mosey on.

Next up, a large department store. Zombies are patrolling the aisles, checking behind clothing racks, looking for any juicy humans they might have missed. They keep mistaking mannequins for living people. They jump on them, growling and howling, then realize their mistake and trudge away sullenly. I get a good laugh out of that, but lose interest after the seventh or eighth time and carry on.

I browse the racks, looking for clean jeans, a new T-shirt and a long-sleeved, heavy sweatshirt. I tear a hole through the sweatshirt and T-shirt to show the cavity in my chest, then pick up gloves and a nice leather jacket, one of the most expensive in the store. I dress in the middle of the shop, not bothering with the changing rooms.

The zombies don't take any notice of me as I strip down. They're not interested in nudity, only brains.

I try on shoes once I'm comfortable in the clothes, but can't easily slip them on because of the bones poking out of my toes. Finally I grab a few pairs of socks and jam them over my feet, letting the bones stick out through the ends.

A good hat is the next item on my shopping list. I don't find anything that I like in the women's section, so I head to the men's department and spot an Australian cork hat. Once I've pulled off the corks and string, it's perfect—with its wide brim, it will shade my face and neck.

"G'day, mate," I drawl in a terrible Australian accent, studying myself in a mirror. "Looking good, sport." I try to wink at my reflection, forgetting again that my eyelids don't work. I scowl, then laugh at my foolishness. "No worries!"

I make my final stop by one of the sales desks, where sunglasses lie scattered across the floor. I root through and find a few that fit me and that I don't mind the look of. When I'm happy with my choices, I put three pairs in my bag and clip the other pair onto the neck of my sweatshirt.

All sorted, I grab some magazines, return to the windows at the front of the store and lie down. I spend the rest of the night reading about showbiz stars who will never glitter again now that the world has gone to hell, glancing up every so often to watch the occasional zombie prowl past outside.

When dawn breaks and the streets clear, I get up, toss the magazines aside, slip on my glasses and hat, pull on my gloves and step out into the brightening day. My eyes tighten behind the shades but gradually adjust. They're not as sharp as they were in the darkness, but protected by the dark glasses, I can see okay.

I move into the middle of the road and stand bathed by the rays of the sun, to test whether or not they irritate me through the covering of my clothes. They do to an extent, and the itching starts again, but it's nowhere near as bad as it was. I can live with it, so to speak.

"Right," I snap. "The day is mine."

And off I set through the empty streets, claiming them as my own. B Smith—queen of the city!

FIVE

In all honesty, it's not much of a city to be queen of. I used to think that London was one of the most exciting places in the world, always buzzing, always something going on. Now it's like walking through the world's biggest graveyard, and an ugly, messy one at that.

The battle between the living and the dead must have been apocalyptic. There are signs of chaos everywhere, broken windows, crashed cars, corpses left to rot outdoors. Many houses and shops are burnt out and fires still smolder in some of them. In other places pipes have burst and streets are flooded.

There are bloodstains everywhere and lots of dried pools of vomit. The reviveds might not be as mentally clued-in as I am, but it looks like they figured out the vomiting part easily enough. I guess even the mostly senseless dead get a shiver at the notion of playing host to a brood of worms, maggots and the like.

The stench isn't as bad as I thought it would be, but it's fairly gross all the same, especially since my nose is more sensitive than it once was.

Birds, rats and insects are feasting on the vomit, blood and rotting flesh. They're enjoying the run of the city now that the zombies have withdrawn for the day. The more alert creatures scatter as soon as they spot me, the birds taking to the air, the rats vanishing down the nearest hole. Only the insects ignore me and go about their business uninterrupted.

The electricity supply varies from street to street. In some it's been cut off and every house is dead. In others it's as strong as ever, lights are on, static crackles from radios, TV sets flicker in shop windows. I consider checking the channels, to find out if anyone is alive and broadcasting, but I can do that later. I want to continue exploring on foot first, not waste the tranquility of the daylight. I can channel surf tonight when the zombies come out in force and I hole up.

I come to a butcher's shop, pause and stick my head inside. Slabs of dried-out meat lie rotting everywhere. A few scavenging flies crawl across the withered cuts, searching for bits that are still edible, but I think they'll struggle.

A pig's carcass hangs upside down from a hook. Its head has been clawed open. I stare at it thoughtfully. I'm guessing that a zombie ripped out the brain, which maybe means we can thrive on animal brains too. I thought only human brains would keep us going, but it's good news if we can absorb nutrients from animals as well—I'd much rather scoop clean the inside of a pig's head than a human's.

This might be why I haven't seen any larger creatures. With humanity out of the way, wild dogs and cats should have the run of the streets. But so far I've seen nothing but rats, birds and smaller specimens. Maybe the zombies killed and ate the brains of larger animals, and all of London's pets have either been butchered or scared off.

I'll have to swing by London Zoo at some point. It's probably been cleaned out already – or the animals will most likely have died of starvation – but maybe I'll be able to gain access to areas off-limits to normal zombies. The good thing about having a working brain is that you can read maps and search for keys to unlock doors, simple tasks that are beyond most of the undead.

As I turn away from the pig, I notice a small red z painted on the frame of the door, a tiny arrow just beneath it. I frown, trying to remember where I've seen something like that before. Then I recall Mr. Dowling daubing my cheek with a mark just like this one.

I glance around nervously. Have the clown and his mutants been here? Might they be watching me now? Mr. Dowling freaked me out big time, especially when he opened his lips and dropped a stream of living spiders over me. I don't want to hang around and risk another run-in with him.

Hurrying from the shop, I come to a set of traffic lights. The electricity is working here and the lights are operating as normal. The red "don't walk" man is illuminated and I automatically stop, waiting for the light to change to green.

After a few seconds, I squint at the light, look left, then right. Nothing moves.

"Of course not," I grimace. "There's no traffic because everyone's dead. You're a bloody moron, B."

I chuckle at my stupidity. Stopping for a traffic light in a city of the dead! I'm glad none of my friends lived to see that. Ignoring the red light, I step out into the road. I'm not far from my old neighborhood. Another hour, maybe a bit more, and I'll be back on –

An engine roars into life. My head snaps round and I spot a car tearing towards me. It had been parked nearby. I'd seen people moving around inside, but figured they were zombies sheltering from the sun.

I figured wrong.

Before I can withdraw to the safety of the pavement, the driver turns on his headlights and I'm momentarily blinded, even wearing the sunglasses. Wincing, I turn my head away and shake it wildly, disoriented and in pain.

Then the car smashes into me and knocks me flying through the air, far down the middle of the road, which up until a few seconds ago seemed just as dead and unthreatening as any other in this ghost city of the damned.

hand over my scalp. Lots of torn flesh but it doesn't feel too serious. The jacket and clothes I picked up earlier are ripped to shreds, but all things considered it could have been a lot worse.

Then the doors of the car open and as four men step out, I realize it's far too soon to be judging this a lucky escape.

The men are dressed in camouflage and black boots. Each totes a rifle and I spot smaller guns and hunting knives

strapped to their legs and chests. They're smiling and laughing, not looking in the least afraid.

"She's up," one of the men says. "You must be losing your touch, Coley."

"I'm not losing anything," the man called Coley snaps. "I was only doing about thirty when I hit her. Didn't want to finish her off too soon. Essex, you want first shot?"

"Don't mind if I do," the man on my far left says and raises his rifle.

I dive for cover behind a nearby car as he fires. He curses and fires again, but only hits one of the wheels.

"You missed," Coley hoots.

"No fair!" Essex shouts. "They're not supposed to hide."

"Not all of them stand still," one of the other men says, and this guy speaks in an American accent. "The survival instinct is still alive in some. Looks like we might have a real hunt on our hands, gentlemen."

"You want to deal with her, Barnes?" Coley asks.

"No," the American says. "Let's give Tag a shot first. This is what we brought them along for."

"What do I do?" the fourth man asks. He sounds nervous.

"Edge over to your right," Barnes says, and I hear him creeping around to my left. "I'll flush her out. As soon as she—"

I don't wait for him to give more orders. Keeping low, I race back towards the butcher's shop, catching the men by surprise.

A couple yell with alarm and fire wildly. Bullets scream past but I keep going.

I'm close to the shop when one of the men hits the window with a bullet and it shatters. As glass sprays everywhere, I fling myself through the hole and roll across the counter before dropping to the floor and taking cover.

"Hellfire!" Essex shouts. "Did you see that?"

"Careful, boys," Barnes drawls. "We've got a live one here. Relatively speaking."

"How do you want to play this?" Coley asks. He sounds excited.

"That depends on these two," the American says. "Do you want to go in after her and risk the thrill of a close encounter, or would you rather we smoked her out?"

As they discuss tactics, I raise my head, get a fix on them, then scout around and pick up a hefty butcher's knife. This is why I came back here rather than flee down the road. I was a target out there, the tools I picked up earlier no use against a group of guys with guns. I hate being trapped like this, but at least I have a decent weapon now.

Shuffling backwards, I search for another way out. There's a door at the rear of the shop, but it's locked and I can't find the key. I hurl myself at the door, hoping to smash through, but it's made of metal and it holds. I only bounce off it, bruising my arm in the process.

"What's she doing?" I hear Tag cry.

"Maybe she's lost her head and is thrashing around," Barnes says calmly. "Or she might be trying to find another way out. Coley, swing round back and make sure she doesn't sneak away."

"She wouldn't be smart enough to think of that," Coley says.

"You'd be surprised," Barnes grunts. "Some are almost as cunning as they were in life."

As Coley circles round, the American addresses the other pair. "This is unusual but not unheard of. Some of these beasts are smarter than others. They recall routines and procedures in some dim corner of their foul, undead brain and act like they did when they were alive."

"How dangerous are they?" Tag asks.

"All zombies are dangerous," Barnes huffs.

"But if this one's more of a threat than most, shouldn't we back off and leave her be?"

"We're hunters," Barnes says stiffly. "We don't withdraw once we've engaged our prey. We have to see this through to the end. If you prefer, you can return to the car and wait for us there, but my advice is to stick together. Never forget that this is a city of the undead. There's safety in numbers. I can't protect you if you cut yourself off from the rest of us."

"I didn't know it was going to be like this," Tag grumbles.

"Quit whining," Essex snarls. "They told us it could turn nasty. We knew the risks coming in. This is all part of the fun, right, Barnes?"

"Sure," Barnes says drily. "*Fun.* That's what we promised you guys and we won't let you down. Coley, you in place yet?"

"Got it covered," Coley shouts.

"Then if you boys will give me a minute..."

There's a long pause. I peer over the counter, trying to see what they're up to, but Tag and Essex start firing as soon as they spot my head. Ducking again, I curse and grab another knife, determined not to go down without a fight and maybe take one or two of these bastards with me.

"Come on," I whisper, gripping the knife tightly. "Meet me on my own turf. Let's see how useful your rifles are up close."

But the American is obviously thinking the same way I am, because even as I'm willing them to advance, he yells a warning to the others, "Clear!"

A couple of seconds later a bottle comes flying through the window. There's a burning rag sticking out of the top of it. I don't know much about weapons, but I know a Molotov cocktail when I see one.

The bottle smashes into the wall and flames billow from it, scorching the shop, roasting the flies, blackening the scraps of meat. I don't wait to be engulfed by the fire. I started moving the instant I caught sight of the bottle flying over my head. As the glass explodes and flames roar around me, I launch myself over the counter and shoot through the window like a human bullet propelled from the heated chamber of the store.

As I crash back to earth, pain flares in my feet and I see that my socks are on fire. Yelping, I toss the knife aside and slap out the flames, then tear off the smoldering socks. I'm so concerned about my feet that I blank out everything else. It's only when I hear a soft clicking noise that I pause, look up and realize that the barrels of three rifles are pointed directly at my head.

SEVEN

Nobody says anything and nobody opens fire. The American is slightly in front of the others, studying me coolly, the mouth of his rifle trained on the center of my forehead. The other two look less sure of themselves. I think of diving for the knife, but I'm afraid that if I move, their trigger fingers will tighten instinctively and that will be the end of me.

"She's smart for a dead bird, isn't she?" Coley remarks, sauntering back into view, rifle slung across his shoulder, grinning viciously. His hair is cut short like a soldier's and he's wearing a pair of designer sunglasses. "Seems almost a shame to kill her."

"It's not really killing, is it?" Tag frowns. He's a thin man with a Scottish accent. Long hair tied back in a ponytail. "I mean, they're dead already, so it's not like we're murdering anyone, right?"

"Don't worry," Barnes murmurs, never taking his eyes off me. "This isn't a crime. Nobody will hold us accountable for what we do here. She looks like one of us but she isn't. She has less right to exist than an animal. It's elimination, not execution. Now, who wants to—"

"Screw you all!" I scream and every one of the men recoils with shock.

"Jesus!" Essex roars. "She spoke! Did you hear that? She bloody *spoke*!"

"I heard," Barnes growls. His dark brown eyes are hard. He's taller than the others, lean and muscular. He's the only one not wearing gloves. His black hair is shot through with streaks of gray and there's a bullet tucked behind his right ear.

"What the hell is she?" Coley asks. He doesn't look so relaxed now, and has trained his rifle on me too.

"I don't know," Barnes says softly.

"Is she alive?" Tag asks.

"She can't be," Essex snorts. "Look at the hole in her chest."

"But she spoke."

"Maybe it was a reflex action," Essex says.

"Reflex action my arse!" I shout, and again they flinch. I push myself to my feet and glower at the astonished hunters. "My name's

Becky Smith. I'm a teenage girl. If you shoot me, there are plenty of people out there who bloody *will* hold you accountable."

Barnes blinks and lowers his rifle a fraction. "Are you a zombie?"

"What does it look like?" I sniff, pointing a finger at the hole in my chest.

"Then how are you speaking?"

"Some of us can."

"None that I've seen," he counters.

I shrug. "Maybe if you asked first and shot later…"

"This is insane," Coley mutters, circling me slowly, keeping well out of reach, nervously eyeing the bones sticking out of my fingers. "Every zombie we've ever seen is a rabid, senseless beast. There can't be an in-between state."

"Well, there is. I'm proof of that."

"There are others like you?" Barnes asks.

"Yeah." Then I recall Mr. Dowling, the mutants, the flame-throwers. "At least, there *were*…"

"Where are they?"

"I don't know. We were being kept underground. Most of the others were killed, maybe all of them. I got away but I think I'm the only one. The clown attacked and everything went crazy."

I stop, aware that I'm making no sense.

"Who *kept* you?" Barnes asks.

"Soldiers. Scientists. They were studying us."

411

"Soldiers?" Essex yelps. He looks around, edgy now. "This sounds bad to me. If the military's involved..."

"We're not doing anything they'd disapprove of," Coley says quickly. "We're zombie hunters, that's all, helping clean up the mess."

"But we're not supposed to be here," Tag mumbles.

"Only because it's dangerous," Coley reassures him. "They tell people to keep away because they want to stop fools being killed or turned into zombies. But nobody's going to give professionals like us any grief for coming in and shooting some of the buggers. We're saving them a job."

"Still," Essex says, pointing his gun away from me, "I think we should split. I don't want to be caught here by the army. They might mistake us for zombies and open fire from afar. I want to leave now."

"We came here to hunt," Coley snarls. "You both begged to join us. We didn't force you."

"I know," Essex says stiffly. "But now I want to stop. Tag?"

"Hell, yes." He lowers his rifle.

"Bloody amateurs." Coley spits with disgust, then cocks an eyebrow at Barnes. The American hasn't budged. "What do we do?"

"If there are soldiers in the area, Tag and Essex are right, we need to get out of here. We're breaking the law. They might let us go with a slap on the wrist. Or they might shoot us dead. We'd be fools to risk it."

"Fair enough," Coley sighs. Lowering his rifle, he pulls a hand-gun and aims it at my face.

"What the hell!" I roar, throwing myself to the ground.

"Coley!" Barnes yells.

"What?" he frowns. "She's a zombie. It doesn't matter whether she can talk or not. She's one of them."

"One of the undead, definitely," Barnes agrees, "but partially one of the living too. I don't know how she can respond, but she's more than a walking corpse."

Coley laughs cynically. "Not much more. I say we kill her. One less zombie is always a good thing."

He takes aim again.

"This is murder!" I howl. "I can talk! I can think! I used to go to school!"

I don't know why I shouted that last line. It just popped out.

"Hush now," Coley purrs. "One little bullet and all your worries will be behind you."

"Hold," Barnes barks. "We're hunters, not killers. We mop up the dead, we don't execute the living."

"She's a zombie," Coley protests.

"But unlike any other we've encountered. She can reason. She can plead for her life. We don't have the right to kill someone who understands what we're doing."

"Not a some*one*," Coley sneers. "A some*thing*. And you might be going soft in your old age, but I'm not about to lose focus. These bastards killed the people I loved. I won't stop as long as they're active and I don't give a damn if they can talk or not."

Coley cocks his gun. Tag and Essex gape like children. Barnes goes on staring at me.

"She said her name is Becky Smith," Barnes says softly.

"I heard." Coley shrugs. "I don't care."

"Have you ever killed something that could tell you its name?" Barnes presses.

"As it happens, yes," Coley says. "That didn't stop me then and it sure as hell won't stop me now. She's a bloody zombie! They're the bad guys, remember?"

"I don't know about good and I don't know about bad," Barnes replies softly. "Until a few minutes ago all that mattered to me was the living and the undead. I thought the world had been divided neatly along those lines and I operated accordingly. Now I see it's not so simple. I can't kill this girl. Even though she's missing a heart, she's too much like a real person."

Coley stiffens. "Are you saying you'll stop me if I try to shoot her?"

Barnes considers that. I start to smile. Then he says, "No," and my smile fades away to nothing.

Coley grins and takes final aim.

"I don't have the right to stop you shooting her," Barnes adds. "You're a free agent, I'm not your boss, you're not answerable to me. And maybe you're right—maybe she is a monster, and we have

414

every right to cull her like a rabid hound. But if you kill her, I'll put a bullet through each of your kneecaps and leave you here for the other zombies to pick apart come night."

Coley does a double take. Barnes's expression doesn't change. If he's bluffing, he's got a first-rate poker face.

"You'd do that to me?" Coley asks softly. "After all we've been through these last six months?"

"I'd have to," Barnes says. "In my view that would be the only appropriate response. If you feel you have to kill this girl, I won't stop you. But be aware of the consequences."

"You'd choose a zombie over a friend?" Coley snarls.

"You're no friend of mine, any more than I'm a friend of yours." Barnes smiles icily. "We're just a couple of guys who hunt together."

Coley weighs his options. I can tell he'd love to put a bullet through Barnes's head almost as much as he wants to put one through mine. But the American has a lethal air about him. He's not someone you go up against lightly.

"Have it your way," Coley finally snarls, holstering his gun. He heads for the car, not looking at any of the others.

"Head on back, boys," Barnes says, nodding at Tag and Essex. In a daze they follow Coley to the vehicle and get in. Coley fires up the engine and revs it angrily. For a moment I think he plans to mow down the American. But Barnes never gives any indication that he's worried. And although the car rumbles forward a few feet, Coley doesn't push things any further.

"You've had a lucky escape today," Barnes says.

"Yes," I gulp. "Thank you."

"In this city, you'd better hope you stay lucky," he mutters, then backs up, keeping his rifle trained on me the whole way, until he gets into the car. As soon as the door slams shut, the car squeals past. The last thing I see of the hunters is an angry-looking Coley giving me the finger.

Then the car turns a corner and is gone, leaving me lying alone in the road, still trembling at my narrow escape.

it would be if I was alive, but it's pretty damn excruciating.

I recall the look of hatred in Coley's eyes as I stumble along. Oddly enough, I don't blame him for wanting to kill me. I probably had that same look when I first saw a zombie. We're monsters, plain and simple. The dead can, by definition, have no automatic right to life.

I make slower progress than before, hampered by my injuries. It's dusk before I turn onto the street where I used to live. Some of the keener or hungrier zombies have already come out of hiding and are on patrol. A few stop and sniff me as I pass, losing interest when they realize I'm more like them than one of the living.

Finally I come to the block of flats where I grew up. I can see from here that our front door is open. We have electricity in this area but no lights are on inside. It doesn't look like anyone's home. Which is a good thing. My greatest fear as I drew closer was that I'd find Mum, eyes glassed over, human flesh stuck between her teeth, lost to me forever in a state worse than death. (I'm not so worried about Dad, as I'm pretty certain he made it out alive. He has the luck of the devil.) I'm not sure what I'd do if I found her and she was a zombie. I'd want to kill her, to end her suffering, but I don't think that I could.

I spot a few familiar faces on the street, neighbors from a past that seems a thousand years removed. Nobody that I really cared about though. Ignoring them, I crawl up the three flights of stairs – as I pass a giant arse that is spray painted on the wall, I slap it for luck and grin fleetingly at the memory of happier times – and limp along the landing, then step inside what used to be my home and shut the door on the outside world.

The flat smells musty. The heating hasn't been turned on for months and none of the windows are open. Most of the doors are closed – a habit of Mum's, she couldn't bear an open door – so the rooms are stuffy.

I do a tour of the flat, making sure I'm alone. No bloodstains anywhere, which is a promising sign. No zombies lying in any dark corners either, which is even better. Maybe Mum made it out after all. Perhaps Dad came for her after I split from him at school, took her somewhere safe. They could be living the high life on some paradise island now.

"Yeah," I sneer at myself. "Dream on!"

I get a pang in my chest where my heart should be when I look into their bedroom. Some of Mum's clothes are laid across the bed, three different sets. She was obviously choosing what to wear that night when the world went to hell. I can picture her standing here, staring at the clothes, trying to decide. Then...

What? Killed by a zombie? Turned into one of the living dead? Taken off to some mystical Shangri-la by her racist, wife-beating knight in shining armor?

I don't know. All I know for sure is that she never made a final choice. The clothes stayed here, strewn across the bed, never to be worn again.

"I miss you, Mum," I moan, and wait for tears to come. But of course they don't. They can't. So in the end I close the door and go to check my own room.

It looks smaller than I remembered, dark and poky. I turn on the light, but that just makes it seem even more claustrophobic, full of ominous shadows. I gaze round. My bed looks the same as it always did, crumpled black sheets, the indent of my head on the pillow. No bookshelves or posters. I didn't believe in cluttering up my room. I liked my space, me.

I spot my iPod lying on the table next to my bed. I pick it up and smile softly. I left it charging the morning I set off to school for the last time, so it's warm to the touch. I scroll through a couple of my playlists, select a song at random and stick my headphones on. I yelp and immediately turn down the volume. It's easy to forget how good my sense of hearing is. Back then I used to set the volume up almost to maximum. If I did that now, I'd deafen myself.

I let the song play to its end, then lay down the iPod and step out of the room. I'd been looking forward to settling in here again, lying on my old bed and staring at the patch of ceiling that I knew so well. But now that I've seen it, I've lost interest. Instead I head back to Mum and Dad's room, sweep the clothes from the bed (I never was overly sentimental), lie back and cross my legs.

"Night night," I murmur after a few minutes, then turn on my side. I can't sleep, not since I was killed, but there's no harm in pretending every once in a while, is there?

NINE

I spend several days in the flat, maybe even a couple of weeks. Hard to tell for sure—one monotonous day blends into another and I lose track after a while. I only leave three times, to feed. On each occasion, being new to the whole brain-eating game, I track other zombies. They shuffle around the streets, sniffing like pigs in search of truffles. Often they go for hours without finding anything, but in the end they usually manage to track down an old corpse with some scraps of brain still left in its head.

I expected the zombies to fight over the meager morsels, but they feed politely, taking turns, waiting patiently while others gorge themselves. Sometimes they get a bit overeager and try to butt in, but always pull back if the feasting creature growls warningly at them.

I hate having to feed on the dried-up, rubbery bits of brain, but it's eat or lose my mental faculties completely. I keep looking for animals, but I still haven't seen any, apart from the birds and rats. I've eaten the brains of a few dead crows and rodents, and even caught a live rat once—I think it must have been sick or lame, because it couldn't run very fast. But they haven't made any real difference. Too small. I'd need to tuck into a dog or a cat's brain to find out if it could do the job that a human's does for me.

The rest of the time I hole up in the flat, recovering. My wounds don't heal, but the dull ache fades from my bones and my thick, jellylike blood combines with the green moss to form thin, wispy scabs around the scrapes. After a few days, I'm good as new (well, as close to it as a zombie can ever be), but I make no move to leave. I can't think of anywhere better to go.

I turned on the lights the first night, when I got tired of lying on the bed, but they attracted curious zombies, so I've sat in the dark since then. A few zombies wander in every so often—I've left the front door open, since one of them nearly broke it down when it heard someone at home and couldn't get in—but they slip out once they've satisfied themselves that my brain's of no use to them.

I check the TV every day but it produces nothing but static. The radio, on the other hand, is still going strong. I never used to listen to the radio – *so* twentieth century! – but Mum always had it playing in the background when she was cooking, ironing, etc.

There are far fewer channels than before. One for official state news, which plays all the time, run by whatever remains of our government and civil service, plus a few independents that broadcast sporadically.

The state reporters give the impression that the military have everything in hand, that they're restoring order, people shouldn't panic, it's all going to work out fine. The independents give more of a sense of the chaos that the world is experiencing. Some of them are critical of the soldiers, claiming they've been opening fire wildly in certain areas, killing the living as well as the dead. A few drop dark hints that the military staged the zombie coup and are eliminating anyone they don't approve of.

I don't pay too much attention to the politics of specific broadcasters. I'm not interested in any particular pundit's opinion. I just want to get to grips with as many cold, hard facts as I can. By switching between the various channels, and filtering out the positive spin of the state channel and the manic gloom of the independents, I fill in a lot of the blanks and get up to speed with what's been going on in the world since my heart was ripped out all those months ago.

Zombies launched simultaneous attacks in most major cities. New York, Tokyo, Moscow, Sydney, Berlin, Johannesburg and scores more, torn apart by the living dead, ruined graveyards of the grand cities they used to be.

The undead spread swiftly. They were almost impossible to stop. Armies everywhere opposed them, but all it needed was for one zombie to infect a couple of soldiers, and soon they were fighting among themselves, forced to break ranks and retreat. Estimates of the numbers lost to the hordes of the walking dead vary wildly, but most reporters agree that it's probably somewhere between four and five billion.

I have to repeat that slowly to myself the first time I hear it, and even then I can't really comprehend it. Four or five *billion*, most of the world's population, slaughtered or reduced to the status of reanimated corpses. How's this planet ever supposed to recover from that?

Nobody knows where the zombies came from, how the disease manifested itself so swiftly, so globally. And, in truth, nobody's overly concerned. Right now their first priority is survival.

When the attacks started, many small islands were spared. Survivors flocked to those on planes and boats. At first the residents accepted everyone. But then a few islands fell when boats docked or planes set down and zombies streamed out of them, having sneaked aboard. After that, the locals in other places began implementing security checks and setting up quarantine zones, opening fire on anyone who tried to bypass the process.

On the mainland continents, millions of people who can't get to the islands have established fortresses wherever they can. In some cases they've barricaded themselves into apartment complexes, prisons, schools or shopping malls.

Even though their forces have been severely depleted, the armies of the world are the sole governors of society now. Most politicians were wiped out in the first wave of attacks, and those who survived no longer have any real clout. It's martial law wherever you turn.

The troops in the UK have been busy reclaiming lost ground from the zombies. They've converted a series of towns and villages across the country into fortified barracks, building huge walls around them, including areas of open fields within the fortifications so that they can cultivate the land and live off what they grow.

The reporters on the state channel are proud of the army's sterling work and every news bulletin includes reports from some of the reclaimed towns, focusing on the resilience of the people living and working there, their struggle to survive, the way they're doing all that they can to rebuild normal lives for themselves.

The independents are more scathing. They say that residents are treated like cattle, forced to do whatever the soldiers tell them. If they resist, aerial units are sent to blow holes in their defenses, to let zombies stream through freely.

I'm not convinced by the wilder reports, but in this zombie-plagued new world, who knows for sure? I keep an open mind, filing everything away.

The army's ultimate aim is to push the zombies back, section them off, then wipe them out. But that will take time. At the moment they're not equipped to engage in a full-on war with the undead. As stern generals keep explaining, their current focus must be on the three *Rs*—Reclaim, Recruit, Recover. Reclaim towns, recruit more survivors, recover their strength. *Then* they can let rip.

It's terrifying at first, thinking of humanity reduced to this, living off scraps, penned into grimy hovels, under constant siege by their former colleagues and relatives, knowing that all it takes is a single breach – one lone zombie in the mix – for everything they've worked so hard for to come crashing down around them.

But after a while, I get used to it. This is the norm now. You can only be shocked by a thing for so long before it starts to lose its impact. Yeah, the world's a dark, terrible place, and it's horrible listening to stories of children eating their parents or mothers chowing down on their young. But, y'know, when all's said and done, you've got to get on with things.

I only keep following the news after the first few days because of one particular story. The army has been making rescue attempts recently. Lots of people are trapped in cities, even after so many months, lying low at night, foraging for food and drink in the daytime while the zombies are at rest.

The military announce a city a few days ahead of a planned mission, telling the people who are listening to get ready. Then, on the morning of the rescue, they declare a meeting point and fly in at an appointed time, usually the middle of the day when the sun is at its strongest. They aren't always able to rescue everyone who turns up, and sometimes zombies attack, cutting the evacuation short. But they've extracted hundreds of refugees and escorted them to secure settlements, and have vowed to carry on.

Things would be a lot easier if the phones worked, but as I found out early on when I tested ours, they're even deader than the zombies. All of the landlines are down and all of the mobile networks too. The Internet is screwed as well. The only way the army can contact trapped survivors is through the news on the radio, but that's a one-way means of communication.

According to the reports, there have been a few rescues in London already. As the capital, it's been granted priority status. They did trial runs in some of the smaller cities first, but now they're hitting London regularly, a different part every time, so as to keep one step ahead of the zombies.

The walking dead aren't as senseless as they appear. They seem to remember lots of functions, such as how to open doors or operate elevators. They've adapted—if they see a car passing a certain spot at a certain time more than once, they can anticipate its reappearance and lie in wait for it.

But they don't seem to understand most of what is said to them. They react to certain tones of voice, recognizing a variety of commands, the way a baby or a dog can. But they're not able to listen to a broadcast and pitch up at a scheduled meeting place in advance.

If the living are to win this war, it will only be because they can outthink their opponents. In every other respect the zombies are a superior force, far greater in number, able to fight without tiring, not needing food or drink to continue. They don't have any weapons, but their bodies are deadly enough, diseased missiles that are much more effective than a bomb dropped in the middle of a confined group of people.

There have been two missions to London while I've been listening, one in the north, one in the west. Both pickup points were out of my way, so I stayed put and let them pass. But it's only a matter of time before they come to the East End or to the city, and I'm determined to go along when a rescue is announced.

There have been no reports of revitalizeds on any of the radio programs. The world doesn't seem to be aware of the existence of zombies like me. I'm not sure how the soldiers will react when I turn up, but I've got to try to tell them about the possible threat that revitalizeds pose.

I've been thinking about Rage a lot, the way he killed Dr. Cerveris, his contempt for the living. If he survived and made it out of the complex, maybe he looks upon the zombies as his allies. It might amuse him to betray humanity. Perhaps there are others like him who've been mistreated by the living, wanting to get revenge and see them brought down.

I don't know if the soldiers will give me a chance to explain, if they'll offer me shelter in return for my help or shoot me the instant they set eyes on me. I suspect it might be the latter. But I've got to at least try to help, because I was one of the living once, and if I don't cling to that memory and honor it, all that's left for me is the monstrous, lonely, subexistence of the dead.

TEN

The call finally comes late one evening. There's going to be a mission to Central London in three days—to make it clear, the reporter says that today is Sunday and the rescue will take place sometime on Wednesday. She's excited when she breaks the news. The other rescues in the capital have all been in the suburbs. This is the first time they've hit the center. They think it might be the largest operation yet, so they're going to be sending more helicopters and troops than normal. But she tells people not to worry, this is just the first mission of many, so if you can't make it this time, stay low and wait for the next.

I head off first thing in the morning. It won't take me three days to walk to the West End, but I want to allow myself plenty of time to overcome any unexpected obstacles along the way, explore the area, find a resting place, maybe meet up with some of the survivors and convince them of my good intentions so that they can act as middlemen between me and the soldiers.

I pause in the doorway of the flat and glance back one last time, nostalgic, remembering Mum and Dad, the bad times as well as the good. And, being honest, there were more bad days than good. Dad was always too free with his fists. Mum and I were constantly walking on eggshells, afraid we'd say the wrong thing and set him off.

But you know what? I'd take them all back in an instant if they were offered, even the days when he beat us and drew blood and kicked us like dogs. He was a nasty sod, there's no denying that, but he was still my dad. I love him. I miss him. I can't help myself.

"I'll come looking for you," I say aloud to the memories of the two people who mattered to me most. "If I survive, and you're out there, I'll try to find you, to let you know I made it through, to help you if I can."

There's no answer or sign that somewhere, somehow, they magically heard. Of course not. I'd have to be a right dumb cow to believe that they're sitting up in a far-off compound, frowning at the ghostly echo of my voice, whispering with awe, *"B?"*

"You're getting soft, girl," I mutter, then slam the door shut and head on down the stairs, whistling dreadfully—I can't carry a tune these days, not now that my mouth is drier than a camel's arse.

I wind my way through the streets, heading west. I've never walked this stretch of London before. We always got a bus or the Tube if we were going up the West End, or a cab on occasions when Dad was feeling rich.

I replace my clothes and jacket as soon as I can, for full protection from the sun. I'm still wearing the Australian hat. That should last me years if I don't lose it. Well, *would* last me years if I lived that long, but I've probably only got about a year and a half, max. Which means this might well prove to be a lifelong hat.

The streets are quiet. I spot zombies in the shade of shops and houses, or resting in abandoned cars or buses. They stare at me hungrily as I amble past. I always make sure I turn so that they can see the hole in my chest. If it wasn't so bright, they'd probably clamber out to make sure I wasn't trying to fool them, but they're reluctant to brave the glare of the day. They haven't thought of wearing sunglasses. They ain't bright sparks like me.

I'm excited to be on the move, to have a goal, even if it's one that could result in my execution. I never did much when I was alive, just hung out with my mates (most or all of them are probably dead now, but I try not to brood about that) or festered in my room. It wasn't a fascinating life by any standard. But it beat the hell out of being held prisoner underground, and the monotony of the last few weeks. I was going stir-crazy in that flat, but I only realize how bad things were now that I've left. You know you've been seriously climbing the walls if the thought of heading off on a suicide mission makes you feel happy!

I lose my way a couple of times, but don't bother checking the map. It's a nice day, I'm enjoying the stroll, no zombies or hunters are hassling me, so what's the rush?

I come to a railway station. Lots of eerie-looking train carriages, windows smashed in, many bloodstains splashed across the metal and glass in more places than I can count. On one carriage I spot a large red z with an arrow underneath, pointing west. It looks like it was freshly sprayed—there's even a smell of paint in the air, or is that my imagination?

I swing a right past the station and follow the road round until I can cut through to Victoria Park. Mum used to bring me for walks up here on the weekend when I was younger. Dad came with us sometimes, but he'd always work himself up into a mood, muttering about all the foreigners on the loose.

He wouldn't mind it now. There's not a soul to be seen, black, brown or any other color. Lots of corpses and bones but that's all. I've got the entire park to myself.

Well... not quite. As I pad past the tennis courts and come to a few small ponds, I spot three skinny dogs lapping water from a pool. I perk up when I clock the dogs and hurry towards them, calling out, "Hey! Doggies! Here!" I make clicking sounds with my tongue.

The dogs react instantly, but not in the way I'd like. Without even looking at me, they take off, yapping fearfully. I race after them, shouting for them to come back, but they're faster than me and disappear from sight moments later. I come to a stop and swear, then kick the ground with anger.

A little later, walking through the park, I regret swearing. I can't blame the dogs for running. These past months must have been hellish for any animal trapped here. If zombies eat an animal's brain as readily as a human's, they'll have gone for every pet in the city. To survive, you'd have to learn to be sneaky, to only come out in the daytime, to avoid all contact with the two-legged creatures that were once so nice to you. I think even Dr. Dolittle would have trouble getting animals to trust him these days.

I spend an hour or more in the park. My skin's itching from the sun, even protected by my heavy layers of clothes, but I press on, determined not to let that spoil the day for me. A pity there's nobody selling ice cream. I could murder a cone right now, even though I'd have to spit out almost every mouthful because I can't digest solids anymore.

I keep hoping the dogs will show again, that they'll realize I mean them no harm, that I only crave their friendship, not their brains—as hungry as I get, I wouldn't kill a dog, any more than I'd kill a living person. I want them to slink forward, give me a closer once-over, learn to trust me. But no such luck. They've gone into hiding and I doubt they'll come here again anytime soon.

Eventually I take a road leading west. There are dead zombies hanging from the street lamps, rotting in the sun. Each has been shot through the head. Many have been disemboweled or cut up with knives. Flies buzz around the stinking corpses. I pass them nervously, wondering if this was the work of hunters like Barnes and his posse.

I don't like the way that the corpses have been strung up. As vicious as the living dead are, they're not consciously evil, just slaves to their unnatural desires. I understand the need to kill the undead, but torturing and humiliating them serves no purpose. It's not like other zombies are going to look at them and have a change of heart. Being a zombie isn't a career choice. The reviveds don't have any control over what they do.

I turn left, then right onto Bethnal Green Road. One of Mum's best friends, Mary Byrne, lived around here. Her oldest son, Matt, was my age, and his brother Joe was just a bit younger. We used to play together when our mums hung out.

More zombies are strung up along the road ahead of me, but I'm not paying attention to them, trying to remember exactly where Mary lived. So it's a real shock, as I'm walking along, when one of the corpses kicks out at my head and makes a choked noise.

"Bloody hell!" I yell, falling over and scrabbling away.

The zombie goes on kicking and mewling, and I realize I have nothing to fear. I get to my feet and study the writhing figure. It's a man. He's been stripped bare. His hands are tied behind his back and a noose around his neck connects to the lamp overhead. But the people who strung up the zombies left this one alive, either for sport or because they were scared off before they could finish the job.

The man's flesh is a nasty red color, where he's been burnt by the sun. His eyes are sickly white orbs. He snarls angrily and kicks out furiously at the world. No telling how long he's been up there, but by the state of his eyes, I'd say it's been a good while.

I should press on but I can't. This guy means nothing to me but I can't leave him like this. I wouldn't do this to anyone, even a savage killer, as he doubtless would become if given his freedom and a human target.

"Hold on, sunshine," I tell him. "I'll find a ladder and come free you."

The zombie screeches hoarsely, limited by the rope around his throat.

"Be patient," I snap. "I won't be long. Just give me a few minutes to go search for..."

I come to a stunned halt. I was turning to look for a hardware store when I spotted something, just past the corner where I cut onto this stretch. I do a double take, but when I look again it's still there.

An artist's easel has been set in the middle of the road, straddling a white line. A medium-size canvas rests on it. And just behind the easel stands a man, holding a painter's palette, gaping at me as if I'd come from another planet.

"Who the bloody hell are you?" I roar, striding towards him.

The man yelps and drops the palette. He turns and runs. I give immediate chase. He's faster than me, but I throw myself through the air, taking long jumps, and a few seconds later I overtake him and draw to a halt, blocking his way. The man screams and turns to run back the way he's come.

"Don't try it!" I shout. "I don't need to breathe, so I can chase you all day and never drop my pace."

The man shudders, glances around desperately for a place to hide or something to defend himself with. Finding nothing, he resigns himself, straightens and turns to face me. He brushes dried flecks of paint from the sleeves of his coat and tries a shaky smile.

"My name is Timothy Jackson," he squeaks, as posh as you like.

"What are you doing here?" I snap.

"Painting." He nods at the easel and beams proudly, forgetting for a moment that he should be trembling with fear. "I'm an artist."

As I stare at him, lost for words, he mistakes my gaze for one of hunger and loses his confidence as quickly as he found it. With a gulp, his arms slump by his sides and he says in a low, miserable voice, "Please don't eat me."

438

ELEVEN

I circle the artist warily as he stands shivering and wincing. He's not very old, maybe early thirties. Medium height, a bit on the thin side, with a long face and dark circles round his eyes. He's wearing yellow trousers, a pink shirt and a tweed jacket. His clothes are dirty, ruined with paint, but look like they came from a top notch shop. He has long, untidy brown hair, but is freshly shaven, not even a hint of stubble. He stinks of strong aftershave, like he bathes in the stuff.

I squint at the canvas on which he was working. It depicts the zombie hanging from the rope. The feet look too big, out of proportion to the rest of the body, but I suspect that's deliberate.

"Did you stick him up there?" I growl.

Timothy laughs nervously. "Hardly. I found him here a few days ago and I've been coming back to paint him at different times of the day, to take advantage of the changing light."

"He's suffering. Zombies can't endure the sun. He's burned and going blind. You never thought about letting him down?"

Timothy blinks and scratches his head. "To be honest, no, I didn't. It's not that I derive any pleasure from his pain—I feel sorry for these poor creatures—but if I'd set him free, he would have come after me and either gouged out my brain or turned me into a monster like him."

I have to acknowledge that he's got a point.

"I'll let you off this time," I sniff.

"If it's not impudent of me," Timothy murmurs, eyes round and filled with curiosity, "what on earth *are* you? I thought you were one of the undead when I first saw you, but then you spoke."

"I'm a revitalized," I tell him. "A zombie who regained its thoughts."

"That's possible?" he gasps.

"In some cases, yeah."

"Does that mean there's a cure for the rest of them?"

I shrug. "I don't think so."

Although, now that I consider it, maybe it does. Perhaps a serum could be fashioned from my blood, one that could restore thought to all of the living dead. If I get rescued on Wednesday, I'll suggest that to the soldiers. I don't mind being a guinea pig, not if

I can help bring peace to the world. Hell, maybe I'll end up being hailed as a hero. B Smith—savior of mankind!

"Enough about me," I grunt. "What the hell is an artist doing in the middle of the road in a city overrun by zombies?"

"Capturing the apocalypse for the sake of posterity," he beams. "I've been doing this every day since London fell. Well, not for the first couple of weeks – it was too dangerous to venture out – but I've not missed a day since."

"And you haven't been attacked in all that time?" I ask skeptically.

"Of course I have," he chuckles. "I've had to race for my life more times than I can count. There are tricks I've learned to employ that help ward off interest – I don't come out if it's cloudy, I douse myself in strong cologne to mask my scent, I make as little noise as possible – but I get spotted and chased two or three times a day on average."

I frown. "How come you haven't been caught yet?"

"A healthy mix of skill and luck," he says, then pauses. "Do you have a name?"

"Of course. I'm B Smith."

"And you're not going to eat me, are you, B?"

"Nah. You don't look that tasty," I laugh.

"You won't snap suddenly, lose your mind and turn on me?" he presses.

"No."

"You're a good zombie?"

I smile. "I probably wouldn't go that far. But I'm not a killer."

Timothy mulls that over, then nods to himself. "In that case, do you mind if we head back to my place? I don't like talking out here in the open. Sounds carry and zombies have a keen sense of hearing."

"Where do you live?" I ask.

"Close by. I never venture too far from my studio. Come, we can chat on the way, and I'd love to show you my work. Are you interested in art at all?"

"Not really," I mutter, and his face falls. "But if it's drawings of zombies and the city, I definitely want to have a look."

Timothy's smile returns full force. "Excellent!" Picking up his easel and palette, he heads down Bethnal Green Road, whistling jauntily, strutting like a peacock.

TWELVE

Timothy looks like a man without a care in the world, but I note the way he casts careful glances at the buildings on either side, keeping an eye out for zombies. He's not as reckless as he appears, although his very presence here proves that he's something of a daredevil.

He comes to the turn for Brick Lane and pauses. "That's where we're headed," he says, nodding at the street that used to contain London's most famous string of curry houses.

"We're not going for an Indian, are we?" I joke.

"Actually I've made use of the restaurants quite a lot," he says seriously. "I ran out of fresh food long ago, but the freezers are still working in many places. I can rustle you up an amazing chicken madras if you're hungry."

"I'm a zombie," I remind him. "I only eat brains."

He considers that. "If you supplied the brains, I could probably do something with them. Mix them up in a korma perhaps."

I burst out laughing. "Anyone ever tell you you're a nutjob, Jackson?"

"Only Mother, Father, my teachers and friends." He sighs. "But they're all dead or eaten now, so I guess I had the last laugh. All joking aside, I love to cook, so if you want..."

"Thanks for the offer, but cooking might rob the brains of the nutrients I need. As far as I know, they have to be raw."

That's nonsense, but it satisfies Timothy and spares me the job of telling him I'd rather eat straight from a corpse's head than risk one of his dishes.

Timothy starts walking again but doesn't turn onto Brick Lane.

"I thought you said we were going that way."

"We are," he nods, "but my studio is about halfway down. It's a narrow, dark street. I've boarded up most of the buildings close to mine, but zombies could be lurking somewhere along the way. I always go down the main road and cut in from there. You have to be careful if you want to survive around here."

At the end of Bethnal Green Road we cut left onto Commercial Street.

"I adored the markets around here," Timothy says. "I often

446

came over on a Sunday and spent the entire day milling around, sketching people, buying things I didn't need, sampling the many local varieties of fine cuisine."

"Fine cuisine?" I snort. "Bagels and curry?"

"Oh, there was much more than that," Timothy insists. "Pies and falafel and jellied eels for instance."

"*You* ate jellied eels?"

"Why shouldn't I?" he blinks.

"I didn't have you pegged for the jellied eels sort. My gran loved them, and my dad and his mates tucked into them sometimes, but I mean, come on, they were disgusting. Cold, bony bits of eel wrapped up in slimy jelly—you wouldn't feed that mess to a dog."

"It was authentic East London," Timothy protests.

"*I'm* authentic East London," I tell him, "and I wouldn't touch jellied eels with a ten-foot pole."

"Well, to each their own," he says with a shrug.

We turn into a street lined with beautiful old houses. It feeds into Brick Lane and we come to a huge building, the old Truman Brewery. Timothy looks around to make sure no one—no *thing*—is watching, then fishes a key out of a pocket and hurries to a large, steel door. He opens it quickly and slips inside. I get an uneasy feeling—maybe this is a trap and I'm not the first revitalized he's lured back—but then I recall his yellow trousers and chuckle weakly. What sort of a bad guy would wear yellow pants?

Maybe it's just because I'm lonely, but I decide to trust my new-found friend. Putting my doubts behind me, I step into the gloom of the building and try not to show any signs of unease as Timothy gently swings the oversized door shut and cuts us off from the outside world.

THIRTEEN

Timothy throws a switch and lights flicker on all over the place. We're in a spacious room, the sort you might find in a warehouse. The windows have all been boarded over to keep in the light and keep out the zombies.

"Most of that was done before I came," Timothy says, nodding at the planks nailed over the glass. "There were five other people sheltering here then, including a security guard who was on duty when the zombies attacked."

"What happened to them?" I ask.

"Two were captured by zombies over the following weeks. The others decided to make a break for freedom. The last I saw of them, they were heading for the river to search for a boat."

"Why didn't you go with them?"

He looks at me as if I'm crazy. "I told you, I'm a painter. I stayed behind to paint."

Timothy leads me up a short set of stairs and into an even larger room. There are canvases everywhere, most of them blank, along with brushes, tins of paint, easels and all sorts of artistic bits and bobs.

"I loved the East End art scene," Timothy says as we stride through the room. "It felt natural that I come here once London fell. I originally meant to make camp in an ordinary house, but when I strolled up Brick Lane and realized this amazing space was occupied by humans and secure, I knew it was fate."

We climb another set of stairs and come to a massive room. The windows have been boarded over here too, though some cracks have been left between the planks to let light through.

"Why the boards?" I ask. "Surely you don't need them this high up."

Timothy squints at me. "Are you *sure* you're a zombie?"

I point to the hole in my chest.

"Good answer. But then why do you know so little about your kind?"

"I was locked up," I tell him. "I only broke free a few weeks ago and I've laid low most nights since then."

"Well," Timothy chuckles, "the good news is that if you like climbing, you're in for a treat. Those bones sticking out of your fingers are extraordinarily durable. They'll dig into wood, brick, all sorts of substances. Determined zombies can scale the walls of old buildings like this."

The room is crammed with canvases, but unlike those downstairs, these have been worked on. A few are hanging, but most stand on the floor, propped against the walls. In some places they're stacked twelve deep.

"When I first moved in, I thought I'd have all the space I'd ever need," Timothy says as we slowly circle the room, studying the paintings. "But I didn't anticipate my muse calling to me so strongly. As you can see, I've been prolific."

The paintings are dark, ominous, creepy, full of zombies, corpses, deserted streets, spooky sunsets. Even though I'm no art expert, they instantly give me a sense of pain, suffering and loss. It's like stepping into a gallery of Hell.

"Do you like them?" Timothy asks, chewing a nail, trying to act as if he doesn't care about my answer.

"They're unbelievable," I sigh, and his face lights up.

"They *are* rather good, aren't they?" he chirps, picking up one of the canvases and beaming at it. It's a painting of a young girl, her head cracked open, brains spilling onto the pavement, face smeared with blood. But the way he gazes at it, it could be a painting of a bunch of flowers.

"To be honest, I was never the most skilled of artists," Timothy admits. "But then the zombies rose up, everyone fled or was killed,

I was left here virtually alone, and something changed. It was like I woke up one morning with a new gift."

Timothy sets down the painting and moves on, looking at the canvases in much the same way that a zombie looks at human skulls.

"We're living in tragic, terrible times. I believe that I've been spared and given extra talent so that I can document the troubles. A higher force guides me, empowers me, protects me when I'm on the streets. I shouldn't have survived this long. The fact that I have . . ."

He falls silent and stares at the dark paintings. I can see that they mean everything to him.

"Do you believe in God?" Timothy asks me.

I shuffle uneasily. "I dunno. I don't *not* believe, but I'm not sure."

"I used to be uncertain too," he says, then waves an arm around at the atrocities captured on the canvases. "But who else could have done this to the world? Only the Almighty could have judged mankind and razed it to the ground in such brute, total fashion.

"I don't know why a loving God would do this to us," he whispers. "But if I keep on painting, and study that which I've created for long enough, I think I can find out."

He steps up to one of the paintings, carefully lays his fingers on it and says softly, "This isn't really the work of Timothy Jackson. These were fashioned by the hand of *God*."

FOURTEEN

I think Timothy's a nutter, but I say nothing. If he wants to believe that God is working through him, I don't mind. As long as he doesn't try to convert me, he can believe whatever the hell he likes.

Timothy shows me round the rest of the building. His sleeping quarters are basic, just blankets and pillows laid on the floor in one corner of a small room. He has a larder full of canned goods and bottles of water, some wine and champagne too. Several small freezers full of bread, meat and other perishables.

He keeps a radio, but only turns it on once or twice a week to catch up with any major breaking news.

"My greatest worry is that they'll bomb London," he says. "There was talk of it in the early days. Zombies are everywhere, but they're especially prevalent in the big cities. According to some reporters, the army chiefs discussed leveling the likes of London and New York. Wiser heads prevailed, but if the rumors are to be believed, the suggestion is still on the table. If they ever go ahead with that, I want to get my paintings out of here. I don't mind if I get blown to pieces, but if the world lost my work, it would be an absolute tragedy."

As impressive as the paintings are, I don't think their loss could be classed as a global disaster. But I don't share that opinion with Timothy.

"Don't you get lonely?" I ask as we sit in the main room and Timothy tucks into a corned beef sandwich.

"Why should I?" he counters, nodding at the paintings. "I have those for company. I work all the time when I'm awake and I only sleep for five, maybe six, hours at night. Although I must admit I've often felt exposed. It's dangerous for me out there on the streets, no one to help if I run into trouble. Maybe that's why you've been sent to me."

"What do you mean?" I frown.

He smiles crookedly. "I don't think we met by coincidence. It was fate. God wants you to become my bodyguard, to ensure my work can continue."

As I stare at him, his smile widens. "You can stay with me. I'll share all that I have, help you find brains, be company for you. We'll be a team, Jackson and Smith, doing the work of the Lord. Neither one of us need ever be alone again."

That sounds both tempting and creepy at the same time.

"Did you have a partner before all this?" I ask, to change the subject.

He nods, his smile fading. "Alan. He was a sculptor. He could create the most lifelike hands."

"What happened to him?"

"He became one of *them*," Timothy says emotionlessly. "I went looking for him in his studio, but he'd already been infected. He chased me. Almost killed me. I had to fight for my life. I managed to drive one of his chisels through his head."

Timothy lays down his sandwich and stares ahead at nothing.

"That was when I created my first painting," he says softly. "I mixed Alan's blood with the paint, careful to don gloves before touching it. I painted him as he was, lying there, teeth bared in a death snarl, the handle of the chisel sticking out of his skull. I wept as I painted, knowing it was beautiful, yet hating it at the same time. Part of me—the part that loves, cherishes, cares—died that day. It was a part that needed to die. It would have got in the way of my work."

He lapses into silence, his expression distant.

"Do you still have that painting?" I ask.

"No. I burned it and scattered the ashes over Alan's corpse. It

457

would have felt like theft if I'd taken it. That moment belonged to him. I didn't want to steal it."

"But you've stolen all of these," I murmur, waving at the canvases.

"Yes," he sighs. "I should feel guilty but I don't. I can't afford guilt or love or anything pure like that. To do my job, I have to be as passionless as the zombies I paint and run from." He smiles fleetingly. "That might be another reason why I've made it as far as I have. Maybe they realize, as they draw closer, that I'm not so different than them. In many ways I'm one of the walking dead as well..."

Later Timothy asks if he can sketch me before he hits the sack. I sit for him patiently while he stares at the hole in my chest and tries to bring it to life on a canvas. He shows it to me when he's done. My face is dimly painted with a mix of dark gray colors. All the focus is on the red and green mess around the hole where my boob should be. I hate the way I look in the drawing.

"You don't like it," Timothy notes, disappointed.

"It's just...am I really that ugly?" I ask.

He shakes his head. "You're not ugly at all. But you're a walking corpse. I have to show that, otherwise it won't ring true."

"That's how I look to you?" I sniff. "Pale, distant, vicious?"

"Not vicious," Timothy corrects me. "I would have said *hungry*. Not just for brains, but for your old life, a cure, the ability to be human again. You hunger for things you can no longer have, and that hunger brings you pain."

I think about that hours later, while Timothy sleeps. I've stayed in the room of paintings, studying them silently, looking for familiar faces. I *am* in pain, all the time, and it's not just because I'm undead. I lost my parents and friends—whether they're dead, alive or somewhere between, I'll almost certainly never see them again. I threw an innocent boy to a pack of zombies. I killed humans when I turned. I failed to save Mark from the zom heads. I have blood on my hands. There's rot in my soul.

By rights, I should huddle up in a ball and howl, beg for pity, forgiveness, release. I should hurl myself off a tall building or find a gun and blow my brains out. In this cruel world, I can only experience more pain, ruin more lives, kill or infect. If Timothy stumbled when he was painting me, and I reached out to steady him, and one of my nails nicked his flesh...

I stare at the monsters in the paintings. I'm no less monstrous than any of them. Maybe I'm worse, still being able to think. They have no choice in what they do, but I have. I could eliminate myself, make sure nobody ever suffered again at my twisted, wretched hands.

But I keep thinking about the possibility of revitalizing the rest of the undead hordes. If my blood could be used to restore consciousness in other zombies, it might help bring order back to this crazy, lethal world.

In the morning, when Timothy wakes, I tell him I have to go.

"You're leaving?" He blinks sleepily. "Did I say something to offend you?"

"No," I smile. "But I can't stay. There's going to be a rescue mission soon. I have to surrender, let the soldiers know I'm different, so their scientists can study me and maybe find a way to help other zombies think clearly."

Timothy hums. "The soldiers would, I imagine, be more inclined to execute you on sight."

"Yeah, I know. But I have to try. You can come along too if you want."

He smiles shyly. "I can't leave. I belong here. I wish you luck, B, but your way isn't mine. If they reject you, please bear in mind that you will always be welcome in my studio."

"Thanks." I chuckle drily. "I'd like to shake your hand, but..."

He chuckles too. "One tiny scratch and I'd be history."

"If I do get out," I say hesitantly, "is there anything you need, anything I can send back to you?"

He shakes his head. "Just tell people about my work." He gestures to the canvases. "We'll all be here, the dead and I, waiting for the world to find us."

"What if they don't want to find you?" I ask. "People might not want to look at paintings of zombies, having seen so many of them in the flesh."

"They will," he insists. He walks over to the nearest painting, picks it up and gazes into the face of a monster. "This is the truth, who we are and where we've come from. People are always drawn to the truth. It demands that we acknowledge it and learn."

He closes his eyes and his face whitens.

"In the end, stripped bare of everything else, as everyone is eventually, all we're left with is the truth."

I don't understand that, so I leave Timothy hugging his painting, eyes shut, lost to a world of madness or truth or whatever you want to call it.

FIFTEEN

I've loads of time on my hands, so I decide to do a bit of sightseeing as I'm making my way towards the center of the city, and cut south towards the river.

I come to the Tower of London and stroll around the moat to the main entrance. Amazingly, I've never visited here before, not even on a school field trip.

As I approach the gate, I spot a Beef-eater standing in the shadows of a hut. He growls and steps forward, squinting in the light. Part of his throat has been bitten out and green moss grows round the hole like a wayward beard. I let him examine the gap in my chest. Once he's had a good look, I start forward, but he stops me.

"Out of my way," I snap, but when I

try to wriggle past, he pushes me back. "I'm one of you, idiot!" I shout, and shove him aside.

The Beefeater slams an elbow into the side of my head as I'm passing, catching me by surprise. I haven't seen any zombies fighting with one another. I didn't think I had anything to fear. Seems like I should have been more cautious.

As I stagger around, the inside of my skull ringing wildly, the Beefeater grabs me and hauls me to the ground. He pins me with his knees and makes a howling, gurgling sound before baring his teeth and leaning forward to chew through my skull.

I thought I'd be able to outsmart a zombie in a one-on-one struggle, but the Beefeater has me at his mercy. All I can do is stare at him with horror as he opens his mouth wide and presses his fangs to the cold flesh of my forehead.

For a few seconds the Beefeater holds that position. My sights are locked on the hole in his throat. If I could get a hand free, I could maybe rip the hole wide open. As I'm considering that, and wondering why the Beefeater has paused, he leans back and looks at me stiffly. To my astonishment he holds up a hand and makes a pinching gesture with his thumb and fingers. Then he cocks his head sideways, questioningly.

"You've got to be kidding," I groan, realizing what the issue is.

The Beefeater snarls and makes the gesture with his fingers again. He's a mindless, cannibalistic killer, but somewhere deep in

that ruined brain of his, an old spark of instinct is driving him to do what he did every working day when he was alive.

"OK," I wheeze. "If you let me up, I'll play ball. I'm a good girl, I am."

The Beefeater squints at me. I offer a shaky smile. He grunts and gets off, studying me suspiciously, as if he thinks I'm going to try to trick him.

Shaking my head in disbelief, I get to my feet and make for the ticket office that I passed on my way. The windows have been smashed in. I lean over the counter and grab a ticket from the nearest machine. Returning to the gate, I hand the ticket to the stickler of a zombie Beefeater. He takes it from me, nods gruffly and returns to his post, letting me through.

Unbe-bloody-lievable!

I go on a tour of the famous buildings, but most are packed with zombies – including a lot of overweight tourists who probably prefer their brains in batter and deep fried – so I stick to the paths for the most part. I'm sorry I didn't come when it was operational. I couldn't care less about the Crown jewels, but I'd have loved to learn more about the prisoners who were held here and all the heads that were chopped off.

I recall the legend that if the ravens ever fled the Tower or died out, the city would fall. I always dismissed that as a story most likely cooked up by a raven-handler who wanted to make sure he was never driven out of a job. But as I wander, I note glumly that there isn't a bird to be seen, apart from a few brittle bones, beaks and feathers.

Coincidence? Probably. But it gives me a mild dose of the creeps all the same. Did some scraggly, wild-eyed soothsayer predict this disaster all those centuries ago? Was this plague of the living dead always destined to happen? Uneasy, I push on sooner than I'd meant to, waving good-bye to the Beefeater as I pass, no hard feelings. In an odd sort of way I respect him. He's stuck true to his principles, even in death. I don't mind that he roughed me up. In his position I like to think that I'd do the same.

I cross Tower Bridge. It hasn't escaped the turmoil unscathed. A plane came down in this area—I guess a zombie must have gotten onboard and caused chaos—and chunks of the wreckage are lying in the river where it crashed. On its way, it took out the two walkways at the top of the bridge, smashing straight through them. The towers that they were attached to weren't damaged. It's as if someone came along and snipped off the connecting tunnels with a giant pair of scissors.

Rubble from the walkways is strewn across the road and footpaths, so I have to zigzag my way across. I pause at the point where the two halves of the bridge meet. How cool would it be if I found the engine rooms and raised the drawbridge!

I grin as I imagine it, then shake my head regretfully. Time might be on my side, but I don't have *that* much to play with. Besides, I'm not a child. I'm on a deadly serious mission. This is proper, grown-up business.

The strangely shaped, glass-fronted mayor's building is gleaming in the sun, half-blinding me. I hurry on past and head for the HMS *Belfast*, thinking I might go for a stroll around the deck. But as I approach, I spot humans onboard. They've barricaded the gangway and several are standing guard, heavy rifles hanging by their sides. As I stare at the living people, bewildered to find them here, one of them spots me, raises his gun and opens fire.

Yelping, I duck out of sight and wait for the bullets to stop. When they do, I take off my jacket and wave it at the people on the boat.

"Ahoy!" I roar, getting all nautical. "My name's B Smith. I don't mean you any harm. I want to –"

The guy starts shooting again before I can finish. Bullets rip through my jacket and one almost blows a couple of my fingers off. Cursing, I drop the jacket, then yank it to safety. I don't know who the people on the boat are, but they clearly like their own company, and when someone's armed to the teeth and quick on the trigger, a wise girl gives them all the space in the world that they want.

I detour via Tooley Street. I remember Dad telling me that the London Dungeon used to be here before it moved. I always loved that ghoulish maze of torment and atrocity, but I don't think I'll ever bother with it again. This city of the dead boasts more than enough public horrors, like the hanging zombie on...

I stop and wince—the zombie who was dangling from the lamppost on Bethnal Green Road! I meant to free him when I left

Timothy's place, but I forgot all about him. It's no biggie. In fact it seems ridiculous to worry about a single zombie in this city of monsters. But if I was in his position and someone had the power to set me free and didn't...

What if you free him and he ends up killing Timothy? part of me sulks as I turn to head back the way I came.

"That's life," I shrug.

The zombie doesn't thank me when I cut him down, or show the least sign that he's grateful. Instead, having paused to sniff me in case I'm worth tucking into, he hurries away, seeking shelter, stumbling into anything in his path, unable to see clearly out of his almost totally white eyes.

Feeling more of a time-wasting fool than a good Samaritan, I retrace my steps and make it back to Tooley Street by early afternoon. Moving on, I slip past Southwark Bridge and cast a wary eye over the shell of the Globe. I never went to a show there – wild horses couldn't have dragged me – but I know all about this place. It's where they used to put on Shakespearean plays every summer.

As I consider the fact that nobody will ever stage a four-hour version of *Hamlet* or *King Lear* here ever again, I break out into a smile and chuckle wickedly— the downfall of civilization isn't *all* bad news!

SIXTEEN

I'm heading for the impressive-looking Tate Modern when I spot a small boat pulling up to the pier. I watch with astonishment as nine people pile out and march towards shore like tourists on a day trip.

But these aren't like any tourists I've ever seen. All nine—four men and five women—are dressed in blue robes. Their arms are bare. Each has a tiny blue symbol scrawled across their forehead. And they chant softly as they progress.

I hang back as the group ignores the art museum and heads on to the pedestrian bridge, which my dad used to call the Wobbly Bridge, since it wobbled so badly when it first opened that they had to close it for months to steady it up.

Something about these people unsettles me. They don't seem to be carrying any weapons, yet they're walking around openly. Hasn't anyone told them about the zombies?

I follow the group onto the bridge, wait until we're halfway across – St. Paul's Cathedral towers ahead of us – then call out to them, "Hey!"

They stop but don't turn. I edge closer, skin prickling, ready to dive over the side of the bridge if they produce guns from beneath their robes and open fire. But although the men and women glance at me as I slip past them, nobody reacts in any other way.

The woman at the head of the group studies me with a solemn expression as I stop before her. She's pretty, but has a pinched, stern face. Her hair is pure white – all the others have white hair too, which makes me think it's dye – so it's hard to judge her age.

"You are one of the restless dead," the woman says, having noted the hole in my chest.

"Yeah."

She cocks her head. "I did not know that the undead could speak."

"Most can't. I'm an exception."

The woman nods, then spreads her arms wide. "I am Sister Clare, of the Order of the Shnax. Have you come to attack us, foul creature of the lost?"

"No."

"You have not come to slice open our skulls and feast on our brains?" she presses, pale blue eyes hard in the glaring sunlight.

"Not unless you want me to," I joke.

"There!" the woman exclaims to those behind her. "The blessings of the Shnax are with us, as I told you they would be."

The people in the robes mutter appreciatively and bow their heads. Sister Clare basks in their adulation, then trains her gaze on me again.

"Are you a vile imp sent to guide us?" she asks haughtily.

"No," I growl, resisting the urge to punch her in the nose. "I saw you getting out of the boat and was curious. I wanted to warn you as well. It's dangerous here. The zombies –"

"We know all about them," she interrupts. "They are why we have come, to test our faith against theirs."

"What are you talking about?" I frown. "Zombies don't have any faith. They're brainless."

"They are instruments of the dark forces of the universe," she corrects me. "By walking without fear among them, we will challenge those who work through their pitiful forms and reclaim this ground that they would steal from us. If you mean neither to help nor hinder us, then step aside or face the wrath of the Shnax."

The woman waves a hand at me and glides past imperiously. The others follow, nodding and mumbling. A few smirk at me. One of the men touches the symbol on his forehead, then points at me as if to say, "I've got my eye on you!"

474

I don't care much for Sister Clare or her sneering tone, but these weirdos have caught my attention. I can't resist following, to find out what they're up to. So, ignoring the fact that they don't care for my company, I trail after them as they cross the bridge and wander into the zombie-infested bowels of the city.

SEVENTEEN

The fearless members of the Order of the Shnax march to St. Paul's and stop outside, chanting happily, beaming at one another. The sun is shining brightly and no zombies are on the streets. It's as if we have the city to ourselves.

Sister Clare leads the group on a full circuit of the cathedral, then heads east. I try to wring more information out of her as they proceed.

"You know you're all going to be killed."

She raises an eyebrow. "You might wish for our deaths, vulgar beast of the otherworld, but you will be disappointed. We have the power of the Shnax on our side. No harm will befall us."

"What *are* the Shnax?" I press. "Some sort of religious group?"

"We are of the true religion," Sister Clare tells me, and points a finger at the sky. "The religion of the stars."

"The stars…" the others echo dreamily, all pointing upwards.

"Celestial beings have always gazed down on us," Sister Clare continues. "Since the dawn of mankind they have encouraged us, rewarded us when we are deserving, punished us when we have sinned. They are the Shnax."

"Aliens?" I laugh. "Give me a break!"

She smiles condescendingly. "Like so many others, you can only mock. That is why you were turned into a pitiful mockery of the human form while we were spared. This world was disgusting, over-crowded with vain, petty humans. It needed clearing so that a fresh, clean civilization could grow out of the ashes of the old.

"The Shnax would never have done this to us, since they are creatures of love, but there are other forces at work in the universe, agents of destruction. The Shnax protected us from them in the past, but this time, for our own good, they let their foes wreak havoc. But they shielded the believers and kept us safe, so that we can guide the others who survived."

I gape at Sister Clare and the lunatics who follow her.

"You think that you know better than us," Sister Clare smirks. "I see it in your eyes, as lifeless as they are."

"Come on," I chuckle uneasily. "You can't really believe that aliens did this or that they're guarding you."

"If not the Shnax, then who?" she asks.

"The government...scientists...terrorists...take your pick."

She shakes her head. "This apocalypse was not the work of humans. No mortal could have subjected the world to terrors on such a diabolic scale. Mankind has been culled. The weak have been cut down and set against the strong. It is the result of a godly hand, but there are no gods meddling in our affairs, only the Shnax."

"Who told you about these aliens? Did you read about them in a magazine? See a show on TV?"

"They contacted me directly," she sniffs. "They spoke to me in dreams to begin with. Later I learned to put myself into a trance and speak with them that way."

"So you hear voices," I murmur.

"Go ahead," she snaps, her smile vanishing. "Laugh at me. You won't be the first. But I told people this would happen. Nobody believed me until it was too late. Now that the worst has come to pass, people are starting to see that I was right. These are the first of my disciples, but they will not be the last. When we emerge from these haunted streets, alive and untouched, more will flock to our side. The survivors will see that I am the mouthpiece of the Shnax, and the world will finally offer us the respect that we are due."

Sister Clare turns to the others and cries, "Out of the darkness of the skies came the Shnax!"

"Out of the darkness!" they respond, heads bobbing, fingers twitching.

The fanatics carry on, wandering aimlessly. I think about abandoning them—I should be heading west, not wasting my time on these maniacs—but I'll feel bad if I leave them without at least trying to make them see sense.

"You can't really believe that aliens will save you from the zombies," I challenge them.

"How else are we protected?" Sister Clare retorts smugly, waving a hand at the buildings around us. "These are the homes of the damned, populated by the lost and vicious hordes, yet no monster comes out to attack us."

"You've been lucky," I argue. "Sunlight hurts zombies. They rest up in the daytime. If you're still here when night falls..." I draw a finger across my throat.

Sister Clare scowls at me. "You know nothing of these matters, child of the lost. Leave us be."

"I know that you're mad," I snap. "And I know you don't truly believe what you're preaching. You'd put your lives fully on the line if you did."

"What are you talking about?" Sister Clare asks, drawing to a halt.

"It's brave of you to come here," I drawl, smiling tightly at the men and women in the robes. "But you'd have come when it was dark if you wanted to prove beyond doubt that you were under heavenly protection. Or you'd go into one of these buildings, packed with the living dead, stand in the middle of them and chant away to your heart's content. But you don't because you know deep down that you'd be eaten alive."

I flash my sharp teeth at them. Sister Clare's face reddens and she opens her mouth to have a go at me. But then one of the men says, "The girl speaks the truth."

Sister Clare's eyes fill with rage. "You doubt me, Sean?" she shrieks.

"No," the man called Sean says without lowering his gaze. "I believe. But we must face our enemy. If the Shnax are looking down on us kindly, as I'm sure they are, we can walk through the ranks of the undead and the whole world will know that what we say is true. Otherwise people will sneer at us, as she has, and claim it was merely good fortune that we passed through these streets unharmed."

Sister Clare licks her lips nervously. I catch a glimpse of uncertainty in her expression. Part of her knows this is madness.

"I can lead you back to your boat," I say softly. "You can return to wherever you were hiding before. You'll die if you go on."

She stares at me for a long moment. Then she spits in my face. As I pull back, shocked, she faces her followers. "The demon wants to lure us back to our boat and send us on our way. She is afraid of us, afraid of the Shnax."

The other men and women start jeering and spitting at me. My temper flares and I flex my fingers, ready to rip them to pieces. I take a step forward, snarling. I think, if Sister Clare stepped away, I'd go for her. But she doesn't retreat. Instead she takes a step towards me, tilting her head back, offering her throat.

"Go ahead, servant of the darkness," she hisses. "Kill me if that is what your foul masters demand. I will die happily in the service of the Shnax."

The others fall to their knees and offer their throats too. I shake my head and lower my hand, remembering Tyler Bayor, recalling my vow to be a better person.

Sister Clare tuts. Then her features soften. "No, it is wrong of me to blame you for what you have become. You were weak, as so many were, but it is not for us to condemn you. You are suffering enough."

Her gaze settles on something behind me. She starts to smile again. "But the imp is right about one thing, brothers and sisters. We *do* need to confront the forces of darkness directly, to prove beyond a shadow of a doubt that we are blessed. Let us face our destiny and show the world that ours is the one true way. Follow me!"

Sister Clare sets off at a jog. The others rise and hurry after her, chanting even faster than before, buzzing now, ready to follow their leader into the jaws of Hell if she demands it of them.

Turning to see where they're going, I realize she's leading them to a place even deadlier than the fabled gates of the underworld. We've come to the threshold of Liverpool Street Station. There are probably scores of zombies down there on the concourse, sheltering from the sun. Sister Clare is at the top of the steps that descend into that murky den of the dead.

"No!" I yell. "Don't do it. I didn't mean to dare you. I believe. You don't have to prove anything to me. Come back."

But Sister Clare only flashes me a smile of twisted triumph. Then she heads down, followed by the others, into the zombie-friendly gloom.

EIGHTEEN

I can't bear to let them go off by themselves, so I race after them, down the steps
into the stomach of what was once com-
muter heaven.

It's not as dark down here as I thought.
The station lets in quite a lot of light, so
most of the zombies in residence have
avoided the concourse. Still, there must
be a hundred or more of the beasts who
were resting in the shade around the main
ring of the station. And every single one of
them is now pushing forward, closing in
on the nine robed, doomed humans.

Sister Clare acts as if she's unaware
of the threat and marches to the center
of the concourse. Her chant turns into a
song and the others take it up, a dull tune

about stars and aliens and how the chosen will be spared the wrath of the skies.

The deluded humans come to a halt in the middle of the station and form a circle, hands linked, feet planted firmly, singing joyously. The zombies push in closer... closer...

Then stop about a yard away.

I stare with disbelief at the white-haired men and women singing loudly, the zombies massed around them but not moving in for the kill, swaying softly as if held in place by the sound of the song. Or by something else?

It's crazy, but I find myself starting to wonder. As I slip through the ranks of the living dead, into the empty space around Sister Clare and her followers, I'm ready to believe. Why not? Their story makes as much sense as anything else in these bewildering times.

"You see?" Sister Clare whispers ecstatically. "They're held in place by the power of the Shnax. They cannot raise a hand against those who are true."

"This is incredible," I croak.

"Yes," Sister Clare says with justified satisfaction. Then she frees her hands and holds them over her head. "We can break the circle now. Let us move among them. Show no fear. The Shnax will protect us as long as we continue to trust."

Not all of the others look so sure about that, but they separate as ordered and edge forward.

The zombies don't budge.

486

"Part, sons and daughters of the darkness!" Sister Clare shrieks, swinging her right arm around like a scythe.

Not a single zombie gives ground.

One of the women loses her nerve and tries to push through, muttering sharply, "Get out of my way!"

A zombie pulls her to the ground. He sinks his teeth into her exposed arm and tears loose a chunk of flesh. The woman screams.

"No!" Sister Clare shouts. "Don't be afraid! Show no fear! We must be strong!"

But it's as if the scream acts as a starting pistol for the rest of the living dead. They surge forward, fingers extended, teeth bared, and throw themselves upon the stunned, defenseless children of the Shnax.

NINETEEN

The tortured death cries of the humans ring out loud. More zombies come running from within the Tube station attached to the railway concourse, not wanting to miss out on the feast.

I throw myself into the middle of the carnage and punch zombies aside, creating a narrow gap. "This way!" I bellow.

I'm closest to Sister Clare, and she hasn't been attacked yet, so she's first past. She reels away from me and pushes through the divide, her face a mask of shock and fear. She starts to pause, but I shove her hard, careful not to pierce her flesh with my finger bones, aware that I'm as much of a threat as any revived.

"Run!" I roar at her, then try to pull some of the others free of the chaos.

Sean, the man who spoke up earlier when I was challenging Sister Clare, is the only one to get close to me. His eyes are bulging. His teeth are bared like the fangs of the monsters around us, but with terror, not hunger.

Then the finger bones of one of the zombies tear into Sean's chest, ripping through his robes, slicing into the flesh beneath. He stops and looks down at the wound. His fingers rise to touch it. All of the tension slips out of him. He smiles wearily at me, resigned to his fate. As I stare at him with horror, he spreads his arms and starts singing again. He carries on singing even when the zombies drag him down and chew through the bone of his skull, although towards the end it becomes more of a gurgling noise and the words are lost, along with the tune.

I don't stay to watch him die. As soon as I realize that the others are beyond help, I race after Sister Clare, determined to do all I can to save at least one of the nine, even though she probably deserves salvation the least of any of them.

Sister Clare was headed towards the stairs, but the zombies pouring through from the Tube station have blocked that route. As she hesitates, I call to her, "I can see another exit at the far end. Follow me."

We set off across the concourse. The way ahead is clear and I think we stand a chance. But then the zombies who couldn't get their hands on the other humans set their sights on Sister Clare and me—in the chaos, they won't be able to tell me apart from one of the living, so they'll tear into me too if they catch us.

A couple of seconds later it's clear we can't make it. Zombies stream into the path ahead of us, blocking the way. I draw to a halt and Sister Clare runs into my back. She tries to break past but I stop her.

"We're trapped."

"No!" she screams. "You've got to save me! Don't let me die!"

"I thought you were happy to die," I grunt, but bitterness won't do either of us any good. I look around desperately as the zombies close in. There's a row of shops to our right. The doors of most are wide open and the shops are totally indefensible. But a security grille has been pulled down over the front of one shop. It doesn't hang all the way to the ground, which means it isn't locked.

"There!" I yell, darting towards the shop. Sister Clare scurries along behind me. The zombies aren't much farther back.

No time to mess about. I throw myself to the floor and push up the grille. As Sister Clare ducks and skids forward, I roll, slam down the grille and leap to my feet.

"I need something to hold this in place!" I shout, but Sister Clare is moaning, lying in a huddle on the floor, hands clamped over her ears. With a curse, I look around and spot a broom with a wooden handle. Grabbing it, I stick it through one of the slots in the grille, then jam it against the wall. It wouldn't hold back any thinking person for more than a few seconds, but the living dead aren't as sharp as they once were. Ignorant of the broom, they tug on the grille, trying to force it up, unable to figure out why it isn't moving.

I back away from the grille and sink to the floor beside Sister Clare. I stare at the zombies glumly. The broom won't hold for long. They'll push through in a minute or two and that will be the end of the human. Probably the end of me as well. The zombies are in a feeding frenzy. I'm guessing they won't pause to assess me, just dig straight into my skull and tear my brain out.

Sister Clare seems to realize she's still alive and lowers her hands, looking up with startled, fearful eyes. When she sees the zombies struggling with the grille, she smiles hopefully. "You've stopped them."

"Only for a while. If you want to pray to your aliens, you'd better be quick."

"There must be a lock for the grille somewhere," she pants, looking around frantically.

I snort. "Even if we could find it and lock ourselves in, what's the point? They won't leave as long as they can hear your heartbeat and smell your brain. Better to die quickly and get it over with, rather than sit here and starve."

"But there might be a way out the back."

"We're underground," I remind her. "My finger bones are tough, but they can't burrow through walls."

Sister Clare makes a low moaning noise, then grabs my arm and glares at me with some of her old determination. "Then you have to convert me."

"What?" I frown.

"Make me like you." She points at the hole in my chest and the bones jutting out of my fingers. "You're different. You can think and speak. If I end up like you, I can continue with my work."

"*Continue?*" I splutter.

"We were weak," she says. "They attacked because they sensed our fear. If I was like you, I need not fear them. I could bring others here and they'd feed on my strength and certainty. We would triumph."

"Are you even crazier than I thought?" I shout. "You've already led eight people to their deaths. How many more do you want to sacrifice?"

"As many as the Shnax demand," she snaps. "They wish to save us, but they can only do that if we're strong. Please, help me, don't let me be eaten, give me the power to continue with my mission."

"Even if I wanted to, I couldn't. I don't know how I –"

"Please!" she screams, not wanting to hear the truth, clasping her hands over her ears again.

I stare at the deranged woman, lost for words. Then a cruel part of me whispers, *Why not? She's doomed anyway. She lured her followers to their deaths and made fools of them. It's only fitting that you should do the same to her.*

"All right," I tell her, pulling her hands away from her ears. "We'll do it if you're sure. Are you?"

"Yes," she gasps.

"Then on your own head be it," I snarl, and pull her in close,

493

as if to kiss her. But instead I bite into her lower lip, drawing blood and infecting her with my undead germs.

"Vile girl!" Sister Clare snaps, pushing me away and wiping blood from her lip. "How dare you press your mouth to mine! I should…"

She raises a hand to slap me. Then she realizes what I've done and backs away, whimpering softly, staring at the blood on her fingers.

"You bit me," she whispers.

"Yeah," I say, feeling rotten now that the moment has passed.

"Will I retain my senses?" she cries. "Will I become like you, not like *them*?" She points at the zombies pulling at the grille.

"Of course," I lie, not knowing if it's true or not, wanting to give her some comfort in her final moments.

"Wonderful," she sighs, leaning against the wall, waiting for the change, probably privately plotting her undead takeover of the world.

Sister Clare shudders. She bends over, gasps, collapses, then screams as her body starts to shut down. I turn away, not wanting to see her teeth lengthen, the bones break through her fingertips, the light fade from her eyes.

The handle of the broom snaps. The grille clatters upwards. Zombies spill into the shop and swarm around us.

But they don't attack, because they can see the human turning. That makes them pause and they sniff me rather than strike. When

they realize I'm one of them, they leave us be and return to the concourse, disappointed and hungry.

After about a minute, I look around guiltily. Sister Clare is staring at me numbly, no hint of life in her expression, green moss already sprouting from the bite mark on her lip.

"Sorry," I murmur. "But you did ask for it."

Making a sighing sound, I blow a regretful kiss to the shadowy remains of Sister Clare, then push through the undead crowd outside the shop, patiently easing my way clear of the crush, past the bodies of the humans who were killed, up the stairs and back into the light of a world that seems even more lost and disturbing than it did an hour or two before.

TWENTY

I make my way west, then hole up in an abandoned coffee shop on Fleet Street when night falls. Every time I think about Sister Clare and her pack of nutjobs – and I think about them lots over the course of the night – I wince sadly. What a waste of life.

I feel guilty too, for biting Sister Clare, knowing it was almost certain that she wouldn't end up like me, that she'd become just another mindless revived.

"The zombies would have killed me if I hadn't done it," I whisper.

"*So?*" I snort.

"I needed to get out," I argue, "to hand myself over to the soldiers, so that they can use my blood to maybe find a way to defeat the zombies."

"Yeah," I retort cynically. *"If they don't shoot me first."*

"I've got to think positively."

"In this world?" I sneer. *"Get real!"*

The night passes slowly. I hear the dead milling around outside, searching for prey, but no screams or gunfire. If any of the living are heading towards the center to be rescued, they're lying low like me. That's not surprising. Only the cunning will have lasted this long. Smart operators like that are hardly going to give themselves away cheaply this close to escape.

As the sun rises and the zombies return to the shadows, I move out and push on, hitting the Strand. Finding a radio in a shop, I tune in to the news channel and wait. It's not long before an excited presenter says that the rescue is scheduled for midday in Trafalgar Square. He tells anyone who is listening to make sure they're present at twelve on the dot, but not to show themselves in the square before that, in case they attract unwanted attention.

I head down the Strand, taking my time. I swing right and check out Covent Garden, once a throng of tourists, shoppers and street performers. I'm half-hoping to find some zombie jugglers, maybe throwing limbs around instead of bowling pins or juggling balls, but the place is as dead as any other part of London.

I pick up new clothes for myself in one of the fashionable

designer shops, so that I look fresh and clean. I think about tearing a hole in my sweatshirt and T-shirt, to expose the empty cavity, but decide to leave it as it is for the moment, so that I can get close to the soldiers before they realize I'm a zombie.

I file down my teeth and the bones sticking out of my fingers and toes. The bones are harder to disguise than the hole in my chest. I pull on a pair of shoes that are three sizes too big for me, and gloves that are more suited to a giant. The shoes are uncomfortable, and the gloves won't hide the shape of the bones up close, but they should get me near and give me a chance to make my case.

I also pick up a pair of watches that would have cost almost as much as our flat in the old days. They're accurate to the smallest fraction of a second, resistant to shock, waterproof, and they automatically adjust for summer or winter time. I attach one to either wrist, so that I can be absolutely sure of the time. I don't want to miss my shot at rescue because of a dodgy watch!

I get to Trafalgar Square five minutes before midday. I'm not the first to arrive. Seven people are already present, three men, a woman with a baby, a girl of eight or nine and a boy a bit younger than me. They're huddled together in the middle of the square, between the two fountains, ignoring the warning not to arrive earlier than twelve. I was expecting warriors, tough men in leathers, carrying guns. But this lot looks like any group of tourists that you would have seen here a year ago.

"Are you one of us?" the woman with the baby shouts when she spots me striding towards them.

"That depends—who are you?" I shout back.

They relax at the sound of my voice. They obviously don't know about talking zombies or they wouldn't be so trusting.

Others come out of the shadows as I draw closer to the group in the center. Two from the direction of The Mall, one from behind the Fourth Plinth, three more–not together, but separately–from Whitehall. They approach cautiously, checking out the buildings as they creep along, keeping to the middle of the road.

I was worried that the people at the heart of the square might grow suspicious if I kept my distance, but to my relief the other newcomers hang back too, not willing to associate too closely with strangers, ready to make a break for freedom if anything goes wrong.

There's no cheerful banter. Apart from the seven in the middle, who mutter among themselves, nobody speaks. Everyone looks wary, studying the others suspiciously, scanning the buildings around the square for signs of life—or, to be more accurate, *un*life.

At twelve o'clock exactly, four helicopters buzz into view overhead. They're military vehicles, armed with missiles and machine guns.

The helicopters do a few circuits over the square, checking to make sure that everyone beneath them is human. Some of the people cheer and wave. I don't. I'm not sure if the soldiers will view me as a friend or an enemy, so I don't want to draw their scrutiny until I have to.

Satisfied with what they see, three of the helicopters set down on the terrace at the top of the steps, between the square and the National Gallery. The fourth remains airborne, hovering ominously, the pilot keeping watch over the others, ready to support them from the air if necessary.

Four soldiers slide out of each helicopter. The pilots remain in place, engines running, rotors whirring. The noise is deafening, especially with my advanced sense of hearing. I grit my teeth and try not to show any signs of distress, not wanting to appear different from the other survivors.

The twelve soldiers advance to the top of the steps. Everyone in the square has started moving towards them. A couple of people are running. But before anyone can set foot on the stairs, two of the soldiers open fire with their rifles and spray the steps with bullets.

As we come to a shocked halt, one of the soldiers moves forward and addresses us through a megaphone.

"No need to panic, people," he barks. "We've done this before, so we know what we're doing. We're going to get all of you out of here, but there are rules you have to obey. We've put them in place

for your safety as well as ours, to ensure no infected specimens sneak through."

"We're not infected!" one of the men yells. "You can see that by looking at us!"

"Looks can be deceptive," the soldier replies. "We don't take risks. I'm sure you can appreciate our position, and the fact that the more cautiously we proceed, the safer you'll all be. We want to get you out of here as swiftly as possible, so listen up and do what you're told."

"This is crazy!" the man roars, starting forward indignantly. "Zombies could be closing in on us while you're wasting time. Let us through."

"If you take one more step, sir, you *will* be executed," the soldier snaps. As the man hesitates, he continues. "We'll do all that we can to help you, but if we sense a threat, we'll eliminate it, no questions asked. You *do not* want to push us."

The man gulps, raises his hands and takes three big steps back.

"OK," the soldier says. "Here's how it works. First you're going to undress. No need to be shy, we've seen it all before. Once you're naked, you'll approach one by one as we summon you, leaving your clothes behind. We'll check you quickly, make sure you're clean, then you can collect your gear and board the helicopters. When we've loaded everyone up, we're out of here."

The other people grumble but begin stripping down, wanting

to escape this city of the dead more than they want to protect their modesty.

I don't take off anything. Instead I wave my hands over my head and call to the soldier. "Sir!"

The soldier smirks at me. "I told you there was no need to be shy. Don't worry, girl, nobody's going to take photos of you."

"That doesn't bother me. But I'm...I'm not like the rest of them."

His smile disappears in an instant. He takes a closer look at me, my hat, the sunglasses, the gloves and shoes.

"Take off your gloves," the soldier growls. Something in his voice alerts the others and everybody pauses and stares at me. The soldiers adjust their guns. They're all pointing in my direction now.

"I don't want to cause any trouble," I cry, not moving in case I set off a trigger-happy marksman.

"Remove your gloves!" the soldier with the megaphone roars.

"I will," I moan. "I'm doing it now." I lower my hands and start to peel off the gloves, slow as I can. "But you're going to see bones. And when I take off my clothes, you'll see –"

"She's infected!" a soldier shouts, and some of the people in the square start to scream.

"No!" I shriek, raising my hands again and waving them over my head. "I want to help. I came here to offer my services."

"Screw that," the soldier with the megaphone snaps. "I told you we don't take chances. Fire!"

Before I can say anything else, every soldier in the square starts shooting, and the nightmarish bellow of their guns drowns out even the ear-shattering thunder of the helicopter blades.

TWENTY-ONE

The soldiers' reaction hasn't come as a complete shock, I hoped this wouldn't happen but I half-expected it. So when I was edging forward a few minutes ago, I carefully positioned myself by one of the fountains, just in case.

As the soldiers rain down hell on me, I hurl myself to my right, into the dried-out fountain. The bullets pound the base. Stone chips and splinters fly in all directions and the piercing whine makes me gasp with pain. But I'm safe for the moment. They can't hit me from where they are, not unless I do something stupid like stick my head up.

The soldiers stop firing and the one with the megaphone shouts at the rest of the people. "This is why we have rules! Get your damn clothes off as quick as you can or we'll shoot the lot of you!"

"We didn't know she was one of them!" a woman screams. "We'd never seen her before. She spoke to us. How can she speak if she's dead?"

"The dead have all sorts of tricks up their sleeves," the soldier says. "Now show us your flesh, and hurry, before the noise brings scores of curious zombies down upon us."

While the people are undressing, I roar at the soldiers, "There's no need to do this. I want to help. If you don't want my help, fine, I'll leave you be. But I'm different than the other zombies. Maybe you can take some of my blood and —"

"I don't want to hear it!" the soldier yells. "Just shut up and play dead, you damn zombie bitch!"

"Up yours, numbnuts!" I retort angrily.

"Right, that's enough," he snarls, then barks a command into his radio.

Overhead, the airborne helicopter buzzes forward. I've seen enough war movies to know what's coming next. With a yelp, I throw myself out of the fountain. My right shoe flew from my foot when I leapt in, and now my left drops away too. But the shoes are the least of my worries. Because as I scramble clear, the pilot hits a button and launches a missile.

The fountain explodes behind me and I'm tossed clear across the square by the force of the explosion. I slam into a lamppost and slump to the ground. My ears are ringing. The hat and glasses have been blown from my head. I'm half-blind and all the way shaken.

Sitting up in a wounded daze, I catch a blurred glimpse of the helicopter gliding in for the kill. I've nowhere to hide now and no strength to push myself towards safety even if I did. Spitting out thick, congealed blood, I sneer at the pilot—just a vague, ghostly figure from here—and give him the finger, the only missile in my own personal arsenal.

There's another explosion. I can't shut my eyes against it, so I cover them with a scratched, bloodied hand instead. Flames lick across the sky and I feel like I'm being sunburnt in the space of a few sizzling seconds. There's a roaring, maniacal sound, as if two huge sheets of welded-together metal are being wrenched apart. Then the dull thudding noises of an impossibly heavy rainfall.

None of this makes sense. The second explosion should have been the end of me. B Smith blown to bits—good-bye, cruel world. But I'm still alive and there's a gap in the sky where the helicopter should be. What the hell?

Lowering my hand, I peer through a dust cloud that has risen in front of me like a shroud. As it starts to clear, I see the wreckage of the helicopter scattered across the ground, mixed in with the remains of the fountain. Some bones jut out of the mess, all that's left of the pilot and any soldiers who were with him.

I gape at the bewildering scene, then look up at the steps. And that's when everything clicks into sudden, sickening focus.

509

A second armed force has spilled out of the National Gallery. Dozens of people, more appearing by the second, race down the steps at the side of the pillared entrance, or leap over the railing to land directly on the terrace. One of them has a bazooka. Smoke is spiraling from its muzzle.

The troops spewing out of the art museum are neither human nor zombies. Most are wearing jeans and hoodies. Their skin is disfigured, purple in places, peeling away from the bone in others, full of ugly, pus-filled wounds and sores. They have straggly gray hair and pale yellow eyes. I can't see from here, but I know that inside their mouths their few remaining teeth are black and stained, their tongues scabby and shriveled, and if they spoke, the words would come out snarled and gurgled.

These are the mutants I spotted in the Imperial War Museum shortly before the zombie uprising, the same monstrous creatures who stormed the underground complex. I know no more about them now than I did then, except for two things. One—they cause chaos whenever they appear. Two—they're led by a foul being even weirder than they are.

As if on cue, as the mutants tear into the startled soldiers, I spot him emerging behind them, colorful as a peacock set against the gray backdrop of the National Gallery. He stands between two pillars, arms spread wide, grinning insanely, the pink, *v*-shaped gouges carved into the flesh between his eyes and lips visible even from here, through the dust and with my poor eyes.

I can't see the button that he wears on his chest, the one with his name on it. But I know that if I could, it would read, as it did when I first met him underground on that night of spiders and death, *Mr. Dowling.*

Send in the clown!

TWENTY-TWO

The mutants swarm round the soldiers and helicopters. They're soon joined by a pack of zombies, who follow them out of the National Gallery, shaded from the sun by long, *Matrix*-style leather jackets, huge straw hats and sunglasses. I'm sure the jackets, hats and glasses were chosen for them by Mr. Dowling.

Two of the helicopters are overrun before their pilots can react. The third manages to clear the ground, but then the mutant with the bazooka reloads, takes aim and fires. It comes crashing back to earth, taking out the bottom section of a building where a bookshop once stood.

The soldiers fight doggedly, first with their guns, then with knives and their hands. But there are too many mutants and zombies. Within a minute the last of the human troops has been cut down and Trafalgar Square belongs to Mr. Dowling and his warped warriors.

A few of the people who came to be rescued have made a break for freedom. They race from the square, hounded by a handful of whooping mutants and hungry zombies. The others are huddled together in the center, surrounded, trapped, alive for the moment but undoubtedly doomed.

Some of the zombies focus on the humans and move in for the kill, but stop when a mutant blows a whistle. I've seen this before—Mr. Dowling's henchmen have the power to command the living dead.

The mutants jeer at the weeping, shrieking humans and stab playfully at them with knives and spears, not interested in wounding them, just in winding them up. I want to try to help, cause a disturbance, break through their ranks and create a gap for the others to escape through. But I can only sit, dazed, ears ringing, legs useless, and watch.

Mr. Dowling trots down the steps of the National Gallery at last, doing a little dance as he descends. The mutants applaud wildly and screech at the humans to clap too.

As the clown nimbly waltzes down the steps from the terrace to the square, I get a clearer look at him. The flesh of a severed face hangs from each shoulder of his jacket. Lengths of human guts are wrapped round his arms, and severed ears are pinned to his trouser legs. A baby's skull sticks out of the end of each of his ridiculously large red shoes. His hair is all different sorts of colors and lengths, torn from the heads of others in clumps and stapled into place. The flesh around his eyes has been cut away and filled in with soot. Two *v*-shaped channels run from just under either eye, down to his upper lip, and the bone beneath has been painted pink. A human eye has been stuck to the end of his nose and little red stars are dotted around it.

The trapped humans stop screaming as the clown approaches and the mutants pull back to let him through. Like me, these people have seen a lot since the world went to hell, but nothing like this. Mr. Dowling belongs to another dimension entirely, one even crazier and more twisted than this undead hellhole.

To conclude his dance, Mr. Dowling leaps into the air and pirouettes, then drops to one knee and spreads his arms wide. The mutants howl their appreciation and stamp their feet raucously. One of them holds up a sheet of paper with a large 10 scrawled across it in red.

Mr. Dowling bows his head and accepts the acclaim with false humility. Then he hops back to both feet and prowls round the humans, grinning at them like a piranha, his eyes twitching insanely, skin wriggling as if insects are burrowing about beneath the flesh.

One of the mutants steps up next to the clown and blows his whistle sharply, waving an arm for silence. I could be wrong, but I think it's the one who tried to kidnap a baby in the Imperial War

Museum on the day when I first learned that this wasn't just a world of normal humans.

When all of the mutants are still, the one with the whistle addresses the sobbing people at the heart of the crush in a choked, gurgly voice.

"Ladies, gentlemen and children—it's showtime! Welcome to the weird, wild, wonderful world of Mr. Dowling and his amazing cohorts. Thrill to the sight of the living dead and their masters. Coo as we rip you from head to toe. Cheer as we make intricate designs out of your gooey innards. Worship as we take you to Hell and beyond."

The mutants cheer again, but the humans only stare in bewilderment. Most of them are weeping openly.

"Please!" one of the men begs. "Spare us! We're not...we won't...anything you ask of us..."

"Hush," the mutant frowns. "Mr. Dowling did not come here to entertain futile pleas. He came to party!"

"Party!" the mutants holler, shaking their fists and weapons over their heads.

When they're silent again, Mr. Dowling points a long, bony finger at the woman with the baby and makes a shrill squeaking noise. The mutant next to him listens carefully, then crooks a finger at the woman and beckons her forward.

"No!" a man next to her shouts. "Take me, not the baby!"

"As you wish," the mutant shrugs. He blows his whistle and a pair of zombies lurch into action, grab the man and drag him to the ground. His screams ring loud around the square, but not for long.

"Now," the mutant says pleasantly, crooking his finger at the woman again.

She stumbles forward, shaking her head, crying, clutching the baby to her chest. "Please," she whispers. "Please. Please. Please."

The mutant makes a soothing, tutting noise, then pries the baby from her and hands it to Mr. Dowling. The clown takes the child with surprising gentleness and rocks it in his arms. The baby gurgles happily, unaware of the danger it's in. Mr. Dowling makes another sharp, questioning noise.

"Is it a boy or a girl?" the mutant asks politely.

"A guh-guh-guh-girl," the woman gasps, eyes on her child, fingers clasped in silent prayer, rooted to the spot, helpless and terrified.

The clown nods slowly and squeals again.

"Mr. Dowling says that he's glad," the mutant translates. "He's not in a boyish mood today. If it had been a boy, he would have dashed its head open and fed its brain to our zombies. But since it's a girl, he's inclined to be merciful."

"He…he's not going to hurt her?" the woman croaks, tearing her eyes away from the baby and looking to the mutant with the slightest glimmer of hope.

"That depends on the choice you make," the mutant says.

"*Choose…*" the other mutants murmur. The word sounds obscene on their scabby, twisted tongues.

"I don't understand," the woman frowns.

"It's very simple," the mutant grins. "The ever-generous Mr. Dowling is giving you a choice. You can choose to spare your baby or your colleagues." He nods at the other humans in the square.

"You mean..." She gulps, eyes widening.

"You got it, sweet thing," the mutant chuckles obscenely. "We butcher the baby or we kill everybody else. Your call. Now—choose."

"*Choose...*" the others repeat again, their pale yellow eyes alive with repulsive yearning.

As the woman struggles with her choice, someone squats next to me and says, "As distasteful as this is, it should be intriguing. Mr. Dowling always puts on a memorable show."

I look around in a daze. The man is tall and thin, but with a pot belly. He's wearing a striped suit with a pink shirt. He has white hair and pale skin, long fingers and unbelievably large eyes, twice the size of any normal person's, almost fully white, but with a tiny dark pupil burning fiercely at the center of each.

"*Owl Man,*" I moan.

TWENTY-THREE

"You remember me," the man with the owl-like eyes beams. "How sweet." He winks, then blows me a mocking kiss.

"This can't be real," I mutter. "I must be dreaming."

"Don't be silly," Owl Man tuts. "You cannot sleep, so it follows that you cannot dream. Therefore this must be real."

"It could be a hallucination."

"Possibly," he concedes. "But it isn't. Now tell me, are you hurt? Can I help you?"

He reaches out a hand. I push myself away from his creepy-looking fingers and wipe dirt and blood from my forehead. "How are you here?" I ask. "The last time I saw you was in my bedroom."

"There's no telling who you might run

into these days," he smiles. "The world was always a small place, but now it's positively boxlike. So few of us left with our senses intact. Our paths cannot fail to cross."

Owl Man stands and stretches. I frown as I study him.

"What are you? I can hear your heartbeat, so you're not a zombie. But you're not a mutant either, are you?"

"Certainly not," he says, sniffing as if offended. "I am..." He pauses, thinks for a moment, then shrugs. "I am, as you so poetically put it, *Owl Man*. That is all you need to know about me for now."

My mind is whirring. There are so many questions I want to put to him, about the mutants, Mr. Dowling, why certain zombies revitalize. I've a feeling that if anyone can answer those questions, it's him.

But before I can ask Owl Man anything, the mutant with the whistle shouts at the woman faced with the impossible choice. "Time's up. Choose or we slaughter them all, baby, adults, the lot."

Owl Man grimaces. "Kinslow is a nasty piece of work, but he keeps things interesting, and that's what Mr. Dowling demands of his followers."

I get the sense that Owl Man doesn't approve of what's going on. But he doesn't try to stop it, just observes the sick show with a neutral expression.

"Hurry!" the mutant called Kinslow croaks. "Choose now or..."

He produces a knife and passes it to Mr. Dowling. The clown laughs as he takes it, then slides the blade up beneath the baby's chin.

"*Them!*" the woman howls, falling to the ground with horror. "Take them! Spare my child!"

The other people scream with fear and outrage, but their cries are cut short when Kinslow blows his whistle again, three long toots. At his command the living dead surge forward and tuck into the hapless humans, survivors no longer, just zombie fodder now.

"This is awful," I groan, turning my gaze away.

"Yes," Owl Man says morosely. "But it's about to get even worse. Look."

Mr. Dowling hasn't handed back the baby. As the zombies finish off the last of the humans and tuck into fresh, warm brains, the clown strides among them, still clasping the infant. Kinslow and the woman trail after him, the mutant snickering, the woman distraught.

"My girl," she whimpers, reaching for the baby.

"In a minute," Kinslow snaps, pulling her back. "You don't want to disturb Mr. Dowling when he's preoccupied. You wouldn't like him if he lost his temper."

The clown comes to a halt over a thin, male zombie who is digging into the open head of the boy who wasn't much younger than me. He watches the zombie for a while, then sticks his left index finger into a hole in the man's throat, where he was bitten when still alive. His finger comes out wet and red. With a soft, choking noise, he puts the finger into the baby's mouth and the little girl's lips close on it trustingly.

"*No!*" the girl's mother screams, sensing the threat too late to prevent it. She tries to throw herself at the clown, but Kinslow kicks her legs out from beneath her and she collapses.

"No! No! No!" she screeches, covering her ears with her hands as the baby's brittle bones extend and snap through the skin of her fingers and toes. "You told me you'd spare her! You promised!"

"We did spare her," Kinslow says, taking the zombie baby from Mr. Dowling and holding her out to the woman who was once her mother. "She still lives, in a fashion. She's as wriggly and alert as ever. Just a little less ... *breathy*. Now take her. She's yours to do with as you wish."

Kinslow presses the baby into her mother's arms. Her tiny sharp teeth, newly sprouted, snap together as she stares at the woman whose brain smells so good and tempting, even to one as young as this.

The woman gazes down on her ruined child for a full minute in horrified silence, the clown and Kinslow waiting to see what she'll do next, everybody watching with wretched fascination except for the feasting zombies. Then, like a person sleepwalking, she undoes the buttons on her shirt and frees a breast. She presses her daughter to it and lets the undead baby bite and feed, murmuring softly to her, stroking her hair, vowing to care for her even in death.

"A touching scene," Owl Man murmurs.

"Bastard," I snarl at him.

"There's no point blaming me," he says. "I wasn't responsible."

"You didn't do anything to stop it though, did you?" I challenge him.

"That's not my role," he says. "We all have a role to play in life, and unlike many unfortunate souls, I am all too aware of what the universe demands of me. I simply follow the path that destiny demands, as we all must."

"Even if it means letting babies be sacrificed?" I sneer.

"Yes," Owl Man whispers and a sad look crosses his oversized eyes. "You may find this hard to believe, but I have done even worse than that in my time. I fear that you might too, over the course of the grim days and nights to come."

"What are you talking about?" I snap.

"Remember when you could dream? Remember the babies on the plane?"

I shiver at the memory. Owl Man also asked me about my dreams the last time we met. "What about the bloody nightmares?" I growl.

"They marked you, Becky," he says. "I was sure you would survive and regain your senses, just as I was certain we would meet again. You are a creature of the darkness, the same as myself and Mr. Dowling. Like us, I fear that you too will end up destined to play a cruel, vicious part in the shaping of the future. Some of us cannot escape the damnable reach of fate."

Before I can ask Owl Man what that means, he stands and calls to Kinslow and Mr. Dowling, "I have someone here I think you might be interested in."

The clown bounds across, Kinslow racing to keep up. Mr. Dowling stops in front of me and beams as if to welcome an old friend.

"You made it out," Kinslow grunts, pulling up beside his master. "Mr. Dowling said that you would. You caught his eye underground. He told me you were the cream of the crop."

"See, Becky?" Owl Man mutters. "*Marked.*"

Kinslow glares at the tall man with the owlish eyes, but says nothing.

Mr. Dowling bends over until his face is in front of mine. The last time he did that, he spat a shower of spiders over me. But today I can't see anything in his mouth, only a long black tongue.

The clown smells worse than an open sewer. My nose wrinkles and I try to turn my face away, but he grabs my chin and forces me to maintain eye contact. As he stares into my soul with his beady, twitching eyes, he squeals a few times, softly.

"He wants to know if you're ready to come with us," Kinslow says. "He knows that you disapprove of many of the things we do. But he's willing to teach you, spend time with you, show you the way forward, share his power with you."

"He's out of his tiny mind if he thinks I'll ever have anything to do with you lot," I jeer. "You're freaks, every last damn one of you. I wouldn't spit on you if you were on fire, even if I *could* spit."

The clown tilts his head sideways and frowns.

"You should kill her for saying a thing like that," Kinslow growls.

"Mr. Dowling decides who to kill and who to spare," Owl Man thunders, his smooth voice dropping several octaves in the space of a heartbeat, his eyes flaring. "Don't ever forget that or speak out of turn again. He makes the calls, not you."

"Of course," Kinslow says quickly, fear mixed in with his apology. "I meant no disrespect. I was merely –"

"Shut up if you want to live," Owl Man says lazily, then looks to the clown. "I told you she would not come with us. Do you want to crack her skull open or let her go?"

The clown stares at me for a few seconds. Then he makes a chuckling, wheezy sound, turns and sets off across the square, Kinslow hurrying to keep up with him.

Owl Man winks at me, all smiles again. "He said we'll probably end up killing you, but not today. He's in a good mood after the game with the baby. Go with his blessing, but bear this in mind— no matter where you go, no matter what you do, he knows you're out there and he can find you any time he likes. You haven't seen the last of Mr. Dowling, Becky, not by a long shot."

Owl Man peels away and follows the mutants and their master. I watch numbly as the clown gathers his posse and leads them from the square. Someone starts to sing an old ballad about murder and revenge, and by the time they pass from sight, they've all joined in, one big, happy party, heading off in search of fresh pickings, leaving me to fester in the square, surrounded by the wreckage of the helicopters and the cooling bodies of the dead.

TWENTY-FOUR

I remain in Trafalgar Square overnight, barely moving, staring at nothing, wishing somebody would come along and free me from this unholy hell of an existence. Zombies trail through the square over the course of the night, scraping dry the skulls of the corpses, ridding them of every last scrap of brain. Some come sniffing to make sure I'm not edible too. I ignore them and focus on the empty feeling inside, remembering the baby, the mutants, Owl Man, the clown, the bloodshed.

In the morning, as the sun rises and the carnage is revealed in all its gory glory once again, I push myself to my feet, pick up my trusty Australian hat that is lying nearby, dusty but undented, and turn my back on the grisly scene. I'm in a universe of pain, and limp badly as I shuffle away, but my wounds aren't fatal. I'll survive, unfortunately.

In a numb daze, I start down Whitehall. It's not an especially long road, but it takes me ages to get to the end, hobbling and limping, dripping occasional drops of thick, gooey blood from wounds I don't even begin to explore.

I pass Downing Street, once home to the Prime Minister. I know he didn't make it out of London alive—the news programs mentioned his loss a few times. He hasn't been missed. His cabinet neither. The army runs the country these days.

I wonder if the PM is still inside Number Ten, a zombie like so many of his voters, resting until dark. I could check—the gate is open and unguarded—and probably would any other time. But I'm too weary to care about such trivialities. This country has fallen. Babies are being turned into zombies and feeding on their mothers. Who cares about stuffy politicians now?

Big Ben comes into view. I pause and stare glumly at the clock tower. The hands have stopped at just before a quarter to five. It doesn't chime anymore. I doubt it ever will again. A dead clock at the heart of a dead city.

As I edge past the Houses of Parliament, I spot a large red z sprayed near the base of Big Ben, an arrow underneath pointing towards Westminster Bridge. I had planned to turn left and crawl along the riverbank, heading back east to more familiar territory, to

BRIDGE
STREET

CITY OF WESTMINSTER

see out my time on home turf. But the arrow intrigues me. I've seen others like it during my march west. I think they might be the work of Mr. Dowling—he sketched a bloodred *z* on my cheek when he visited me in my cell in the underground bunker—but I'm not sure. Maybe they were sprayed by humans, survivors hoping to guide others to their hideout. If so, they might be more interested in my offer of assistance than the soldiers were.

Silly old B! Still keen to help the living. Will I never learn?

I move forward, wincing, dragging my left leg, half-blind and itching like crazy. I should have found new clothes and glasses before I came out onto an exposed bridge, but I wasn't thinking clearly. No matter. I push on regardless. I won't be in the sun for long. There will be plenty of shadowy corners for me to rest in on the south side of the river.

I'm surprised, as I advance, to note that the London Eye is still revolving. At first I think it's a trick of the light, so I stop and watch it for a minute. But no, the capsules are moving slowly, just as they did in the old days when every tourist in London made a beeline for its most popular attraction. Today, though, the capsules are deserted. The Eye might be open for business, but it doesn't have any takers.

As I drag myself off Westminster Bridge, I think about the London Dungeon, a place I visited several times when I was alive. I passed its original home earlier in my journey, and now here I am at its subsequent location in County Hall. Maybe that's the place for me. I'd fit in perfectly among all the waxwork monsters.

"No," I whisper. "You're too grisly. You'd give the rest of the freaks a bad name."

Shuffling on, I come to the turn for Belvedere Road, which separates the buildings of County Hall, and spot another red *z* with an arrow beneath, pointing up the road.

I stare wearily at the arrow. I need to feed. It's been a long time since I last ate. I can feel my stomach tightening, my senses beginning to loosen. If I don't tuck into some brains soon, I'll regress and become a mindless revived. If I'm going to follow these damn arrows, I need to make sure I'm in good shape to deal with living humans if I run into any.

St. Thomas's Hospital is just behind me, so I turn slowly and make for it. I assumed a hospital would offer rich pickings, but as I work my way through the wards, I find that isn't the case. Others have been here before me and scraped the remains of the corpses dry.

But I've got a bit more up top than your average zombie. As far as I know, any hospital this size has a morgue. And I'm guessing they were normally situated on one of the lower floors, so the staff didn't have to wheel corpses through the rest of the hospital, spooking the life out of everybody.

I find the morgue after a short search but it's locked. It takes me far longer to track down keys for the door, but eventually I find a set in a nurses' cabinet and let myself in. It's brighter and cleaner than I anticipated, no stench of death at all.

The morgue is refrigerated and the electricity is still working. I don't find as many corpses as I thought I might, but four are lying on slabs, ready and waiting, and there are probably a few more tucked away out of sight. If I don't stray from this area in the near future, I can come back and search again. But right now I have more than I need. Time to dine.

I mutter a quick apology over the body of a woman in her early twenties, then chip through her skull with my finger bones and pry out bits of her brain. I eat mechanically, forcing down the food. When I've eaten my fill, I let myself out, lock the door behind me, and throw up in the corridor. I place the keys back where I found them, then return to Belvedere Road, moving more easily than before, but still very far from normal. If my bones and flesh don't heal – and I've no reason to think they will – I'm going to be hobbling like this until the end. No more long jumping or sprinting for me.

I limp along, head low, feeling sorry for myself. As I come to one of the entrances into the main building of County Hall, I notice a small red *z* sprayed on a wall, the arrow beneath it pointing inwards. I stare at the arrow for a long time, then shrug, mount the steps and push open the unlocked door at the top. If this is a trap, so be it. I'm too tired to worry.

The shade of the building is a welcome relief after being out in the sun. To my surprise there are no zombies here. I thought a massive, dark area like this would be bursting with the undead, but I seem to be the only soul making use of the place.

I wind my way through a warren of corridors and rooms with unbelievably high ceilings. This is like a palace. I never knew there was so much to it. I've been to the aquarium and games arcade at the front of the building in the past, and the London Dungeon, of course, but had no idea that all this existed farther back.

Many of the doors are shut and won't open. If I wanted to, I might be able to force them apart or find keys if I searched, but I'm content to simply wander where I can, stepping through every door that opens to me, ignoring the rest.

After a while, I come to a room overlooking the river. I edge up next to the panels of cracked glass and gaze out at one of the best views in town. To my left lie Big Ben, the Houses of Parliament and Westminster Bridge. To my right is a bridge for trains, and just beyond that, Waterloo Bridge. Huge, ornate buildings line the bank on the far side of the river. The London Eye is directly ahead of me, imposing and graceful, still turning smoothly, silently, like some windup toy standing tall and proud among the ruins of the city.

I take off my hat and let it drop to the floor. Rubbing the back of my neck, I lean my head against the glass and make a sighing sound. I feel more alone than ever in this immense building, like I'm in a tomb.

Then, as I'm glumly considering where I should turn next, from just behind me, out of the shadows of what was an empty room when I entered, somebody coughs politely and says, "Good morning, Miss Smith. We've been expecting you."

To be continued…

SINK YOUR TEETH INTO THE NEXT INSTALLMENT OF DARREN SHAN'S ZOM-B SERIES.

AVAILABLE NOW
HOWEVER BOOKS ARE SOLD

TURN THE PAGE FOR A SNEAK PEEK!

ONE

I whirl away from the window that over-looks the Thames. A man has entered the room through a door that I didn't notice on my way in. He's standing in the middle of the open doorway, arms crossed, smiling.

My survival instinct kicks in. With a roar, I hurl myself at the stranger, ignoring the flare of pain in my bruised, broken body. I curl my fingers into a fist and raise my hand over my head as I close in on him.

The man doesn't react. He doesn't even uncross his arms. All he does is cock his head, to gaze with interest at my raised fist. His smile never slips.

I come to a stop less than a meter from

the man, eyeing him beadily as my fist quivers above my head. If he'd tried to defend himself, I would have torn into him, figuring he was an enemy, as almost everybody else in this city seems to be. But he leaves himself open to attack and continues to smile.

"Who the hell are you?" I snap. He's dressed in a light gray suit, a white shirt and purple tie, and expensive-looking leather shoes. He has thin hair, neatly combed back, brown but streaked with gray. Calm brown eyes. Looks like he's in his forties.

"I am Dr. Oystein," he introduces himself.

"That supposed to mean something to me?" I grunt.

"I would be astonished if it did," he says, then extends his right hand.

"You don't want to shake hands with me," I sneer. "Not unless you want to end up with a taste for brains."

"I was an adventurous diner in my youth," Dr. Oystein says, his smile widening. "I often boasted that I would eat the flesh or innards of just about any creature, except for humans. Alas, ironically, I can now eat nothing else."

I frown and focus on his fingers. Bones don't stick out of them the way they poke out of every other zombie's, but now that I look closely, I see that the flesh at the tips is broken, a small white mound of filed-down bone at the center of each pink whorl.

"Yes," he says in answer to my unvoiced question. "I am undead like you."

I still don't take his hand. Instead I focus on his mouth. His teeth are nowhere near as jagged or as long as mine, but they're not the same as a normal person's either.

Dr. Oystein laughs. "You are wondering how I keep my teeth in such good shape, but there is no magic involved. I have been in this lifeless state a lot longer than you. One develops a knack for these things over time. I was brought up to believe that a gentleman should be neatly groomed and I have found myself as fastidious in death as I once was in life.

"Please take my hand, Becky. I will feel very foolish if you do not."

"I don't give a damn how you feel," I snort, and instead of shaking his hand, I listen closely for his heartbeat. When I don't detect one, I relax slightly.

"How do you know my name?" I growl. "How could you have been expecting me? I didn't know that I was coming to County Hall. I wandered in randomly."

Dr. Oystein shakes his head. "I have come to believe that nothing in life is truly random. In this instance it definitely was no coincidence that you wound up here. You were guided by the signs, as others were before you."

I think back and recall a series of spray-painted, *z*-shaped symbols with arrows underneath. I've been following the arrows since I left the East End, sometimes because they happened to be pointing the way that I was traveling, but other times deliberately.

"*Z* for zombie," Dr. Oystein says as he sees my brain click. "The

543

signs mean nothing to reviveds, but what curious revitalized could turn a blind eye to such an intriguing mystery?"

"You know about reviveds and revitalizeds?"

"Of course." He coughs lightly. "In fact I was the one who coined the terms."

"Who are you?" I whisper. "*What* are you?"

Dr. Oystein sighs. "I am a scientist and teacher. A sinner and gentleman. A killer and would-be savior. And, if you will do me the great honor, I would like to be your friend."

The mysterious doctor waves his extended arm, once again inviting me to accept his hand. And this time, after a brief hesitation, even though I'm still suspicious, I lower my fist, uncurl my fingers and shake hands with the politely spoken zombie.

me, examining my wounds. "My father was English but my mother was Norwegian. I was born in Norway and lived there for a while. Then my parents moved around Europe – my father had itchy feet – and I, of course, traveled with them."

I try not to jitter as the doctor slips behind me. If he's been concealing a weapon, he'll be able to whip it out and strike. My shoulders tense as I imagine him driving a long knife between them. But he doesn't attack, just continues to circle, and soon he's facing me again.

"I heard that your heart had been ripped out," he says. "May I see?"

"How do you know that?" I scowl.

"I had contacts in the complex where you were previously incarcerated. I know much about you, but I hope to learn more. Please?" He nods towards my top.

With a sigh, I grab the hem of my T-shirt and lift it high, exposing my chest. Dr. Oystein stares at the cavity on the left, where my heart once beat. Now there's just a jagged hole, rimmed by congealed blood and a light green moss.

"Fascinating," the doctor murmurs. "We zombies are all freaks of nature, each a walking medical marvel, but one tends to forget that. This is a reminder of our ability to defy established laws. You are a remarkable individual, Becky Smith, and you should be proud of the great wound which you bear."

"Stop it," I grunt. "You'll make me blush."

Dr. Oystein sniffs. "Not unless you are even more remarkable than the rest of us. Without a heart, how would your body pump blood to your pale, pretty cheeks?"

Dr. Oystein makes a gesture, inviting me to lower my T-shirt. As I do so, he steps across to the window where I was standing when he first addressed me. County Hall boasts one of the best views in the city. He looks out at the river, the London Eye, the Houses of Parliament and all the other deserted buildings.

"Such devastation," he mumbles. "You must have encountered

horrors beyond your worst nightmares on your way to us. Am I correct?"

I think about all of the corpses and zombies I've seen...Mr. Dowling and the people he tormented and killed in Trafalgar Square...his army of mutants and his bizarre sidekick, Owl Man... the hunters who almost killed me...Sister Clare of the Order of the Shnax, the way she transformed when I bit her...

"You're not bloody wrong," I wheeze.

"The world teeters on the brink," Dr. Oystein continues. "It has been dealt a savage blow and I am sure that most of those who survived believe that there is no way back, regardless of what the puppets of the military might say in their radio broadcasts."

"You've heard those too?"

"Oh yes. I tune in whenever I am in need of bittersweet amusement." He looks back at me. "There are many fools in this world, and it is no crime to be one of them. But to try and carry on as normal when all around you has descended into chaos...to try to convince others that you can restore order by operating as you did before...That goes beyond mere foolishness. That is madness and it will prove the true downfall of this world if we leave these people to their sad, petty, all-too-human devices.

"There *is* hope for civilization as we once knew it. But if the living are to rise again, they will need our help, since only the conscious undead stand any sort of chance against the brain-hungry legions of the damned."

Dr. Oystein beckons me forward. I shuffle towards him slowly, not just because of the pain, but because I've almost been mesmerized by his words. He speaks like a hypnotist, slow, assured, serious.

When I join him at the window, Dr. Oystein points to the London Eye, turning as smoothly and steadily as it did when thousands of tourists flocked there every day.

"I consider that a symbol of all that has been lost but which might one day be restored," the doctor says. "We keep it going, day and night, a beacon of living hope in this city of the dead. But no ordinary human could operate the Eye—they would be sniffed out and besieged by zombies. We, on the other hand, can. The dead will not bother us, since we are of no interest to them. That lack of interest is our strength and humanity's only hope of once again taking control of this planet.

"You are not the first revitalized to find your way here," Dr. Oystein goes on. "There are others – weary, battered warriors – who have crawled through the streets of bloodshed and nightmares in search of sanctuary and hope, following the signs as you did."

"Are you talking about zom heads?" I ask.

"Yes," he says. "But we do not use that term here. If you choose to stay with us and work for the forces of justice and mercy, you will come to think of yourself as we do, not as a zom head but an *Angel*."

I snort. "With wings and a harp? Pull the other one!"

"No wings," Dr. Oystein smiles. "No harp either. But an Angel nonetheless." He moves away from the window, towards the door. "I have much to show you, Becky. You do not have to accompany me – you are free to leave anytime that you wish, and always will be – but, if you are willing, I will take you on a tour and reveal some of the many secrets of the newly redefined County Hall."

I stare at the open doorway. It's shadowy in the corridor outside. There could be soldiers waiting to jump me and stick me in a cell again.

"Why should I trust you?" I ask.

Dr. Oystein shrugs. "I could tell you to listen to your heart, but…"

The grisly joke eases my fears. Besides, there's no way I could turn back now. He's got me curious and, like a cat, I have to follow my nose and hope it doesn't lead me astray.

"All right, doc," I grunt, limping over to him and grinning, as if I haven't a care in the world. "You can be my guide. Just don't expect a tip at the end."

"I will ask for no tip," he says softly. "But I *will* ask for your soul." He smiles warmly as I stiffen. "There's no need to be afraid. When the time comes, I believe you will give it to me gladly."

And with that cryptic remark, he leads me out of the room of light and into the vast, dark warren beyond.